MURDER MUST EXTREME

Book One *of* The DCI Dixon Investigations

Elizabeth Rex

CHAPTER 1

The persistent ringing of the phone jolted Ann from her delightfully erotic dream. Irritated at the abrupt awakening, she reached over in the darkness, took hold of the phone and pressed it to her ear. She muttered a sleepy, 'Hello'.

The urgency in the voice that replied caused Ann to sit bolt upright.

"Sorry to wake you, Guv, but can you get over here as soon as possible?"

She recognised the voice immediately. It was Sergeant David Hughes on the line.

"We're at the home of a Mr Tom Casey who's been murdered," Sergeant Hughes said. "Address is 27 Chapel Street, Belgravia. Scenes of crime officers, SOCO, are on their way. Coroner's here already."

Ann memorised the address before replying, "Oh alright, I'll be there as soon as I can."

She let her gaze linger, a little regretfully, at the athletic shape of her partner's body beneath the sheets; she was still fast sleep, her chest gently rising and falling with each breath. Quickly, albeit reluctantly, Ann scrambled out of bed, pulled on some clothes and hurried off out of the door to her car which was parked in front of the house.

The rain pelted down as Ann Dixon sped through the London streets to the address in Belgravia. She slowed as she approached the house where she could see two squad cars pulled up. She parked her car in front of the house, next to a car that she recognised as the coroner's and walked towards the front door. As always, her long, shapely legs and the distinct turn of her head caught the attention of the police officers milling around outside.

SOCO had arrived and were assessing the crime scene inside.

Ann ducked beneath the police cordon of blue and white tape and walked to the front door of the house where Sergeant David Hughes came forward to greet her. He handed her some overshoes that she slipped on and then walked into the house. The scene inside the house defied description. The naked, bloodstained body of the victim that hung upside down from the banister resembled a grotesque carcass at an abattoir. Rivulets of blood pooled beneath the victim's head. The bloodied figure could only be defined as human by the position of his arms and legs splaying outwards. The victim had been placed in an upside-down position secured by ropes. His face was almost completely obscured by the blood that had cascaded over it from the numerous wounds on his abdomen and legs.

"Hi, Ann," Tim Jones, the coroner, greeted her. "Glad you could come. Your Super asked us to call you as you have experience with this type of murder. The victim is Tom Casey, the owner of the house. His housekeeper, Mrs Smith, found him at 6.15 this morning and alerted the police."

According to Tim, the copious amount of clotted blood around the trauma sites on the body suggested that Tom Casey had been tortured and for a considerable length of time.

"I would imagine death was between 4am and 5am," Tim continued.

Ann looked at him.

"Any idea of the cause of death?"

"I would say virtual exsanguination," Tim answered, "with probable strangulation."

He looked at her steadily for a moment before adding, "I'll be able to give you more detail after the post-mortem. There's a distinct pattern of an inverted cross on his neck that might have been made by the ring the murderer was wearing at the time of the strangulation."

Ann took a few tentative steps forward to have a closer look at the body.

Whilst she did so, Sergeant Hughes explained that the knots in the rope suggested that the killer might have served in the navy. She noticed there were multiple cuts visible on the torso and legs.

The extensive bleeding and formation of clots around the wounds suggested that the cuts were made while the victim was still alive. It was clear that the murderer intended to inflict severe suffering prior to death.

She observed the tastefully furnished room, with notable paintings on the wall, and which paid testament to the exquisite taste of the owner. And Ann could see, with her many years' experience of such brutality, that this had all the hallmarks of a revenge killing. The room was now in complete disarray with chairs overturned, drawers pulled out and the contents strewn all over the floor.

Ann surveyed the rest of the room. Large blood stains and patterns of smaller, splattered drops on the sheer white carpet looked like a macabre painting. The SOCO guys bagged and labelled all the items they found lying around the floor. They photographed the scene, the victim and any items of relevance.

"You might want to look at this, Guv," David said, handing her a book. "It's some kind of code book; found it stuck to the underside of the desktop."

"OK, tell them to bag it," Ann instructed. "I'm sure we'll find someone to decipher the code. Let's go talk to the housekeeper."

She turned and walked towards a woman who was casually dressed in a green, loose cotton dress that had clearly been through a few too many wash cycles. She was sitting in a chair with a supporting police officer and looked distressed.

"Mrs Smith," Ann said, introducing herself in the most comforting way she could, bearing in mind the nature of her job. "I am Detective Chief Inspector Dixon. My colleague, Sergeant Hughes, and I promise not to detain you longer than necessary and the paramedics are waiting to attend to you when we are done."

Linda Smith sniffed and wiped a hand across her nose. She nodded.

"What time did you get to the house this morning?" Ann asked her, keeping her tone light but professional.

"I'm just his housekeeper," Linda sobbed. "I arrived for work this morning at 6.15 and discovered him there, hanging up. Terrible… terrible…"

Ann smiled gently, trying to encourage her to say more.

"My employer was a lawyer," the woman blubbed, choking back her tears. "He lived alone; he was single; wouldn't hurt a fly."

"And can you tell me when you last saw Mr Casey alive?"

"At 6pm. I cooked him his dinner as usual."

"And did you notice anything different about him, any unusual tension that struck you as odd?"

"No, he seemed fine. Same as normal."

"I know this is hard for you, Mrs Smith, but can you tell me what exactly was 'normal'?"

"A pleasant man, never complained much." Linda stalled, breaking down into tears again and her voice caught in her throat.

Ann waited patiently for Linda to compose herself. "Take your time," she said.

Linda said, wiping her eyes, "He seemed happy enough."

"And did he eat his meal with anyone else?"

"No," Linda sniffed. "He dined alone. He asked me to prepare the table just for him."

"And Mrs Smith, can you tell me, did he often dine alone, or did he have friends join him sometimes?"

"He usually had a friend join him to play bridge."

"OK, you're doing very well. Thank you, Mrs Smith, you've been very helpful."

Linda managed a grateful smile and brushed a hand over her hair.

"And I just have one more question," Ann said gently, leaning forward slightly as if to emphasise the importance of her request before Linda broke down again and almost made further questioning impossible. "Did Mr Casey have family, do you know?"

"Yes," replied Linda, "he had three other brothers. He also had a sister, but she died some time ago."

Ann nodded.

"And do you by chance have his brothers' contact details?"

Linda reached down to her bag that lay at her feet, rummaged about and pulled out a small notepad from a zipped pocket. She looked pleased with herself for being able to contribute something of importance. "George Casey is his elder brother," she said, and gave Ann the contact details.

Ann thanked Mrs Smith and told her the police would be in touch if they needed any more information. Ann and David then returned to the scene of the crime. An enormous bookshelf on the far wall housed an impressive array of books amongst which, Ann noticed, were a vast number of hardbacks on the occult.

The murdered man was still wearing his Cartier watch and his wallet and mobile phone lay on the coffee table near to the body. He clearly hadn't been murdered for material gain.

Ann instructed the forensics team to speed up the gathering of evidence – the coroner was keen to get the body to the mortuary. A man's boot print, approximately size 10, was found at the edge of the carpet. All the items collected were duly photographed, labelled and bagged.

"I also want all kitchen knives collected, tagged and bagged," Ann added as a final instruction.

Tom Casey was heavily built – it took four policemen to lift his body off the banister when it was then placed in a body bag to be transferred to the mortuary.

"I'll call you when I'm ready to do the post-mortem," said Tim.

"Come on, I'll walk you to your car," David said to her.

Ann smiled her acquiescence and they headed for the door.

"I see you still have your Renault," he remarked as they stepped outside, "and still in pristine condition."

"Yes," said Ann, "it gets so little use, that's why. I drive around in cars from the Central London Police Division most of the time."

David climbed into the driver's side of her car and Ann jumped into the passenger seat. As soon as she was inside her car, she was besieged by a group of reporters and bombarded with a flood of questions from the media.

"You'll have to wait for an official press release from the superintendent," she said. "There's been a murder and it's too soon to draw any conclusions about the case. Now," her voice became brusque, "please get away from my car, I have work to do."

The reporters continued to surround the car like a mob of protesters, ignoring her request. She urged David to drive away swiftly. "Bloody vultures, they can smell carrion far better than the feathered species."

David gave a wry smile. "I guess they're only doing their job."

"Let's find Stephen Edwards and ask him to deal with the press."

"Good idea, Guv; I'll see if he's in his office while you park the car."

"OK, that will buy me time to grab a quick cup of coffee, too," she said, smiling as she envisaged the magic black liquid which she often, against advice, substituted for food.

After she had parked the car, she returned to her office and hastily poured herself a large cup of coffee from the machine. It gave her an instant lift and pacified the pangs of hunger, at least to some degree and if only temporarily. Sitting at her desk, she raced through her emails and replied to the urgent ones before dialling the number of George Casey, the elder brother of the victim whose number Linda had given her.

There was a short ring and then a man answered. "George Casey, can I help you?"

"Hello," said Ann, "this is Detective Chief Inspector Ann Dixon of the Central London Police Division. I wonder when it would be convenient to see you, Mr Casey. It concerns your brother, Tom."

"Good Lord, what crime has Tom committed?" came the response.

"Well, I cannot tell you over the phone as it is a delicate matter," Ann replied, "but it is very important that I see you urgently."

She heard the intake of breath as if George was taken aback at her words before he said, retaining an air of professional cool, "I'll give you the address and you can liaise with my secretary about my availability."

Ann scribbled down the address and managed to secure an appointment with George for 3pm that same day. Just then, David popped his head around the door. "The Super is in his office, if you're ready to see him now, Guv."

Ann grimaced at the thought of meeting with her boss. Stephen Edwards disliked having women in the police force and hated them in authority. As a result, he always managed to erode Ann's confidence and reduce her to a mumbling wreck during their meetings and, worse, he knew damn well the effect he had on her. Her hands were clammy with anticipation.

David sensed her anxiety and said, "It's OK, Guv, he seemed in a good mood when I saw him a few minutes ago."

"Huh," she said, grimacing, "that will change as soon as I step into his office."

David shrugged, pursing his lips, and said nothing.

"Oh well, better get it over with," she said as she rose a little unsteadily and headed for Edwards' office, "no point in delaying the agony."

She knocked and waited to be invited in.

"Come in!" boomed Edwards' voice.

Ann walked in, greeted him and sat down in the seat in front of his desk.

"There's been a murder," she said. "Our victim, Tom Casey, is a 45-year-old white male. He was tortured, then murdered in his home. The housekeeper found the body at 6.15 this morning. The victim has three brothers and a sister who is deceased. Victim must have let his killer into the house because there was no sign of a forced entry. The extent of the injuries suggests the victim was tortured for a considerable length of time. The position of the body was hung upside down from a banister. The large collection of books on the shelf suggested a link to the occult." Ann paused and took a breath. "The extent of the torture suggests a revenge killing. The coroner thinks cause of death was strangulation and he will tell us more after the post-mortem."

Edwards stared at a notepad on his desk without looking up.

"I have contacted one of the siblings," Ann continued, keeping her voice steady, despite the tension knotting her stomach, "George Casey, the elder brother. I haven't told him about his brother's death. I have an appointment to see him this afternoon at 3pm."

"I see," Edwards said to the notepad, "and the media?"

"We had the press at the victim's house this morning demanding answers. I wonder, Sir, if you could call a press conference at your earliest convenience, please."

Edwards did not look at Ann for the entirety of her speech. Instead, he continued to doodle on the notepad. To attract his attention, she felt forced into asking him more directly and purposefully if there was anything more he needed to know about the case. *Damn the man. Why does he feel the need to undermine me in this way?*

He looked up at her at last. "Dixon," he began, "the CLPD does not pay you to speculate. I need hard evidence and don't take a bloody lifetime gathering it. I want a result in the shortest possible time and don't fuck up. I'll sort out the press. Now get out of my office, I'm very busy."

Ann, furious at his disinterest and lack of respect, remained civil and calmly left the room.

David joined her in her office instantly noticing her upset.

"See?" Ann seethed. "He's an arrogant pig and he gets worse. He thinks we must tolerate his rudeness because he's the stressed father of a child with special needs. He's oblivious to anyone else's needs."

David frowned, then brightened, turning his features into a wide smile. "Hey," he cajoled, "how about I buy you lunch after you've interviewed the Casey guy?"

"That sounds great; let's get the team together in the incident room. I need to brief them on the murder."

David then set about informing his colleagues that Ann had called a meeting at midday. They began setting up photographs and details of the murder on the board and on computer screens in the incident room. The officers gathered promptly and two teams, headed by Detective Inspectors Ian Roberts and Alfred Tobin, were present.

Ann called order as the officers continued to talk among themselves. She banged a book on the table forcing them to stop chattering and look up at her.

"Alright everyone, our murder victim, Tom Casey, a 45-year-old white male was tortured then murdered at his home at 27 Chapel Street, Belgravia. There was no forced entry, so we assume the victim let his killer into the house. The motive was not burglary even though the chaos at the scene of the crime suggests it was. The victim's Cartier watch, laptop and phone were still in the house." She pointed to the photos that had been taken at the scene.

Ann paused to survey the group gathered in front of her. "It appears," she continued, "that the killer might have been looking for something. It might have been the code book that we found stuck under a desk." Again, she pointed to the screen where the image of the book was displayed. She didn't let the features on her face move. "Forensics have informed me that the book is written in witches' code. Presumably one or more of the brothers might be able to decode the book. The killer must have missed it in his panic to find it as he hurriedly pulled out the drawers of the desk."

She paused and took a breath. "Our officers discovered the book by chance when they replaced the drawers of the desk and saw it carefully stuck under the desktop. Someone obviously knows about its existence and is keen to have it."

She noticed they were listening attentively, waiting for her to continue.

"Perhaps the victim was tortured to reveal the whereabouts of the book or the murder possibly was a revenge killing, judging by the degree of torture, and," she took a step nearer the screen and indicated the close-up images of Tom Casey, "the mark on the victim's neck, an inverted cross, and his being strung upside down, suggests a link to the occult."

Ann took a step back from the screen. "There were also a large number of books on the occult on his bookshelf." Someone coughed. Ann waited for them to clear their throat and went on. "The degree and savagery of the murder I would say suggests some kind of revenge."

Looking at the officers she asked, "Are there any thoughts on the murder or any questions?" while scouring the room. Various questions were asked about items found at the scene and she answered them one by one.

"OK," she said to them at last, "here's what I want you to do."

She organised the team into units and assigned them various tasks.

"I want DI Roberts and his team to question work colleagues and friends of Tom Casey."

Ann then turned towards a tall, dark-haired man to the left and made a gesture with her arm. "DI Tobin," she said, "needs to interview the neighbours and friends who accompanied Tom Casey to his various social engagements. Check if anyone saw anything out of the ordinary. I want you to interview Mrs Smith, the housekeeper, again. She was too distraught on the morning of the murder to give a comprehensive statement. She'll be able to tell you what is missing. She may even be able to give you more information, too."

She twisted her head back to face the whole team again. "Sergeant Hughes and I will interview all the brothers. We are meeting with George Casey, the elder brother, today."

A short silence followed while she allowed them to digest the instructions.

"If there are no more questions," she said, breaking the silence, "I'll arrange another meeting when I have the post-mortem and forensic reports."

She straightened her back, exuding an air of confidence. "Now get on with it and quickly, the Super wants a rapid result."

As she turned to go, she noticed DI Roberts and Tobin pause outside the incident room. Detective Inspector Ian Roberts turned to his colleague, and she heard him say, "I can't stand that cow. Who the hell does she think she is ordering us about like she does?"

"She might be a woman," DI Tobin replied, "but I reckon she has more balls than most men in that position. I'd like to remind you, too, that she has an impressive record."

From the other side of the doorway, Ann observed the way Ian looked at his colleague, opened his mouth to say something then closed it again.

"If you bothered to read her profile," she overheard DI Tobin whisper, "you'd know that she was one of the first UK detectives who got a murderer prosecuted by the analysis of plant DNA."

Ann continued to eavesdrop on them without them realising.

"OK, am I supposed to be impressed?"

"Well, her persistence resulted in solving a murder case which baffled the senior members of the force. She got the conviction using plant DNA to solve what was a confusing murder case and which stumped the best of her male colleagues."

"OK, OK, so she's cleverer than us lot; still gets me bloody irritated."

"That may be but her impressive service for MI6 prior to her joining the force and her training with the special forces has contributed to her achieving some quite astounding results in her career."

"Alright, so you're clearly enthralled."

DI Tobin looked at him.

"I'm just giving you the facts. She also speaks five languages fluently. Name any man in the force who can match her."

"Jesus!" DI Tobin exclaimed, putting a hand to his cheek. "Do I have to put up with this? It still doesn't make her a bloody man."

"Well, before you judge her for her gender, look beyond that and you might be astonished at her professional talents."

Ian raised his eyebrows. "I'll be stunned," he said, unable to stop mocking. He thrust out his chin. "What about that arrogant prick, her sergeant?"

Ann stared as DI Tobin glared at him then shook his head.

"David Hughes thinks he's been elevated to the rank of DI," said Ian.

"Hughes is not just a pretty boy either," DI Tobin countered. "He served in the Royal Engineers for five years before joining the force. He served in Iraq and has proved himself admirably in the force."

Ian hunched his shoulders and said nothing.

"Ann requested that he join her team because of his impressive record," DI Tobin said, narrowing his eyes. "Their relationship is totally professional because, as you know, she has a female partner."

"Who cares about their bloody great achievements? I still can't stand her."

***

On the way to Surrey, she didn't mention to Sergeant Hughes the conversation she had overheard between the two detectives.

They drew up in front of an attractive mock Georgian detached house near Esher. "You'll never be able to afford this on your salary, Guv," teased David.

Ann tossed her head. "I'm very happy in my humble home, thank you," she said.

"Wish I could afford it," David muttered.

They walked through the landscaped garden to the front door and rang the doorbell. A large, bearded man opened the door. Ann stuck out her hand to greet him and said, "You must be Mr George Casey, I'm Detective Chief Inspector Ann Dixon, and..." she indicated her colleague standing a step behind her, "...this is Sergeant David Hughes."

George Casey shook Ann's hand and ushered them both into the house. He motioned for them to sit down and offered them a drink. Ann declined and so did David.

"So, now what has my brother done that makes your visit so urgent?" George asked them, sitting himself comfortably in the richly padded, bottle green velour armchair opposite them. Beside the chair, Ann observed, was a gold drinks trolley on top of which were three cut-glass decanters filled with what she assumed to be sherry, red wine and brandy. She then noted two cut-glass polished tumblers sat beside the bottles.

"I am afraid I have bad news, Mr Casey," Ann began, "your brother, Tom, was murdered last night."

George jolted forward. His eyes widened whilst he managed to sit back again and maintain his composure.

Ann looked at him and continued.

"This isn't very nice for you, I understand, but I have to tell you that your brother was tortured before he was killed."

George absorbed the news, quietly, and without further reaction except for the change in his eyes that gave away his troubled thoughts.

His silence, Ann observed, betrayed his shock.

"George, can you tell me, did your brother have any enemies that you knew of, or someone you know who might have wanted to harm him?"

George shook his head and looked at the floor.

"Tom was well liked by all his colleagues and friends," he eventually said. "I don't know who could have done this."

Ann took out a small notepad and pen from a pocket on the front of her jacket. "Did your brother owe anyone money or was involved in financial schemes which might have put him at risk?"

George lifted his head to look at Ann. She noticed how his eyes had glazed over as if the truth of what she was saying was too hard for him to digest.

Ann probed further. "Did a disgruntled client from his legal business bear a grudge, perhaps?"

He twisted his hands together in his lap. "My brother lived a clean life and would not have put himself at risk in any way."

Ann nodded and asked George to confirm that Tom had never married.

George pursed his lips into a thin smile. "He never found the right girl."

Ann studied his expression for a few seconds, before asking, "When did you last see your brother alive?"

George thought for a moment then said, "I think about a week ago."

"And what was that for?"

"Tom asked me about a hedge fund investment he was interested in pursuing," replied George, keeping his voice level. "He had become rather bored with his job and wanted to pursue something more exciting."

Ann made a few notes.

"And you get along well with all your brothers?"

"Yes."

"And did Tom get along OK with your other sibling?"

George's eyes brightened a little. "Yes, absolutely. Jake and Nathan share a house in West London. There has never been any animosity amongst us brothers." He paused for a second, looking sightlessly into the distance. "And we all loved our sister, Yvonne, when she was alive."

"When did she die?"

"Three years ago," replied George, bringing his eyes back to Ann. "Seems like yesterday; I still miss her."

Ann nodded in sympathy.

"There was no family conflict at all then?"

"The only person who caused friction in our family was our brother-in-law, Mr Luke Cowan, a surgeon."

Ann's eyes darkened. She leant forward in her chair a little. "Your brother-in-law?"

"Yeah."

"In what way did he annoy you?"

"He was obsessed with Yvonne." George put a finger to his chin as if considering his words. "Luke resented the fact that we brothers were close to her, he thought we protected her too much. He became arrogant."

Ann stared at him. "Did your confrontations with Luke lead to violence at any time?"

"Well… let's say it got very close to physical stuff at times," George said, "but it never ended in anyone getting hurt."

"Where would I be able to contact Mr Cowan?" enquired Ann.

"He's based at Chelsea and Westminster Hospital," George replied emphatically. "My secretary has his number. I'll ask her to let you have it."

"Thank you." Ann scribbled down some more notes and looked up. "I would also like to interview your two brothers. Can you give me their contact numbers too, please?"

"Sure." George reached for his cell phone that was on a wooden circular table beside his chair. He pulled out the top drawer of the table and took out a Biro and pad of paper. He scrolled through his phone and began writing down the names, addresses and contact numbers of his brothers.

"Mr Casey, can you tell me where you were last night between three and six o'clock this morning?

"Yes, I had dinner with friends and then went to my private club until 4am."

Ann looked at him closely. "And can your friends corroborate your whereabouts?"

"Yes, indeed." George scrolled down his phone contacts again, scribbled a number on the pad of paper, ripped off the page and handed it to Ann. "Here is my friend, John's, telephone number."

Ann took the piece of paper from him. "Thank you."

George said, "John drove me home around 5.30am, stayed for a drink then left."

Ann made a few more notes, slipped her notepad and pen back into her jacket pocket and said, "George, we'll need you to come to the mortuary to identify your brother's body as soon as possible."

George nodded in agreement.

An arrangement was made for him to call at the police station the next day.

Ann thanked George for his cooperation and told him she would be in touch if the police needed any more information. They shook hands and she left, accompanied by David.

They climbed into the car.

"Hedge fund," David grumbled, pursing his lips. "Huh, they should rename it 'unlimited fund'," he commented, rolling his eyes. "Did you see the Lamborghini parked outside?"

"Just be happy with your lot in life and stop envying other people," Ann said, sounding annoyed.

"Yeah."

"And speaking of happiness," Ann said, "how about some food?"

"Good idea."

"Well, at least that's got you smiling."

She quickly spotted a café, parked the car and asked David to order the food.

He returned with two large burgers, and they sat in silence in the car whilst they ate.

When they had both finished eating, Ann scrunched up their food parcels, stepped out of the car to deposit them in the litter bin and then returned.

"So, what did you think about George Casey?" she asked David as she turned the ignition.

"I was wondering if maybe George had exaggerated the animosity of the family towards Luke Cowan."

Ann smiled and agreed, looking in her side mirror before indicating to turn right.

"And that's another reason why I think it imperative that we obtain Luke Cowan's side of the story," she said.

"Yes, you're right," David agreed.

Ann dropped David off at his home before returning to her office where she did some more work on her laptop before heading home.

An enticing fusion of spices wafted through the living room from the kitchen as Ann entered the house.

"Hmm, that smells divine; what are you cooking?" asked Ann on entering the kitchen. She gave Josie a welcoming kiss.

"Your favourite," replied Josie with a cheeky grin.

"Sounds just what I need."

"And when you have eaten it all you can have some of my delightful cuisine, which has been made with special love for you," Josie responded with a knowing grin. "You can show your appreciation by conjuring up a suitable dessert."

Ann laughed. "Ooh, I like the sound of that," she said, touching Josie on her bottom. Then she danced off to the shower, softly singing to herself.

After she had showered and changed, they sat down to dinner catching up on the events of the day. Ann told Josie about the murder victim, omitting all the gory details.

The doorbell rang.

"Are you expecting anyone?" Josie asked her.

"No, and I don't know of anyone who would arrive unannounced," replied Ann.

Josie went to answer the door and Ann heard her emitting a joyful whoop.

"Oh, Adam," Josie's voice shrieked from the hallway, "how wonderful to see you!"

Ann immediately recognised her brother's voice; she stood up and rushed to the door in time to see Josie flinging her arms around the tall, handsome, blond caller at the door.

She stepped forward and embraced her brother who grinned at their delight in seeing him.

"Oh, my favourite girls, I've missed you so much."

Ann and Josie smiled.

"When did you get back?" Ann asked, looking up at him. "I was expecting you *next* month."

"I left because things in Afghanistan were becoming quite tense for us journalists," replied Adam.

"Have you finished writing your book?" urged Josie.

"Yes, my third and my last, I hope," he said.

Josie stood back and looked at him. "You've lost weight," she said, almost in admonishment. She leaned forward and took hold of his hand, leading him to the dinner table. "You've arrived at just the right time, we've just started to eat dinner," she said. "Let's give you some proper food."

Adam, Ann knew, had seen many atrocities in the war zones of Bosnia, the Gulf War and Afghanistan. He was her only sibling, and they were close. She also loved the way he adored her partner, Josie.

They chatted amiably together during the meal, catching up on one another's news.

"Where are you staying?" Josie asked.

"Well, I wondered if I could bed down here for a few nights as my flat has been rented out," Adam replied.

Ann and Josie both sealed their approval. "That's absolutely fine by us."

***

The following morning, Ann sat at her desk and began reviewing the details of the murder. Her concentration was broken by a member of staff who informed her that George Casey had arrived to identify his brother's remains. Ann immediately stopped what she was doing, went to meet him and led the way to the mortuary.

George went through the motions expected of him with such a procedure. He maintained his composure throughout the brief inspection. This was quite remarkable given that the battered corpse barely resembled the brother he once knew. Only his dark, heavy brows knitted together in a deep frown.

"Do you have any leads on the killer?" George asked Ann afterwards. His normal healthy florid complexion had a waxen, pale look.

"Not at present," said Ann, "except to say that your brother let his killer into the house. It suggests he might have known his attacker. We doubt whether it was a burglary because expensive items belonging to your brother were not taken, although the disarray at the scene of the crime suggests the killer was searching for something."

George gave her a questioning look; his dark, brooding eyes slightly widening. He waited for her to go on.

"We suspect it might have been a book written in some sort of code that we think the killer missed," Ann explained, "because we found the item stuck under the desktop and the drawers of the desk had been pulled out." She looked at him with intent. "Do you know anything about this book?"

George remained wordless for a few moments. "Do you think I could possibly have the book?" he asked unexpectedly. "You see, my brother was very meticulous about his books and I know he would have wanted that kept by the family."

Ann said, "I am afraid I cannot do that as the book forms part of the evidence and must remain with the forensics department until we have completed our investigation."

She regarded him quizzically. "It would be helpful, though, if we can find someone who can decode the book." She continued to study his features. "I am sure the book has some connection to your brother's death."

George frowned.

"I wouldn't be able to decode the book and I don't know anyone who can help you," he said with a studied gaze, "but I would like it returned to me as soon as your investigations are complete, Inspector."

"I will make a note of your wishes," Ann said.

George shuffled his feet, reached into his pocket and drew out a piece of paper. "Here is Luke Cowan's number," he said, handing the notepaper to Ann.

Ann politely thanked him for coming to identify his brother and escorted him out of the building. She was keen to interview the other two brothers and, of course, Luke Cowan. She surmised that the answer to the killing might be lurking within the family.

Ann went to find David to remind him that they should arrange to see the brothers as a matter of urgency. He told Ann that he had managed to contact the younger brother, Nathan, who explained that, as he and Jake shared a house, he would arrange for Jake to be present at the meeting, too.

"I managed to arrange the meeting with both brothers on Thursday at 7pm," David announced later, looking pleased. "Are you able to make that day and time, Guv?"

"I'll just check," she said, and flipped through her diary. "Yes," she said, getting to the right page, "I'm free from 5pm. Let's meet at my office around 6pm on Thursday. We should be able to get to West London by seven."

***

David parked the car at an attractive, terraced house in Fulham. Ann climbed out and went to ring the bell.

A tall, athletic looking man answered the door. Ann identified herself and flashed her badge to confirm her identity. The man introduced himself as Jake Casey. He invited Ann and David into the living room and called to his brother, Nathan, to join them.

Ann informed the brothers of Tom's demise and offered her sympathy. Nathan broke down in tears at the news, but Jake remained unemotional.

Ann asked where the brothers were on the night of Tom's murder.

"I work as a paramedic," Jake began, "and I was on duty that night."

Nathan said he was at the pub until midnight, after which time he went to his girlfriend's home where he stayed till the next morning.

David remained in the background, listening, without saying a word.

"OK, I'll need names and contact numbers to check your alibis," said Ann.

"Yes, of course," Jake said.

Nathan nodded.

"How well did you get along with your brother, Tom?" Ann asked them.

"I got on well with Tom," Jake replied. "We didn't live in each other's pockets, but we got together quite frequently at family gatherings and for the odd drink." He waved a hand. "We had our differences, what family doesn't? But not to the extent of needing to commit murder."

She turned to Nathan. "And what about you, Mr Casey; did you get along with Tom?"

"Yes," Nathan replied, "I was very close to my brother." His eyes clouded. "He was like a father to me after our parents died."

Ann paused for a moment then asked, "I understand from your brother, George, that none of you get along with your brother-in-law Luke Cowan. Is that correct?"

Jake's face hardened. "Yeah," he said, "the cunning bastard; he should have died instead of our sister."

Ann fixed him with her stare.

"There wasn't a moment's bloody peace when he was around," Jake said. "Yvonne was irritated and affected by the way in which he disagreed with us brothers. We got into many verbal battles with Luke. And my brother, Tom, despised him with a vengeance." He paused to take a breath and reflected. "In as much as it devastated us, it was a kind of relief when Yvonne died because it cut the connection we had with Luke."

"Really? In what way?"

"He thinks too much of himself, that's what. He thinks everyone is beneath him. We could now, at last, get him out of our lives."

David began to survey the room, taking a step towards the bookshelf along the far wall.

Ann turned to address Nathan. "And do you share your brother's opinion?" she asked him.

"Not really," said Nathan. "I had no fights with Luke. I know he loved our sister and I guess that was good enough for me."

"Oh, for heaven's sake," Jake said at that, and turned to Ann. "I'm afraid my brother is far too tolerant."

David turned his head back towards them, observing the scene.

Ann listened intently, making notes as they spoke. Jake, she observed, did most of the talking, interrupting Nathan in mid-conversation sometimes and answering for Nathan before he had a chance to reply.

After she had taken all the notes she could, she thanked the brothers and reminded them that she would need to take a cheek swab for their DNA to exclude them as suspects.

David waited until they had reached the car before he spoke.

"Do you think Jake interrupted his brother because he wanted to stop him from divulging anything?" he asked Ann.

"I don't think so," Ann said. "On the one hand, the guy is arrogant and seemed to want to belittle Nathan, assuming Nathan was not intelligent enough to answer the question for himself." She gave a light shrug and glared at the road ahead as she turned the engine. "But on the other hand, you could be right – it might be part of a cover-up."

"And another thing," David said, "did you notice the number of books on the occult on *their* bookshelf?"

"I'm not surprised," said Ann. "George Casey had enough books on the occult to fill a modest library and his brothers clearly share the same interest."

She braked as she reached a set of lights on red.

"Let's get in touch with the formidable-sounding Mr Cowan," she suggested, easing her car into the right-hand lane as she pulled ahead when the lights turned to green.

"Shall I ring him, Guv?"

"No, let me do it as I think this guy will insist on speaking to a senior member of the team."

Pulling up in a side road beneath the overhang of a leafy tree, Ann dialled Luke's mobile number that rang for a while before he answered. Luke Cowan sounded charming on the phone and not at all like the self-righteous character the brothers had portrayed him to be. He agreed to meet with Ann and nominated the hospital lecture room as he was on call and unable to go home.

David redirected the satnav and they set off in the direction of the hospital.

Mr Luke Cowan was an eminent orthopaedic surgeon. He was tall and his fit, muscular body strained against his fitted shirt. His fair hair was swept back giving him a rather handsome, somewhat dashing appearance.

In the lecture room, Ann moved forward to shake Luke's hand and introduce David to him. Luke motioned them to sit down. He pulled up a chair opposite them.

He fixed his gaze on Ann as she spoke and began informing him of his brother-in-law's death by murder.

His piercing blue eyes unsettled her. He had a disarming smile that she supposed he used as part of his seduction strategy. David noticed how Luke frequently diverted his gaze to Ann's shapely legs. This act alone began to nurture in David an intense dislike for the man.

Luke continued to gawp at Ann without flinching, except when his eyes were drawn back to her legs. As she briefly outlined the circumstances of Tom's death, he seemed, Ann thought, utterly devoid of emotion.

He reclined in his chair and measured his words as he spoke. "Why are you telling me this?" he asked. "I have nothing more to do with the Casey family after the death of my wife. I cut all ties with the brothers after she died."

"Mr Cowan, it is routine police procedure to question everyone who is involved with the family, even ex-in-laws, not to mention informing all family, past and present, in the first place," Ann explained.

Luke Cowan ran his glance up and down her as if resenting having to defer to a woman. David silently observed him.

"Can you verify where you were between 3am and 6am on Thursday, Mr Cowan?" enquired Ann, ignoring his eyes travelling up and down her body appraisingly.

"I was in the operating theatre until 11pm, then went to the office to catch up on some paperwork," he replied matter-of-factly. "After that I went to sleep in the doctors' room."

"Can anyone vouch for your whereabouts?" Ann asked him, beginning to get the measure of the man.

"Yes, a colleague, Dr Worthing, met me in the corridor as I emerged from my office around 2am." He sounded haughty as if pleased to have scored a point over her questioning.

"I will need the contact number of your colleague, please," Ann responded, maintaining her official on-duty tone. She heard David move slightly in his seat but did not look his way.

Luke slid his hand into his jacket pocket and pulled out his phone with the action of a man for whom this was a minor, piffling procedure. He scrolled down and read out the number and location for Dr Worthing. His voice sounded weary, almost lazy.

"You don't believe I had a hand in Tom's death, do you?" he asked, in a tone that was mildly mocking, as if at any moment he would wink at her, pleased with his little joke.

"No," Ann said, "but I understand you had many disagreements with the victim and with his brothers and we do have to exclude you as a suspect."

"Oh, I get it," Luke said, looking pointedly at his watch, an expensive gold-encrusted timepiece. "So, they've told you about our *disagreements…*" he emphasised the word to make his denigration clear, "…haven't they, Inspector?"

Ann merely looked at him and said nothing.

"And did they tell you also how possessive they were over their sister? Did they explain how they ruled her life? Did any one of them tell you how insanely jealous they were of my love for her, my love for *my wife*?" His brooding blue eyes had suddenly darkened, burning into hers as if at any moment real flames would be seen erupting in their depths.

And as he spoke, the veins, stood out prominently on his forehead as he tried to stifle that inherent anger, an anger that had clearly been smouldering for some time.

Ann spotted an opportunity to catch him off-guard and immediately asked the question, "Did your animosity towards your brothers-in-law drive you to the point of committing murder, Mr Cowan?"

The effrontery of her question brought Luke to his feet. His previous calm composure was replaced with explosive rage. He moved swiftly towards her, shouting into her face, inches from his own, "How dare you! How dare you make such an accusation?"

The outburst swiftly mobilised David to his feet. He placed himself between Ann and her would-be assailant. She stood still and calmly qualified her statement by saying, "It is a perfectly reasonable question, Mr Cowan."

Ignoring David's presence, he glowered at her.

"It is very well documented," she continued, "how powerful, repressed emotions can drive some people to commit murder."

"Perhaps they neglected to tell you," Luke said, "about their sister's ex-boyfriend, Sam Cain."

Ann listened carefully to his response and said nothing, watching his face as he spoke.

"Oh yeah, the brothers gave Sam the beating of his life when they discovered he was sleeping with their sister."

"I see."

"Good. Because you should be asking Sam how much he hates the brothers." Luke appeared to calm and took a step back. "That's where you should be looking for the murderer, Inspector, not here."

Ann regarded him thoughtfully. "Where will we find this Mr Cain?" she asked.

"His landline number will be in the phone book," replied Luke with an audible sigh. "I don't have his mobile number."

"Thank you," Ann said, and made a mental note of the name. "However, we will still require your fingerprints and a swab for DNA testing. You understand we must formally exclude you from the list of suspects, Mr Cowan."

"Bloody hell!" Luke exclaimed, tossing his chin. His scathing tone fell just short of fury. "That's it, isn't it? You lot love to chase the wrong people and let the real criminals enjoy their freedom."

Ann remained still and studied him.

"And when do you propose to do your samples?"

Ann remained unfazed by his derisive tone.

"Tomorrow, if you are free, please," she replied.

"Yes, if it's necessary." He once again made a pointed gesture to check the time on his watch. "I have to attend a meeting right now," he said, his voice brusque. "I'll be available should I be needed for any more questions."

Ann remained polite then thanked him and they left.

"This guy has a very short fuse," David said in the car afterwards. "It would not be difficult to provoke him and I reckon he has enough anger towards the brothers to do serious damage."

"He certainly is a volatile character," Ann said. "Let's see what forensics have found."

"Yeah, agree."

"And" added Ann, "when we meet with this Sam Cain, he might just provide a missing piece of the jigsaw."

Once back in her office she began to document her interview

with Luke Cowan. She had completed most of her paperwork when the phone rang. It was Tim Jones, the coroner, reminding her that her presence in the mortuary was needed for the post-mortem examination on the body of Tom Casey.

She apologised for being late and hurriedly went to the mortuary, pulling on protective clothing before entering the room where Tom Casey's body lay on the slab. Tim was busy dictating into a recorder suspended overhead. He had confirmed that the cause of death was asphyxiation due to strangulation. He also confirmed his findings by stating that the victim's hyoid bone had been fractured during the strangulation. He drew attention to the circular pattern on the right side of the victim's neck. He suggested that it resembled a pattern of an inverted cross that might be the impression of a ring. Tim deducted that the killer had used his hands to strangle the victim and that he wore a ring, which seemed to have been turned around on his finger, facing the inside of his hand. The imprint of the pattern had been transferred to the victim's neck as the killer clasped his hands around it and squeezed with tremendous force, whereupon the hyoid bone had fractured. An impression of four fingers on the side of the neck confirmed that the victim was indeed strangled. The presence of petechial haemorrhages in the eyes also suggested cause of death as strangulation. A trace of glove powder suggested that the killer wore gloves.

"There are bruises at the side of the mouth where the linen strip kept the mouth gag in place," he pointed out. "There is a pattern of bruising around the shoulders and around the groin, also across the body. This is consistent with the rope that held the victim onto the staircase. There are further bruises on the wrists and ankles where he was probably restrained. Your murderer knows how to tie his ropes. He could have had naval training."

Tim pointed to the missing strips of flesh that were cut out from the victim's thighs. "These missing pieces of flesh presumably were kept as trophies by the killer," said Tim. "There are holes in the bones of the legs and arms that appear to have been made by an electrical drill. The drill bit found at the scene fits the holes in the legs. Linear cuts matched to a chisel found at the scene that was used to join up the holes drilled in the bones by dragging the chisel along the drill holes. The victim's hands and feet were a bloody mess as the bruising and bleeding suggested that the industrial staples that had been inserted were done pre-mortem, causing great damage to bone and flesh. The victim's penis is slit in four sections, from the tip to the root; splayed open, it resembles a starfish."

Tim paused, losing his professionalism a little. "Hmm!" he grimaced. "Must have been bloody excruciating – the poor sod was still alive when this was done."

"All the hallmarks of a personal grudge and a punishment, I would think," said Ann.

Tim continued, "There were numerous linear cuts all over the body, which suggested that the killer began the torture with the small cuts, possibly done with a razor or scalpel that caused profuse bleeding. The intermittent clotting around the sites suggests the cuts were made ante-mortem. The killer then made deeper incisions to the dermis that he knew would cause severe pain. The condition of the organs suggests the victim was a relatively healthy individual."

Tim's final comment was that he assumed, judging by the precision of the strips of flesh cut from the body, that this must have been done by a skilled butcher or someone with medical knowledge as the incisions missed the major blood vessels in the abdomen, causing maximum pain and delayed death.

He told Ann that he had sent off samples of blood and bone marrow taken from the drill bit and chisel found at the scene. Toxicology reports did not reveal any drugs in the victim's system. Alcohol levels were minimal.

Ann remained at the mortuary to discuss the details of the case with Tim for some time after the completion of the post-mortem.

Tim promised that he would send Ann a detailed, typed report as soon as he could. She thanked him and left, returning to her office to complete all her paperwork regarding the post-mortem. She recalled details of her interview with Luke Cowan and tried to piece together parts of the puzzle; she recalled what he had said and his impromptu and abrupt reaction to her questioning. Ann made a note of the contact details for Sam Cain, which Luke had given her, picked up the hand receiver from the office landline and dialled the number.

A male voice answered. "Hello, this is Sam Cain."

"Mr Cain, I am Detective Chief Inspector Ann Dixon," Ann said into the mouthpiece. "I wonder if you could spare the time for me to visit you. I am investigating a murder."

There was a brief pause on the other end of the line.

"Are you sure you have the right number?"

"You are Mr Sam Cain of 12 Bentley Road, Battersea?"

"Yes, that is right."

"I will get right to the point, Mr Cain," said Ann. "A man named Tom Casey, whose sister you once knew, has been murdered and we need to interview you and everyone who was close to the Casey brothers."

There was another brief silence after which Sam Cain offered, "How about 10am on Wednesday?"

"That would be good for me, too, thank you; I will see you then."

At that second the ringing of her cell phone interrupted her thoughts. She glanced at the screen before answering it.

"Hi, busy lady, fancy a game of squash?"

"Hello Clive, good to hear from you. Oh yes, I would love a game. Maybe I can get rid of some of the stress that is taking over my life right now. What time?"

"6pm any good for you?"

"Perfect."

"And if you're free afterwards, we can grab a bite to eat," suggested Clive. Clive Hammond was Ann's friend and colleague whom she had worked with when they worked for MI6.

Ann readily agreed and called Josie to inform her that she would not be home for dinner.

Ann enjoyed the rigours of playing squash. It provided a healthy opportunity to lash out at the frustrations pounding in on her via a simple racquet and shuttlecock, thereby releasing the tension. Sweating profusely and breathing heavily as she battled to keep up with Clive's command of the game, Ann finally collapsed on the squash court, smiling whilst admitting defeat.

Later, whilst eating, Clive remarked, "Your case, I see, is dominating the news these days."

"I wish it wouldn't. It's become the bane of my life," Ann said. "And I get nil support from my super. He's the rudest bastard on the planet."

"Maybe you should consider returning to MI6 with us," suggested Clive encouragingly.

"Absolutely not, I'm done with that lot. I love my work. I just wish I didn't need to deal with such a mindless idiot as my boss."

"You were a fantastic operative and I am sure a great cop. Don't allow them to get to you. Just follow your instincts."

"Your advice is welcome," Ann said, "and thank you for the compliment."

After they had eaten and parted company, Ann returned to her office. The phone rang. It was the forensics' pathologist who informed her that they were able to lift off a good set of fingerprints from the drill bit and the chisel found at the scene of the crime. She was also told that the blood and bone marrow found in the groove of the drill bit was a match to Tom Casey.

The next morning, Ann mobilised her team to get fingerprints and cheek swabs from the Casey brothers and from Luke Cowan. She told them she would also take swabs and fingerprints from Sam Cain.

The following day, David accompanied Ann to 12 Bentley Road. She stood at the door for a few minutes while David parked the car before ringing the bell. A stocky man answered the door. Ann introduced herself and Sergeant David Hughes to Sam Cain who invited them in.

She swiftly glanced around the living room before taking a seat next to David on the sofa. Ann wasted no time in getting to the point of the matter. She repeated the reason for her visit and asked Sam if he could substantiate his movements on the day Tom Casey was murdered. He duly told her that he was at home, but there were no witnesses to support his claim. When questioned about his relationship with the Casey brothers, Sam explained how they beat him when they realised he was dating their sister. He expressed deep loathing for the brothers and showed Ann the scars he still bore because of the beating.

"You see," Sam said, "the Casey brothers thought nobody was

good enough for their sister. They hated me because they thought I wasn't wealthy enough to marry her."

"Surely, Mr Cain, you must have built up a certain amount of resentment towards the Casey brothers if they beat you and humiliated you over time?" Ann probed. "Isn't that a strong enough motive for murder?"

Sam shuffled uncomfortably. When he replied, Ann noted how his words fell over one another in a slight stammer. "I did-disliked the brothers, but not enough to murder one of them. They're a wicked bunch. You should speak to their old n-neighbour in Nottingham."

Ann gave him a questioning look.

Having controlled his nervous stammer, Sam continued. "His neighbour could tell you how cruel they were to animals, torturing and murdering those poor creatures during their satanic rituals. They also tortured the girls who were naïve enough to venture into their clutches. Who knows, one of them could have murdered their own brother."

"Do you know about the existence of a code book that belonged to Tom?" asked Ann.

"I don't know about a code book," Sam replied, "but I do know that Tom had many books on the occult. I don't know about that book, though. Talk to Jack Slade, the neighbour. He knew the brothers well enough. He may even be able to tell you about the book in question."

He gave her a direct and forceful look and then turned his head slightly, averting his eyes and facing into the air.

"He has enough dirt on them to put them all in jail. And Jack Slade will give you an eyewitness account of what the brothers did to their sister." At that he appeared to stall and shifted nervously in his chair, entwining his fingers together in his lap. He finished by saying abruptly, "And I am *not* saying another word."

Ann waited for him to recover from his outburst. "What do you do for a living, Mr Cain?"

"I work for an insurance company," Sam responded, looking more at ease. "It's rather boring work, but thankfully I can lose myself in my love of woodwork." He made a gesture with his arm and for a moment looked proud. "I've made most of the furniture in this room."

Ann faced towards an elegantly constructed coffee table; it was made of soft walnut with intricately carved fluted legs. There was a matching cabinet to her left that stood tall and majestic with fitted doors, neat hinges and delicate handles.

"You are indeed very talented, Mr Cain, judging from the furniture I see here; your work is tasteful and looks well-crafted."

"Thank you," Sam beamed. "I do all the work in my shed at the back of the house."

Ann looked at him before asking him the same question.

"Mr Cain," she said, "we will need you to come to the police station for our forensics officer to take your fingerprints and swabs for your DNA so that we can exclude you from the investigation."

Sam nodded and said nothing.

"We will need to speak to you again," she added, "so please don't leave town." She then asked for Jack Slade's address, which he gave her willingly.

Her phone rang as she got into the car. It was Edwards. She rolled her eyes towards David as she held the phone.

"Dixon," Edwards barked down the phone to her, "I've organised a press conference for this afternoon at two in the briefing room. You had better be there!"

"OK, I'll b–"

She barely had time to finish her sentence when he put the phone down.

"Rude bastard. I hate it when he does that to me," Ann said, frustration making the skin on her forehead crease into a frown.

She glanced at her watch and realised they had just about an hour before the press meeting. "Let's try to contact Jack Slade while we're waiting."

The two of them headed off in the direction of her office. She listened while David dialled the number Sam had provided. After a few minutes, a frail voice answered the phone.

"May I speak to Mr Jack Slade, please?" David asked.

"Yes, this is he. Whom am I speaking to, please?"

"This is Sergeant David Hughes from the Central London Police Division, Sir. I wonder if I could come to your house to speak, please, and at your earliest convenience?"

There was an absence of any sound when Jack Slade asked, "Why do you need to see me, Sergeant?"

"We are investigating a murder of one of your ex-neighbours and we thought you might be able to tell us a bit about the background of the Casey brothers."

When Jack replied, there was an edge of consternation in his voice.

"I don't know if I can do that, Sergeant Hughes," he said, "those boys are a bad bunch and it's not my life's worth to get involved."

Noticing that David did not respond straightaway and irritated at his procrastination, Ann took the phone from him and introduced herself to Mr Slade.

She spoke in a charming, almost seductive tone, pausing where necessary.

"Hello, Mr Slade, I am DCI Dixon. So sorry to bother you; we understand your concerns about helping the police, but I can assure you, your help will be invaluable to us and, of course, everything you say will be kept in the strictest confidence."

Her enticement worked and he agreed to meet with them early the next morning.

David wrote down the address as Ann repeated it.

"Thank you, Mr Slade, and we look forward to meeting with you tomorrow," she said into the phone.

David smiled.

"Ever thought of working for the United Nations, Guv?"

Ann swung around at the remark, laughed, and hit him playfully on the head with a folded newspaper.

"Watch your mouth, Hughes," she admonished him. "Ever imagined yourself back in uniform?"

He tossed his head and pursed his lips.

Ann threw a look at him and altered her tone. "Now," she ordered, "get hold of a decent car and one that will drive us to Nottingham tomorrow."

David nodded and scribbled something down on his notepad.

Ann added, "And we'd better grab some lunch in the canteen, there's no knowing how long the press meeting will last."

During lunch, they discussed the meeting with Sam Cain and worked out a strategy for their next move.

"Better not be *too* direct with the questions when we meet with Mr Slade," Ann warned, "he may clam up if he feels threatened." At that, David recalled her earlier tone on the phone to him.

They mulled over the evidence so far and spent some time going over the details of their interview with Sam.

The briefing room, meanwhile, was filled with the buzz of eager press waiting patiently for the superintendent to appear.

A momentary hush prevailed when Edwards at last entered the room. He outlined brief details of the murder, omitting details that would harm the progress of the case. His statement was immediately followed by a barrage of questions.

"Superintendent, do you have a suspect?"

"Why was the victim tortured?"

"Do you have any leads yet?"

"Why has it taken you so long to release a statement to the press?"

Edwards waited for a suitable pause in the questioning before answering in his no-nonsense professional tone.

"We do not have a crystal ball to lead us to a suspect or tell us why the victim has been tortured," he replied. "My officers must be given time to pursue information and rely on scientific evidence to help them find the killer."

He took a breath while watching them scribble down their notes before continuing.

"The police do not have an obligation to keep the media informed day and night whenever a crime is committed. They need time to process the evidence, which hopefully will result in the killer being caught, and they will keep the press informed."

Edwards looked around, surveying them, scanning his eyes across the room. "I have no further information at present, except to assure you that my officers are doing everything possible to find the murderer who committed this heinous crime."

He took a few steps back, raising his chin slightly. "Ladies and gentlemen," he said pointedly, "if there are no further questions, I am now concluding this meeting."

Edwards raised himself from his seat and began walking out of the room. Some persistent members of the media continued to fire questions at him. Edwards tightened his lips, remained silent and walked out of the door.

Ann and David followed hastily before the journalists began to question them.

"Who the hell was that short journalist who refused to back down? David asked.

"That's the poison dwarf from *The World News*, Amy Baker," Ann replied. "We have crossed swords many times and she hasn't forgiven me. No doubt she will follow this case doggedly, purely to score points with her boss and hopefully try to get me discredited."

"She sounds a nasty bit of work; you should steer clear of her, Guv," said David, pointing out the obvious.

Later, Ann completed her backlog of paperwork and headed home. Josie was away for a few days, so she indulged in a takeaway dinner and a glass of wine and settled for an early night.

The following morning, David collected her at 7am and they set off for their meeting with Mr Slade. They reached Edwinstowe, Nottingham, at 10.30am. The house was hidden from view amongst a clump of trees near the edge of the forest. From the outside, it appeared in a state of neglect. Paint peeled from the guttering and there were large cracks along the outside walls. The garden was overgrown with weeds and there were rusted car parts strewn at the rear of the house.

Ann and David took a brief look around before knocking the doorknocker. There was a momentary pause before a rather bedraggled-looking man opened the door.

"Who are you?" he enquired.

"Good morning," greeted Ann, "we are from the CLPD." She flashed her identity badge. "We'd like to speak to a Mr Jack Slade, please. I believe he lives at this address." She kept her voice light and friendly without sounding too cheerful.

"*I* am Jack Slade," he said, taking a cursory glance at her ID badge. "Come in."

Ann followed him into the house with David a few steps behind.

Jack invited them to sit down. The inside of the house was unkempt and in urgent need of a clean. Jack apologised for the untidy state of the house, explaining that he neglected to keep it tidy after the death of his wife three years ago. He offered them tea, which Ann politely declined, explaining that they had had coffee on the way over.

"So, which one of the Casey brothers has died?" Jack enquired.

"Tom. He was brutally murdered last week," explained Ann.

"Hardly surprises me; he got what he deserved."

"That's quite a harsh statement, Mr Slade," exclaimed Ann.

"Not at all, if you knew how wicked all the brothers were."

"Mr Slade, we have information about the brothers having tortured animals and women. They also apparently practised satanic rituals. Can you give us your version of events?"

"Oh ay, I'll tell you about the Caseys alright," he said.

He got up from his seat and walked to the window. He pointed to a large white house a few hundred yards from his own.

"That is where the Casey brothers lived with their parents. Their mother was an actress and spent lots of time away from home. Their father was a lawyer for Lloyd's of London, so he commuted each day. The boys were cared for by a nanny. What you say is true – they are wicked. They tortured and killed small animals in the forest, including some of the neighbours' pets.

Ann blinked.

"How do you know so much about their behaviour, Mr Slade?"

"The boys used to take my tools and hide them in their garden shed to annoy me," he replied. "I would go looking for my stuff in their backyard. That's how I happened to see what they got up to when their parents were away." He paused for a moment before saying, "They brought girls in off the streets, tortured them and then held sexual orgies with them. They moved their activities into the basement of the house because the women screamed so much. They finally moved their rituals to the forest where they had the freedom to continue their perverse practises undisturbed. The most unforgivable crime was the sexual abuse of their sister. I only know about what they did because she ran away from them one night and sought refuge at my house. She was terrified and told me not to say anything to anyone."

Ann had been scrutinising his face as he spoke.

"The boys had a cousin, James," Jack went on, "he was as evil as the rest of them." He looked away for a moment then brought his eyes back to Ann. "I suppose his father being a Nazi might explain his cruel streak. He mixed with drug dealers and some very shifty fellas."

Ann remained silent, listening to him.

"Their mother and father were killed in a car crash just when the boys started their careers. We heard that they were practising satanic rituals in the forest. Nobody dared go to watch what was going on; it was thought they posted guards near the ritual site and the guards stopped anyone getting close. It was said the guards were a force to be reckoned with, so nobody ventured near the scene."

"Did you witness firsthand what was going on?"

"The terrible things that were done to the women by those lads is beyond belief," Jack responded, without answering her question directly. A tear ran down his cheek unchecked as he appeared to be remembering the distress of their sister.

"Mr Slade," Ann said, continuing to observe him, "the police would label you a voyeur for watching these activities and possibly an accomplice for not reporting the abuse."

"Believe me, Inspector," replied Jack, still managing to avoid giving her a direct answer, "I would rather spend time in jail than suffer the wrath of the Caseys."

"Do you remember anything else, Mr Slade?" asked Ann, feeling she was unlikely to elicit further response.

"Yes, for all their violent behaviour, George Casey and his brothers created a beautiful rose garden at the back of the house, and they tended it every day."

"Really?" Ann's eyes widened at this.

"I couldn't believe that men who embodied such perversity could produce such a beautiful garden," Jack went on.

"Did you know any of the girls who were brought to the house?"

"No, they were foreign girls who lived rough on the streets. Choosing such girls gave the boys carte blanche to use and abuse them as they pleased. They were vulnerable and easy targets."

Jack appeared to be thinking for a moment.

"I do remember a Russian girl named Saskia, though. She befriended my son and that's why her name sticks in my mind. She got friendly with the Casey boy and was seen at their home frequently."

He went silent for a few seconds and lowered his eyes to stare at the floor.

"Then Saskia suddenly vanished, and we never heard about her again."

He brought his head up and looked at Ann again.

"Perhaps you should speak to my son, Andrew. He would be able to tell you more."

"Thank you; where does your son live?"

"Well, he lives on the Costa del Sol in Spain, but he comes to see me at Christmas."

"We would like to speak to your son," Ann said. "Do you have an address in Spain for him?"

Jack shuffled over to a chest of drawers, riffled through some papers and produced his son's address and telephone number.

"Perhaps you could warn your son that we will be in touch," Ann advised, "and thank you for your help," she said while handing him her business card. "Here's my contact number. If you remember anything more that may help in our investigations," she said, unwilling to stress him any further, "please get in touch."

"Wow, these Caseys are a bad bunch," exclaimed David after they had left.

"Sounds a bit like the Mafia," agreed Ann. "We need to have another meeting with the rest of the brothers."

They got back to London by early evening. Ann could not escape her meeting with Stephen Edwards. She headed for his office as soon as she arrived.

"Where the hell have you been?" he demanded. "I've sent numerous messages and tried calling you several times."

"Sorry, Sir, we've been busy interviewing," she replied, keeping her voice as steady as she could. "Sergeant Hughes and I have just come back from a meeting with the former next-door neighbour of the Casey brothers when they lived in Nottingham."

"I trust it wasn't a wasted journey," Edwards said.

"No, on the contrary, it was most useful as we discovered facts about the Casey brothers that are valuable to our investigation."

This aroused Edwards' curiosity and he pressed her for more information. She told him what Jack Slade had said. She was amazed that it held Edwards' attention to such a degree that he did not interrupt her as she spoke. When she had finished, he asked if the information had brought her any nearer to finding the killer. She told him that she was still awaiting the outstanding forensics results and promised to keep him informed of all matters pertaining to the case.

"Well, keep me posted and give me a shout when you've heard from forensics," Edwards said somewhat kindly.

***

Josie was late for a meeting with an important client. She raced to her appointment, speeding across a red traffic light in her haste. The driver of an ambulance that came out of the hospital gates was unable to apply the brakes in time to avoid a collision. Josie's car was rammed from the passenger side but thankfully nobody was hurt.

The tall, handsome driver stepped out of the ambulance, checked Josie was OK and then grinned as he mocked her driving skills. She was too embarrassed to reprimand him for criticising her driving but felt incredibly lucky he was not on his way to an emergency.

He stuck out his hand and introduced himself as Jake Casey.

"I am so sorry," said Josie apologetically. "I was speeding to a meeting, and I should not have been driving so fast."

"No real damage to the ambulance," said Jake glancing across at her vehicle, "but your lovely red Porsche has taken a bit of a knock."

"Let's swap details and I'll get my insurance to sort it out," Josie said.

"No need to stuff up your no-claims bonus," Jake said with ease. "I have a better solution," he began as he appraised her, "and that's if you would agree to have dinner with me, I'll tell my boss I was hit by a guy who drove off."

"Oh, I don't think I could do that," replied Josie, taken aback at his suggestion.

"Well, why not?" Jake Casey asked looked down at her. "A pretty woman like you must be beating the men away from your door."

"I am in a relationship so I can't accept your invitation," replied Josie, looking at him steadily.

"For heaven's sake," responded Jake, "it will only be dinner, not a marriage proposal. A small price to pay for my silence, don't you agree?"

Josie thought for a few seconds and then reluctantly agreed to meet him for dinner in a few days. They exchanged phone numbers, but Josie warned him not to call her. He teased her about being afraid of her partner.

Nonetheless, she drove off feeling terribly guilty for planning to do something behind Ann's back. *Oh well*, she thought, trying her best to brush off her decision as nothing more than a harmless gesture of goodwill, *no harm done; it will only be dinner*. But she couldn't shake the feeling off. She was wracked with guilt. She knew Ann would be incensed at her for entering into a covert arrangement but there appeared to be something genuine about the man she had met – quite literally – by accident. She hurried home, her thoughts in turmoil.

***

Pleased that she had survived her meeting with Edwards, Ann headed for her office, completed additions on her laptop and left for home.

"I hope you have prepared a hearty meal, I'm starving," she said as she entered the house.

"Of course, my darling, I have prepared your favourite," replied Josie.

"Good, I'll just jump into the shower and then you can have all my attention!" Ann shouted as she ran upstairs to the bathroom.

Josie, too impatient to wait, followed Ann into the shower whereupon they engaged in a frenzy of passionate love-making that left them breathless.

"Oh, someone *was* starving," remarked Josie afterwards, grinning cheekily.

"I guess it serves me right for deserting you in the early hours of the morning," quipped back Ann.

The two women got dressed and headed for the kitchen. They caught up on their news and Ann talked briefly about her trip to Nottingham.

The following morning, the familiar sound of David's car hooter sounded outside. Ann dashed about collecting the files she needed to take with her for the day's work.

"Sorry to keep you waiting," she said to him as she climbed into the car. "I never remember to put things where I can find them in the morning and then it's a frantic scramble to get everything together."

Josie waved them off at the door, watching as David's car disappeared down the road towards Ann's office.

***

"I managed to get George Casey to meet with us this morning," David informed Ann when they were in her office. "He was not exactly pleased, but he did at least agree."

"Good," said Ann, "we'll have a coffee and then go to his house."

When they arrived at George Casey's house he was still in his dressing gown. He seemed irritated but remained civil and invited them into the living room.

"Thought I had told you everything I know at our last meeting, Inspectors," he informed them.

"You were indeed very helpful," agreed Ann, "but we need to clarify a few things we have learned from someone else who is also helping us with our enquiries."

George swung around sharply at that and demanded to know whom Ann had been speaking to. Ann had already made a note in her pad that his attitude was not quite the same as it had been when they had first met.

"Never mind who it was," said Ann, drawing herself up, "we need *your* version of the story."

George Casey stared at her. "I don't like your tone, Inspector," he said. "What have they been saying to you?"

"Let's say we know about the satanic rituals in the forest and the encounters with foreign girls by you and your brothers, Mr Casey," Ann said, watching his features carefully.

"We are normal, healthy men with an interest in women; since when has this been a crime?"

"Yes, I agree, but we have been told that your relationship with the girls defied the terms of normality. We believe that you and your brothers used the girls in your rituals and that you tortured the women to satisfy what can best be described as your perverse needs."

George gave her a dirty look. "That's a preposterous accusation!" He stuck his hands on his hips. His face, crimson with anger, looked as if he had sat in the sun too long. "And what evidence do you have to support your accusations?" He had thrust out his bottom lip as he spoke. "Because I will consult with my lawyer about bringing charges against the police for slander."

"We do have a credible witness who will testify against you," Ann informed him.

Her statement forced George to back down. He managed to compose himself and said, "I am quite within my rights to practice as a Satanist in this country. You will find it hard to prosecute me on the grounds of my unorthodox religion."

"Of course," said Ann, "I am aware of that, however, there is the question of you and your brothers having had an incestuous relationship with your sister."

She paused, watching him steadily. "She related her rather harrowing ordeal to our witness."

Ann continued to look at him closely, observing every flicker of his eyes as she spoke.

"Do you have a feasible explanation for this accusation, Mr Casey?"

George shifted uncomfortably in his seat. He was silent for a few moments before replying, "You don't have a case, Inspector. My sister is dead. Where is the evidence?"

"Don't be so sure of that, Mr Casey," she said. "You may be surprised how the law can make a case stick, given the right circumstances."

He gave a wry smile at her confidence.

"Let me tell you," he said, showing equal confidence, "no-one will ever testify against me."

Ann raised a cynical eyebrow.

"So, I daresay," she said, "you will have them silenced if they do?"

"Those are *your* words, Inspector," George Casey retorted, "not mine."

He jabbed a finger towards her. His tone was emphatic.

"And my answer to your question is," he said, "'no comment'."

Ann realised they would not get the information they had hoped for, so she thanked George for agreeing to meet with them and they took their leave.

"I wanted to thump him at one stage, Guv," said David when they were in the car.

"No point in doing that, David," she said. "George Casey has wealth and power. He probably uses force to ensure people toe the line. And we did promise Jack we would be discreet."

The phone rang just as Ann got to her office. It was Peter Drew on the line.

"Got some fascinating news, Ann," said Peter. "The fingerprints on the drill bit belong to Sam Cain."

"Really?"

"Yep, and the blood and bone marrow belong to Tom Casey."

Ann asked if Luke Cowan had been in to tender his fingerprints and DNA yet. She was told he had done so very early that morning and his DNA was no match to any of the forensics evidence at the scene of the crime. Ann immediately went to the incident room to find the senior officers who were assigned to the case. She found DI Tobin at his desk.

CHAPTER 2

"Alf, I just had a call from forensics. They have matched the fingerprints on the drill bit and the chisel to Sam Cain."

Ann took a step towards the door then turned her head back to Alf.

"I'm off to see Edwards now to get an urgent warrant to search his house."

She spoke in a brusque tone, confident and precise.

"Contact the rest of the team, fill them in and tell them to be on standby to accompany me to the house when I have the warrant."

David joined them in the incident room and was briefed about the latest details.

"Stick around, David," she said to him, "I want you to accompany me to Sam Cain's house. But first, give me a few minutes to brief Edwards."

The news had already reached the superintendent by the time Ann walked into Edwards' office.

"Dixon," began Edwards, in sarcastic mood, "I believe you have a suspect."

"Yes, Sir; I do."

He looked at her expectantly.

"And what else?"

"I'm on my way to arrest Sam Cain," she said, swallowing hard to maintain a dignified courtesy. "I need you to get a warrant issued to search his property, please."

"Alright, you can pick it up in the morning," Edwards said, "and make sure there are no hitches!" he growled, to signify their meeting was closed. "Now get on with it."

Ann didn't hesitate to leave the room.

"Bastard," she muttered to David. "He gets worse with each passing day. A smile would probably crack his face."

"Come on, Guv, you know he'll never change," David said. "Now, let's go and tell Sam Cain the bad news."

"We'd better check on his whereabouts first," Ann said.

David agreed and called Sam to inform him that the police wanted to pay him a visit on an urgent matter. Sam replied that he was at home and would be happy to help with their enquiries.

He was pottering in the garden when they arrived. He looked at them quizzically as they got out of the car and walked towards him.

"Good afternoon, Mr Cain," Ann said, greeting him amiably enough. "There has been a dramatic development, which I need to inform you about."

Sam eyed her suspiciously.

"We have matched your fingerprints to a drill bit and chisel used to torture Tom Casey," she said and paused significantly, watching him all the time she spoke, "and his blood was found on the drill bits."

Sam just stared at her with unflinching eyes.

"I would like you to accompany us to the police station," Ann said, "for further questioning in connection with the murder of Tom Casey."

Sam made a move as if to back away.

"Cuff him, Sergeant Hughes!" ordered Ann and she turned and led the way to the car.

She addressed Sam.

"A warrant will be issued to allow the police to search your home."

Sam looked stunned. He attempted to protest but clearly thought better of it. He followed the officers in silence, into the car.

They drove him to the holding cells where both Ann and David accompanied him to the interview room. Ann went into the room alone with Sam.

She informed him that their conversation would be recorded. He nodded in acknowledgement of her statement. The bright light in the room accentuated his pallor.

"It is 10.30am on the 11th of March 2005. I am in the interview room with Mr Samuel Cain who has been brought in as a suspect in the murder of Tom Casey," Ann said for the benefit of the recording.

She then read Sam his rights ensuring that this, too, was logged onto the recorder.

"Mr Cain," she began, "are you aware of the serious nature of the charges you are facing?"

"Yes, I think so," he responded, "but I'm innocent." He spoke with a slightly anxious stammer. "I would never resort to murder even if the Caseys and I had our differences."

"You have no alibi on the night of the murder and your fingerprints are on the weapons found at the scene of the murder," Ann went on, ignoring his protest. "Can you explain how they got there if you claim you are innocent?"

Sam blinked and said nothing.

"You had motive and opportunity," Ann continued. "We know that you could not have lifted Tom onto the staircase by yourself, so did you have an accomplice, Mr Cain?"

Ann leaned forward across the table in an intimidating manner, hoping to unnerve him.

Sam's shoulders hunched. He looked awkward. He began to shake.

"I didn't do it. I didn't murder anyone. You must believe me."

"The evidence seems to link you to the murder of Tom Casey," Ann said, her eyes never leaving his face. "We will need to keep you here in the holding cells until we have searched your house. If we find more incriminating evidence on your property it will enable the prosecution to build a very strong case against you. You will then appear in court and be formally charged."

Sam's distress and the fact that he could offer no additional information to either confirm or refute the charges against him brought the meeting to a swift close. Ann formally terminated the interview and instructed the officer in charge to take Sam back to the holding cell.

The buzz of the CID team could be heard along the corridor as Ann approached the briefing room. Instead of shouting to get their attention she banged the door loudly. There followed immediate silence and they settled down to listen to her.

Ann began by informing them that she had Sam Cain in custody on the strength of the fact that his fingerprints were found on two of the murder weapons and that she was waiting for a warrant to search his home.

"OK," she said when she had finished, "now I need to hear what you have found out."

Detective Inspector Alfred Tobin told her that his team had interviewed Tom's neighbours. He said that the neighbour heard loud voices on the night of the murder. They also reported hearing classical music played around midnight. They did not take too much notice as they were used to Tom playing his music loudly; however, the music lasted for three hours until 5am, which they thought was unusual. They did not see anyone leave the house. They also did not see any strange cars parked at the house.

Tobin went on to inform her that Tom Casey's laptop and mobile phone did not have any significant information relevant to the murder.

Detective Inspector Ian Roberts reported that he had interviewed Tom's work colleagues, a close friend and associates of his company. There were very positive comments about him, and nobody could think of a motive for his death. He added that he discovered that Tom's bridge partner was also his lover, but that she was away in Scotland on the night of the murder. Linda Smith, the housekeeper, confirmed that nothing had been stolen from the Casey home.

Once Ann had searched Sam Cain's house, she informed the team that she would convene another briefing afterwards.

The team gathered in groups and began to discuss their assignments. The warrant was granted later that day and Ann, David, DI Roberts, DI Tobin and the forensics team descended on 12 Bentley Road. Ann sent her officers to various parts of the house and instructed them to be meticulous in their search. Many books relating to rituals of the occult were found on the bookshelf. Sam's clothes, together with many other items in the house, were bagged for evidence. Ann and David concentrated on the tools in Sam's garage. David found a workbench and an array of chisels, screwdrivers, nails, a staple gun and a drill. David then called Ann over to witness the collection of tools.

"Right," Ann said, making a sweeping gesture with her hand, "I want you to bag all these tools."

The forensics officer glanced at the number of tools in the garage and groaned at the command.

"Get it done!" Anne snapped.

The officer gave a small nod of acquiescence. He had already noticed what appeared to be a size 10 footprint visible in a smear of grease near the door.

"And I don't bloody care if you are here all day!" Ann barked at him. "I want you to do a thorough job."

The search lasted seven hours before Ann and her team locked the house and took all the evidence they had collected. Ann had a good working relationship with the head of the forensics laboratory, Peter Drew. Despite her exhaustion, she went to meet with him and implored him to get the samples processed urgently. They discussed details of the case over a cup of coffee in his office.

"Old Edwards been on your back again, Ann?" Peter asked with a wry smile.

Ann rolled her eyes. "When is he *ever* reasonable about time limits?" she said. "I'm quite certain he's pushing for a result in view of the fact it is me who is heading this investigation."

Peter grinned.

Ann said, "Well, put it this way, if it was a man in charge, no doubt it would have been different."

"Huh," grunted Peter, "don't allow that old fart to get to you. Stand up to him. This is your investigation and when you have caught the killer, Edwards will reap the benefit and you'll be lucky if he says thank you."

He put his arm around her for support.

"Listen," he said, with a note of reassurance in his voice, "I won't let you down. My team will work overtime to get you the results… and by tomorrow afternoon."

True to his word, the results arrived promptly at 2pm the next day. She walked to the incident room where David and Ian Roberts were examining some details on the board.

"Listen up, guys," she announced, "I have the forensic reports from Sam Cain's house. Get my team here now, please."

She briefed David and Ian on the reports while waiting for the rest of the team. It was short notice, so only eight members of the CID could attend the meeting.

"Thanks for coming," said Ann, addressing those present. "I now have the reports on samples and the items collected from Sam Cain's house."

She looked around at the faces staring up at her.

"The drill and staple gun had been washed," she went on, "but contained small traces of blood and bone marrow, which was a match to Tom Casey. The fingerprints on the staple gun and drill matched those of Sam Cain. The shoe print had traces of blood belonging to Tom Casey and carpet fibres from the carpet at the scene of the crime, but the shoe size did not match that of Sam as he wears a size 8 shoe. I do think, therefore, that he might have had an accomplice. The fact that it would have needed two people to lift the victim onto the staircase indicates this."

She paused, allowing them to digest these facts before continuing.

"I can confirm that, according to these results, we *do* have a murder suspect and Sergeant Hughes will accompany me to the holding cells where I am going to formerly charge the suspect."

Ann gathered her bag and papers as she prepared to leave the room. She made her way to the holding cells with David. She seated herself opposite Sam in the cell and informed him that the forensic department's results confirmed that his drill bit contained blood, bone marrow and tissue samples of Tom Casey, and that she was charging him with the murder.

"Mr Cain," she said, matter-of-factly, "you have the right to remain silent. Anything you say will be taken down and will be used in evidence against you." She peered at him, checking he had heard her. "You have the right to appoint a lawyer. If you do not have one the court will appoint one for you."

Sam Cain stared at her. He looked in total disbelief that he had become a key suspect in a murder case and was being charged.

Ann watched as, in the space of a few seconds, he sank to the ground, appearing to be crushed by the news.

"I did not murder Tom Casey," he protested.

She waited until he had composed himself sufficiently to speak and then informed him that he would be held in prison until he was due to appear before a judge to be formally charged, and that he would then be moved to a secure prison. She advised him to contact his lawyer in the meantime.

Sam Cain looked a pathetic figure as he sat bent double in the brightly lit cell. Overcome with shock, he seemed unable to comprehend anything she said. Ann was puzzled by this and felt a measure of pity for him. She did not think he appeared as a heartless killer, but then, she supposed, you never knew… he could have been driven by exceptional circumstances to commit murder.

Ann and David returned to her office. She was surprised that she did not feel triumphant at finding the murderer. It all seemed so surreal. She slumped in her chair.

"Catching killers is exhausting stuff," David remarked, watching her. "You look like you could do with a double whiskey."

"I agree," she responded quickly, and smiled, "but a strong coffee will do just as nicely."

They chinked coffee cups as David offered his congratulations. "I'm sure the boss will be pleased," he said.

"Don't remind me," she said, unable to match his bright tone. "I had better inform misery guts personally before he gives me an earful."

She traipsed off to Edwards' office, willing herself to feel triumphant but, at the same time, she couldn't help envisaging his discomfort at her success. Nonetheless, she offered him a genial smile as she entered his office.

"What do you want?"

She was taken aback by the abrupt tone even though the sneer was obvious.

"I came to inform you, Sir," she announced as confidently as she could, "that we have arrested Sam Cain for the murder of Tom Casey." She paused, looking at him across the desk.

"His prints were found on the murder weapons in his garage and his drill bit had Tom Casey's blood and bone marrow on it."

Her statement distracted him from his paperwork. He looked up and said, "Splendid work, Dixon. Pull up a chair and update me."

His unusually civil manner disarmed her.

"Well actually, Sir, there's not much more to tell. I will have a full report on the case on your desk tomorrow morning."

He looked annoyed at her brevity, as if he had hoped for more.

"The team are joining me for a celebratory drink at the Horse and Hounds in Pimlico at 7pm, Sir," Ann added. "You are most welcome to join us."

She left the room with a sense of satisfaction that she had perhaps conveyed to Edwards the humiliation of being dismissed.

The news of the arrest and the charge spread through the station like wildfire. The police station was virtually deserted as most of the force had migrated to the pub. The officers crowded around the bar. They cheered Ann as she walked into the pub. She acknowledged their enthusiasm with a knowing smile and joined them at the bar.

After a few minutes, she was joined by Peter Drew who offered his own compliments for her diligent work. She duly thanked the team for their hard work and support.

Then someone shouted, "Three cheers for the Guv!" Everyone then joined in the singing of 'For She's a Jolly Good Fellow'. David then proposed that Ann should buy everyone at least two rounds of drinks to which she swiftly responded, "Don't push your luck, David, you'll be back on the beat tomorrow."

The officers roared with laughter and pointed a warning finger at David. She turned her head to the door and was taken by surprise to see Edwards walk into the pub. He joined her at the table.

"Seems like you've done a good job, Ann – congratulations."

Even though she'd invited him it made her flesh crawl to sit in such proximity to a man who had always treated her so appallingly and who, she thought, now wanted to be nice to her because her hard work made him look good.

"I've arranged a briefing with the press and TV crew in the morning at 8am," Edwards informed her. "Meet me in the briefing room at 7.30."

She nodded.

"OK, I'll be there." Then she thanked him and made her excuses to get away because she needed to go home. He tried to persuade her to stay but she declined and called to David to drive her home.

In the car she was pensive.

"What's on your mind, Guv?" David enquired, sensing her mood.

"Something's missing about this case," she replied. "I don't understand the bit about there being superimposed glove prints on the murder weapons. Why would Sam handle the weapons with bare hands, then use gloves? It just doesn't make any sense."

"Maybe he used gloves to hold the weapons while he was washing off the blood and forgot to remove all his fingerprints," David surmised.

Ann shrugged.

"Look, Guv," David said as the car drew to a halt outside her home, "you nailed the villain. The forensics evidence is irrefutable. Get a good night's sleep and things will look different in the morning."

When she entered her home, Josie was asleep. She climbed into the bed, snuggling up beside her. She had not bothered to undress. Sleep overwhelmed her.

The following morning, Josie had already left when Ann scrambled around the bedroom trying to put together a suitable outfit for the press meeting.

"Oh God Josie, why are you never around when I need your help?" she muttered to herself.

David's persistent hooting of the car horn outside only added to her stress and she shouted out of the window for him to stop being so bloody impatient.

Five minutes later she jumped into the car, still applying her make-up.

Ann turned to question him as she adjusted her jacket. "Do I look alright to face the cameras, David?"

He threw her a swift glance and reassured her that she looked very smart. She scrambled out of the car realising she was already 10 minutes late. David feasted his eyes on the way her dress hugged the curvaceous contours of her body before he alighted from the car.

Edwards glared at her as she entered the room, already in critical mood.

"Why the hell can't you get out of bed on time in the morning?"

"Sorry Sir," she said and, to cover up his preoccupation with her late arrival, said, "Do you have the report I left on your desk yesterday?"

"Come on, let's go and face the press," was all he replied as he led the way into the briefing room.

They were met by a sea of flashing lights and Edwards began to release his statement.

"The CID murder squad, led by DCI Ann Dixon, yesterday arrested and charged a man with the murder of Tom Casey. He will be formally charged by a judge over the next few days and moved to a secure prison. Are there any questions?"

The media jostled and pushed for position around Edwards and Ann, their microphones held aloft, beginning to fire questions.

"How did you catch the killer, Superintendent?"

"The murder weapons contained evidence linking the killer to the murder," Edwards replied.

A second reporter fired a question.

"DCI Dixon's previous reports stated that the police suspected there might have been two killers. Do you think the murderer in custody acted on his own or did he have an accomplice?"

"We are still continuing our investigations and will continue to question the suspect in an attempt to establish if he had an accomplice," Ann answered the female reporter who was called Amy Baker.

"The nature of the killing suggests a link to the occult," Amy probed, questioning her further. "Do you think you should be pursuing Satanists connected to the victim to find a possible second killer?"

"We cannot draw any conclusions about a second killer at present," Ann replied, "and it would not be worth wasting police time and money pursuing weak leads which do not guarantee an arrest."

Realising that Amy Baker was angling to trap him with her questioning, Edwards brought the meeting to a close and thanked everyone for their time.

This sparked even more questions and with howls of protest, but he was determined not to answer any more questions. He and Ann exited swiftly through the side door. Edwards told Ann that he was pleased with their performance at the press meeting. He told her he would let her know when Sam Cain would need to appear in court to be formally charged.

They parted in the corridor, and she walked to her office. Her phone rang as soon as she sat down at her desk.

"Who is the greatest detective in the world?" asked the cheery voice on the other side.

"Josie, it is *so* good to hear from you," Ann said. "I missed seeing you this morning. I wanted to tell you before you heard it from the media."

"It's OK, and I'm so proud of you," Josie said, "and by the way, I'm going to have dinner with a client tonight, so if you are early don't wait up for me."

"OK, see you in the morning."

Josie let out a big sigh.

"And I guess I will just have to join the queue of all your admirers," Ann said.

"Well, don't sound so glum," Josie admonished her, "I will make it up to you, I promise."

"Promise, promises. I will hold you to that," Ann said.

At that moment, David knocked and entered carrying two steaming cups of coffee.

"You read my thoughts, wonderful man," Ann said, smiling at him.

She took the cup from him, nurturing it in both hands and savouring the first warming mouthful. Her mobile rang as she downed the last drop, relishing its invigorating strength. It was Chief Superintendent Michael Heath.

He offered his congratulations and invited her for a drink at the pub in half an hour's time. She agreed but told Michael that she had promised Josie she would be home early.

After the call she turned to David and said, "Come with me, then I can sneak off while you keep him company," she begged him.

David agreed and they drove off to the pub. Michael Heath was beaming all over his face as he shook Ann's hand and kissed her on the cheek.

"We are proud of you, Ann; great job, well done," he said enthusiastically.

"This is Sergeant David Hughes," Ann said. "He worked hard on the case, too, and should be rewarded.

Michael ordered the drinks and they wandered off to sit at the tables outside the pub.

Ann updated Michael on the details of the case. She thought for a moment and then said, "Please will you promise not to share with Stephen Edwards what I am about to tell you."

"You have my solemn word – fire away," Michael replied.

"I think there are a few discrepancies which casts doubt on Sam Cain's guilt," Ann said tentatively. "I cannot put my hand on my heart and swear that he committed the murder. If he did, I think that he was just the lackey and not the main culprit. I believe we should gather further evidence in fairness to both him and to justice."

Michael listened intently and nodded. Then he smiled and said, "You had better keep mum about your thoughts because you know Edwards will have your guts for garters if he knows there is division in his camp."

"Yes, indeed, and that is the reason I advised Sam to hire a good defence lawyer. And in the interests of justice," she assured Michael, "I will also continue to gather information about the case."

***

Josie parked her car and headed up the steps of the restaurant. Jake got up from his seat and greeted her with relish.

"I was afraid you would change your mind and not turn up," he said.

"Well, as I am the guilty driver, the least I could do was comply with your request."

"Did you get to patch up your lovely Porsche?"

"Yes, they did a really good job," Josie replied. "Can't tell it was damaged now."

"That's good," Jake said. "And what are you having to drink?"

"A glass of white wine would be nice, please."

Jake suggested Prosecco.

"Lovely, that would be very nice."

"What do you do for a living?" Jake enquired as they sipped their drinks.

"I'm a fashion designer," replied Josie.

"Bright lights and glamour and lots of money – very impressive."

"You forgot to add that it takes plenty of hard work and mountains of stress, too."

"And what does your partner do?"

Josie hesitated before replying, "She's in the police, a detective chief inspector."

"Then I had better watch my step," Jake said, smiling. "And what a coincidence, I recently met a DCI who happened to be investigating the death of my brother."

Josie looked at him.

"Your partner wouldn't happen to be the gorgeous Ann Dixon by any chance?"

Josie blushed as she confirmed Ann's identity. "Yes, she is."

"Well, fancy me crashing into the detective's other half," he laughed. "What did she say when you told her we were having dinner?"

"I am not going to tell her," Josie said, feeling the first flicker of nervous tension. "She will be very upset if she knows I accepted your invitation. Please, let's keep it quiet."

"OK, I promise," Jake said. "And may I ask, where did you meet the sexy detective?"

"We met at a charity function," Josie explained. "Ann has a friend, Clive Hammond, who also happens to be *my* friend. I didn't know that they met when they both served in MI6. Clive's brother is in fashion design, so he invited them both." She spoke with a hint of girlish enthusiasm. "Clive was the matchmaker for Ann and me. He arranged it so that I would give Ann a lift home that night, we fell hopelessly in love and the rest is history."

"Are you the same age?"

"Ann is five years older than me, and our love is very strong."

Josie went still for a second, feeling guilty.

"I hope you're not going to tell Ann that I have told you our life story," she said, suddenly wishing she hadn't spoken quite so candidly.

"Absolutely not; my lips are sealed," Jake reassured her, then added, "and you know what? It's just not fair. There are you, two stunning women, blissfully happy in a relationship while here I am, a lonely guy who would give his eye teeth to have either one of you."

Josie merely studied him.

"I don't see how someone like you, with your good looks, cannot hold onto an attractive woman," she remarked.

"Problem is that they don't stay," Jake replied.

"You'll just have to tie them down, so to speak, before they *do* escape," Josie commented, laughing.

Dinner progressed pleasantly enough, and she soon found that Jake's sense of humour and charm allayed her anxiety about the meeting. They laughed and chatted late into the night.

As they were leaving the restaurant, Josie said, "Well, I hope I have paid off my debt by having dinner with you."

"Well, I don't know about that," he teased, "you might need to pay it off in instalments."

Josie, who suddenly became serious at his remark, visibly stiffened.

"Only joking," Jake said, touching her lightly on the arm as if to emphasise his little joke, "but no harm in keeping in touch, is there?"

Josie nodded in agreement and then fell silent.

"Maybe we can just speak from time to time," he suggested, turning to go, when, to her surprise, he stopped, leant forward and kissed her on the cheek before she headed off towards her car. She had the feeling his eyes were on her back as she walked away.

She felt regretful. She couldn't shake off the notion that she had done something terribly wrong in having dinner with Jake. Unable to control her shame, she phoned Adam and asked him to join her for a drink.

Adam, who expressed concern at the urgency in her voice, sped over to meet her.

"Everything OK, Josie? You sounded stressed," he said as he joined her at the bar where they had agreed to meet.

"Sit down, I have to talk to you."

"Go on then, don't keep me in suspense."

"Adam, I have done a terrible thing."

He looked at her inquisitively.

"I smashed into the ambulance driven by Jake Casey, the brother of Ann's murder victim. It was my fault, but he suggested I blame it on a hit-and-run driver and in return I had to have dinner with him."

"Hmm," murmured Adam, looking pensive, "a bit of a predicament, I agree."

"Oh God, I am so afraid of telling Ann," Josie said, sounding distraught. "I only found out who he was at the dinner. He confessed to having met Ann through the investigation into his brother's murder and, like a fool, I told him Ann was my partner."

She looked at Adam with pleading in her eyes.

"Please believe me it was just dinner," she said. "Nothing else happened. I did it just to buy his silence."

"I understand but Ann won't see it like that," Adam said, knowing his sister well.

"Oh Adam," she cried, "I'm so sorry I agreed to dinner. Do you think I should confess to Ann?"

"No," Adam said gravely, "that's the last thing you should do. She would never trust you again."

He paused to think for a moment.

"Did Jake ask to see you again?"

"No, he only wants to call me to speak occasionally, as he said, the way good friends do."

"That doesn't sound too bad," Adam said more cheerily and added with a cautionary tone, "but don't let Ann catch you out if you do."

Josie sighed and she looked tired.

"Don't worry," Adam said, "you've done nothing wrong short of bumping into an emergency vehicle. Just keep his calls curt and if he doesn't comply, I will persuade him not to do otherwise."

Josie hugged Adam, thanked him and drove home feeling better. She slept on the sofa as she could not face Ann that night. She pretended to be in a deep sleep while Ann tried to wake her the next morning.

"Hmm, must have been some dinner to leave you comatose," Ann muttered under her breath.

***

The reporters and members of the public were in a frenzy outside the prison gates as the van carrying Sam Cain drove past. Cameras flashed and clicked; there were shouts of 'Murderer!' as the van sped through the prison gates. The reporters chased after the van in their cars and rushed towards it while Sam was spirited away to the court for the short hearing. A jacket was flung over his head as he emerged from the van and entered the court through the side door.

Despite the precaution, some reporters managed to take photos of the prisoner. He appeared deeply distressed from some of the photos that appeared in the papers the next day. But Sam Cain had an excellent lawyer who challenged the evidence against him with impunity. The lawyer managed to prove Sam's innocence beyond reasonable doubt. The size 10 footprint of the shoe in his garage was not Sam's as he wore a size 8 shoe. The superimposed glove powder on the murder weapons suggested someone had worn gloves when handling the drill bit and staple gun. The evidence from Sam's next-door neighbour, in seeing a tall man leave Sam's garage on the night of the murder, confirmed that a second person had access to Sam's tools.

The evidence was only admitted after Sam was already in custody. One of the neighbours went on a business trip the day after the murder and had not been available for questioning immediately afterwards. The police were only able to interview him on his return. The strongest evidence for his defence was that Sam could not have lifted the large-framed Tom Casey onto the banister by himself. The presence of the superimposed glove powder cast doubt on the evidence that a suspect would use his tools without gloves and leave his prints and then use gloves to handle the tools he used to inflict the torture.

Sam's neighbour, who had seen a tall man leaving the shed around 5.30am, provided the final proof needed to overturn the evidence against him. Sam's lawyer presented a strong case for his defence. The judge was unable to refute the evidence presented to him. The case did not go to trial. The judge dismissed the charges based on the new evidence for the defence. It was a relieved and elated Sam who was released from prison that day.

Subsequently, his sister accused Ann of gross negligence and incompetence and vowed to sue the police. Ann Dixon was pleased at the outcome but had to hide her true feelings from Stephen Edwards who was clearly vexed at the prospect of resurrecting an investigation that he felt should have been put to bed.

Ann and David shifted uncomfortably in their seats at his office as he gave them his verdict on their bungled arrest.

"You can have the pleasure of facing the media with the Commander," he warned Ann, continuing ad nauseam about the shortage of resources and the strain on the CLPD's finances.

The pair felt relief when he concluded the meeting and could leave his office but not before he had issued a stern warning that they were only to return when they could secure a viable conviction.

David and Ann headed off for the nearest coffee shop where they could at least gather their thoughts and recover their self-esteem.

"Miserable bastard," said David as he savoured the invigorating sips of coffee.

"Well, we will just have to re-examine all the evidence and return to the scene of the crime," replied Ann who sounded contemplative. "There has to be something we missed."

They returned to her office where she again laid out the entirety of evidence to pour over every detail, looking for a connection to Tom Casey.

"We know that Jake and Luke wear gloves in their jobs," Ann said. "Let's exclude Luke because he only uses powder-free gloves because of his allergy to glove powder." She looked momentarily perplexed. "Jake is the only one who wears size 10 shoes," she went on. "We have examined his shoes, and none have a sole matching the print in Sam's garage. We need to consider if the perpetrator had an accomplice or that he was a very strong man."

When they had finished, Ann called a meeting with her team. She pointed out all the details they had that were relevant to the case and impressed upon them the urgency to find further evidence. She told David that they ought to interview Jake and Nathan again and enquire about their cousin, James.

Ann organised a meeting with the brothers for later that week.

Jake seemed peeved at another interview, especially when she informed them that Sam was acquitted of the charge of murder.

"I don't know what more you think you can learn from us, Inspector," he said waspishly. "We have told you everything we know."

"I need to know more about your cousin, James," Ann explained, keeping her voice level. "Do you know where he is right now?"

"He left for Brazil," Jake replied without much expression. "He has business interests in Brazil."

"Do you know anyone who might be able to tell me where he is living in Brazil?" Ann persisted.

"He has a sister, our other cousin Susan, with whom he stays in contact," Jake responded. "She will be able to tell you more about his whereabouts."

"Thank you. Do you know specifically why he went to Brazil for his business?"

"James is half-German," Jake said. "His father, our uncle, was a Nazi during the war. After the war he fled to Brazil where he bought a house and lived there until 1965."

Ann waited for him to continue.

"Then he changed his name to Muller and came to England where he met and married our aunt."

Ann had been looking at him closely.

"Do you know whether James participated in the satanic rituals with your brothers?"

"I am aware that James and my brothers belonged to a sect who met regularly to practise their rituals in the forest, but I never joined in with any of it."

Jake scratched the side of his head and thought for a minute.

"Sam Cain hung out with them in the beginning," he continued, looking at the ground, "but after he had a run-in with my brothers, he was excluded from the rituals."

"Really?"

"Yes. He might be able to tell you more than I can."

"That's very helpful of you, Jake; thank you."

Jake gave the semblance of a smile.

"We found a book with coded symbols at Tom's house," Ann said. "It seems that the killer was searching for this book on the day Tom died. Do you know about this book, and do you know what it might contain?"

Jake stayed silent for a few minutes before replying. Ann remained patient, waiting for him to respond. "No, I did not know about the book." His eyes slid sideways, avoiding Ann's keen gaze. "I don't know what the symbols mean."

She had a strong feeling that Jake knew more than he was prepared to say. Ann gazed at him directly, hardening her eyes slightly.

"Nathan," she said, turning to address his brother, "can you tell me anything about this book with the symbols?"

"No – can't. My brother was completely excluded from everything connected to the rituals because he was the youngest and therefore very vulnerable."

"Excuse me, Mr Casey, I have asked Nathan," she said curtly. "I'm sure he can answer for himself," Ann said.

"Well," Jake began, "my brother gets very upset at being asked questions he doesn't even understand."

Ann nodded her acquiescence.

"My brothers and I have always protected Nathan and shielded him from the evils of the world," Jake explained.

"That's very noble of you," Ann said, annoyed at his constant interruption, "but I still need a reply from Nathan. He is an adult and can answer for himself."

Ann smiled politely, fearing that Nathan might be the cause of an argument. "I understand your protection of your brother."

Before the exchange could continue between herself and Jake, Nathan intervened by saying, "I never knew what my brothers did in the forest although I knew they went there with some girls."

Jake glared at him, clearly annoyed that he was giving Ann more fuel for questions.

"Ah, so there *were* girls involved in the rituals," Ann said. "Tell me more."

"I never met the girls," Nathan said, "but I used to hide and watch from a vantage point when my brothers took them to the forest."

Ann nodded and gave him a benign smile, saying, "Well, that wasn't so difficult, Nathan, was it?"

The ringing of Ann's mobile broke their conversation. Forgetting to check who was calling, Ann accepted the call.

"Do you remember me, Inspector?" asked the voice at the other end of the line.

Ann walked into the garden to continue her conversation in private, gesturing with a hand for David to continue interviewing.

"Oh God, Josie," replied Ann, when she realised who it was.

"Hasn't madam forgotten something?" continued Josie cheekily.

"Oh no!" exclaimed Ann as she realised she had missed the launch of Josie's new designs.

"Well, may I ask, when will Her Ladyship be putting in an appearance?"

Josie appeared to enjoy rubbing salt into Ann's wounds as she squirmed with shame for disappointing her.

"See you in about an hour," Ann said.

"Just remember, you will have to pay a forfeit of *my* choosing," Josie teased.

Ann smiled to herself and promised Josie she would try to hurry to make it in time for the launch.

David overheard some of Ann's conversation even though he continued to talk to Jake. The expression on his face told of his silent envy of his wish to have been at the other end of the phone. Despite trying his best to hide this fact, his body language gave him away. He wore the expression of a man whose mind was constantly haunted by the shapely body of the woman whose company he found himself in daily. If one could dissemble the thoughts echoing through his head at such times, it would surely have been hope that by some miracle she would become aware of his feelings and reciprocate them.

Sadly, for him, she remained aloof, seemingly oblivious to his intentions. Theirs, as far as she was concerned, was a strictly working relationship.

After a while, Ann returned to the room, her cheeks a warm tint of rose. She hastily apologised for her brief absence and continued questioning Jake.

A few minutes later they were leaving, reminding Jake to contact them if he remembered any significant details.

David went quiet during their journey, so much so that Ann enquired if he was feeling alright.

"I'm fine, Guv," David replied, "just a bit tired."

Ann turned to look at him. *He doesn't look tired at all!*

She dropped him off at the station and sped off to meet Josie at the launch. Her chic, black trouser suit complemented her neatly cropped blonde hair.

As she entered the venue it was as if all eyes were transfixed on her. Her front forelock fell onto her forehead; the way she tossed her head back to flick it from her forehead was mesmerising – for most women, an ordinary gesture.

Josie moved forward to greet her, announcing her arrival proudly. She kissed Ann on the cheek, hugged her and pushed a glass of champagne into her hand.

Ann enquired how the launch had progressed so far.

"Great!" exclaimed Josie. "There's been lots of positive feedback." Her eyes shone, sparkling excitedly beneath the crystal lights. "We should have quite a few orders, I think."

Ann warded off the attentions of admirers, both male and female, while Josie mingled.

Ann found it most amusing at the speed at which her male admirers fled when they learned of her profession. Some of the female guests seemed more intrigued about what she did for a living and tried even harder to seduce her. The evening progressed pleasantly as she followed Josie around and who proudly showed her off to the fashion glitterati.

***

Ann awoke early the following morning and sipped a cup of coffee as she turned her thoughts to what Nathan Casey had revealed about the meeting of the occultists in the woods. She knew that she had to witness the rituals for herself, and she had to speak to George Casey.

A pair of arms embraced her from behind and a kiss into the folds of her neck announced Josie's presence.

"Early bird, how do you exist on four hours sleep a night?" Josie asked.

"A lot on my mind, I suppose," then Ann groaned. "Damned murder case is complicated."

When Ann talked about the satanic rituals of the Casey brothers, Josie looked concerned, knowing that in her determination to solve a case Ann frequently put her life on the line.

The doorbell rang. Josie opened the door to David who stood at the threshold drenched from the bucketing rain.

"Come on inside," said Josie, greeting him.

David wore a serious expression on his face.

"I need the guv to accompany me to a crime scene," he said. "It's urgent."

"Who is it, Josie?" called Ann from behind.

"It's your lovely sergeant needing your urgent attention," Josie replied, turning her head back.

Ann shot out of her chair, grabbed her phone and bag and joined David at the door. They raced off towards the car.

"Tell me on the way," Ann requested as she jumped in the passenger seat.

"You are going to find it hard to believe this, Guv," David said, "but George Casey has been murdered at his home."

"What?" Ann looked at him, panicked, with a sudden jerk of her head that thrust her chin forward. "What the hell is going on?"

As David drew up at the scene of the crime, Superintendent Edwards and DI Tobin were already there. Edwards walked towards the car just as Ann and David had parked.

"Keep that lot at bay," Edwards instructed, pointing to a group of reporters who were standing nearby. "Tim Jones says the victim looks pretty smashed up."

He gave Ann a sharp look that told her he was not to be argued with. "Take a look and get the report to me first thing tomorrow morning!" he snapped.

Ann and David pulled on their overshoes and went into the house. Tim was bending over the body in the bedroom. He looked up as they entered.

"Seems like the same modus operandi as the one who did

Tom Casey in," he said, and added, "cause of death suffocation by strangulation – the familiar pattern of the inverted cross."

He looked up at them.

"Percy, the gardener, found the victim at around 7am this morning. Apparently, he's worked for George Casey for the past 15 years." He rubbed the side of his chin. "He says Jake Casey visited George around 6pm last night. Better leave the questioning for later. He seems very distressed about the murder at present."

Ann was ushered into George Casey's bedroom. His battered, bloodied body was sprawled in a heap on the floor. His hands and feet had been crushed and broken and there was extensive bruising on the body. The bed sheets revealed evidence of sexual activity, the sheets soiled with body fluids and a streak of blood.

"Make sure you get all the evidence," she said and examined the scene with David to make doubly sure that nothing was missed.

The rest of the house seemed undisturbed. There were three wine glasses on the coffee table in the dining room. The forensics officer collected the fingerprints from the glasses.

As Ann descended the stairs towards the living room, a DCI from the Surrey CID office was standing in the hallway.

"Who the hell are you?" he demanded, giving her a fierce stare.

Her face clouded. She could not disguise her irritation. "I am DCI Dixon; who the hell are you?"

"What are you doing on my patch?" he yelled at her.

"Well, if you can bring yourself to ask my Chief standing at the door," she retorted indignantly, "you might learn more and acquire some manners on your way over there." Then she muttered in an audible rasp, "You bloody insolent arsehole."

The man strode off angrily and went to speak to Edwards.

"That's put him in his place," she said, twisting her lips to emphasise her note of triumph.

"Good for you, Guv," said David.

The reporters waited patiently for Ann to emerge from the inside of the house. When she at last appeared, they rushed towards her and fired a wave of questions at her.

"DCI Dixon, was George Casey murdered by the same man who killed his brother?"

"Do you think you have a serial killer at large?"

The questions continued to be fired in rapid succession, leaving her no time to answer any of them and little desire to do so.

"It is too early to draw any conclusions at this stage," she replied, and with the intent of reassuring them she added, "Superintendent Edwards will release a formal report after the post-mortem."

Her statement seemed to placate them and they dispersed, drifting off rather reluctantly.

Tim apologised to Ann for the behaviour of the DCI from the Surrey Police. He explained that Edwards did not tell him Ann had been drafted in to head the case. He informed her that he would let her know about the date of the post-mortem.

Ann and David stopped off at a café for lunch where they could discuss aspects of the murder in privacy, uninterrupted.

"We had better build a watertight case, David," she warned, "because we're going to have that bastard, Edwards, breathing down our necks at every step."

David gave a wry smile and nodded his agreement.

They returned to Ann's office where she began to build a profile of the case, relying on input from David.

"Get the team in for a briefing this afternoon and tell the forensics team I need their feedback by tomorrow," she said. "Then meet me here at my office in an hour." She pushed a tendril of hair behind her ear. "First call will be the remaining Casey brothers to inform them about their brother's death."

David joined her an hour later. They tracked Jake down at work. He was shocked at the news but maintained his composure. He explained that he had stopped at George's house and was invited to join George and his daughter, Elaine, for a drink at 6.30pm that evening.

"Elaine was spending a few days with her father. I left around 9pm and went home," Jake told Ann. "Nathan was at home too, so he would be able to confirm my story."

Nathan duly confirmed that Jake had come home around 9pm on the evening of the murder.

A buzz of excited voices signalled the team of men were ready and prepared to take on the new case. They all filed into the briefing room.

"We have another murder," Ann told them. "I gather you have heard about the recent murder of George Casey. He has been murdered in virtually the same way as his brother, Tom, a few weeks ago. It is the same modus operandi – tortured and then strangled, leaving the imprint of an inverted cross. His ears are missing. The killer has presumably taken them as trophies. The victim was not alone during the attack. His daughter, Elaine, had been visiting him, but she was nowhere to be found. We don't know if it was a double murder or if the killer has kidnapped the daughter. The brothers that are left, Jake and Nathan, both have alibis. I was unable to contact Luke Cowan as he is away at a medical convention. I will inform George's ex-wife, Eve, who has remarried. We really have a serial killer at large."

She blinked a few times then added, "OK DI Roberts, you need to organise your team to interview the neighbours for their feedback. Check for strange cars or persons entering or leaving the house."

Ann shot DI Tobin a glance. "Get your men to interview the gardener, friends and colleagues of George Casey," she instructed. "He had golf buddies and some associates at the races, apparently. He also had a few female lovers whom he saw casually. Check if they have any grudges."

She scanned round at the faces looking up at her.

"If there are no questions we will meet when I have news from the post-mortem and forensics. Now get on with it!" she barked.

Her mobile rang. She checked that it was not Edwards before answering. It was the detective constable at the police station.

"Guv," he said, "we just had a call from a woman called Eve Marshall. She says she's Elaine Casey's mother. She's concerned that she has been unable to contact her daughter since yesterday. I told her we only investigate if the person has been gone 24 hours, but she was very insistent that we find her daughter."

Ann said nothing, anticipating there was more.

"I thought you might want to handle it in view of her daughter having the same surname as your murdered man."

"Interesting," she said. "Yes, you're right."

Ann took down the contact details, thanked the constable and phoned the number provided. A tearful Eve Marshall informed Ann that her daughter had indeed been visiting her father, George Casey, yesterday and that she had not been contactable since early evening.

"It is very out of character for my daughter not to answer her phone," Eve said.

The realisation that Elaine's disappearance could be linked to her father's murder turned Ann's stomach. She paused for a moment before asking Eve if she could meet with her urgently.

"Yes, of course, Inspector; please come around in the next hour. We are at home."

Eve rattled off details of her address, which Ann scribbled down, thanked her and said she would call at the home shortly.

David popped his head around the door. "Everything OK, Guv? You look as though you've seen a ghost."

"I have just spoken to Eve Marshall, ex-wife of George Casey," she explained, unable to conceal her fears for Elaine's safety. "She has reported her daughter, Elaine, missing since she visited her father yesterday."

"Bloody hell," David said. "Are you thinking what I am thinking?"

"Yes, David," she replied, her voice quivering slightly, "we might have two new murders on our hands now."

David blinked.

"Come on," she said with a sense of urgency, "we've no time to lose. Get the car – we're going over to see Eve Marshall right this minute."

On the drive to Finchley in north London where Eve lived, David put his foot down. For once, Ann did not reprimand him for speeding.

An attractive petite woman answered the door. Ann introduced David and herself.

"Have you found my daughter, Inspector?" Eve's cheeks were tear-stained, and her voice shook with fear.

"I am afraid not," Ann replied. "I am terribly sorry to inform you, but your ex-husband has been murdered. It happened at his home, last night."

Eve became visibly distressed, trembling uncontrollably as she digested the news.

"Did whoever it was harm Elaine?" she asked, bloodshot and pleading eyes gazing at Ann, "she was with her father for a few days."

"Mrs Marshall," Ann began, keeping her tone light, "we do not know where your daughter is at the moment."

Eve Marshall stared at her, to David, and then back at Ann again.

"All we know at present, according to Jake," Ann continued, "is that the three of them had drinks at 6.30pm last night and then Jake left for home, alone."

She waited until Eve was composed before continuing her questioning.

"Would your daughter have gone off somewhere else without telling you?"

"Elaine was a creature of habit," Eve said, beginning to choke on her words again. "She would not have done anything out of character." She sniffed and when she spoke again her voice came out with a scratchy undertone. "She was close to her dad so she would have wanted to spend all the time she could with him."

Ann nodded and made a note.

"Even though my husband and I were divorced," Eve said, swallowing hard as if a stone was lodged in her throat, "George and I did not deny our daughter the love and care she deserved."

Ann didn't doubt that at all. She pressed on with her enquiries.

"Did your ex-husband have any enemies that you are aware of?"

"No," replied Eve promptly in barely a whisper, "nobody that I know of."

Ann considered for a moment before asking the next question.

"Mrs Marshall," she began, speaking slowly, "we have reason to believe that your husband dealt in the occult. Did you know about these rituals that he and his brothers and friends performed in the forest?"

Eve raised her brows and dropped her bottom lip, reeling back in shock.

"Good God, no!" she exclaimed. "I knew that George had books on the occult and had an interest in the subject, but I never knew he indulged in such dark practises."

"I understand this must be difficult for you," Ann said, "but do you have a photograph of your daughter that we could borrow, please?"

Eve nodded, then disappeared, reappearing a few minutes later with a photo of her daughter that she handed to Ann.

There was the sound of the front door opening and Eve's husband stepped into the room. Eve introduced him to Ann and David.

"My husband, Harold, is also very close to Elaine," said Eve.

Ann directed her gaze towards Harold and asked him where he was the previous evening between 11pm and 4am. He said that he was at home with his wife. Eve confirmed that they watched TV until midnight, after which time they went to bed.

"When did you last see Elaine?" she asked Harold.

"Eve and I dropped her off at George's house two days ago," he replied.

"Did you ever have any arguments with Elaine?"

"Whatever are you implying, Inspector?"

"Mr Marshall," Ann said firmly, "sometimes young girls do things out of the ordinary. No matter how well you think you know your daughter, she may do unpredictable things like disappearing for no apparent reason."

Harold gave her a doubtful, slightly resentful look.

"Did you ever argue with Elaine or have irreconcilable differences?" Ann persisted.

Harold continued to ridicule her suggestion. "That's preposterous," he said, looking at her with scorn, "we both love Elaine and I have never argued with her or caused her to be unhappy. My wife will vouch for that."

Eve put her hand on his shoulder and nodded in agreement.

Ann smiled in acquiescence. "Does your daughter have a boyfriend or a special friend?"

"She is studying to be a lawyer and did not want to be distracted, so she only has a few good girlfriends," explained Eve.

"We would need to interview some of her close friends," Ann said. "I would be grateful if you can give us contact numbers." All the while Ann was saying this, she hoped more than anything that Elaine would just step through the door with a cheery 'Hello'.

Eve stood up, went to a drawer in a cabinet, took out an address book and handed over the details of Elaine's closest friends.

"May we have a look around your daughter's bedroom?" Ann asked, with a polite smile. "We may find a clue to her disappearance."

Eve hesitated for a moment then agreed and led the way to Elaine's room. It was spacious and tastefully decorated. There were school photographs of Elaine displayed on the dressing table. A collection of teddy bears sat on the bed.

Ann rested her eyes on a laptop sitting on a desk at one end of the room and asked if they could take the laptop as it may hold some important information.

Eve consented, albeit reluctantly.

Ann asked if she could have a hairbrush or comb belonging to Elaine for the forensics scientists to examine.

At this point Eve became indignant.

"What do you want with my daughter's hairbrush?"

"We need to establish if the hairs on your daughter's brush match the hair found at your husband's home."

Eve grudgingly handed over the hairbrush. Ann informed the Marshalls that the CLPD Kidnap Unit would liaise with them to set up a trace/intercept on their incoming calls that would be monitored by the technical support team. She also informed them that officers of the Kidnap Unit would park their operations van near their home, to which Eve objected vehemently.

"This is an intrusion on our privacy!" she cried.

It took a great deal of persuasion on Ann's part to convince Eve that it was in the best interests of finding her daughter and that she would be advised to assist the police in whichever way she could by agreeing to their methods of surveillance. Harold, who had been standing silently beside Eve, agreed with Ann, and with some firm but gentle coercion they finally convinced Eve to agree to the plan.

CHAPTER 3

Ann thanked Eve for her help and promised that they would do their very best to find her daughter.

She waited until they were in the car before she spoke to David.

"Jesus, David, this case is more complex than we thought."

"Do you think the murderer has abducted the daughter?"

"That is possible," she agreed. "Let's see what the boys at forensics have found."

They sped off to forensics but were disappointed when the chief pathologist said he would only have all the information for Ann by the following morning. David and Ann departed and headed for her office. Stephen Edwards' dark office indicated that he had left for home. Ann sighed with relief that she did not have to confront her boss who had been trying unsuccessfully to contact her all day. She asked David to join her for a working dinner as Josie was away at a fashion show in Paris and she hated cooking.

David nodded in agreement, and they headed for a little Italian restaurant in Victoria. David phoned ahead to reserve a booking while Ann completed some work on her laptop. Then he dashed to his locker where he splashed on some aftershave, combed his hair and checked his appearance in the mirror before joining Ann outside her office.

They sped off to the restaurant together and were ushered to their seats by a waiter. David perused the wine list and asked Ann what she would like to drink.

"Rioja would be nice," she said.

David thought her choice was excellent and told the waiter to bring the wine. They surveyed the menu. Ann chose the butternut-filled ravioli with seared salmon and wild rocket. David opted for lasagne and a Mediterranean salad. Having placed their order, they sat back and savoured the wine.

Ann looked across the table at David and asked him if his girlfriend complained about his long hours at work. He replied that he did not have a girlfriend as his unsociable hours chased away all the women he had met. She sympathised with him and advised him not to give up so easily.

He smiled then said, "I suppose I am still waiting for the right girl."

"Don't worry," Ann replied, "she's out there somewhere."

The expression on David's features read as if in plain print: 'So near and yet so far', but when he looked at Ann, he managed to conceal his feelings.

"Your partner is a fashion designer, hey Guv," he said.

"Yes, she's held in high esteem in the fashion world."

David looked at her steadily while listening.

"She attained her degree in London and then spent some time in Milan and Paris gaining experience," Ann said, looking proud as she added, "and last year she was awarded an MBE for her contribution to fashion."

"It must be difficult to maintain a relationship when you are both so busy," David said.

"Josie travels a great deal," Ann answered, shrugging off his question, "but it works well for us as I work such long hours, too."

Embarrassed that he had perhaps probed into Ann's private life too much, he changed the subject and asked her, "Do you think that doctor bloke, the Caseys' cousin, might not have gone to South America and is committing these murders?"

"Well, anything is possible right now," Ann replied. "I think we need to establish if James has re-entered the United Kingdom and before the murders were committed."

She used her serviette to make a rough sketch of the details of the case. Their dinner arrived and they ate without speaking much.

After the meal, they resumed their discussion. David stifled a yawn, at which point Ann announced it was time to go home. She reminded him not to be late in collecting her in the morning as they had an early start. David promised he would not disappoint her, said goodnight and drove off into the night.

True to his word, David arrived early to collect her the following morning. Their first port of call was the forensics lab. Peter Drew, the head of the forensics lab and chief pathologist, invited them into his office. He brought them a coffee from the machine in the corridor and the group sat down to discuss the forensic department's results on the murder of George Casey.

Peter revealed that the fingerprints on the wine glasses were a match to George, his brother Jake and an unidentified person. The bed sheets contained semen that belonged to George. The streak of blood belonged to a female who shared DNA with George Casey.

"Now, brace yourselves for this revelation," he said. "The DNA taken from the vaginal fluid on the sheets, on George's penis and also a few strands of hair on the bed belong, possibly, to his missing daughter."

"What the hell does that mean?" demanded Ann.

"It seems to point to the fact that daddy had sex with his daughter before he was killed," explained Peter.

"Jesus Christ!" exclaimed David.

"Carry on," Ann addressed Peter, almost impatiently. "What else?"

"Blood at the scene all belonged to George," said Peter. "A sliver of material at the scene, on the sheets, is from a SOCO suit, so we are assuming that our murderer wore a protective suit. The size 10 bloody boot print at the scene is army-issue, so we might be looking for someone in the army or ex-army."

He looked up at them, allowing them to take in this information before continuing.

"We also found part of the broken finger of a rubber glove that had a partial print," he said. "The print belongs to Jake Casey."

Ann listened to the new evidence with a look of astonishment. She took copies of the reports and made some notes as Peter continued. She glanced at her watch, remembering that she had to be at the post-mortem midmorning. She thanked Peter for the report then sped off to the mortuary.

"Sorry, delayed at forensics," she apologised as she rushed into the examination room.

Tim dictated into the recorder as he commenced the post-mortem.

"This is the body of George Casey, a white male and in good

physical health," he began. "There are numerous bruises on the body suggesting the victim was repeatedly beaten with a blunt instrument after being subdued with a stun gun. The fingers of both hands are crushed. Degree of damage suggests use of a hammer or a similar heavy weapon. The toes of both feet are crushed. Both legs are broken above the ankles, probably with a sledgehammer and a block of wood wedged between the legs. Metal spikes driven through both knees. There is profuse blood loss and the clotting at the sites suggests the wounds were inflicted while the victim was alive."

He glanced at them to check they were OK before continuing in the same level tone.

"Severe bruising on the face and body, several broken ribs and broken facial bones," he said, "suggests a beating of unparalleled brutality and while the victim was alive."

He paused again for two or three seconds, allowing his words to sink in.

"His ears are missing, possibly taken as a trophy by the killer. I would say cause of death is asphyxia due to strangulation. Victim has petechial haemorrhages of the eyes. There are two identical black marks on the side of his neck. They look like burns from a stun gun. I would guess this was the killer's method of subduing the victim before the torture. The bruises on the neck, gloved fingers and, of course, the unmistakable murderer's signature – the imprint of the inverted cross pattern."

Peter rubbed his chin thoughtfully.

"I would guess the killer put the ring on over his gloved finger to get a clear pattern of the ring. Please help me to turn him onto his front now," he instructed.

The victim's back was as bloodied and bruised as his front.

"Note the trauma to his anus. He was sodomized with an implement that had rough, raised spikes on the tip. I would hazard a guess that his rectum has been severely damaged by the implement. I won't know until I have opened him up."

Peter proceeded with the 'Y' surgical incision extending from the victim's throat to the pubic bone. This exposed all the organs in the thorax, abdomen and pelvis. He began his commentary as he removed and examined each individual organ.

"The lungs are punctured by the broken third, fourth and fifth ribs. The liver and the spleen are ruptured, which indicates blunt force trauma, probably a large weapon like a baseball bat," he reported, looking down at the victim during the inspection.

"Your killer's a sadistic bastard, Ann," he said, now lifting his eyes to hers. "Seems he is sending us a message each time he kills."

Ann merely blinked at the news.

Peter asked, "Do you have any ideas who the murderer might be?"

Ann shook her head and told him she thought the killings were possibly linked to a satanic cult to which the brothers belonged.

The toxicology report was unremarkable. There was a moderate amount of blood alcohol level. He was on antihypertensive medication. There were no class A drugs in his body.

"Well, that's all I have for you now," Peter concluded. "I will send you a written report when I have completed the post-mortem."

She thanked him and headed for her office with David following behind.

Ann turned her head back towards David and said, "We'd better have another coffee," and then she grimaced, "I don't think we're going to get lunch today."

David fetched two coffees from the machine and placed them on Ann's desk. She sat down and checked her notes as she sipped her coffee.

"Have you reminded the boys about the briefing at 3pm today?" she asked.

"Yes, Guv, I sent them all messages and left a reminder on the notice board," David replied.

"Well done," she said, smiling. "OK, drink your coffee, we got to shoot off before Edwards gets back from lunch." She pulled a face. "He'll go ballistic if he asks for the reports and I don't have them ready yet."

They entered the incident room where a team of officers waited to be briefed by Ann. The CID squad who dealt with kidnapping was also present. Ann had photographs and details of both murders displayed on two boards.

"Good afternoon team," she addressed them. "Listen up; we

have two murders and a possible kidnapping."

Ann took her officers through the crime scene evidence and elaborated where appropriate. "Sick fuck!" was one of the comments emanating from some officers when Ann informed them that evidence suggested George Casey had had sex with his own daughter.

"I don't want inane comments, guys, only intelligent, positive feedback, please," requested Ann.

"We don't know if George was forced to have sex with his daughter by the killer, so reserve your judgements, gentlemen, please, until we know the facts."

She spoke in a loud, assertive voice.

"I want you to interview Jake Casey as his fingerprints were on a wine glass at George Casey's house and on a broken finger of a rubber glove," she instructed. "Bring him to the station for questioning."

There was a murmur of assent before Ann went on.

"I want you to interview the ex-boyfriend, Sam Cain, and the brother-in-law, Luke Cowan, too. Also, check on whether the cousin, Dr James Muller, returned to England in the last month."

She rubbed her left temple that had a tiny pulse.

"Check the hospitals," she said, "just in case Elaine Casey was admitted at any time and get a team with sniffer dogs to search the woodland near the house."

She swung her eyes around the room. "I don't want a stone left unturned."

Ann folded her hands in front of her in a decisive gesture. "If there are no questions, hurry up and get a move on."

The detective inspectors divided their men into groups and allocated various tasks to them. She reminded the men to get in touch with Interpol and circulate the photo of James Muller, and to check with the border squad to ensure James had not left the UK. She provided them with copies of Elaine Casey's photo and requested that a search be launched for her whereabouts.

"DS Hughes and I will interview Luke Cowan," she said. "It is vital you do not speak to the press on any account." Her eyes darkened while her face hardened in defiance. She was in control and needed to show it. "Stephen Edwards will do the official press release tomorrow."

A hum echoed throughout the room as the police discussed the tasks with their colleagues.

Ann dealt with the individual queries from the officers before they embarked on their investigations. Then she turned to speak with David. While they were busy planning their next move, her phone rang.

It was the traffic police who informed her that George Casey's Lamborghini had been found abandoned a few streets from his house.

Ann frowned, then turned to David and asked, "Why the bloody hell would George's car be abandoned only a few streets from his house?"

She immediately informed the forensics officers and asked them to supervise the delivery of George Casey's car to the pathology garage. They complained that it was short notice but agreed; they clearly did not want to increase Ann's stress levels.

"Let's try to get an interview with Luke Cowan today," she told David.

He nodded and immediately phoned Luke. The phone was on voicemail, and he left a message for Luke to contact him or Ann at his earliest convenience.

David was surprised when Luke returned his call just 10 minutes later.

"To what do I owe the pleasure?" Luke's sarcastic tone grated on him when he answered the phone.

"DCI Dixon would like to interview you as another of your brothers-in-law has been killed," said David.

He paused and heard the slight intake of breath on the line.

"We would like to know when it would be convenient to meet with you, Mr Cowan?"

"Why don't I meet you at the hospital canteen around 7pm?" Luke suggested. "We can have a civilised discussion there over a cup of coffee."

David checked the time suited Ann then agreed with Luke, they would meet him at the hospital at the suggested time.

Ann spotted the disconcerting look on David's face as he ended the phone call.

"Mr Cowan is not your favourite person, is he?" she asked.

"No," he snorted, "he gets up my nose with his condescending manner."

"Hmm, must be a guy thing," Ann mused. "I don't allow him to rattle my cage."

David murmured something inaudible.

"Best I do the talking," Ann said, "just to make sure you don't end up beating each other up."

He looked at her and gave a lopsided grin.

"You could be right there."

Ann smiled at that.

"Let's grab a bite to eat before we swan off to meet your favourite person," she said with a mischievous grin.

They ordered Mexican food from a nearby takeaway, ate it quickly, then drove off to the hospital. The crowded, noisy hospital restaurant was not the ideal place in which to conduct an interview, but Ann had to contend with the time and place afforded them. It was better than some places she could think of.

After a few minutes waiting, Luke sauntered up to them in his overly casual way as if demonstrating they were being a little dramatic; this was a mere pleasantry and nothing to do with him. He ushered them to a side room next to the canteen with a leisurely sweep of his hand; it was a gesture intended to emphasise his thinking, not seeing the irony in acting in a drama and one of his own makings.

"Ah, it is the lovely Detective Inspector," he said to Ann by way of greeting, sounding what might be termed demeaning and sexist by some.

He shook Ann's hand.

"How nice to see you again."

David mumbled a greeting as Luke looked at him, almost as an oversight. Luke's overt manner irritated him.

He asked what they wanted to drink, ordered them and then fetched three coffees from the counter.

"Well," Luke began, swallowing the hot liquid in a rasp, running his tongue across his lips as if it was beer he was drinking from a pint mug, "what can I do for you this time, Inspector?"

"George Casey was also murdered two days ago," Ann informed him, keeping to a sober tone. "We need to interview all those immediately connected to him to exclude them from our list of potential suspects."

"Oh dear, the Casey brothers appear to be dying like flies," Luke said. He seemed to be enjoying himself as if this was a game of *Cluedo*.

"No need to be facetious, Mr Cowan," Ann said, "murder is a serious matter. I need to know where you were two nights ago between 11pm and 4am."

Luke wore an undisguised smirk on his face. "I was at a medical convention during the day and spent the night with a woman," he said.

"Can we have the contact details of this woman, to verify your statement?" Ann asked.

"Yes, of course, but you do realise," he said, "that by interviewing this young lady you may be ruining my chances of a relationship?"

"I apologise about that," Ann said, "but there is nothing I can do; the police have to do their work in order to be in a position to arrest the killer."

Luke gave an irritatingly insouciant shrug of his shoulders.

"So, each time a Casey brother dies," he responded in the same sardonic tone as before, "you are going to chase away my girlfriends with your questions?"

At that he stood up in front of Ann in a confrontational manner, puffing out his chest in a self-important gesture of challenge that was mixed with his arrogant, assumed dominance.

David briskly jumped in between them and warned Luke to sit down.

Luke backed down and laughed.

"Well, Inspector," he mocked, addressing Ann, "you seem to have quite a feisty Rottweiler to protect you."

David moved to strike him, but Ann stopped him in time.

"You should watch what you say, Mr Cowan," she said. "We are doing our job, and I will remind you that *your* job is to help us in our investigation, not to thwart that."

Her tone of voice indicated that she would not tolerate his impudence.

Luke apologised and asked if they had any more questions.

"We will contact you if we need to ask any more questions," she said, and thanked him for his time.

She then accompanied David to the car.

"You shouldn't have stopped me then, Guv," David gritted his teeth. "A good beating would have taken that clown down a notch or two."

"If you *had* beaten him, you would be giving out parking tickets instead of doing this job," she said, and reminded him, "restraint is the name of the game."

Later, Ann said with a pleading note in her voice, "It's late and I am completely bushed. Please can you drop me off at home, David?"

"Sure, nothing more we can do tonight anyway," he said, and they drove off in the direction of her house.

"I'll call you in the morning after my meeting with Edwards," Ann said as she got out of the car.

"Good luck," answered David before he sped off into the night.

***

Ann could tell that Josie was back from Paris by the trail of designer carrier bags that littered the living room floor.

Then Josie appeared, wrapped in a towel, just as Ann entered the kitchen. They ran towards each other, hugged and kissed.

"Hmm, you smell divine," said Ann as she kissed Josie's neck.

"New French shower gel – divine," Josie stated.

"And I smell of the morgue," quipped Ann, curling her lips in a mock grimace as she began to undress. "Yuk. I think I'd better head for the shower, too."

She ran upstairs leaving Josie to wrap a new towel over her wet hair and scour the fridge for some food. Ann never cooked and whenever Josie was away the fridge would always be left with just a few dried bits and pieces.

"What would you like for dinner?" she heard Josie shout from the bottom of the stairs.

"Can't hear you!" Ann called back. "Be out of the shower in a jiffy."

After her shower, she entered the kitchen.

"How was Paris?" she asked Josie.

"Fabulous and very inspiring." Josie sounded excited. "I met a new designer and I'm going to hire him for my company. His name is Pierre. A charming and very handsome man."

Ann raised a brow. "Oh, trying to make me jealous, are you?"

"Got to keep you on your toes, my darling," Josie teased. "Makes the relationship more interesting."

"I see."

Josie changed the subject. "Any leads on the murders?"

"No, it's becoming a minefield with so many possibilities and no definite leads," replied Ann.

She gave Josie a synopsis on what had been happening and found they had similar theories on the murders. She had always maintained that Josie should have worked on the force as her logic always made sense.

Their discussion seemed to last for hours until Josie got up and said, "I am officially declaring you off-duty." She grinned cheekily. "We are going to watch a soppy romantic film and afterwards you must promise to be a very bad girl."

They settled in to watch the film and then fell asleep on the sofa till dawn.

Ann awoke first. She stood up and groaned with discomfort as the soft sofa had made her back ache. She glanced at the clock and panicked as she had barely half an hour to get to her meeting with Stephen Edwards. As usual, she dashed about like a woman possessed, struggling to find the clothes she wanted to wear.

"The world is conspiring against me," she complained to Josie, who had been woken by Ann's noisy efforts to get dressed. "I can't find my shoes."

"Bunk off work and come back to bed," Josie suggested, creeping back under the duvet.

"Can't; I have a meeting with the ogre, Edwards, this morning. He'll kill me if I don't turn up."

"Well, if you don't turn up, how can he kill you?" said Josie.

They both laughed at that. Ann knew that Josie was forever great at making her happy, which was why she was with her.

She hurriedly kissed Josie and dashed out the door, cursing at the heavy traffic as she sat idling and watching the minutes tick by. All hope of getting to the meeting on time was fading fast. When she finally got to her office to collect her reports, Edwards' voice boomed down the corridor as he had heard her speak and ordered her into his office.

Whenever she delivered a report he would ignore her verbal rendition and read the written report for himself. He never praised any of her efforts but was quick to condemn her omissions and mistakes.

"Where the hell have you been for the past few days?" he demanded. "Did you not get my messages?"

"Sorry, Sir, I've been up to my elbows in work. We have *two* murders: *two* Casey brothers and the possible kidnapping of the latest victim's daughter."

Edwards peered over the reports and looked thoughtful.

"Have the team come up with any sound leads for the murders?"

"No, Sir, I've ordered my men to bring in Jake Casey as he was the last to have seen his brother and niece alive."

She paused to steady herself and take a breath, trying her best to remain calm in front of his hostile glare.

"A finger of a rubber glove with Jake's partial fingerprint was found at the scene of the murder," she began. "He has an alibi – his brother, Nathan – who claims they were both at home at the time of the murder."

Edwards continued to study her. "Go on," he urged. "What else?"

"The forensics report confirms that George Casey had sex with his daughter before he was murdered," she said. "We don't know if it was consensual sex or if he was forced to do it by the murderer. A partial size 10 army boot print seems to belong to the killer. I have put out a nationwide search for Elaine Casey. We have no evidence she has been killed. We think she has been kidnapped by the murderer because she probably witnessed the killing. George Casey's car was found abandoned a few streets away from his house. I am waiting for the forensics lab to send me a report of their findings in the car."

She stopped for two seconds to look up at him. He nodded for her to continue.

"We are waiting to hear from Interpol to see if they managed to track down George Casey's cousin, James Muller, a doctor who used to work at Chelsea and Westminster Hospital."

"Why do you need to interview this man?" asked Edwards.

"He is the doctor who participated in the satanic rituals with the Casey brothers, and we believe that he may be complicit in the murders because the brothers know about his involvement in the rituals."

Edwards gave her a sardonic look. "And you know this *how*, exactly?" His scathing tone was not missed by Ann.

"The young Casey brother, Nathan, revealed James' participation in the rituals, but he won't testify," she went on, suppressing her annoyance at his reaction to her hard work. "If we subpoena him, he might change his story."

"Jesus, what a family!" exclaimed Edwards. "I have the bloody press release at 2pm today. Be there," he ordered, "and I mean, on time!"

Ann nodded in agreement and promised to meet him at 2pm in the press room.

"I think, Sir," she added, "it is time to bring in a forensic psychologist."

Blinking at her suggestion, she continued, "I know of a very good profiler, Savannah Carey," she informed him. "She helped to bring a serial killer to justice very successfully, quite recently. She is rather unorthodox in her methods but if it brings us a result it would help us to prosecute the bastard who has eluded us thus far."

Edwards directed his eyes at her with some annoyance that he had not thought of the profiler first. Instead of complimenting her conscientiousness, he reprimanded her for proposing that he spend more CLPD money.

"Oh look, for heaven's sake," he said, twisting his features into an unpleasant scowl, "bring in whoever you bloody like, but if it blows up in your face I'll have your guts for garters."

David was waiting outside the door. Ann's flushed face bore the scars of an unpleasant meeting with her boss.

"How did it go?" he whispered to her.

"Bloody awful," replied Ann as she nudged him in the direction of the coffee machine.

The pair of them helped themselves to coffee and headed for her office. She brought David up to date with her meeting with Edwards and outlined what he had asked her to do.

David said that he would contact the profiler later that day. He told her that forensics wanted them to call in at the lab because they had an update on their examination of George's car.

"An exciting update, I hope?" Ann asked, but more to herself. "We had better go there after the press release," she suggested. She pressed her lips together in a submissive grimace and added, "I was reminded not to be late."

Ann peered over the reports to familiarise herself with all the details; she anticipated that she would be asked questions by the reporters even though her boss would head the interview.

The press room buzzed with the excited chatter of impatient newsmen. Stephen Edwards called them to order and began his report. He explained that the two murders bore the hallmarks of the same killer. He also told them that the disappearance of Elaine Casey was linked to her father's murder. His statement released a barrage of questions, all directed at Ann.

"DCI Dixon, is this the work of a serial killer?" asked a reporter in the front seat.

"We are treating these murders as linked, but we can only arrive at a definite conclusion once we have processed all the evidence," replied Ann.

"How soon do you think you are going to catch this killer, or do you think he has outwitted you, Inspector?"

"Has the CLPD procrastination resulted in a second murder?"

Waves of questions were fired persistently at Ann.

"The CLPD and all our affiliated teams are doing their very best to find the killer and bring him to justice," she responded, tight-lipped.

"Do you think it is a personal vendetta against the Casey brothers, Inspector Dixon?" asked a female reporter.

"Well, the fact that two brothers were murdered in quick succession suggests a grudge or a score to settle," replied Ann matter-of-factly.

"DCI Dixon, do you think Elaine Casey has also been murdered, or has she been kidnapped and being held somewhere?" asked Amy Baker, *The World News'* reporter.

"We have no evidence to suggest that Elaine has been murdered. There is a distinct possibility that she may have been kidnapped, but we are not sure at this stage," Ann replied.

Ann remained steadfast in her replies, much to the chagrin of her boss who appeared somewhat overwhelmed by their probing questions. Sensing that the reporters were not satisfied with their explanations, Stephen Edwards informed the press that he was calling an end to the interview due to lack of time.

A roar of disapproval echoed around the room and some reporters persisted with their questions. Finally, Edwards' voice boomed across the room.

"There will be no more questions; this meeting is adjourned!"

The reporters flocked towards Ann in the hope of gaining a few last fragments of news. She remained firm and refused to answer any more questions. Then she grabbed her coat and headed for the door with David close behind.

They dashed for her car with the reporters in hot pursuit. David grinned as they reached the safety of the car.

"The boss didn't like being shown up, hey Guv?" said David.

"Well, *I* didn't tell the reporters to only ask me the questions."

"No, but he's green with envy; you're clearly more popular than he is with the press."

"Tough luck, that's his problem," said Ann. "We need to be wary of that Amy Baker, though. She's like a bloodhound, always sniffing out juicy bits of news and then using it to her own advantage. She's never forgiven me for the bruising encounter we had with the last investigation, and for being disciplined by her boss for using unlawful tactics to obtain information. I will also let you know that she is pretty pissed off because I rejected her advances."

"Ouch, that must have been a blow to her ego. She rates herself as irresistible."

Ann raised her brows in acknowledgment of his comment.

"Just remember: no private interviews to anyone," warned Ann.

"I promise to keep my head down and my lips sealed."

"Let's shoot over to forensics," she suggested, "I want to hear what they found in Casey's car."

Peter was peering into a microscope when Ann and David tracked him down.

"We fine-tooth combed George Casey's car," said Peter, looking up at them. "Strands of female hair belonging to a relation of George Casey, probably his daughter, Elaine's hair. It was found on the back seat of the car. Front seat had fibres from a SOCO suit. Also found mud and blood on the accelerator and at driver's side of car. The blood is a match to George Casey. Fingerprints on the steering wheel are no match to anyone we have on file. Possible indication that killer drove Elaine in George's car to wherever he took her then drove the car and abandoned it where we found it."

Peter scratched the side of his face and looked at his notes beside his microscope, then back at Ann.

"You had better ask the neighbours if they saw anyone leaving the house or heard a car driving off at around 4am that morning," he said.

"I have my men already working on that side of things," replied Ann, and thanked Peter for his report before heading for her office.

Detective Inspector Tobin was waiting for her as she opened the door.

"I have Jake Casey in the interview room, Guv," he said. "I thought you may want to sit in on the interview."

Ann nodded and followed DI Tobin.

Jake looked dishevelled as they entered the room. He had been on night duty and seemed in need of sleep.

Ann greeted him and proceeded to turn on the tape recorder. She stated the date and time, and the names of the persons present at the interview.

"Jake Casey," she said to him, "we have brought you in for questioning as part of a glove with your fingerprints was found in the bedroom where your brother, George Casey, was murdered two days ago. Can you explain how a glove with your fingerprints happened to be at the scene of the crime?"

Jake looked up in surprise. "What do you mean, my 'glove'? I only went to my brother's house that night to have a drink at 6pm with him and my niece, Elaine," he declared. "I came straight from work." He took a breath and continued, "I do remember finding a pair of gloves in the pocket of my uniform, which I had used on duty, and discarding them in the kitchen bin."

Ann studied his face and said nothing.

"George reprimanded me for bringing bacteria into his house," Jake said with an impish grin.

Ann pressed him further.

"So, how do explain why only *one* finger of the glove was found in the bedroom where the murder occurred if you say you put *both* gloves in the kitchen bin?"

"I went to have a drink with my brother and his daughter and left at 9pm," Jake answered. "*You* are the detective; *you* work it out."

She looked at him, making a mental note of his unnecessarily defensive tone.

Jake added, "My brother, Nathan, can verify that I got home around 10pm and went to bed."

"Nathan has confirmed that you were home by 10pm, but he went out around 10.30pm so that means you don't have a complete alibi," Ann said. "And what was part of your glove doing in George's bedroom where he was tortured and murdered?"

"I don't know," protested Jake.

Ann stared at him.

"I think you sneaked out of the house before 11pm and returned to George's home where you tortured and murdered him," replied Ann.

Jake looked affronted. "Why would I do that?"

"Because you resented George for having sex with your sister, a resentment you harboured for years."

DI Tobin leaned forward to grab Jake by the shoulder. Ann cautioned him and reminded him that his methods would be regarded as police brutality. David and Detective Constable Terence Holmes were watching the interview in the room next door.

Terence Holmes leaned over David's shoulder and whispered,

"Still got the hots for DCI Dixon, I see."

"Fuck off, you bastard; you wish you could bang her – admit it!" retorted David. "Isn't *that* what you are doing when you go off on those long investigations together?"

"I'll bet you come in your pants every time she shows off her legs," mocked Holmes.

"Fucking bastard," exclaimed David, and he lunged at Holmes, punching him so hard that he fell against the table.

Ann heard the noise, switched off the tape and left the room to investigate. She could not believe her eyes when she saw the two men embroiled in battle like a pair of overgrown schoolboys.

Her voice rose to a shout. "What the bloody hell is happening?"

David got up from the floor. "Sorry, Guv, this bastard made a very personal remark and it got to me." He hung his head, trying to disguise his embarrassment.

"And what do you have to say for yourself, Holmes?" asked Ann.

"Not my fault, Guv, your boy can't cope with the truth, that's all."

"And *what*, exactly, do you mean by that?"

Holmes indicated towards David with his arm. "Better ask pretty boy here," he replied. "He ought to tell you why."

"Whatever the reason, this is no way to behave," Ann said, her voice becoming firmer. "I suggest you settle your differences outside of work."

Both men apologised to her. Holmes left the room and David asked to be excused to tidy up in the men's room. Ann returned to the interview room, embarrassed that she had to apologise to Jake. She turned the tape recorder back on and resumed questioning him.

"Mr Casey, forensics have revealed that the code book found at your brother's house has been written in witches' code. Can you tell me what the code means?"

Jake shifted uneasily in his chair. His voice sounded hesitant.

"I don't know anything about codes."

"Oh, come on; don't play the innocent. You were as heavily involved in satanic worship as your brothers. You are facing a possible murder charge, Jake. If you cooperate, the judge might commute your sentence."

"M-murder," he stuttered, looking confounded.

"Yes, murder," Ann responded, "and for that, you are looking at a life sentence."

Jake remained silent for a few moments. "I know some parts of the code," he said, "but if I reveal it to you, they will kill me."

"Who are '*they*'?"

Jake ignored the question and said nothing.

"We will offer you police protection if you help us," Ann said.

"Bollocks!" he yelled. "You know you can't guarantee that for the rest of my life."

"So what alternative is there?" she said, studying him. "You'll just have to trust me and start spilling the beans."

Jake looked at his feet.

"I tell you what we'll do," she said to him, "we have enough evidence to get a warrant to search your home. You will have to spend 24 hours in police custody while your house is being searched. You will have 24 hours to decide whether to assist us or not. The choice is yours."

Jake demanded to see his lawyer. "You have the wrong man, Detective," he said. "You'd better be damned sure of your case because you remember how you cocked up the arrest of Sam Cain?"

Ann informed him he would be allowed to contact his lawyer later that afternoon. In the meantime, he was taken to the holding cell.

Ann turned to Tobin and told him of the fight that had taken place between David and Holmes and that in future she wanted them kept apart at work.

Tobin agreed and assured her he would have a word with Holmes. She signalled for David to accompany her to her office. They walked in silence. When they were in her office she turned to David and said, "You will tell me in your own time what happened at the interview office today. But let me warn you, if it ever happens again, I will replace you and that is a promise."

David listened intently to her but remained silent for a few moments. Then he promised to keep his temper under control and apologised for his lack of judgement.

"Now go and get us some doughnuts," she requested, "I need plenty of sugar for my meeting with Edwards."

She prepared herself mentally for the encounter with Edwards before she knocked on his office door.

"Yes, who is it?" boomed Edwards, his voice sounding agitated.

Ann opened the door and peered inside.

"Stop skulking outside and get in here," Edwards instructed. "I hear you have Jake Casey in custody."

"We found a glove finger with his prints at the scene," Ann declared. "He also does not have a watertight alibi for his whereabouts after 11pm. He was the last person to see his brother alive. A warrant would enable us to possibly find more evidence."

"Does he have a motive?"

"Well, yes, he does," she replied. "He was also involved in the occult rituals and he resented George having exclusive rights to sexual encounters with their sister. I believe this caused a great deal of resentment between the brothers.

"But he has a partial alibi," countered Edwards. "His brother was with him on the night of the murder until 10pm."

"Yes, but his brother went to bed after 10pm, so if Jake sneaked out, he could have travelled to Surrey in 45 minutes. I have the men checking the local cabs, just in case he went by taxi."

"OK," Edwards began, placing his interlocked fingers irritatingly on the desk in front of him, "so we get the warrant and find nothing. You can't convict him on the evidence of a glove print if he admitted to leaving his gloves in the bin at the house. The boot print at the scene also suggests another person was in the house and could have planted the glove finger at the scene."

"Yes, Sir, that is why we need to search the house to find more evidence."

"Get the bloody warrant and make sure you don't fuck this up, Dixon. We already have negative press reports, no thanks to that Amy Baker."

Ann always felt she had run a marathon after a meeting with Edwards. He drained her of all energy and confidence. She added the last updates to her laptop and headed home. She knew that Josie would be working late from home that evening as she had deadlines to meet for a new line of fashion. After a shower, she poured herself a glass of wine and slumped into the armchair.

Her phone rang.

It was Edwards.

He informed her that he had a warrant to enable the police to search Jake's house. He reminded her to be thorough in their search. He didn't want the police to bungle yet another investigation.

Ann promised to do her best and contact him as soon as they had finished the search and then turned on her laptop to ensure she had documented the latest details pertaining to the case. She was aware that both the police reputation and hers rested on the outcome of this case.

Ann turned off her laptop and went downstairs.

"You are not allowed to work when your brother is visiting," Josie said in mock admonishment.

"Spoke to my boss," Ann explained. "Couldn't get out of it."

"Hey, your case is really making headlines," said Adam. "Do you think it is the work of a serial killer?"

"Not sure," Ann replied. "We think it's a personal vendetta against the Casey brothers. A grudge, perhaps, or someone trying to stop the victims from revealing incriminating information."

"Oh, for heaven's sake, don't encourage her, Adam," put in Josie, "she spends too many hours at work as it is."

"It's a fascinating case, you must admit," said Adam. "I wouldn't mind tagging onto some of it myself."

"Hang on a minute, Sherlock Holmes, who appointed *you* to the CLPD?" Ann said in jest.

"If you two don't stop talking shop," warned Josie, "I won't get tickets for *Tosca* next Saturday."

This statement got their attention, and they asked if she was serious about going to the opera.

"Would I joke about something so close to my darling's heart?" declared Josie. "I take it you will both be able to attend?"

"Oh yes, we would love to," they chorused in unison.

Adam stifled a yawn.

"You're sleeping here tonight, and I won't take no for an answer," said Ann.

Josie added her support.

Adam was too tired to argue and settled for the sofa bed in the living room.

Ann and Josie chatted into the early hours before falling asleep. Ann only regretted her large consumption of wine and getting into bed at 2.30am when her alarm sprung into life at 5.30am.

"Oh God, my head is going to explode," she complained as she turned on the cold water in the shower to revive herself. The shock of the water hitting her warm skin made her shudder, but it had the desired effect as she felt more alert as she emerged from the shower. She hastily scrambled her clothes together and got dressed.

David was parked outside the door as she left the house at 5.50am.

"Good morning David," she greeted him, "I hate these bloody early mornings."

"Morning Guv, we're going to collect the warrant on the way to the Casey house, aren't we?" he asked, ignoring her comment about the early starts.

"Yes, the forensics chaps will meet us there."

At that moment her mobile rang. The look on her face and the expletive she uttered told David something terrible had happened.

"Jesus Christ! We need to get over to the station," she said, and let out an exasperated sigh. "Jake Casey was attacked in the showers and is in hospital."

David looked stunned at the news. He immediately obeyed, turned the car around and headed for the police station whereupon Ann jumped out and hurried towards the holding cells where she had last seen Jake.

The sergeant met her on the way. She demanded to know what had happened. The constable who had been assigned to guard Jake was called into an office to explain. On noticing Ann's anger, he looked terrified as if he thought he might be physically attacked.

He stuttered as he spoke.

"J-Jake was fine until he went to have a shower. I left him to get on with it and when I came back half an hour later, he was lying unconscious, face down in the shower." He stopped to take a breath. "He was taken to St Bartholomew's Hospital."

Seeing that this could have been prevented, Ann ordered, "I want the names of everyone who was on duty last night and this morning!"

The constable and sergeant assured her that the list of names would be supplied to her later that morning. Ann asked to be shown where Jake was found and immediately ordered the forensics officers to examine the scene of the attack and take samples. DI Tobin joined her at the scene of the incident, and they discussed the details of the attack.

"Come on Alfred, we need to find out how badly Jake has been injured," she said.

Ann was most unpredictable in her moments of anger and Alfred did not attempt conversation as they sped off to the hospital. They headed for the ward where Jake had been admitted. A policeman sat outside the intensive care unit as David and Ann entered.

A nurse and doctor were taking a sample of blood from Jake. The doctor looked up at Ann as she approached the bed. She flashed her identity card and introduced herself. A man called Dr Evans told her he was taking charge of Jake's care. Ann asked about the medical details.

Dr Evans informed her that Jake had sustained a subdural haemorrhage due to a severe blow to the back of his head. There was substantial brain damage. He said that they had operated to remove most of the blood clot and had to wait for the swelling on the brain to subside before they could ascertain whether there was long-term damage. The doctor said he was unable to say how long it would take. Ann pulled a disconcerting face at the prospect of the unknown time factor.

"I understand this man was arrested on suspicion of murder, Inspector," said Dr Evans.

"Yes, but it is more complicated and having an injured suspect makes my work doubly more difficult."

Ann thanked the doctor for his help and went to instruct the constable on guard outside the door that she wanted the number of officers doubled and the identity of all non- hospital staff vetted.

A noisy group of reporters were waiting outside the hospital gates as Ann and David emerged.

"How badly is the suspect injured, Inspector?" asked one of them.

"He is stable, in intensive care," Ann replied. "That is all I can tell you."

They ignored her statement and persisted with their questions.

"The CLPD is very careless to allow a suspect to be attacked!" someone shouted. "What do you have to say about that, Inspector?" asked another reporter.

"The Central London Police Division will call a press conference soon," Ann responded, "and at which you can ask any further questions you have."

They crowded around the car like a pack of wolves, continuing to hound her with questions.

"Put your foot down so we can get away from this lot," she told David. "The bastards never give up."

David grinned. "I know what you mean."

"And I'll have to tell Edwards the latest news before he hears it from someone else. Let's stop at his office."

As soon as she stepped into the building, as if on cue, one of the sergeants announced, "The Super wants to see you urgently."

"I'm on my way to his office now," said Ann a little breathlessly.

She instructed David to wait in her office while she braced herself for Edwards' wrath.

"What the hell is going on?" he raged. "You'd better have a bloody good response."

"I can only tell you what I know," said Ann, feeling her throat go dry.

"This is going to give the press a field day!" Edwards' voice boomed back at her. "We're going to look like incompetent idiots."

"I have ordered a full investigation and report," said Ann. Her voice came out in a slight rasp as she tried to overcome the bitter taste that had entered her mouth. "Got forensics working at the holding cells right this minute, and I've spoken to Jake Casey's doctor who says he cannot predict the rate of recovery from the head injury. I've also increased the security at the hospital."

"Do we know why Jake was targeted?"

"This might seem implausible," Ann said carefully, "but I think he was attacked because there is an accomplice in the murders."

"I want to know who was in or around the interview room

yesterday," Edwards said in a crisp bark. "I want everyone questioned never mind who they are."

Ann nodded in agreement and said she would have a report on his desk by the morning. After the meeting she went to her office and sat down, nursing a well-deserved mug of steaming hot coffee. David was on his mobile and ended the call when Ann appeared.

"God, this is such a bloody fiasco," she said, placing the coffee mug on the desk beside her. "It's fucked up everything."

"I'll chase up the list of names of the staff on duty yesterday at the holding cells," David said, looking at her face.

"Thanks, I'd appreciate that," said Ann, "and we'll need to pick up the warrant and get to Jake's house this afternoon. Tell everyone the time has been rescheduled and ask Nathan to be at home so we can gain access."

"Will do," said David. "I just spoke to Nathan who was very miffed at being kept waiting three hours before being told his brother had been attacked and we were not going to pitch."

"Just be nice to him and win him over," advised Ann. "We can't afford to alienate him now."

David immediately began following her instructions by phoning around. Ann got on with preparing the report she had promised Edwards. The phone rang two hours later. It was DI Tobin informing them that he and a team of forensics officers were inside Jake's house.

Ann and David hurried off to the car and headed for West London. Ann cursed at the heavy traffic that slowed them down.

As David pulled up in the drive, Nathan stood at the front door looking dejected.

"I am so very sorry about what has happened to your brother," Ann said, "and I want you to know everything is being done to find Jake's attacker.

"That's exactly what you said when Tom died and since then another brother has died, a niece is missing and another brother badly injured," Nathan responded in an unmistakably cold tone. "It doesn't inspire me with confidence, and it gives me very little trust in your ability to do your job, Inspector."

Ann felt stung by Nathan's criticism and direct condemnation of her. She knew, too, that DI Tobin had overheard his comments and some of the forensics officers. Embarrassment and shame flooded her.

She thought about a suitable retort but desisted, took the front door key from Nathan and proceeded to instruct her officers to begin their work. The forensics officers' first visit was to the upstairs bedrooms, bagging and labelling Jake's clothes. They focused their attention on Jake's shoes as they were a size 10, the same size as those found at the murder scene. Ann's attention was drawn, specifically, to the photographs on the wall of Jake's bedroom; they were photos of him while serving in the Territorial Army. They searched the cupboards thoroughly, looking for weapons and items related to the murders. They found a cloak and a few candles in a box under the stairs.

Ann examined the entry and exit points of the house and considered the possibility of someone leaving without disturbing the rest of the building. Exit was possible via the kitchen door and from the bedroom or living room windows as they opened easily without making a noise.

She spotted the shed at the bottom of the garden and sent a forensics officer to inspect it. The shed door was unlocked. It contained several gardening implements and bags of fertilizer. Then, in the semi-darkness of a corner of the shed, the officer spotted a pair of boots. They were army-issue boots caked in mud. The boots leaned against a large mallet. The mallet had mud and what appeared to be dried blood on it. He called out to his colleagues. Ann heard the shout and rushed to the shed.

"Found these boots and this wooden mallet, Guv," said the officer.

"Bag them and get them to the lab," Ann instructed.

They continued the search, finding items relating to practises of the occult in the basement. A pentagram drawn on the floor of the basement suggested that rituals might have occurred there. The team spent many hours combing through the house, carefully searching every corner. Satisfied that they had collected all that they came for, Ann announced that they should wrap up the search and she would meet with them later.

David drove her back to her office.

"The boots and the mallet are an important find and I hope will match the boot print found at the scene," Ann said. She then promptly slumped into her chair with exhaustion. It was 7pm.

"I think my stomach thinks my throat has been cut. I've had no food today. I'm absolutely famished."

She put a hand on her stomach as if in protection then sat up wearily, rubbing her left temple.

"Just give me half an hour to get this report done, then we can grab some dinner."

She checked her phone for messages. There was a message from Josie reminding her to come home for dinner, telling her not to eat out. She phoned her and asked if she could bring David along, as they were both so hungry. David looked up from his paperwork and began waving his arm, indicating a rejection to the dinner invite. Ann ignored his refusal and told Josie to prepare for an extra person for dinner. When she came off the phone, she informed him that she would not take no for an answer. Josie loved to cook and entertain.

"I will not have another word on the subject. Now, get done so that we can get out of here!" she ordered.

They whizzed out of the office by 8pm and sped off to Ann's home. They were greeted by Adam who had also been invited to dinner. Ann introduced David to Adam. Josie came out of the kitchen, kissed and hugged Ann and said, "There will be no food for any guests who discuss work." She then ushered them to an immaculately laid dinner table.

"You've forgotten the place names," David quipped.

Josie responded by swatting him over the head with a dishcloth.

"I hope you don't have any food fads, David. I've cooked a French dish and I hope you'll enjoy it."

"I'm not fussy, I'm too starving for that – any food will be just fine."

"Whatever it is, Josie never disappoints," said Adam. "She's an excellent chef. I keep urging her to open a restaurant if she wasn't so busy designing clothes."

"You are too kind, darling Adam," Josie said. "I doubt whether my culinary skills can compete with all the great chefs out there."

They tucked into a starter of smoked salmon, figs and light garnish. This was followed by coq au vin served with petits pois, potatoes and vegetables. The dessert was crème brûlée, which was followed by cheese, biscuits and coffee.

Convivial and light-hearted banter was tossed between them during the meal. David and Adam hit it off and discovered they had many shared interests.

"I suppose Ann doesn't give you much time off," enquired Adam.

"Well, that's just the nature of our work," explained David. "I pursue my hobbies and interests during my days off or while on leave." He began to talk about his interests and passions outside of work.

Ann was quite surprised to learn that David played squash and did boxing. She was also surprised that he shared a love of photography and canoeing with Adam. The two men chatted away like old friends, while Josie flirted across the table with Ann.

"You should invite your sergeant more often, Ann," suggested Adam, "then you'll learn more about his various pursuits of pleasure."

"Chance would be a fine thing," said Josie, "she works them into the ground; every second is accounted for. We are very lucky that her ladyship has deigned to join us tonight."

Ann watched as Adam and David exchanged phone numbers.

"I don't think it's a good idea for you to socialise with my sergeant, Adam," she remarked.

"Why ever not?" asked Adam, arching his brows. "I don't have a pal who I can drag along when I want to chill out. And I don't complain when *you* go off playing squash with your MI6 heartthrob, Clive Hammond."

"Mind your own business and stop telling the world about my social pursuits," retorted Ann sharply, and turned towards David. "And just remember, David, work first. No gadding about with my brother and phoning in sick to get time off."

"Told you she would put a damper on the fun," Josie chipped in, trying to make light of the conversation. "Time off does not feature in this lady's book."

The wine flowed freely and when Ann noticed David getting inebriated, she reminded him that he needed his full senses for work in the morning.

David checked his watch and announced that he ought to be getting home. He thanked Josie for a superb dinner. Ann called a taxi and David left half an hour later.

"Nice bloke, your sergeant," said Adam.

"I don't want you filling his head with promises of adventure," said Ann as she thrust out her chin, "he has an important job to do."

Adam moved close to Ann and whispered, "Your sergeant idolises you."

Ann drew back, disarmed by his comment.

"Haven't you noticed how he watches you?" Adam continued, keeping his voice low. "I'd guess that he more than admires you."

"Don't be ridiculous," Ann said, a little above a whisper. "David and I are a great team; we have a good working relationship."

Josie entered the room.

"Who is having a relationship?" enquired Josie.

"I was just telling Adam what a good professional relationship David and I have," Ann said, twisting round to face her.

"Yes, he is a great guy," Josie said. "I wish he could meet a nice girl."

Adam thanked Josie for the meal and announced he was going to bed. Ann and Josie chatted while they finished washing the dishes. Josie embraced Ann and they kissed passionately.

Ann broke away and said, "No second dessert tonight, we have a guest, remember?"

"Oh damn, I forgot," exclaimed Josie, then grinned impishly. "Never mind, there is always the weekend."

The following morning, Ann called at David's house to collect him for their visit to the hospital to check on Jake's progress.

CHAPTER 4

The good news was that there had been no deterioration in Jake's condition. He was stable but remained unconscious. Ann asked to be kept informed of any significant improvement, gave her thanks and left the unit. Just as she emerged from the intensive care unit door, Eve and Harold Marshall arrived.

"Well," said Eve, so that Ann could overhear, "isn't this nice, the Inspector visiting the hospital when she should be out there finding my daughter."

"Mrs Marshall," Ann began, "the police are doing everything in their power to find your daughter. We have her photo in all the newspapers. My officers have interviewed many people who are friends or associates of your daughter. I would ask you, please be patient and less critical of the police."

"The police have made no progress in their investigations of two murders!" shouted Harold. "How the hell can we trust them to find our daughter?"

Ann remained composed and politely promised them that she would do her very best to find Elaine. They snorted and walked off.

"Phew!" David let out a breath. "He certainly woke up on the wrong side of the bed today."

"They're understandably anxious," said Ann. "Come on; never mind them for now. Let's get over to the holding cells. I want to interview those idiots who allowed Jake to be attacked."

They were greeted by the constable on duty at the reception desk at the station.

"Inform all the staff here that I want to see them in the main office in five minutes!" ordered Ann.

"Yes, Guv," he assured her.

"Get hold of DI Tobin. I want him here, too."

The men went to the assigned location promptly and Tobin

appeared 10 minutes later.

Ann proceeded to address the room. "Right, I want to know how someone can walk into a police station and clobber a prisoner over the head without any of you lot noticing," Ann demanded to know.

They looked at her. A silence prevailed. No-one said a word.

"DI Tobin, you oversaw the holding cells on the night of the assault. Where were you and, more importantly, where was the constable guarding Jake Casey?"

"I had gone off to get something to eat and I left Constable Drake to stay with Jake," he explained.

Ann turned to Drake.

"What do you have to say for yourself, Constable Drake?"

"Jake Casey asked to have a shower," said the constable. "We were not busy, so I checked with Sergeant Pollock here if it was OK to take Jake to the shower."

His hands fidgeted nervously as he spoke.

"I left him in the shower for 30 minutes and went off to wait for him in the office down the corridor," he continued to explain.

"You have omitted to tell us that the reason you went to wait down the corridor was because you and a female officer were having sex in that office." Ann didn't let her stare falter. "You were so immersed in your sexual activity that you were unable to see when a stranger, posing as a maintenance man and with a fake identity, slipped into the shower and floored Jake Casey. Is that not what happened?"

Constable Drake looked aghast. It was clear Ann had hit upon the truth.

His cheeks were pale, and he began to stutter.

"I'm s-sorry, Guv," he began to admit, "it was a terrible lapse of judgement on my part, and I am truly sorry."

"You see, I have good officers who are loyal to this force and who tell the truth," she said. "Your appalling behaviour has injured our prisoner and has given the press a field day, questioning the credibility of the police."

She scanned the room, her eyes hardening to a stare.

"Superintendent Edwards wants to see all of you," she told

them, and then to Drake she said, "and I can tell you my reprimand is the least of your concerns compared with how he will discipline you, Drake, and possibly dismiss you from the force."

Constable Drake appeared to tremble.

"I want a comprehensive report of the incident on my desk by the morning," Ann instructed. "Now get out of my sight."

"Fucking arrogant dyke. I hate her!" cursed Drake under his breath to Tobin. "I wish someone would put her in her place."

"Watch your mouth, Drake. *You* were in the wrong and she is only doing her job. Your negligence has dropped all of us in it, especially me as I was accountable for the security of the holding cells."

"What do you really think will happen to me?" Drake asked.

"Well, a reprimand, if Edwards is in a good mood, but I suspect he will make an example of you as a warning to other potential misconduct," Tobin replied matter-of-factly. "I would start to pack your bags. I think you'll be shown the door, my son."

Edwards wanted DI Tobin and Sergeant Drake in his office at 2pm that afternoon. He was incandescent with rage and didn't mince his words in telling them how furious he was at Drake's behaviour and Tobin's negligence.

"You can clear out your lockers, both of you. You are no longer part of this force. Now get out of my sight!" he growled.

The two men listened in silence, knowing any attempt to explain would incur Edwards' wrath even more. They left hurriedly.

"That bastard thinks he can treat me like dirt," Tobin said. "I never wanted to be a policeman anyway."

"I did it to please my father," complained Drake. "I wish I'd never bothered now."

"Oh well, now you got your wish," Tobin joked. "You can contemplate your future while signing on the dole."

Drake pursed his lips in desultory acknowledgement.

"I wouldn't advise contemplating any type of revenge, though," said Tobin. "Life as a locked up ex-policeman is a grim one, indeed."

***

Ann and David met with the CID squad in the incident room where they discussed their latest findings on the two murders and the kidnapping.

DI Ian Roberts led the feedback.

"We had an eyewitness who was walking his dog on the morning of the murder of George Casey," he began. "He says that around 4.15am he saw someone in George Casey's drive carrying something which looked like a large sack over their shoulder and putting it into the front seat of a Lamborghini, which was parked in the drive. The man said he hid behind a tree. He watched as the car drove off and, as the streetlight shone on the car when it drove past him, he saw a woman slumped in the front seat. He thought she looked asleep or very drunk as her head rolled from side to side. He was unable to see the face of the driver as it was too dark."

"Why did he not come forward with the information sooner?" asked Ann.

"He said he had just moved into the neighbourhood a few weeks ago," answered DI Roberts, "and he only came forward when he read about it in the papers."

"We must assume that Elaine Casey is still alive and being held captive somewhere," said Ann.

"All the interviews with her friends and her associates yielded no clues," said Roberts. "We discovered that she had a secret boyfriend who said they kept their relationship quiet until Elaine had passed her exams at the bar. He said her parents did not want her studies interrupted. George had an alibi for the night of Elaine's disappearance."

"What have you dug up, Roberts?" asked Ann.

He recapped about the finding of a part of Jake's glove and which had his fingerprint, at the scene of the murder. He told of Jake's flimsy alibi and the fact that he was the last person to see his brother alive.

"I have just picked up the report from Peter Drew at forensics," Roberts continued. "The boots belonging to Jake Casey, which were found by the garden shed at his house, contained mud from George's garden and blood belonging to George. Carpet fibres were from the carpet in George's car and a hair belonging to a relation of George Casey, presumably his missing daughter, Elaine."

He looked at them before going on.

"We interviewed Casey's hedge fund associates. He did not seem to have enemies, but the view was that they knew that George had powerful friends. They carefully mentioned that he had links to the underworld, so nobody would dream of trying to harm him."

"Has anyone spoken to Sam Cain?" enquired Ann.

"Yes, I spoke with him," said Roberts. "He was out chasing girls with his brother on the night of the murder and spent the night with a woman who has confirmed his story."

"I don't want you to rest on your laurels and assume that we have no more work to do," said Ann, "just because Jake Casey is a suspect."

Roberts nodded.

"Our suspect was attacked in the shower of the holding cells last night by someone posing as a maintenance man," said Ann. "He is unconscious and has been taken to intensive care. The idiots who were guarding him allowed this to happen and dropped us all in the shit. We have no idea when Jake Casey will recover but this will not halt the investigation."

A buzz of disquiet filtered through the room.

"OK, there's no need to dwell on what is done," Ann said. "All I am asking of all of you is to do your job with commitment and professionalism. The public and the press will be unforgiving if more ignorance and stupidity occurs. I am asking for total discretion and dedication from all of you."

The team nodded in agreement.

Ann pressed her lips together before continuing. "We have grounds to go over every bit of the property," she said. You may have missed something."

She regarded them defiantly, her eyes appearing to scan each face in turn as she held their attention.

"I don't want any one of you speaking to the media," she warned. "The superintendent will handle all press releases."

There was barely a murmur amongst them. After the briefing, the team left the incident room and chatted amongst themselves as Ann gave orders to the senior officers.

David told Ann that Peter Drew wanted to speak with her at her earliest convenience.

"Thanks David, tell him I will see him in the next 30 minutes," she said.

She checked her watch and remembered that Josie had booked opera tickets for them at 7.30pm, but she wanted to know what Peter Drew had to say. She sauntered off to his office, hoping he had encouraging news about the case.

"Drag up a chair, Ann, I need you to hear this," Peter said with some hesitance. "I examined the shoes we think belong to Jake Casey. I let his brother identify them. Nathan is not one hundred per cent sure if the boots belong to his brother, but he said Jake has a pair like the ones we have found in the shed. If you look carefully, you will see that the boots are caked in mud almost up to the laces. We have checked the boot prints left in the mud in the garden of George Casey's house. We are sure that these boots made these prints as the mud on them has the same geological composition as the mud in George's garden. The blood belongs to George. The pattern of mud on the boots and the depth of the prints in the mud in the garden suggests that a man with a height of 6ft 3ins, weighing 12 stone and carrying a weight of around 8 stone."

Ann stared at him and blinked. "That is some discovery. Very good. Anything more you can deduct from this discovery?"

"The killer," continued Peter, "must have carried Elaine Casey from the house to the car, across the muddy flower bed. This is consistent with the eyewitness seeing a man carry what looked like a sack of potatoes over his shoulder and into the front seat of the car. The soil in the flower bed had been loosened by the gardener and the water sprinklers came on at 3am. The soil had about two hours' worth of soaking, which, if you walked in it would leave deep prints. What we now need to do is to establish Jake Casey's height and weight and, of course, Elaine's weight when we find her."

"OK," said Ann. "I will get Sergeant Hughes to find out from the hospital and get the information to you as soon as possible."

She looked at her watch. "Look, I must dash. Going to the opera tonight – *must not* be late!" She paused and added, with a wry expression, "Or I will be severely reprimanded."

When she arrived home, she charged through the front door of her house, glancing nervously at the clock on the wall of her hall.

She had barely an hour to get ready.

"Hurry up, slowcoach!" Josie said as Ann raced to the bathroom.

"Get me a glass of wine!" she called to Josie as she went up the stairs two at a time to the shower. "I need something to calm my nerves."

Josie was applying her make-up in front of the mirror in the bedroom when Ann came through the door after her shower. She thought Josie looked tantalisingly provocative in her little black dress that accentuated her striking curves. Ann lifted the hem of Josie's dress and slid her hand along the top of Josie's stockings, trailing her fingers past the suspenders to her crotch. Ann sighed as she anticipated the potential for an erotic evening.

"Oh God, please stop," Josie squealed, "you're driving me mad with desire."

"Well, it's all your fault," Ann whispered, "you smell utterly divine; good enough to eat."

"Oh God, don't start," Josie groaned, as if an erotic wave had just passed through her, "or we'll never get to the opera."

She pushed Ann away just as Adam popped his head around the door and enquired if they were ready to go. He smiled knowingly as he witnessed their embrace, apologising for spoiling their fun.

"Weren't you taught to knock on bedroom doors before entering, cheeky sod?" Ann asked.

"Just think of all the fun I would miss if I did that," he answered.

Ann drained the last drop of her glass of wine, put on the finishing touches of her make-up and raced downstairs after Josie and Adam.

"Have you got the tickets, Josie?" Adam asked.

"Yes, check everything. Jesus, Adam! Do you trust *any*one?"

They stopped off at a restaurant after the performance, enjoying a hearty meal of lemon roast chicken with a Spanish-style chorizo stuffing, accompanied by liberal amounts of champagne.

On arriving home, Josie, a little inebriated, said, "Adam, are you coming in to put us to bed?"

"No, my darlings," – he winked – "I am going to leave you to continue the unfinished business you started earlier this evening."

"Go on home, you are a wicked, suggestive boy," Ann said.

They hugged and kissed him goodnight and went indoors. It was with feverish and joyous anticipation that Josie pulled off Ann's clothes. Both women were highly charged. When their bodies were exhausted from their orgasmic tsunami, they lay in each other's arms reminiscing about the love that bound them so securely.

But their hopes of having a Saturday morning lie-in were dashed when a car hooted outside. Josie cursed at the noise, got up and looked outside the window.

"Bloody hell!" she exclaimed. "What does Hughes want at this time on a Saturday morning?"

Ann sat up in bed rubbing the sleep from her eyes. She slipped on a dressing gown and went to open the front door.

"Who chased you out of bed this morning, David?" asked Ann.

"Sorry to disturb you, Guv, but we have had an anonymous tip-off from a caller. Jake Casey has a lock-up garage near King's Cross. We were unable to reach you as your phones were switched off."

She pulled her dressing gown more tightly around her, folding the belt more securely around her waist.

"DI Tobin and the team are already at the scene." David's eyes slid down Ann's body as he spoke, making it obvious he was aware of her half-dressed state.

She galloped upstairs, got dressed and her and David raced over to meet the rest of the team. The area was cordoned off with tape. Tim emerged from the grubby garage wearing his SOCO suit.

"Hi Ann," he said. "The body found in the boot of the car is that of a young woman in her early 20s. It appears to have been stored in a freezer, wrapped in heavy-duty plastic and then put in the boot of the car."

Tim led Ann to the open boot. He pulled away the plastic covering the body. It revealed a naked woman lying in the foetal position. Ann gasped as she recognised the face of the deceased woman to be that of Elaine Casey. Her skin was marbled and extremely pale. Ann had so hoped and prayed that the woman had been kidnapped, not killed as well. Elaine's parents' faces briefly flashed into her mind.

"Decomposition has been delayed," Tim said, "due to the body having been frozen. I think the body was kept in a freezer for some time, then dumped about two days ago. You can see the freezer burns where the skin was in contact with the cold surface of the freezer."

"Do you know the cause of death?" Ann asked.

"A wound below the sternum suggests a puncture of the aorta," Tim replied. "Exsanguination, probable cause of death. The forensics team worked diligently, collecting and labelling samples, taking photographs and collecting evidence."

DI Roberts joined Ann and began updating her on his findings.

"The car is registered to Dr James Muller," he said. "The lock-up is in Jake Casey's name. We assume that the men shared the garage."

"Get the car and everything to the forensics garage," Ann instructed.

The teams then spent more hours collecting evidence. Ann arranged for refreshments to be served to the teams to help revive their flagging energy after hours of painstaking work. When the forensics team had satisfactorily completed their work, they placed the body in the body bag and moved it to the police mortuary.

Ann ordered urgent DNA tests as she wanted to establish the identity of the victim. The garage was sealed off and locked and she arranged for a 24-hour police surveillance outside.

The media stood around at a discreet distance. They waited for Ann to walk to her car then raced towards her.

"Who have you got in that garage, DCI Dixon?" asked Amy Baker.

"It is an unknown woman at this stage," Ann replied. "We will need to wait for the pathologist and the forensics team to establish identity."

"Do you think the body is that of the missing woman, Elaine Casey?" asked a second reporter.

"Read my lips – haven't I just said we need to establish identity – we do not know whose body it is!" Ann almost shouted. "And for now, I am not answering any more questions. Stephen Edwards will be issuing an official press release later. You will need to be patient till then."

"Do you think it is another serial killing?" asked Amy Baker, ignoring Ann's request for them to wait until the official release. "I think you've been rumbled, Inspector, and I think you've lost your edge."

"I don't care what the hell you think!" Ann spat, resenting the girl's spiteful comment and added, unable to suppress her anger, "The police are doing their utmost to solve this case."

At that point, David opened the car door and coaxed Ann into the passenger seat, reminding her that there was no point in arguing the toss with the press.

"Bastards, they never give up," Ann said. "Just like rats, gnawing at your soul."

"As I said, not worth getting into a spat with the press," said David. "They'll only use it against you and then you'll be judged as the aggressor."

Ann folded her lips together and shrugged.

"Let's speak to Peter to get us an urgent report on the forensics," she suggested, "and our next priority is to contact Eve Marshall and ask her if we can visit."

They called at Peter's office. He smiled as Ann walked in.

"Coming to egg me on for your results, hey Ann?" he asked.

Ann smiled.

"I will have them ready by this afternoon," he said.

David accompanied Ann to the incident room where they began preparations for the briefing of the team on the body found in the garage.

"Schedule the briefing for 9am tomorrow; we should have all the information by then," Ann said.

Peter rang her around 2.30 that afternoon.

"The dead girl is confirmed as Elaine Casey," he informed her. "Her DNA matches the hair and blood we found at the scene of her father's murder."

"Fuck!" exclaimed Ann. "Now I have the onerous task of telling her mother."

She thanked Peter for the prompt information and dialled Eve Marshall's number.

"DCI Dixon here, Mrs Marshall," she said when Eve answered. "I wonder if it would be convenient to call on you, today? There have been some new developments, but I need to discuss them with you in person."

There was a brief pause.

"If you don't have news of my daughter, then you would be wasting my time coming to see me," Eve responded.

"Mrs Marshall, I would not be ringing you if I did not have important information to share with you. Please let me see you in person as the information I have is highly classified and cannot be said over the phone," Ann explained.

She could hear Eve asking her husband if it was OK for Ann to call at the house. "I see no harm in the detective coming here," she heard Harold say to Eve.

"Alright," Eve said, returning to the phone, "but you'd better come before 4pm as we have an appointment."

"We will get there as soon as possible, traffic permitting," replied Ann.

She ascended the steps to the Marshalls' front door with some trepidation. Harold Marshall opened the door.

"Hello!" Harold greeted her cheerfully. "Inspector, do come inside. Can I make you a cup of tea?"

Ann shook her head and sat down opposite Eve, composing the statement she was about to make in her head.

"Mrs Marshall," she began, "I am afraid I have bad news about your daughter." She paused for the beat of a second, watching Mrs Marshall's face. "We were led to a garage where her body was found locked inside the boot of a car."

Ann braced herself for the reprisals amidst the flood of emotion that she expected would follow.

Eve leant towards Harold and clung to him as the bad news took a few seconds to sink in. She let out an ear-piercing scream and leapt out at Ann, aiming to hit her in the face.

David stepped forward and intercepted the blow, getting struck in the face instead of Ann. Eve became hysterical, screaming and cursing as Harold and David tried to restrain her from attacking Ann.

Ann looked on resignedly, understanding Eve's rage, not even trying to defend herself.

It took 20 minutes before Eve finally sank into a chair, sobbing uncontrollably, repeatedly saying Elaine's name.

When Harold was satisfied that it was safe to leave Eve sitting by herself, without restraint, he went to make tea. When he returned, placing a cup in front of Ann without asking her, he enquired, "Do the police have any idea who the garage belonged to?"

Ann answered his question cautiously, unable to give too much away at this stage. She assured him that they would let him know as soon as the police discovered the identity of the garage owner. She informed them that she would arrange when it was convenient for them to formally identify their daughter.

"Do you know how long Elaine has been…" he hesitated, finding it difficult, "been dead?" Harold asked.

"I'm afraid it is up to the coroner to determine the time of death," Ann said. "We will need to wait for the post-mortem results before we can be sure of that."

"Post-mortem?" shouted Eve, suddenly becoming alert again. "Nobody is going to cut up my daughter!"

"I am afraid the law states that a post-mortem has to be performed in cases of sudden or unexplained death or cases of suspicious death," Ann said.

"Are you saying our daughter was murdered, Inspector?" asked Harold.

"The circumstances surrounding Elaine's death suggests foul play," she said.

They sat in silence drinking their tea while the Marshalls tried to come to terms with the news of their loss.

Ann was the first to break the silence.

"Thank you for your time, Mr and Mrs Marshall," she said. "I am so sorry I could not bring you better news. My team and I at the station will be available at any time you have any queries."

Both Ann and David felt a sense of relief when they reached their car.

"Quite a wild reaction from Eve Marshall," David said, "she nearly had your eye out."

"Look at the situation from *her* point of view, David," said Ann. "Her only daughter visits her father, she disappears and ends up dead in the boot of someone's car. All those agonising days of waiting and hoping end in a statement that makes her world come crashing down."

David said nothing.

"You and I would react in a similar fashion," Ann said without looking at him. "Maybe not so vocal, but visibly outraged and beyond upset."

David looked down at his feet and said, "Yeah, you're right."

Ann said, "Imagine her reaction if she knew that the car and garage belonged to her in-laws."

"I can't imagine."

"Let's hurry back to the office," Ann suggested, "I need to fill Edwards in on the latest details."

Her heart sank as she walked down the corridor to her office and saw Edwards waiting for her, leaning against her office door.

"In my office, now!" he demanded, ignoring her protests to see him in an hour.

She followed him, without a word, and sat down in his office.

"What the hell is going on, Ann?" he yelled. "I get a call from the commander telling me that he was informed about a dead woman found at a lock-up garage belonging to Jake Casey and a James Muller. You can imagine the headlines tomorrow. It's going to make the police look like a bunch of amateurs."

"We don't know all the details yet," said Ann, her voice coming out more subdued than her usual confident tone, "but I assume that both men were involved in the murder." Then she became more assertive. "Tim says the state of the body suggests that Elaine was kept in a freezer after death, then wrapped in plastic and put in the boot of the car. So, if Jake killed her days before he was arrested, James possibly could have transferred the body to the boot of the car in the garage."

"And just how did you arrive at this conclusion?" asked Edwards, unable to contain his sarcasm.

"We have evidence to support the fact that Jake Casey was at the murder scene," she said emphatically. "He did not put Elaine in the car at George's house because circumstantial evidence supports the fact that a heavier, taller man carried Elaine to the car. Our eyewitness substantiates this fact. Tim Jones was not able to establish the post-mortem interval because the body had been frozen and left in the car for approximately two days. We need to wait for the post-mortem to find out more. If we have some way of knowing that James was in London at the time of the murders, we can categorically say that he was an accomplice to the murders."

Edwards listened, without interrupting.

"Have you briefed your team?" he asked.

"I have a briefing scheduled for tomorrow afternoon. By then, Tim will have done the post-mortem," she said. "I'm meeting with Jeremy Doyle, the guy from Interpol, tomorrow evening. He might have some news about James Muller."

"Well," hissed Edwards as if speaking between his teeth, "I don't care what it takes to get a result, but you bloody get to it and wrap this fiasco up as soon as possible. In the meantime, I have the chief superintendent breathing down my neck."

He glared at Ann. This admonishment, however, seemed to placate Edwards and he allowed her to go, warning her to keep him abreast of everything.

David was waiting in her office when she had finished her impromptu meeting with Edwards.

He raised his brows when she appeared.

"Rough going, was it, Guv?"

Ann curled her lips. "Bloody man is so impatient and rude."

Her phone rang. It was Tim Jones.

"Hi Ann, just ringing to say I'll be performing the post-mortem on Elaine Casey at 8.30 tomorrow morning. Do you think you can be there?" he asked.

"I wouldn't miss it for the world. See you at 8.30 prompt."

Turning towards David, Ann asked, "Did you hear that? PM being done tomorrow. Pick me up around seven o'clock and I'll treat you to breakfast."

"I'll be there on the dot."

"And please ensure the team know about the briefing at 3pm tomorrow."

"Will do."

"Looks like it's going to be a hell of a day," she said. Then she looked at her watch and yawned. It was 9pm. "And for now, *I'm* going to call it a day, David. My brain has gone to sleep."

"Want me to drop you off?" he asked.

"No thanks," she responded, "I'll grab a cab; I'm meeting Josie and some friends for a drink in Islington."

The cab dropped her off at the Fox and Hounds pub in Islington. She threaded her way through the crowd to the table where Josie sat with her friends from the fashion world and who beamed with delight as she spotted Ann heading in her direction.

Ann kissed her and gave her a gentle squeeze.

"This is my partner, Ann Dixon," Josie announced as she introduced Ann to her colleagues. They smiled back and each shook her hand in turn.

"Josie says you are working on a serial murder case," announced a girl named Tamara.

"Yes, you'll no doubt read about it in the papers," Ann replied. She gave Josie an admonishing look as she pinched her thigh under the table.

"Let's give my partner a break from work, shall we?" suggested Josie. "I am quite sure she doesn't want to be reminded about work when she's here to enjoy herself."

The conversation switched to more conventional matters and the awkward moment passed. The evening at the pub passed amicably, with Ann saving her reprimand of Josie for when they were in the return cab home.

"Are you telling the whole world that I am working on a serial killing?" she asked her.

"No! My darling, Tamara Smith who asked you about your work was a former lover of *The World News* reporter, Amy Baker. Perhaps you would like to know that Amy Baker left Tamara for a constable on your team. So! Tamara's presence at the pub was no coincidence. I think Amy, who knows you and I are together, planted her. I think Tamara thought she could catch you off guard and hoping you would reveal some information that she could then pass on to Amy."

"Oh, I have turned you into quite the sleuth, haven't I?"

"Indeed, I am not just a pretty face. I *do* watch your back, more than you realise."

"Do you know the name of the constable she is dating?"

"I don't, but I could find out."

That night, Ann lay awake for some time, mulling over what Josie had told her about Tamara Smith's link to one of her constables. She realised now where Amy Baker might have got her classified information from, and which had been printed in the paper.

***

"Good morning, Guv," David greeted her as she climbed into the car in the morning. "Have you seen the papers today?"

"No, what do they say?"

David showed her the headlines, which read: 'Casey family virtually decimated by serial killer. Are the CLPD procrastinating while a family is being brutally murdered?'

Ann skimmed over the article that implied that she was being outwitted by the killer and seemed to be out of her depth at solving the case. The article also contained forensic facts that had not been released to the press.

"Bastards, I'll show them who is incompetent," she vowed. "And I found out last night that Amy Baker is dating one of the CID officers on my team." She took her eyes off the print and looked up at David. "Find out who he is; I'll skin him alive and have him chucked off the force."

David said he had no idea who it could be but would make a special effort to enquire for Ann.

"It could certainly explain why the newspaper published details not officially revealed to the press," he said, biting on his lower lip.

"Yes, and precisely why Edwards had my guts for garters because he assumed it was *me* who had leaked information to Amy Baker 'to cement my status with the media', he called it." Ann tossed her head. "I think we have a mole leaking sensitive and highly classified information and I want him found."

David looked thoughtful, digesting what she had just said.

"Let's have breakfast at that workmen's café in Eccleston Street," Ann suggested.

They drove in silence as Ann continued to read the

inflammatory article in the paper. At the café, they ordered a substantial breakfast; Ann feared it might be her last meal for the day. When they'd finished, they hurried to the mortuary.

Tim looked up as they arrived.

He talked into the tape recorder as he began his examination of the remains of Elaine Casey. "This is the body of a white female, aged 23. Decomposition was delayed due to being deep-frozen. Considerable body mass loss suggests this woman was starved or refused to eat over some length of time, prior to her death. There is no rigor mortis present. The length of time that the body was kept in the freezer is unknown. I cannot give you a date or time of death. I would surmise three weeks, plus or minus. There is evidence of bruising on face, wrists, ankles and thighs. There is a deep cut below the sternum, probably pierced the aorta. It appears that the wound was carried out with a 6-inch blade dagger. The blade width is two inches. There is a 4-cms cut over the jugular vein on the right side of her neck." He paused for a second, took a breath and went on. "Cause of death, exsanguination due to incisional cut of aorta."

Tim peered over the body thoughtfully.

"Ann, the manner in which this poor girl was killed suggests it might have been ritualistic," he said. "Don't quote me on this, but you should go with your gut feeling and check out the Caseys' satanic pursuits as you had originally intended to do."

She looked at him. Tim continued to speak into the tape. "The hair of the victim contained seeds, grass and insects. It suggests she was left in the woods before being put in the freezer."

After taking photographs of the wounds, he began washing the body. There was a measure of sadness in his face as he performed this task. Ann always admired the professionalism and empathy with which Tim performed his post-mortems. It couldn't be an easy job.

He stopped washing the body as he stumbled onto what resembled a leaf in Elaine's hair. He collected the leaf debris cautiously and put it in the forensics bag. When he turned the dead woman's head to the left side to continue washing her body, he noticed something stuck in the left ear. He lifted it out gently with a pair of forceps. "Hmm, looks like a type of beetle," he said. "How odd, there was no evidence that any insects had visited the body.

Perhaps this one crept in while the body lay on the ground to be moved. Let's see what forensics have to say about it."

His assistant helped him turn over the body as he continued washing it. "Livor mortis on the back suggests she died face up," Tim said.

He then began the process of opening the body and examining all the organs as he carefully removed them, weighed them and continued a running commentary on their condition.

"The victim's organs appear in a good state of health," he continued.

When he began to inspect the pelvic organs, the colon and rectum, he paused and expressed concern at what he found.

"Massive bruising of the vagina and a tearing of both vagina and anus suggests either repeated, violent acts of rape and sodomy. The labia majora are missing. These have probably been taken as trophies."

Tim gritted his teeth in anger.

"The sick bastard who did this," he muttered, "must be found."

He examined the empty cavity of the thorax and abdomen after he had removed all the organs.

"Hmm, I thought as much, the blade that pierced the aorta was wielded with so much force that it cut into the vertebra. See here," he pointed out to Ann, "the muscle and tissue are scraped off the bone."

Ann nodded in silent acknowledgement.

Tim took blood samples and scrapings from under Elaine's fingernails, bagged and labelled them and sent them to forensics.

"Please make her face as decent as possible," Ann said. "Her mother is understandably very fragile at present. It will be extremely upsetting for her to see her daughter like this, and I don't want her freaking out by her battered face."

"Don't worry, my technician is good at his job," assured Tim. "He'll ensure that Elaine looks good for when her mother does the identification."

David had managed to pop in and out between spells of nausea during the post-mortem, much to Ann's amusement.

Tim promised to send Ann a concise report on the post-mortem. She thanked him and promised to be in touch if there were any queries. It had been a long morning.

Ann looked at her watch with a gasp of consternation. She had barely 30 minutes to prepare for her briefing with the team. She checked her emails, relieved to discover that Tobin was unavoidably detained and would not be able to make it to the briefing.

"Thank God for that," said Ann under her breath; however, on the one hand she knew she would now have to rush to do the briefing, aware she was not fully prepared. On the other hand, she was pleased because she wanted to get the full forensics report on Elaine to present to her team.

David breezed into her office with a tray of coffee and mouthwatering doughnuts.

"You're an angel," she said, munching appreciatively into her doughy heaven.

Ann phoned Jeremy Doyle to reschedule her meeting with him for early afternoon. She was in luck because he had a slot in his diary for the time she requested.

"David," she said, wiping away a trace of jam from the corner of her mouth, "I want to ask Edwards if he would fly you to Spain to interview Jack Slade's son about the Russian girl, Saskia, who hung out with the Caseys," said Ann.

"I can't imagine him forking out money for an air ticket," David said. "He'll give us a long lecture on the constraints of his budget."

"Fuck his budget," replied Ann, and took another bite of her doughnut. "If he wants us to solve this case he'll need to spend money."

"All I can say, Guv, is good luck with that one," said David.

"David, I have to follow every lead." She finished the doughnut and began pressing her forefinger into the remaining random sprinkle of crumbs on the plate. "All our reputations are at stake here, even his. We look like shit in the public eye at present."

They worked out a rough plan for the team in preparation for the briefing, which Ann postponed for two days later.

"Come on, let's get a move on, we're meeting with Jeremy at The Traveller's Hotel on the Euston Road. The traffic shouldn't be too heavy at this time."

Jeremy Doyle was a tall, slender man with sharp eyes. They met in the bar of the hotel that was unusually quiet at this time of day.

"Nice to meet the woman I've heard so much about, face to face," said Jeremy with a broad smile.

"Hopefully only good things about me," said Ann.

"Mostly good things, and the bad was only mildly bad."

"Aha, that's what I like to hear, only the truth," Ann said, beaming.

She turned to introduce David as he stepped forward to shake Jeremy's hand.

David ordered a round of drinks while Ann and Jeremy set about the business at hand.

"You seem to have a hell of a difficult case, Ann," Jeremy said.

"It's been a bloody nightmare," replied Ann. "Thus far, we have two murdered brothers, an unconscious brother and a dead daughter of one of the murdered men."

Jeremy studied her over the rim of his glass.

"Our efforts of finding the killer have been frustrated because the sly bastard has been planting so-called evidence that sent us chasing the wrong people," she said. "There is a possibility that there may be two murderers working together. We think that the unconscious man might have had an accomplice, possibly James Muller, who unfortunately has not been found to date."

She showed Jeremy some of the information on her laptop to get him up to date on what they had gathered thus far.

"Did you get the photos I sent to you of James Muller?" she asked him.

"Yes, thanks; we've begun processing the information," he replied. "So far, we can tell you that James Muller has been in London until a few days ago when he left for Brazil. We have no leads as to where he lives in London. He is not employed at any hospital or clinic as far as we are aware. He has not contacted his sister, Susan, since he left." Jeremy took a sip of his drink. "We have circulated his photograph throughout the country and at all major ports and airports. We are also working closely with the FBI in Brazil as they have a greater network over there."

He replaced his beer glass on the table, glanced at David, and then swung his eyes back to her.

"A few days ago, we received a report that James Muller left Britain under the alias of Carlos Mendes. He travelled on a Portuguese passport. He seems to have something to hide. If he has been here for three months there is no doubt, I think, that he is involved in the killings."

He drank from his glass again and swallowed.

"I'm going to head up a team to Brazil and meet with some guys from the FBI," said Jeremy. "Do you have any idea why Jake Casey was attacked?"

"We are not absolutely sure," said Ann, "but I have a hunch that he knows something his accomplice does not want him to reveal." She twirled the stem of her glass on the table. "If they did the killings together, then his accomplice might fear he will turn as a witness for the state. If it is about the contents of a coded diary written by his deceased brother, Tom, the diary must contain evidence implicating the accomplice."

"What chance does Jake have of regaining consciousness?" asked Jeremy.

"The doctor said a good chance, when all the swelling on his brain has subsided," Ann replied, looking back at him.

"Have you checked that James is not employed at any of the army bases?" David asked and took a glug of his beer.

"Hey, that's somewhere we had not explored," said Jeremy. "I'll get on to it tomorrow."

"I don't care if you have to kidnap James Muller to question him," urged Ann. "Find him and get some answers." Her eyes narrowed. "I don't care what it takes, but I am accompanying your team to Brazil."

"We would love to have you come along, but your boss might not agree due to the cost of the trip," Jeremy said.

"Sod the top brass, I'll pay my way with my own funds."

The beer and drinks had flowed freely during their long meeting. When Ann began to see double, she called time on their meeting and thanked Jeremy for his contribution to the investigation.

Later, when they were alone, she whispered to David to save her blushes by getting her home before she fell over and disgraced herself. He had to hold onto her to help her out of the car and into the house. He also appeared to enjoy the moment, holding Ann close to him. He breathed in as if savouring the heady fragrance of her perfume.

She leaned on him, totally inebriated. Josie, looking surprised, helped David get Ann into the house. Ann mumbled a few incoherent words before collapsing into a stupor on the couch in the living room.

"David, you won't pass a Breathalyser test either," said Josie. "Sit down and have some coffee to sober up."

She covered Ann with a blanket. Adam came downstairs when he heard the commotion.

"Hi, David," he greeted him. "Nice to see you again. Thanks for getting Ann home safely."

"Oh, it's a pleasure. We had a heavy meeting with someone from Interpol. The meeting went on for five hours and I guess we didn't realise how much we had drunk," David said.

"If you're OK, I'll see you to the car," Adam said.

Just as soon as they got outside, Adam tugged at David's sleeve and said, "Hold on, don't go just yet. I have some important news I must tell you. It concerns the case, but I can't tell you right now. Let's arrange to meet in Scotland. Dream up a story for Ann. Tell her you're going fishing with a friend."

"OK, I'll ring you when I've secured the weekend," David promised. He chose a suitable moment when Ann was momentarily distracted to ask for the weekend off.

"Oh, I see, so you've met a nice girl, have you?" Ann teased.

"No, Guv, I'm going fishing with my brother."

Ann stared at him.

"You've never mentioned him before."

"He's been away for a while, we just made contact in the last few days."

"OK, as long as it is only two days away," Ann insisted, intense piercing eyes on David, "I need you here promptly on Monday morning."

"Now, go and find me that forensic profiler's contact number while I collar Edwards about sending you to Spain," she instructed.

***

"If it is about the post-mortem on Elaine Casey," Edwards sounded curt, "I have already received the report."

"It is about another matter," Ann replied, standing in front of his desk.

Edwards stood up to face her. "If it is about supplying more officers, the answer is 'No'."

"During our interview with the Caseys' old neighbour, Jack Slade in Nottingham," Ann said, ignoring his answer, "we found out that the Casey brothers befriended foreign girls and lured them into their house where they probably subjected them to all manner of perverse sexual practises. Jack's son, Andrew, who now lives on the Costa del Sol in Spain, knew one of the Russian girls who visited the Caseys; she disappeared suddenly without a trace while the Caseys were living at their old house." She pulled at her left ear lobe. "I would like you to fund Sergeant Hughes' flight to Spain to interview Andrew Slade."

Edwards swung around with an indignant expression.

"How the hell do you think I am going to justify spending money to send your sergeant to Spain on a fact-finding mission that won't bring us nearer to solving these murders?" he exploded angrily.

Ann felt her breathing quicken and tried to control it.

"That's where you are wrong, Sir," she said, her bold assertion astonishing her. "The brothers' shared interest in the occult is the key to solving these murders. Someone attacked Jake in the hope of killing him to silence him. Andrew Slade grew up with the Casey brothers and he should be able to shed some light on the Caseys' perverse practises. He had a Russian friend who might be a witness to the Caseys' practises and Mr Slade's son is the only one who may have the answers."

Two seconds ticked by. They held eye contact.

"Please just give me a chance to explore what I consider to be a serious lead," she said, trying to keep her voice from sounding beseeching. "Take the money out of my salary if the CLPD are too cash-strapped to support my request."

Edwards sat down and said, "I will speak to the commander and get back to you."

Ann smiled broadly and thanked him.

She rushed into her office and phoned David, excitedly telling him there was a chance that her request might be approved. There was a message on her mobile to contact Peter. Keen to know the outcome of the forensics results, she went to see Peter at his laboratory. He was typing a report when she arrived.

"You have got to sit down to hear what I am going to tell you," he said. "In fact" – he smiled mischievously – "I think you are going to have to buy me dinner for all the hard work I've done."

She gave Peter a quizzical look.

Peter said, with a look of near triumph, "The sand found on the wheels of the car and from Elaine's body bag found in the boot was traced to sand from Sherwood Forest. A knife with a 6ins blade was found hidden under the carpet of the boot. It contained old blood and DNA of two different females." He looked at the PC screen in front of him. "We also found petrol in 5-litre cans in the boot." He looked at her. "I am guessing that whoever killed Elaine intended to torch the car with the body inside." He returned to the screen on his desk. "The entomologist had a look at the beetle found in Elaine's hair. It is a darkling beetle native to Sherwood Forest. The species are found elsewhere in the United Kingdom, but the fact that the beetle had microscopic traces of soil endemic to Sherwood Forest narrows down the location of the beetle as having lived in Sherwood." He looked briefly at some notes on the desk beside him. "The leaf found in Elaine's hair is from the sessile oak trees native to Sherwood Forest. The soil found in Elaine's hair is endemic to Sherwood Forest."

He glanced at her as if to clarify she was taking it all in. "The report from her blood sample is even more astounding." He turned back to study his report on the screen. "Her blood and stomach contained a combination of teonanacatl and ololiuqui. These substances are found in plants grown in Mexico and other parts of South America. The Aztecs are known to have given the people chosen to be sacrificed the mushrooms and seeds to ingest to make their victims hallucinate before they were killed. The victims knew their fate but were disabled by the effects of the plants they were forced to ingest. The effects of these hypnotic plants are like ecstasy. The victims suffer blurred vision, euphoria, increased sense of hearing, altered concentration, hallucinations and a sense of oneness with a divinity of their belief. A dose of 4 to 8mg is effective. Teonanacatl is an alkaloid mescaline." Again, he looked at her, studying her expression. "The effect gives the victims a feeling of inebriation, being possessed of some entity, with hallucinations. The Royal Pharmaceutical Society lists these natural drugs under the Class A: Dangerous Drugs section."

Ann stared across at the screen, momentarily transfixed by his findings.

Peter continued, "These plants are found in other parts of the world, but the species found in Elaine's stomach contained soil endemic to Mexico. So, it is my calculation that these natural drugs were brought from Mexico, possibly by your Dr Muller."

"A lot of discovery here, Peter," Ann responded. "So, what is your overall conclusion?"

"I think Elaine was murdered in Sherwood Forest in some bizarre satanic ritual and kept in a freezer before being brought to the garage. The killer planned for us to find the body. I also think it was the killer who told Tobin about the garage."

"Good God!" Ann exclaimed when he had finished. "It is abundantly clear that we are dealing with extremely dangerous and clever criminals who will stop at nothing to get what they want."

"Precisely."

"We cannot possibly allow them to get away with these crimes. I will pursue them to the ends of the earth to bring them to justice, I swear it."

Tim put a consoling arm around her, reassuring her that she would succeed, but also reminded her to proceed with caution.

She took the forensics report with her to her office to update her files and share the news with David. He could hardly believe his eyes as he read the report given to him by Ann.

"I want everyone at the briefing tomorrow," Ann said, "including the forensics team. I want a full report from all my officers and nobody is to leave the room until I am absolutely finished."

David nodded in agreement and informed her that he had already made it abundantly clear that it was an important meeting, that everyone needed to be there on time and ready to make a valuable contribution to the investigation.

Edwards popped his head around the door of her office and told her that he wanted to be present at the briefing.

"OK, Sir, I'll send you the forensics report later today," Ann said.

"I believe the findings are quite incredible," Edwards remarked. "I look forward to reading it." And at that, he turned and left the room.

"David, do we know who owns the Caseys' house in Nottingham?" Ann asked.

"Jack Slade said that George Casey bought the house and paid the rest of his siblings for their share. I think I recall Jack saying that part of the animosity amongst the brothers was because George bought the house."

"Let's find out from Eve Marshall if she has access to the house," Ann suggested.

"Good idea."

"I'll ring her now and get the ball rolling," Ann declared, and she dialled Eve's number.

Harold answered.

"Mr Marshall, I wonder if it would be convenient to pay Mrs Marshall a visit as there is some very important information we need?" Ann asked him.

She heard him relay the question to Eve and overheard the caustic reply.

"You must understand, my wife is still very angry with the police," Harold Marshall said. "She says she will think about your request and get back to you, Inspector."

"Thank you; I would be grateful if she could let us know at her earliest convenience."

"Damn difficult woman," Ann said as she came off the phone. "I think I'll send DI Roberts and yourself to question Eve." She let out an irritated sigh. "Perhaps not seeing me might elicit a more positive response."

"OK, I'll contact DI Roberts as soon as Eve gives us the go-ahead," replied David.

The time had flown, and David did not hesitate when Ann

persuaded him to join her for a meal at a pub near Sloane Square. It looked as if it was going to be a long night filled with discussion about the case. David didn't look too bothered about this; it gave him a legitimate excuse to be with Ann and to admire her in secret.

They sat at the tables outside the pub to avoid the deafening din inside, which forced them to shout at each other to be heard. Just as fate would have it, David glanced over Ann's shoulder and spotted Josie's colleague, Tamara, with DC Terence Holmes. He moved closer to Ann and whispered to her to move away from the table, to avoid being seen by Holmes.

After a while, they went over to David's car across the street from the pub. Ann stood by the passenger door whilst David went to the driver's side.

"Was that DC Holmes I just saw with Tamara Smith?" she asked.

"Yes, it was. He must be the mole in our team," David said, looking at her across the roof of the car before unlocking the door. "I can guess why he is dating Tamara. He has a gambling problem. I wouldn't be surprised if she is funding his habit."

He climbed into the car and reached across to the passenger side to open the door for her.

"I am sure Tamara is using him to get information that she's passing onto Amy Baker," he said. "That's how *The World News* can print the finer details on our murder cases."

"I want Terence Holmes tailed," Ann directed. "I also want his house bugged. The bastard is not going to ruin my investigation because he needs to fund his gambling habit."

From where the car was parked, they could observe DC Holmes and Tamara in animated conversation at their table, without being seen. The pair looked so engrossed in their conversation they seemed oblivious to everything else. They watched as Tamara leaned in close to Holmes as if they did not want to be overheard. They were soon joined by another man who brought them a round of drinks.

Ann, who had begun to feel a creeping sense of anger at the thought of how they might be plotting to undermine her, said, "I'm going to speak to surveillance and nail the bastard who is passing information to Amy. I will not allow them to make fools of the force. We are already viewed in a bad light in the eyes of the public as it is."

CHAPTER 5

After watching them for 20 minutes, Ann announced that she wanted to be taken home.

"Remember the briefing is at 8am," she said to David. "Please collect me at seven o'clock."

When she got into the house, she found Josie fast asleep. She tiptoed around the room then snuggled up behind Josie's back, kissing her on the neck as she moved closer.

Josie stirred. The manoeuvre never failed to ignite Josie's passion. The resulting exchange of sexual fury consumed them and continued until they were both spent. They hugged and kissed and continued to touch and stroke each other until they both drifted off to sleep.

The hooting of David's car woke Ann in the morning, and she fell out of bed, horrified that she had not heard the alarm. She ran to the door to let David in, apologising profusely for being late. Then she dashed into the shower, shouting for Josie to get up and help her find some clothes to wear.

Josie came into the shower with a smile on her face. She handed Ann a towel and said suggestively, "See what happens when you seduce an innocent girl?"

"Hmm, and I can still taste you," murmured Ann. "Now, get out of here and help me get dressed by finding me some suitable clothes to wear."

Josie laid out a smart suit with matching accessories. Ann dressed hurriedly then bounded downstairs, grabbing her phone and laptop.

As she kissed Josie goodbye, their combined radiance reflected in their faces and was not missed by David whose expression of envy was unmistakeable.

"We can get coffee on the way," she said to David, a little breathlessly.

They stopped at Ann's office to collect the reports and relevant information for the briefing. Stephen Edwards was already seated in the briefing room when Ann arrived. The rest of the team filed in steadily until everyone was present.

Ann had arranged all the photos and notes about the killings and kidnap on the incident board at the front of the room. She stood up and thanked them for attending.

"We have a very complex murder investigation," she began. "I am grateful for all your input and diligence, but I don't want you to be influenced by the negative comments in the media." She skimmed around at the faces watching her. "The latest murder of Elaine Casey brings us to the conclusion that there may be two killers. We have arrived at this conclusion because the eyewitness described a larger, taller man putting Elaine Casey into the car on the night George Casey was murdered. The depth at which the boots worn by the man sank into the mud in the flower bed suggests that it was a taller, heavier man and not Jake Casey who kidnapped Elaine." Someone coughed and Ann waited until the person had cleared their throat, before continuing.

"The fact that her body was found in the car belonging to James Muller, in Jake Casey's garage, means we must assume that these men are jointly responsible for the killing. The murder weapons used to kill George Casey were found in Jake's lock-up." There was an audible murmur of voices following this statement. Some of the team shook their heads in disbelief and muttered their disgust.

"I want DI Roberts to contact the Forestry Commission of Sherwood Forest to grant us permission to do a search for the spot where Elaine was murdered."

"I can do better than that, Guv," DI Roberts replied, "I have found out that George Casey had a private ownership public service with the Forestry Commission. George had his own woodland that he cared for, but which was supervised by the Forestry Commission. I think we should find out where it is in the forest and get a search warrant based on the findings of the death of Elaine."

The murmurs in the crowd ceased. No-one spoke. The information DI Roberts had produced was valuable and the team had previously always looked down on him.

"Good work, Roberts," Ann commended him and smiled at Edwards as she said, "I am quite sure Superintendent Edwards will get us the warrant to search the woods."

Edwards scowled and said he would need a few days to get the warrant.

"If you have any queries concerning the drugs used to sedate Elaine," Ann said, "then speak to Tim who should be able to answer any questions you have." She looked around the room again. "Our task is very complex as we don't have either of the killers in custody," she went on. "Jake is still unconscious, and James Muller is in Brazil."

"What has Interpol said?" asked DI Roberts.

"I spoke to Jeremy Doyle who says that James Muller had been in London over the last three months but left on a Portuguese passport under the alias, Carlos Mendes, a few days ago," Ann replied. "Jeremy is meeting with the FBI in Brazil to gather more information. I have asked Superintendent Edwards to ask for funding to send Sergeant Hughes to interview the Caseys' old neighbour, Andrew Slade, about one of the girls who was possibly used in their rituals. I also want to get permission from George Casey's wife to search the Caseys' old house that he now owns."

Edwards then addressed the meeting, endorsing what Ann had said and surprising her by announcing that he had managed to get approval for Sergeant Hughes to travel to Spain for the interview.

"OK, good. Let me now introduce our forensics profiler, Savannah Carey," she said. "Ms Carey has a great deal of experience with the profiles of serial killers."

Savannah stepped forward and acknowledged Ann's introduction. Her long blonde hair and curvaceous figure would no doubt have caught the eye of every officer.

Savannah's self-confidence in her appearance matched her confidence at doing her job. "Hi team," she said, ignoring the barely disguised expressions of desire in front of her. "I was called in to assess the profile of your perpetrator. It is my opinion, after having studied the details of the murders, your killer is operating alone. He behaves normally but his psychotic behaviour manifests when he is challenged. He enjoys the buzz of being pursued by the law, hence the red herrings he has left, diverting the focus of the police.

He is extremely clever and manipulative. He probably had a very controlling parent during his early life and has built up a sea of hate against anyone who prevents him from getting his way." Savannah paused, allowing them to take their eyes off her, for a moment at least, and digest the information. "He is a professional man who conducts himself respectably in his everyday life," she continued, "but is capable of extreme violence when the need warrants. He craves control in all situations, but when his power is challenged he will go to any length to maintain it. The degree of torture suggests that it is a revenge vendetta. It suggests that the murderer knew his victims. The attack on one of the brothers suggests that Jake Casey might have some information the murderer wants to suppress. If the murderer has an accomplice, it would be someone of lesser intelligence and subservient to the killer who makes all the decisions about the murders."

The officers questioned Savannah about various aspects of the perpetrator's character. She answered their questions confidently and reassured the team that she would be available for discussions about the case whenever they needed her. The officers swapped various pieces of information they had gathered and shared it with one another. The whole room buzzed with conversation as the team chatted excitedly about details of the case thus far.

Ann and Edwards spoke to the other senior officers in the team, questioning them about their enquiries. The meeting dragged on for four hours, after which Ann, sensing that matters were ending, announced that it was evident that under no circumstances was anyone allowed to speak to the media.

"God help anyone who is found to leak information to the press or anyone outside this force," she warned.

There was a hushed silence as they assimilated her warning.

"I am proud of your lot," she said, "so don't let the team down. If there are no more questions, get out of my sight and come back with good results."

She gave them a conciliatory smile as they walked past her and filed out of the room.

Edwards came up to Ann and thanked her for a successful briefing. He asked about Savannah's professional background. Ann informed him that Savannah had a degree from Oxford and had helped to solve cases on several murders. She told him that Savannah was highly respected for her work.

"Well," he said, "she had better know her stuff with our case."

She reassured him he would not be disappointed and thanked him for getting the funding for the trip to Spain.

"Just make sure it is not a wild goose chase," he warned Ann, "or there will be no end to what you will suffer."

"It will be a valuable trip, I assure you, Sir," replied Ann.

David joined her as they walked to her office, pausing at the machine in the corridor to each get a coffee.

"We can phone Andrew Slade today and ask him when it will be convenient for you to come," Ann said.

"OK, I'll do that right now."

"Grab a pen so that you can jot down all the details for your trip to Spain."

It was a while before the phone was answered. Ann introduced herself to a female voice and asked for Andrew. She was told that she was speaking to his wife, Rita, and that he would come to the phone shortly.

Within seconds, Andrew took the phone from his wife and greeted Ann pleasantly.

"My father warned me that you would be ringing, Inspector," he said.

"Yes, I wondered when it would be convenient for Sergeant David Hughes to come over to Spain to interview you about Saskia?"

"Next week would be fine. I'll give you the details of how to get to our place," he said.

Ann repeated the address and the details for the directions. Then she handed the phone to David to continue the conversation with Andrew.

Ann took back the phone from David when he had finished the conversation and said to Andrew before he rang off, "My sergeant will be on duty, so no sangria or any other form of alcohol, please. I don't want to have to read in the papers that a member of my team was incapable of doing his job because he was inebriated."

A chuckle filtered through the phone. Ann smiled and turned

to David, "Please don't get back late from your weekend break," she said, "I need you here on Monday. We need to tie up some loose ends before you go."

David nodded in understanding.

"For now," Ann said, "I need to talk to Eve Marshall so we can gain access to George's house in Nottingham. I'll try phoning her in the morning."

It seemed the briefing had inspired the team to continue their investigation with renewed vigour. DI Roberts contacted Sam Cain for another interview in the hope that he would gain more information about how Jake and James managed the garage. DC Terence Holmes was the only one who came away from the briefing bearing a grudge. He was incensed that Ann had made such an issue about the information leaked to the press.

"Arrogant bitch!" he could be heard muttering to anyone who would listen. "Did you see her looking at me when she said that? She made it look as if *I* had spoken to the press."

"And *did* you reveal classified information to the press, Holmes?" enquired Roberts, raising a brow.

"No, I bloody didn't," Holmes replied.

"Well, you *are* banging Amy Baker's ex-girlfriend, aren't you?"

"So, what if I am? It doesn't mean I need to open my mouth to get her laid."

"If you have friends in the media you'll be considered a risk to confidentiality, even though you say that you are not discussing details of the murders."

"OK, so I have to curtail my private life to please the CLPD?"

"Yes, you do, as a matter of fact. As an officer in the police, you are judged by the company you keep and your discretion concerning your acquaintances is crucial to the stability of the force," Roberts reminded him. "And if you are talking to the likes of Amy Baker, I will personally deal with you."

Holmes uttered an expletive and walked out of the office.

Roberts phoned Ann and told her that he had questioned Holmes about his association with Tamara and that Holmes denied leaking the information. Ann replied that Holmes was lying and that she wanted Roberts to arrange to have Holmes tailed.

Roberts promised to keep her informed. Stephen Edwards arranged to meet with Chief Superintendent Michael Heath to discuss the progress of the investigation and about the warrant for searching the woods. Michael liked Ann and admired her professionalism immensely. He listened attentively while Edwards told him about the difficulties the officers had encountered during the investigation. Just as he was about to condemn certain aspects of Ann's method of investigation, Michael stopped him and reminded him about Ann's impeccable record over the years and about the time when her male colleagues were confounded by the evidence in a previous murder. Ann came up with a solution that solved the case.

"Stephen," Michael began, "you cannot allow your misogynistic prejudices to blind you to Ann's talent. She has survived tremendous odds like chauvinism and homophobia and has triumphed in bringing the criminals to justice, despite everything. There is no guarantee that the CLPD would have made more progress if a man headed the investigation."

Edwards looked at him.

"Ann Dixon can hold her own against any male police officer," Michael continued. "She worked for MI6 for a short while. She has trained as a special forces officer. Her track record in the force has been most commendable. She has the highest number of successful arrests that led to prosecutions in the UK."

Edwards blinked, rubbed his chin and remained silent.

"I will get you the search warrant, but you must promise me that you will give Ann your total support," Michael continued, "no matter what prejudices against women you might harbour."

Stephen Edwards listened to what Michael said and nodded his head in agreement.

"OK, I can't change overnight but I will try to be more civil to Ann," he said, and looked down at his desk. "I will wait for the warrant and let you know how the lads got along."

Meanwhile, Ann had managed to get Eve to meet with her at the Marshalls' home.

At first, Eve remained sulky when they first started talking, but Ann managed to win her support by making the priority of the meeting about catching Elaine's murderer. It took all her diplomatic skill to reveal to Eve, in the best way she could, that Elaine had been killed in Nottingham and that the police suspected that George's empty house might have been used to keep her body until she was moved to London.

"So, you see, Mrs Marshall," Ann said, "it would be a great help to us if you gave us permission to search your husband's old house." She gave her a warm smile to reassure her. "Our officers will take great care not to damage any valuables which may be in the house. You can also check on when the officers have finished each day."

The pain of losing her daughter was making Eve cry with a flow of bitter tears as Ann spoke. Eve spent an hour in contemplation and discussion with Harold before she agreed to let them search the house.

Ann signed for the keys and thanked the Marshalls for their cooperation. She promised that she would keep them informed of any important findings. Eve hung onto her every word, hopeful that someone would pay for murdering her beloved Elaine.

Ann came down the steps of the Marshalls' home in good spirits. Just as the car door slammed shut, she smiled at David and told him that she felt sure they would find something significant at the house.

"David," she said, "I want us to be at the house in Nottingham on Monday morning. I'll give you the afternoon off today so you can have a longer break, but please don't let me down. I need you to be there with me."

"Oh thanks, Guv." He swayed on his feet slightly, drunk on his enthusiasm. "I can leave earlier and get to my brother's by tonight."

"OK, now bugger off and have a good time before I change my mind."

*****

David caught sight of Adam. He was shuffling his feet whilst repeatedly glancing up at the digital clock above where he stood on the platform. He ran towards him.

There were nine minutes left before the 3.45 to Glasgow departed.

"You guys love to live life on the edge," said Adam by way of greeting.

They jumped on the train just as the last call to board came over the speakers.

"Sorry," said David, breathless from the effort of rushing, "I left my keys at work and had to get them and then, of all the bad luck, I ran into your sister who wanted to ask a hundred questions." He looked at Adam mischievously. "I've never told her so many lies to get away."

He followed Adam into the carriage to find their seats.

"Going off with you feels like cheating on the boss," he chuckled as he made himself comfortable.

Adam grinned.

"We all know why you feel that way," he said. "Admit it; you fancy my sister like crazy and think nobody notices."

David said nothing.

"And you have to remember any lies you tell," Adam added, "because Ann has a strong memory with a talent for tripping you up if you can't repeat the lie."

The train pulled out of the platform.

David continued to remain silent, trying to control his awkward embarrassment.

"I'll hire a car to get to the fishing grounds outside of Glasgow," Adam said.

The prospect of not having to think about work for two whole days helped David take his mind off Adam catching him out.

"Do you get to see much of your brother?" Adam asked, after a while.

"No, we don't speak to each other. We had a terrible argument some time ago."

"Must have been a big fight if you're not speaking," said Adam.

"I'll tell you about it sometime, but let's not talk about that now."

"OK, mate, don't stress; let's change the subject."

A few minutes passed during which neither spoke, but it was a comfortable silence.

Adam was the first to break it.

"Actually, I have a confession to make," he said. "This is not a fishing trip. That was a ruse to get you to meet someone who has vital information about your case."

David just looked at him across the table that separated them.

"I have a contact in MI6," Adam went on, "a guy called Nigel Phillips. He knows Rachel Levine, an agent with Mossad whom I worked with a few years ago."

Adam was shuffling in his seat, uncomfortable at his deception.

"Oh, I see, so here I was psyching myself up for a weekend of leisure," David groaned.

"Sorry about ruining your weekend, mate," Adam admitted, "but when you realise how important the information is that Nigel has for your investigation, you'll feel better."

"It had better be," David sighed, stifling his regret.

"Cheer up, it won't all be work. We'll have a good piss-up and go horse riding while we are here."

The train rattled, clunked and clicked on as the journey sped by until they were pulling into Glasgow station.

After they alighted, they stood waiting just outside the station entrance. After five minutes a tall, muscular man walked up to them, smiled at Adam and stuck out his hand.

"Good heavens, Adam, you're looking good. Got a good woman keeping you in shape; is that how you do it?"

"You don't look so bad yourself," laughed Adam and gestured towards David. "Meet Sergeant David Hughes."

Nigel shook David's hand vigorously.

"Come on," Nigel said, leading them to his car, "you must be famished. I'll treat you to dinner."

After a lavish three-course dinner washed down with numerous pints of lager, the three men retired to Nigel's home.

"Your room is just off the kitchen," Nigel explained and made an apologetic gesture. "I hope you don't mind sharing. The other spare room is stacked with all my diving gear."

"We don't mind that," Adam said. "Just need a place to kip. It doesn't have to be The Ritz."

Nigel lit the gas fire to warm the room and brought in a few bottles of wine to keep them going while they talked.

"I was going to call Ann Dixon," he said, "but Adam didn't want her to see the true picture until I had talked to you." He looked at them both. "Your murder suspect came on the radar of MI6 through our Mossad contact, Rachel Levine. They're very interested in James Muller aka Carlos Mendes because of his links to Hezbollah through the Mexican drug cartel, Los Zetas." He poured them all a glass of red wine and corked the bottle. "There's a Brazilian drug link, too, but James is directly involved with Los Zetas." He took a sip of his wine, swallowed and replaced the glass on the wooden table around which they sat. "There's no love lost with this strange alliance; their only interest in one another is the money – vast sums of money through the drug trade that supports Hezbollah for the sale of arms, Los Zetas for drug money and Muller's neo-Nazi troops for their fascist campaign. Muller is vital to Los Zetas because he ensures that their money is laundered. They protect him as if he was a bona fide gang member." He shrugged. "Hezbollah don't care who shares their bed, if it supports their need for arms against the Jews. So even though members of this unholy alliance do not share one another's passion for their different causes, together they are a mighty force because of their commitment to the common purpose of making lots of money. This is the true driving force that makes them formidable enemies." He picked up his glass but did not drink from it, looking at both David and Adam. "Rachel Levine and her colleagues are working on a very daring plot to kidnap Muller and fly him to Israel. It is a virtual impossible task, but it can be done if we all work together."

David and Adam stared at him, slightly uncomprehendingly.

"You must realise," Nigel continued, putting his glass back down on the table, "that this is likely to be a very dangerous mission." He rubbed his hand distractedly along the wooden edge of the table. "I'm afraid that lives will be lost during this mission."

David nodded. Adam cast his eyes down.

"The most important reason to find Muller," Nigel said, "and bring him to justice is that our double agent in Brazil has told us that Muller knows Ann has put out an alert for his arrest. He is planning to take her out. We must act before he does."

Adam looked up and blinked.

"And what is the action?" David asked.

"The team, if everyone is agreed," Nigel said, "would consist of you, Jeremy and another MI6 colleague, Rachel and two DEA agents. Ann must not be allowed to accompany the team as it is too dangerous."

"Hopefully, Nigel, you can convince Jeremy to exclude her," Adam said.

"Forget it," David intervened, "Ann has made it abundantly clear to Jeremy that she is going."

"Shit, that means I definitely have to go, too," put in Adam. "I must protect my sister as well as the DEA agents and two local Brazilians who are working undercover in the Los Zetas camp."

Adam frowned. "David," he said, "you need to tell Jeremy that Nigel called, and you answered the phone. Contact Jeremy explaining that Nigel needs to speak to him urgently. Make some excuse that Nigel did not have Jeremy's direct line and as the matter was of the utmost secrecy, he needed to call Nigel."

"He has to tell Ann, omitting the fact that Adam is involved of course," Nigel added.

There was a brief silence as David and Adam assimilated what they had just been told.

"Pretty intense; makes one's hair stand on end just envisaging the dangers," said Adam, breaking the silence.

"The obstacles are not insurmountable," said Nigel, "but we need to plan the operation with military precision and work together as though our lives depended on it."

He turned to Adam. "Ann must never know you are behind all the surreptitious planning, Adam," he said.

David said, "She'll make our lives hell if she ever finds out."

Adam nodded.

"Nigel will introduce Rachel to Jeremy," he said, "and Rachel will mention that they have an operative called Ben Hajiof, who is me with an Israeli identity."

Nigel looked at him and said, "Jeremy must not disclose Adam's true identity as Ann will definitely not agree to Adam's involvement."

Adam twisted his lips into the semblance of a smile.

"Jeremy is partial to sound suggestions," he said. "He is not as arrogant as his colleagues." His eyes lit up as he added, with a confident tilt of his head, "And he is our best bet to hopefully get all of us in the team to Brazil."

The three men talked well into the early hours of the morning. The next day they had a hearty brunch then went horse riding. The rest of the day was spent consuming vast amounts of alcohol.

***

David groaned. The piercing sound of the alarm clock reverberated in his ears like a shrill whistle. He rubbed his eyes blearily. The consistent *thump-thump* in his head made him curse at the thought of Monday morning and having to get up and go to work. Then he remembered that he had promised to collect Ann early. He jumped out of bed, rushing to avoid being late, hoping his headache would dispel the distraction. It didn't. The gum he chewed also did little to mask the smell of alcohol on his breath from the heavy drinking session he and Adam had had last night before returning to London.

He stopped at Ann's home, hooted the car horn as usual and waited. She greeted him cheerily as she got into the car.

"Bloody hell, I needn't ask if *you* had a good weekend, my nose tells me that it was a good one," she announced, immediately screwing up her nose. "And the chewing gum hasn't worked either."

He shuffled uncomfortably and apologised.

"I hope you are sober enough to do your job this morning," she remarked.

"My brother and I had a late drinking session last night, that was all," David said. "I feel fine this morning."

Ann did not respond to this and suggested they go to the station and join the rest of the team who would be travelling to Nottingham.

"DI Roberts and his sidekick, Holmes, will be going too, so I don't want a repeat of what happened at the station a month ago," she said and shot him a stern look. "Is that crystal clear, Sergeant Hughes?"

"Yes, Guv," David replied, sounding contrite. "I will stay out of his way."

The CID team were milling around at the station when they arrived. Ann checked whether they had all the equipment they needed for the search. The forensics team would also accompany them. Ann briefed them on the search and warned them to be careful not to damage any items inside the Casey home as she was accountable for loss and damage of items inside the house.

Time was tight. They were ferried to the helicopters and flown to Nottingham where they were met by the Nottingham CID who provided transport for the team to the Casey home in Edwinstowe. They disembarked from the cars and walked up the long garden path to the house. The house was in an immaculate condition even though it was unoccupied for most of the time.

Ann turned the key in the front door, opened it and led her men into the house. The furniture was covered with white sheets. The place looked as though nobody had lived in it for some time, but every piece of furniture was tidily arranged in the room. A thick coating of dust clung to the floor and shimmered on the white sheets as Ann switched on the light to the gloomily dark living room. A pair of shoe prints was visible leading from the front door towards the rear of the house. The thick layer of dust delineated the outline of the shoe very clearly.

Ann ordered the forensics team to take an impression of the shoe prints. They moved forward and examined the prints before proceeding to take the impression. "Looks like a man's size 10 shoe print," said an officer.

Checking it was safe to proceed further into the room, Ann led the team to the next room. The forensics team went ahead and asked the CID to be careful where they walked in the house; they did not want any evidence destroyed – the house might have been a crime scene. They entered a large dining room that led off into another living room and a spacious kitchen. Stairs led to four large bedrooms, a study and two bathrooms. Everything was in pristine condition. It looked as though a housekeeper maintained the rest of the house and in an immaculate condition.

Ann said, "I want every corner of this house searched."

There was the sharp sound of David's voice as he called out. He had found a door leading to what looked like a cellar. The door was heavily bolted. A small glass window in the top of the door had a metal grid over it. Ann and some members of the team rushed to see what David had found.

"We'll need to cut the bolt to get into the cellar," Ann said, fixing her eyes on the lock.

A constable cut the large lock off the door with a bolt cutter.

Cautiously, David opened the door, peering carefully into the dark, not knowing what he would find. The rest of the team followed. The blackness hindered their search. Ann called for a torch and told the men not to move. She shone the light into the cellar and was shocked at the sight that greeted her. There were chains, manacles, knives and a bed.

"Get the forensics team in here right away." There was an urgency in her voice now, which crackled with command. "And the rest of you get out of here now."

The forensics team filed into the cellar. Ann shone the torch until they had found the light. They gasped as it revealed a macabre array of what appeared to be torture instruments. Dark patches on the floor appeared to be blood. The crude metal bed also contained stains. There were a few items of dirty crockery and cutlery and some stale bread. A bag that contained soiled women's clothing lay in a heap at the end of the bed.

Ann and David surveyed the room while standing at the door while the forensics team photographed and collected the items that they thought were significant to the investigation. Ann shone her torch onto the ceiling of the cellar. A blood-spattered pattern was visible. In the cellar were an assortment of daggers, candles, cloaks with satanic insignia and a rope. One of the forensics officers found a large freezer hidden in an alcove of the cellar. It was covered with a cloth. When they opened the freezer, it contained blood. A layer of thick ice betrayed that it was still switched on and in working order. They also found a chainsaw that was caked in dried blood, with fat and gristle clinging to the blade.

The forensics team continued photographing the cellar and collecting items of interest. The rest of the team searched the garage and gardens for anything remotely connected to the murders. The search took a long time. Ann organised refreshments for the crew.

The Nottingham CID officers mingled with Ann's team and discussed aspects of the case. Ann called a halt to the search at nightfall and told the men they could continue the following day.

"Come on, you lot," DI Roberts announced with a cheerful smile, "all roads lead to the local watering hole. See you there in an hour."

The team chorused their approval and departed noisily from the house. The group congregated at the Black Swan pub an hour later. Local police members joined them, making it quite crowded inside the small pub and their noisy banter annoyed the locals who frequented it.

Nonetheless, for a few precious moments the men from the CLPD were able to unwind and forget about pursuing their grisly investigation.

"Listen up, all of you," Ann warned after a while, "I don't want you lot pissed out of your skulls tonight. You need to be on your game tomorrow."

Her warning came too late for her sergeant who had consumed quite a large amount of alcohol; he called Ann by her name, after which she swung around and gave him an admonishing look.

Despite his drunken state, he clearly had not forgotten Adam's warning about never dropping his guard around Ann. He looked terrified, quickly made his excuses and left for his hotel.

The team arrived back at the house the next morning whereupon they found a secret trapdoor that led from the cellar to the rose garden. The door could only be opened from the inside of the cellar. The CID team searched the garden. A shed contained some burnt-out wooden torches that were strewn haphazardly amongst the gardening tools. The forensics team took fingerprints from the torches.

Ann surveyed the rose garden with a keen interest and was very tempted to have her team investigate the garden also, but knew she had to adhere to just searching the house.

Pleased with their discoveries, the team were certain they were nearer to solving the case.

Ann received a call from Edwards informing her that he had managed to get a warrant from Nottinghamshire Wildlife Trust to search Treswell Wood within Sherwood Forest, which was managed by George Casey. The project was run by trustees who gave permission for the police to search the woods.

"That was the boss," Ann said, turning to them after the call. "We have just got permission to search Treswell Wood."

A disgruntled groan echoed around the group; their faces filled with dismay at yet another day working in inclement weather.

"OK, I'll get you fed and watered first, then it's back to work," Ann informed them.

At the prospect of imminent food, the mood transformed to one of enthusiasm. Ann used the lunch break to discuss the strategy of the search in the woods. The geologist had mapped out where the sessile oak trees grew in the woods. Ann instructed them to search for any clearing that would suggest a meeting place for the Satanists.

After lunch, she divided the officers into teams and instructed them how to proceed with the search. They were transported to the woods by the local police, disembarking at the edge of the dark, dank and rather forbidding enclave. The teams separated and went their respective ways according to the plan set out by Ann.

It was some time before the men were able to penetrate deep into the woods. Just as Ann began to despair that their search would be fruitless, an officer shouted to signal that he had found something. His colleagues rushed over to where he stood. When they reached him, they saw a clearing hidden behind a clump of large oak trees. A sawn-off tree trunk stood in the centre of the clearing. There was a pentagram drawn on the ground near to the trunk and several footprints on the periphery of the trunk. Additionally, found on the ground surrounding the trunk were dark, red stains. The forensics team examined the red substance more closely, guessing it would be blood. They collected a sample, bagged and labelled it. The officers conducted a meticulous search in the undergrowth for the darkling beetle, which they knew to be indigenous to Sherwood Forest and which was found in Elaine's hair; they found many samples. A few leaves of the sessile oak were also collected.

Photographs were taken of anything assumed relevant to the investigation at the site. An exhausted team of officers emerged from the woods as daylight faded. The samples and items collected at both sites were carefully packaged and despatched by helicopter to the laboratories at the CLPD.

Ann was pleased that they had found what they came for. There was a last count to ensure all the team were accounted for prior to their departure, to the hotels where they were staying.

At one of these hotels a meal was followed by a cabaret and evening entertainment that was organised by the local police force.

There were no constraints on the consumption of alcohol. David steered clear of Ann as he knew he had no control over his words when he was inebriated. The entertainment continued into the early hours of the morning. Ann had also consumed a considerable amount of alcohol, but she managed to stay on her feet for most of the night.

The following morning, they were wrestling with hangovers and sleep deprivation for the journey back to London by helicopter.

Ann's first meeting of the day was with Edwards and Michael Heath.

"Good to see you, Ann," Michael greeted. "How did the search go in Nottingham?"

"Very well, Sir," she replied, holding her hands by her sides, managing not to fidget with her jacket. "I do believe we have significant finds linking Elaine's murder to Nottingham. Our forensics boys should come up with some interesting facts based on the items we found. I'll let you know as soon as Tim sends his report."

"Do you think it will make it clearer as to who the killer is?"

"I cannot say for certain – one suspect is out of the country and the other is unconscious – but if their DNA or prints are on any items found in the cellar of the Caseys' house it will strengthen our case against our suspects."

"Jolly good and well done," Michael said. "I shall look forward to seeing the forensics report."

He turned to Edwards. "Don't you agree, Stephen? Ann deserves credit for her hard work so far."

Recalling his previous promise, Edwards forced a smile and nodded his agreement.

"I'll get the report to you as soon as forensics send it to me," Ann promised.

Afterwards, she turned to David and said, "Come on over to my office, we need to prepare you for the trip to Spain."

In her office, she slumped into her chair and sighed with relief. She was beginning to make some headway with the case at last. David entered the office a few minutes later with two cups of coffee; he sat opposite her, fully focused on the task ahead.

Ann opened a file on her desk that contained an air ticket and some documentation. She handed David the ticket and began briefing him on the details of his trip.

"You leave in five days," she told him, and added pointedly, "please get to the airport in good time as you are notorious for being late."

David sat back and sipped his coffee, ignoring her remark.

Ann continued, "You fly to Marbella. Andrew will collect you at the airport. He will hold a card bearing your name at the arrivals lounge."

David perused the contents of the file and reassured her he would find out as much as he possibly could about the Russian girl whom Andrew had known.

A knock on the door interrupted their conversation. David opened the door and was surprised to see Savannah.

Seeing his surprise, Savannah said, "I was in the building and thought I might catch you before you leave."

"Come on in," David said, "the guv hasn't left yet."

"How can we help?" Ann asked her as Savannah walked into the office.

"I was keen to know what you uncovered in Nottingham. We have a great deal of interesting forensics evidence. We're just waiting for SOCO to do the analysis and get back to us. The house and forest had evidence of satanic practise and torture. Come along to my meeting with the team when I reveal the SOCO results."

"I was about to leave," Ann said, adding more brightly, "but David can have a half-day off." She gestured to him. "David, why don't you take Savannah to lunch?"

David looked at his watch and then back at Ann.

"I can't join you," she said, as if reading his thoughts, "my partner is desperate to see me after being away." She rolled her eyes and smiled. "I'll be in the doghouse if I don't get home in time."

David nodded but looked decidedly annoyed at Ann's presumption that he wanted to have lunch with Savannah. This was further exacerbated by being spotted with Savannah by Holmes who then quipped, in earshot of Savannah, "I see you've settled for second best. Better luck next time, mate."

David gritted his teeth and remained silent.

Savannah looked at him. "What cheek!"

David nodded, subdued by his embarrassment.

"I gather that chap is not your favourite person?" Savannah remarked.

"He irritates the hell out of me."

"A professional rivalry?"

He tried to wave the notion away with a movement of his head. "It's a personal thing; that bastard knows how to get me angry. He nearly got me chucked off the force when we came to blows once."

"Sounds serious, then. What does Ann think?"

"I prefer to leave Ann out of the equation," David replied a little tersely. "Let's have lunch and not talk about it further."

"Sorry," Savannah said, "I shouldn't be intruding."

CHAPTER 6

Ann raced up the stairs pulling off her clothes as she headed for the bathroom from where Josie had called out to her as she came through the front door. Josie was lying in the bath, covered in foamy bubbles. Ann climbed in with her and smothered her with kisses. After a minute or two they climbed out, hastily dried themselves, and disappeared to the bedroom where they spent the next hour making love.

"Well, Inspector" – Josie gave her a cheeky grin – "as your absence seems to have given you a good appetite, I think you should go away more often."

"Your brother will be here soon and you know how he hasn't learned to knock before entering," Ann commented. "Let's get dressed and go down to the kitchen."

In the kitchen, Josie chatted about her forthcoming trip to New York. Ann listened with a disapproving scowl.

"I'll only be gone five days," Josie said, seeing her expression.

Ann filled the kettle and talked about the events going on in Nottingham. Josie listened intently, adding her comments as the story unfolded. She warned Ann to be careful as she considered that the whole case sounded fraught with danger. Then Josie seized the opportunity to broach the subject of beginning IVF treatment to have the baby they longed for.

"Ann," she began, reaching into the cupboard and passing two mugs across the worktop to her, "don't forget you need to be flexible so that you can accompany me to the IVF clinic for the implantation."

Ann poured the tea.

"Of course; when is your appointment?"

Josie smiled with obvious delight. "Next week."

Ann swung around. Josie looked at her.

"You *are* still interested in us having the baby, aren't you?"

Josie went to the fridge and passed Ann the milk, surveying her reaction.

"Thanks." Ann stirred milk into the tea, allowing herself to think before responding. "Yes, I am, but you must realise I can't guarantee being free at a moment's notice."

"That is exactly why I want to discuss it now," Josie said with a hint of vehemence, "because you'll never make the time, will you; your work takes up all your time."

Ann observed her.

Josie took the milk back to the fridge and, turning back to Ann, said, "Do you still want this baby or not?"

"Don't be ridiculous, of course I do, but I also need enough notice to be with you."

"Well, real life is not as simple as that," countered Josie, beginning to raise her voice. "I can't simply command my hormones to perform when Ann Dixon is available."

The steam from Ann's mug of tea wafted in front of her face as she held her mug up. She did not speak.

Josie looked at her pointedly.

"Oh look, don't bother," she said, replacing her own mug of tea on the worktop with a small thump so that some of the liquid spilt. "I'll just drag Adam along because I know you won't be around when you're needed. And while we're on sensitive subjects" – her voice held an edge of annoyance – "when are we having our civil union?"

Ann drank from her tea and swallowed. "Gosh, you got out on the wrong side of the bed today, didn't you? What with all this talk about sensitive issues."

"Good heavens, Ann," Josie said, fighting tears, "I love you so much. All I want is to cement our relationship with a special union and a baby we can have together. Don't you see that?" She fled to the bedroom and shut the door.

Instantly regretting her insensitivity, Ann ran up to their room and sat on the bed beside Josie. She put her arms around her and began comforting her.

"I am so sorry, Josie," she said with genuine warmth, "I didn't mean to be so cold." She drew back a little and found she couldn't meet Josie's eyes. "I suppose I'm afraid of the commitment, in a way, and about what my colleagues at the station might say when they find out." She leant forward and kissed Josie on her forehead, wiping away her tears.

Josie half-smiled through her tears and said nothing.

"Tell me when you need me to accompany you to the clinic," Ann said, "and I'll be there, I promise."

Josie's smile widened.

Ann looked at her and asked quizzically, "Why are you so insistent on the civil union?"

"You know how my family have virtually ostracised me since discovering I'm gay," Josie said, unable to hide the hurt in her eyes, "and I don't want them having any claim on our baby if anything should happen to me. The civil union will ensure that you are the legal guardian."

"Hard for you, I know."

Josie said, "You and Adam are my only real family."

Ann's eyes fell on the framed photo on the dressing table next to the bed. It had been taken on Adam's birthday, the three of them at a restaurant laughing with joy, one girl either side of Adam, wrapping an arm around each shoulder.

"I have leave in two weeks' time from Monday," Ann said. "How about we tie the knot during those two weeks?"

"Can we have Adam as a witness, please, please, please?" begged Josie.

Ann shook her head and laughed. "Yes, alright, or I will never hear the end if Adam is not included."

Josie hugged and kissed Ann and danced around the room with abandon.

"Anybody home?" Adam called up the stairs just at that moment.

"We're in the bedroom," replied Josie.

"Oh no, you are not at it at this time of the day, girls?" enquired Adam.

"Stop assuming things. Do you think our entire lives revolve around sex?" said Ann, flinging a pillow at him as he popped his head around the door.

He grabbed another pillow and engaged the girls in a pillow fight, which they won – as they invariably did – and had him begging for mercy.

"Then what are you both doing at home so early?" he asked as they made their way downstairs to the kitchen.

"I had work to do on my laptop," replied Ann, "and Josie is just chilling out after her trip to Milan."

"I must say, you both look fabulously happy; what's happened?"

Josie smiled and glanced at Ann for approval to share their good news. Ann sighed happily and nodded for her to tell Adam.

Josie beamed. "Ann and I are going to get hitched this month." She reached up to her spice rack on the wall, selecting jars of basil and oregano.

"Oh, great news!" he exclaimed, clapping his hands in the air. "So, my favourite girls are tying the knot at last." He made a move forward and scooped them in his arms. "Have you named the day?"

"No, we haven't, and I don't want you telling a soul; I really mean that, Adam," Ann implored, handing Josie the milk from the fridge. "You know how much flack I have had from my work colleagues. The last thing I need is to have gossip ringing through the police corridors about my forthcoming civil partnership."

"Oh, for heaven's sake, Ann, you are surely not going to be dictated to by an ignorant bunch of coppers who have nothing better to do than engage in idle talk." Adam put his hands on his hips. "Your personal life is your own and you don't have to consider anyone else's opinion."

To Adam's surprise, Ann swung round and glared at him.

"You have no idea what I have endured," she said while giving the tea towel hanging on a hook by the fridge a fierce tug, "so for the moment, will you please shut up about my private life?"

An awkward moment followed. As always, Josie used her knack for diffusing potentially volatile situations. She hugged Ann and Adam and announced that it was time to eat dinner, which she had prepared earlier, and which had been stewing nicely in the slow cooker. She turned and began to butter chunks of crusty bread.

A call from David asking Ann for a lift to the airport interrupted the conversation. Ann explained to him that she had an early meeting and told him to arrange the lift with DI Tobin, at which point Adam interjected and offered his help.

Ann reluctantly handed him the phone and heard him arrange a pick-up time for David. When he had finished the call, she asked, "Since when have you joined the Central London Police Division, CLPD?"

"It's on my way to Reading," he replied. "It's fine."

"I am not as daft as you think, Adam. I don't trust you and David Hughes as far as I can spit." She gave him her penetrating gaze. "My gut instinct tells me you are up to something."

He was unable to look her in the eye.

"Problem with you, sis, is that you are never off duty," he said, keeping his voice level. "You should believe in your flesh and blood more readily."

She dismissed his explanation with a shrug and walked away.

***

The following morning, Adam hooted impatiently outside David's flat. David came running out towards the car clinging onto his cup of coffee.

"Come on, get in," Adam urged him, "your boss will never forgive me if you miss your plane."

"Bloody hell, she must have given you some stick for volunteering to take me," said David, grinning as he slumped into the front seat of the car.

Adam looked in the driving mirror then indicated to turn right. "She bloody well wiped the floor with me for offering to take you, then accused us of scheming behind her back."

"I swear she operates with radar," David said.

"What are you going to do in Spain?" Adam asked, his eyes fixed on the road ahead.

"I must interview the son of the Casey brother's neighbour. He was a friend of a Russian girl with whom the brothers were friendly and who vanished without a trace. Ann thinks the girl might have been murdered by one of the brothers."

"Gosh, sounds like heavy stuff." Adam pulled out to avoid a cyclist. "Have you had any news from Interpol about tracing James Muller?"

"No, so far they've drawn a blank."

"I know I can help them to find the guy," Adam said, slowing as he approached traffic lights. "My South American contacts are very efficient."

David looked across at him.

"I'll wait for your return from Spain and then I'll make some excuse to Ann that I need to go to Israel," continued Adam.

He pulled into the car park, got out of the car and accompanied David to the check-in desk. They shook hands and promised to meet on David's return. There were no delays and the flight left on time.

David sipped his drink as the flight got underway and read through the instructions that Ann had provided for interviewing Andrew. After a while, he nodded off to sleep and, the next thing he knew, he was awoken by the stewardess announcing their arrival at Malaga Airport.

While standing in the queue at passport control, he removed his jacket – too hot despite the air-conditioning. He looked about him then spotted a stocky man with a disarming smile who held up a board with his name on it. He walked towards the man, stuck out his hand and asked, "Are you Andrew Slade?"

"Yes, you must be David Hughes."

The two men shook hands and walked off in the direction of the car park. Andrew stopped as they reached a red Ferrari.

"Welcome to Malaga," he said and then invited David to get into the car.

"Thanks, I've never been in a Ferrari before," David confessed.

"Hah, this is my pride and joy." Andrew eased the car into the traffic as the engine purred into life. "My wife says my car is the other woman in my life."

"I'm an avid racing fan," David said, "but my work prevents me from racing my stock car."

"What a shame; you must come and stay with us when they race at Monte Carlo."

"Thanks, I'll keep that in mind."

They sped along the Golden Mile, a glitzy, charismatic stretch of coastal paradise teeming with scantily clad ladies who never failed to entice the millionaires who cruised around in their fancy cars.

"David," Andrew began, keeping his foot steady on the accelerator, "we need to conduct our talks away from my home. I beg you not to mention any of this business in front of my wife. She doesn't know about my life in Nottingham. I don't want her knowing anything about the Casey brothers. It's a part of my life I would rather forget. I'll tell you what I know when we go out alone."

David nodded his understanding.

After 20 minutes they arrived at an exquisite Spanish villa, which peeped out from the trees. The pool shimmered in the morning sun, shaded in parts by palm trees.

Andrew led the way into the spacious living room inside the villa. They were greeted by Andrew's wife, Rita, who shook David's hand and invited him to make himself at home. He sunk into the plush leather settee in the living room and, after being offered an enticing array of various cold refreshments, he opted for a beer. Andrew's two children appeared and cowered shyly behind their father when Andrew introduced them to David. After being shown to the guest room – a vast, luxurious room with private balcony – Andrew offered to show David around the villa when he had finished his drink.

David gawped in awe as Andrew guided him round, listening to the commentary about the special features of the place and how it was built. He was informed about the time that lunch would be served but asked if he could skip lunch as he wanted to rest instead. He did not emerge from his room until 6pm. Andrew was relaxing on the sun lounger by the pool while his wife and children were enjoying the pool itself. Andrew announced that they would all be going to have a meal at his favourite restaurant later in the evening.

The group sat and chatted companionably around the pool until 8pm when Rita announced that the children were hungry. They set off for the restaurant around 9pm. Andrew parked outside a place called Pangea, one of the most luxurious restaurants in Puerto Banús. The place oozed wealth and status. Andrew was well known to the waiters who ushered them to their table.

Rita struck up a conversation with David while they waited for their drinks. "Andrew tells me you are here to quiz him about the shady dealings of his ex-business partner," she said.

David, totally unprepared for her question after what Andrew had said, stammered a reply. "Yes, we have quite a bit of dirt on this bloke, and we thought Andrew might be able to help," he lied.

Rita wished to press on with the matter, but Andrew intervened and asked her to allow David time to enjoy the evening; they would discuss the matter at an appropriate time. Thankfully, she switched to another topic. David made polite conversation as they ate their meal. They left the restaurant around midnight and headed for home.

It was a pleasure the following morning to be woken by brilliant sunshine that streamed through the partially opened curtains. David lay in his bed and thought, *I could get used to this lifestyle.*

Andrew knocked on his door and enquired if he wanted to go for a drive along the coast. David shouted back that he would love to but first needed a quick shower.

"Take as long as you need," Andrew replied. "I'll wait for you on the terrace."

They drove out past the ruins of the old Arab wall in the Orange Square that had been built in 1485. They passed ancient, stately buildings, tall trees and exotic plants and, as they approached the coastal road, manifestations of every water sport came into view. Andrew pulled off the main road to a quaint little café that served a scrumptious breakfast.

David looked up from his coffee and said, "You nearly dropped me in it last night. Why did you not warn me that you had given your wife a story about a business partner?"

Andrew laughed out loud.

"Lucky you were quick on the draw and dug yourself out of the hole," he replied.

"OK, now we need to talk about serious business," David said.

"We'll drive to a quiet spot, and you can ask your questions."

Andrew drove to a secluded spot surrounded by trees with not another human in sight. David explained that he needed to record their interview.

Andrew shuffled around in his driver's seat, hesitant about

divulging what he knew. He appeared nervous.

"Are you absolutely sure that whatever I reveal to you will not be traced back to me?"

"I promise you that whatever you tell us will be kept in the strictest confidence," assured David.

When he was satisfied that Andrew was ready to be interviewed, he switched on the tape, established the date and time and stated Andrew's full name.

"How long have you known the Casey brothers, Mr Slade?"

"All my life as we lived next door to the family in Edwinstowe, Nottingham."

"Can you tell me about the Russian girl, Saskia, who was your friend and also an acquaintance of the Casey brothers?"

Andrew cast his eyes down.

"Saskia was an illegal immigrant whom I met in a pub in Nottingham." He looked up. "I was entranced by her beauty and her charm, but she also appeared very anxious and rather naïve when we first met. She told me that she had recently arrived in England and lived with friends in Nottingham. Her English wasn't very good, but we were able to engage in conversation without too much difficulty. I later discovered that her so-called friends were none other than the Casey brothers." Andrew paused and stared for a moment at the dashboard in front of him. "Saskia and I began meeting regularly and as time progressed, she began to trust me; she revealed that she was grateful to the Casey brothers for rescuing her from a gang of Albanian pimps who had her working in a brothel." He began to stroke the steering wheel with his forefinger and thumb. "She was terribly ashamed of her past and said she could never return to Russia because she was unable to prove to her family that she had become a professional model." He stopped stroking the wheel and glanced at David, avoiding looking at the tape. "I suppose I became attracted to her beauty and vulnerability."

"Go on," urged David after a few seconds of silence, prompting him to speak again.

"We eventually fell in love, but I didn't want to progress to a physical relationship. She was damaged by her time at the brothel. I wanted her to feel ready to take our relationship to the next level."

He paused and appeared to reflect. "We shared a great many interests and I discovered that she was very bright. She regretted not going to university and her parents had clearly wanted her to have a good education. She confessed to getting mixed up with a wayward boy at school who got her onto drugs that eventually resulted in her meeting a man who promised her a modelling career in England. She discovered to her horror that the man was in fact an Albanian pimp who had procured her for work at a brothel. She managed to get away and ended up meeting Tom Casey who allowed her to stay at his home."

He let out a sigh and paused for a few moments.

"Saskia would disappear for days or weeks. I got used to her gypsy lifestyle. And then she phoned me after a short absence and told me that she was pregnant and needed to have an abortion as she was not able to support a child." For a moment he looked part-angry and part-sad as he said, "I discovered that the father of the child was Tom Casey. I was unable to do anything about her situation; I knew that taking on Tom or any of his brothers would be tantamount to suicide. I asked her how she could allow Tom to get her pregnant when we were in a relationship. She confessed that she needed money and asked Tom who suggested she agree to have sex with him and get pregnant." He frowned. "Tom told her that his cousin, a doctor, needed babies for research and that she would be paid two hundred pounds for having the baby aborted. I offered to take her to an abortion clinic, but she declined at first, saying that she was terrified of going through the abortion process."

He sat upright, his body appearing tense as he spoke.

"I did not see Saskia for weeks after our discussion. She did not return my calls or text messages. Then, just as I had given up hope of ever seeing her again, she came into a café I frequented. She looked drawn and tired. She was embarrassed at not having contacted me and at first gave me a half-baked story about visiting a friend in London. She finally confessed to having had the abortion, but not at the clinic." He looked down into his lap. "She said that Tom's cousin, James, did the abortion and paid her two hundred pounds for the 24-week-old foetus. I protested that the abortion could not have been carried out properly as it would have been if done at a designated clinic." He drew his head up and stared through the screen. "Saskia hesitated for several minutes before telling me that she remembered going through the abortion process but was not shown the baby. She thinks she might have been drugged at the time that the baby was taken away. When she awoke, she asked to see the baby but was told that Dr James had to take the baby to the hospital without delay; he did not want to lose vital information for their research. Saskia, in her ignorance, was convinced that she had made a good contribution to medical research, so much so that she introduced her cousin, Olga, to the brothers. She said she thought she had found a good, honest way of making money. I was horrified but was unable to intervene as it would have put Saskia at considerable risk. I tried to dissuade her from allowing the doctor to perform any more abortions, as I told her it should be done at a proper clinic or hospital."

He shot a glance at David and paused a few moments more.

"Dr James was her hero and, no matter what I said, it fell on deaf ears. The two Russian girls wrongly believed the Caseys were good to them and agreed to the dangerous practise of getting pregnant and having frequent abortions. The girls didn't care as they had somewhere to stay and were being paid for what they assumed was their contribution to research." He looked out of the side window. "I felt sorry for Saskia, but I was deeply hurt, too, as I had fallen in love with her by then. Anyway, the next time we met, Saskia was distressed. She told me that Olga had disappeared, and she could not tell the police because they were illegal immigrants. She told me that Olga was pregnant and was due to have the abortion in two weeks' time."

He brought his eyes back to the front again, staring at the steering wheel that his right hand now gripped. David noticed Andrew's knuckles were white.

"George Casey told Saskia that Olga had not come home," Andrew continued, "but Saskia knew Olga not to be irresponsible and would not have gone elsewhere. Saskia said there were other homeless girls who lived with the Caseys who got pregnant and had abortions performed. I remember an Irish girl named Mary O'Reilly who was besotted with George Casey and took whatever he said as gospel. She spent a great deal of time at their home. She looked pregnant the last time I saw her and then, like the other girls, she disappeared without trace. I still remember where she stayed with her mother as her father had died in an accident.

"Anyway, Mary was very wayward and gave her mother a hard time controlling her." He looked across at David. "I can give you her address if you would like."

David nodded and murmured his thanks but didn't want to break the flow of Andrew's story.

"Mary had a cousin, Ellen O'Brien, who also hung out with the Caseys," Andrew continued. "Saskia feared that we would lose touch, so she gave me her brother, Yuri's, contact details in Moscow. I kept it safe in case I plucked up the courage to make contact one day." Andrew frowned. "When she vanished 15 years ago, I was too afraid to contact her brother as I felt they would have held me accountable if anything had happened to her. I was also afraid because I knew about the abortions and might have been implicated in what the Caseys were doing. I was terrified of reprisals from the brothers because they were so violent." He briefly hung his head, quickly glanced down and then concentrated his gaze out the window. "I thought it best to remain silent even though it came at huge personal cost because" – his voice had lowered to barely a whisper as he fought to suppress his emotions – "I really loved Saskia."

Andrew opened the car door to take some deep breaths, got out, slowly walked a few paces from the car, turned, and walked back. He climbed back into the car again, avoiding eye contact with David who noted Andrew's obvious distress at talking to him and revealing so much.

Andrew gazed into the distance through the windscreen of the car. David gave him time to recover, then spoke into the tape signifying the end of the interview. They drove back to the house in silence, each immersed in their own thoughts, with the sun sinking over the horizon.

His children ran up to greet them as they got out of the car. Rita jokingly said she had sent the police out to find them as they had been gone for so long. David explained that Andrew had had a great deal of explaining to do as the case was complicated and

Andrew had to give a concise account of what had happened. The explanation placated her, and she announced that dinner was prepared.

David and Andrew opted for double whiskeys and went to sit beside the pool.

"It must have been a gruelling day if you need double whiskeys to calm your nerves," Rita commented.

The men smiled and carried on with their conversation. After a delicious Spanish paella washed down with plenty of wine by the men, Rita retired to bed with the children and left the men to continue their chat during which Andrew explained to David his rather chequered career in the construction business; he told him of his narrow escape from bankruptcy after his business partner defrauded millions of his company money.

The following morning, David arose at the crack of dawn to enjoy a swim. After, Andrew took him to the airport for his flight to London. In the car, they discussed the final details of the information on the Russian girls. David thanked Andrew for his cooperation and hospitality and boarded the plane.

Adam met David in the arrivals lounge as he emerged through the exit.

"Come on, let's grab a coffee before we hit the road," Adam suggested as he carried David's carrier bag with the alcohol.

"Oh, that's for you, by the way," David said, looking at the bag. "I thought you might like some old Famous Grouse."

"Thanks, my supplies are running low, as it happens."

David smiled.

Adam asked, suggestively, "So, how many Spanish belles did you conquer?"

"Your sister gave me such a stern warning about partying that it put me off even contemplating having a wild time."

Adam pulled a face.

"Anyway, it was a tight schedule," David replied. "Andrew had taken a few days off specially, so we had to utilise every spare moment. The trip was worth it, though, as it yielded information vital to our investigation. And before you interrogate me, I am not giving you a single detail. You already know too much."

Adam laughed and said in genial mood, "Her ladyship requests the pleasure of your company. I was instructed to deliver you to her straight from the airport, immediately you arrived."

David didn't respond.

"You promised to keep me posted about the happenings in Brazil," Adam added. "You *will* keep your word on that, won't you?"

"Yes, I'll keep you posted," David replied, "but if Ann finds out you're going with me your name will be the last one on my lips when Ann thrusts in the dagger."

Both men chuckled at the visual image conjured up by David's statement. They left the airport and headed for Ann's house. She was working on her laptop when they walked into the living room.

"How was Spain?" Ann enquired.

"It was a very useful trip," David replied. "Information will, I think, advance our investigation."

"OK, we'll go over the details later. Meanwhile, Josie has prepared lunch. Let's eat before we get to work."

Just then, as if on cue, Josie swept into the living room and welcomed David with a hug.

Adam fetched some wine and filled up the glasses as Josie began to place the food onto the table. They tucked into her Sunday roast, chatting away during the meal. David impressed everyone with his vivid details of the millionaire lifestyle of Andrew Slade. Adam was especially interested in Andrew's invitation to David to join him for the Monaco Grand Prix.

"You are definitely in the wrong job, Hughes," Ann said, "always yearning for the greener grass in another man's garden."

Josie momentarily forgot that she was not to speak about the wedding when she blurted out to Ann that she had contacted a marriage officer who was willing to perform their wedding in the Lake District. She continued chatting about it enthusiastically, oblivious that everyone had stopped talking and was staring at her.

Ann's expression clouded to anger. Only then did Josie realise her mistake. It was too late. David shifted uncomfortably in his chair.

Adam, sensing the change in atmosphere, said, "Ann and Josie are tying the knot, but don't want it to be public knowledge yet. And as you have just found out inadvertently, perhaps the girls would need a second witness at the wedding?"

Adam glanced across at Ann who wore a deep frown on her face.

"Nothing in this house is private anymore, is it?" she spat, banging her fist on the table. "It's like living with the media."

Josie and Adam got up and moved to her, wrapping their arms around her with apologies.

Determined not to appear unreasonable, Ann said, "Well, David, since you inadvertently found out about my private life, I am sure you know that you will be expected to exercise the most stringent discretion."

"I am very happy for you both and I would be honoured to be a witness if needed," said David.

"Please let him be a witness, Ann," begged Josie.

Ann suppressed a wry smile. "Alright, if it will stop you two behaving like a couple of spoiled kids."

Josie eagerly began giving details of the forthcoming marriage. The venue was to be at a country house in the Lake District in three weeks. David and Adam put the date in their diaries. Josie asked everyone to remind Ann to keep at least two days free before the wedding.

"Enough of this now, David, we have work to do," Ann said, leading the way to her study with David following behind.

Ann turned and asked him if Andrew was cooperative to which he told her that he had been very helpful and had answered all the questions without hesitation.

"Let's hear the tape," Ann suggested.

David played back the tape and they both listened to Andrew's testimony in silence. When the tape had finished, Ann commented that she would need to meet with Michael Heath to ask for permission to travel to Moscow to find Saskia and interview her.

"It's going to be a tall order, Guv. I can't see them getting more money for our trip."

"I'll fight tooth and nail to get us there. If they want a result I will leave no stone unturned to solve these murders."

David murmured something.

"I have arranged a briefing on the findings in Nottingham,"

Ann said. "I've asked Peter Drew to deliver his findings directly to my team at the briefing at 1pm tomorrow. You had better get home now so that you can be fresh and alert tomorrow." She looked at him as she ushered him to the front door. "And thanks for going to Spain and getting the information."

Josie and Adam waved to him as he got into his car and drove off. Josie hugged Ann as she sat down beside her on the sofa.

"I haven't excused you for the unforgivable breach of trust today," Ann said to Josie, and then she turned to Adam and said, "and don't you look at me with those doleful eyes, Adam, because you are also included in that."

Adam looked contrite.

"In fact, no more cuddles and kisses for at least a month until you have both repented," Ann added.

***

David arrived promptly to collect Ann on Monday morning. She ran through the schedule for the day to ensure they met with their deadlines. Her first appointment was with Peter Drew at 8.30.

"We have some shocking evidence collected at the house in Nottingham," Peter informed her. "The cellar yielded most of the evidence and it seems it was used as a torture chamber by the Casey brothers. The most disturbing find was the presence of foetal blood belonging to 15 babies found in the cellar."

The group examined the forensics department's details and began preparing their presentation at the briefing later that day. Ann informed Peter that she would be presenting details of the taped interview with Andrew Slade at the briefing.

Ann repeated the time of the briefing and left with David.

"Next stop, meeting with the monster," Ann said, "but let's first get some caffeine for courage," She grabbed a coffee and they headed for her office.

Stephen Edwards was surprisingly good-tempered when Ann entered his office a few minutes later.

"Word has it that the investigation is going well," Edwards said as he motioned Ann to sit down.

"Yes, indeed, Sir; we have made excellent progress. The trip to Spain delivered invaluable information on the case and I have just spoken with Peter who has a wealth of forensics evidence which undoubtedly will advance our investigation." Ann was buoyed up with confidence. "I'd be most grateful if you, and possibly the Chief, could join us for the briefing at 1pm today."

"I'll try to get the Chief at the briefing," Edwards said with equanimity. "Look forward to hearing what Peter has for us."

Ann felt elated by Edwards' good temperament, hoping it wouldn't suddenly reverse when reality kicked in again, like it did when you woke from a dream.

The briefing room buzzed with excited conversation as the officers shared information and discussed it among themselves.

Ann called everyone to attention when she was sure that all were present. She thanked her team and the forensics unit for their diligent work and welcomed Peter and Edwards to the meeting.

She was pleasantly surprised that the Chief had made a special effort to be at the briefing, as Stephen had implied. She addressed the team by saying that she would leave Peter to tell them about his forensics evidence found at the house in Nottingham and Sherwood Forest.

Peter pointed to the relevant photographic evidence from the sites, with a running commentary of what they had found. He indicated the bed and a set of chains found in the cellar. The items contained human hair, tissue and blood belonging to the murdered Elaine Casey. He explained that her skin was also found in the freezer kept in the cellar. From this evidence, they now knew that Elaine was held hostage in the cellar before her death. He added that she was murdered in a clearing known as Treswell Wood because the improvised altar contained large amounts of Elaine's blood. He said that the same species of indigenous oak leaf and beetle found in Elaine's hair were from the woods.

Peter paused to allow his audience to assimilate the information before continuing. He expressed his concern that hair and samples of blood found in the cellar belonged to as many as five different women and 15 different foetuses. Foetal blood had also been found near the tree stump in the woods. The forensics team, he explained, were able to collect fingerprints from the wooden torches found in the cellar and shed of the property. Some of the fingerprints were a match to Tom, George and Jake Casey. The shoeprint in the hall of the house was indeed a man's size 10 shoe and matched the shoeprint found at both crime scenes. He mentioned how they also found traces of semen from some unknown males. One was a match to Jake Casey.

Peter's report was followed by a stunned silence. Only Ann's voice asking for any questions mobilised the men into speaking.

"What do you think happened at that house, Guv?" asked DI Tobin.

"I would like Sergeant Hughes to tell you about his interview in Spain before I answer your question," she replied.

David played the taped interview with Andrew Slade. When the tape had finished running, Ann asked if it had made the forensics evidence any clearer.

Some of the team members nodded, indicating that they had a better understanding, while some pressed for more answers. She urged that it was imperative that some of the girls were traced to verify what had been done with the bodies of the babies. She emphasised the importance of finding James Muller and instructed DI Roberts to return to James' sister to extract more information; finally, she asked David Hughes to accompany him to the interview.

Knowing full well that tracing witnesses who would contribute to the gathering of evidence was vitally important, Ann seized the moment to request funding for a trip to Moscow. She also expressed the need to explore every lead to finally conclude the case.

Peter Drew, realising Ann's brilliant move, supported her on the idea of travelling to Moscow.

Stephen Edwards shifted uncomfortably in his seat as he realised he had been put on the spot by Ann's suggestion and would have been seen as mean and uncooperative if he refused outright. He looked to the Chief for support as he *had* promised, albeit half-heartedly, to assess the available funds. The Chief rubbed salt into the wounds by saying he was sure they could squeeze out some money from the CLPD somewhere.

Ann gave the address of Mary O'Reilly to DI Tobin, instructing him to trace her or her cousin. She gave DI Tobin details for Saskia Stravinsky who lived at a shelter in Nottingham before she met the Caseys. She then enquired if anyone had checked on Jake Casey. She was told that he remained in a coma but that his condition was stable. A member of the team asked Ann if Interpol had tracked down James Muller yet. Ann replied that she had a meeting with Interpol later that week and would ask them to step up their enquiries as James Muller needed to be found. She added that there was no doubt that James had a hand in the murders and was accountable for illegally aborting the foetuses and possibly killing them, too. The team began dispersing after they had taken their instructions.

Michael Heath walked over to Ann, patted her on the shoulder and said, "Splendid work, Ann. I am proud of you."

Not normally one to be embarrassed, Ann blushed at the compliment. "It's thanks to my team who have worked very hard to get us this far."

"Give me a call in a couple of days," Michael said to her, "I'll try to get you funding for your trip to Moscow."

"Sir, will it be possible for Sergeant Hughes to accompany me?"

"Yes, of course, Ann; you'll need your right-hand man with you." He patted her on the shoulder a second time and left the room.

Stephen Edwards had overheard the conversation and made it clear that he was not in favour of the Moscow trip.

"What the hell do you think you'll achieve by going to Moscow?" he asked.

"We have a contact number and address," Ann replied astutely. "I believe we'll succeed in finding the Russian girl. She may be our only witness to the murders in the woods."

When he had gone, she turned to David and said, "Come on, David, we have a trip to prepare for." She grabbed her coat and added, "Let's get some lunch; I'm famished."

They sauntered off to a pub in Victoria that was still serving lunch at 3pm.

"Michael is going to get enough money for both our tickets," announced Ann triumphantly.

"That must have put Edwards' nose out of joint," quipped David.

"He damn nearly had a heart attack when Michael said he would get the money."

They waded through shepherd's pie and peas with crusty bread, pausing in between mouthfuls to comment on the briefing.

"David, I want a thorough interview with James' sister," Ann declared. "I suspect she knows more than she's willing to say. I don't know whether it's because she's afraid of him or is protecting him. Perhaps I should go with you to assess her."

David nodded, listening.

"Ring her today if you have her number," Ann said. "I'd quite like to see her as soon as possible."

David found Susan Muller's number and promptly dialled it. A crisp voice replied. David identified himself and asked when it was possible to meet with Susan. She was reluctant to meet with any of the police. Ann took the phone and explained that she wanted to accompany her sergeant as they had some new information. Susan finally agreed after some persuasion.

Ann scheduled the meeting for the following morning. David and Ann went their separate ways after lunch and agreed to meet at the station in the morning.

***

Susan Muller, looking distinctly irritated, answered the door to them. "I suppose you had better come inside."

She motioned for them to sit down as they entered the living room, and said, "I don't know what you think I can possibly tell you after the exhaustive questioning I endured the last time with your officers."

Ann had to reclaim Susan's loss of confidence in the police. With some rapid thinking, she invented a ploy, hoping to change Susan's mind.

"Miss Muller," she began, "I am very concerned that, as you have not heard from your brother, any number of things might have happened to him. I don't know whether you realise but South America is a dangerous continent. The law as we know it is not practised democratically." She drew a breath and looked at

Susan. "The killing of innocent people happens every day and the police over there are bribed to look the other way in most cases. You know that the drug cartels of Mexico also have jurisdiction in Brazil and there is no policeman brave enough to challenge these thugs who rule many of the South American countries. There has been kidnapping of the local people and foreigners and some of them have been killed. We are concerned for your brother's safety. We know that your brother had foreign friends and we need to trace these friends to find him. Did your brother ever mention the names of people he knew?"

Susan's expression changed to one of bewilderment. Her eyes darted from Ann to David, but she was unable to reply.

"We have reason to believe that James is in Brazil," Ann pressed, "but we are not sure of his exact location. Does he perhaps have a relative in Brazil?"

Tears began to well up in Susan's eyes. "Do y'think he has been harmed?" Susan enquired.

"Well, at present we don't know, but it will help us if you tell us where he might be in Brazil. We could help him if he is in trouble."

"We have an uncle in Curitiba." Susan sounded hesitant. "His name is Jürgen Muller. James may be with him." Her eyes darted sideways from Ann's face. "I do not have a contact number." She suddenly stiffened. "Please promise not to tell my brother that I told you about my uncle, please."

"Susan," Ann began as gently as she could so as not to frighten her into backing off, "has James hurt you in any way?"

"No, no," she protested, "he would never do that."

Ann thought that Susan looked as if she was trying to convince the police, and herself, that her brother was incapable of violence. She pressed on with the questions, probing steadily, aware of the girl's obvious vulnerability.

David sat in silence, quietly admiring Ann. She was making the person being interviewed feel that they were the most important person in the room and that their role was vital in securing the safety of their loved ones.

Ann's approach also secured her the answers that had eluded the officers at the previous interview. Her performance further solidified the professional bond between her and her sergeant.

Ann asked to use the toilet and, after she had reached the top of the landing where Susan told her it was situated, she slipped into Susan's bedroom. She deftly removed some hairs from Susan's hairbrush and put them safely in a plastic bag. She returned to the toilet, flushed it, and joined Susan and David in the living room.

Ann thanked Susan for her time, gave Susan her card and urged her to phone if she needed to talk or had any important information. Susan smiled in agreement, taking the card from Ann and bidding the detectives a warm farewell.

"Well done," said David as he eased into the driving seat of the car.

"Yes, I thought that went rather well," she admitted with satisfaction, "and I stole some of Susan's hairs to give to forensics."

"How lucky that you found a brush or comb in the room," David said. "We also now have a name and place to begin with."

"David," Ann said, "I want you to arrange another interview with Sam Cain. We may be able to squeeze something more from him. And now, please drop me off at home. I have just remembered Josie has invited me to some party to lure new clients to her fashion house."

Just at that moment, Ann's phone rang. It was Josie in a panic about them being late for the party. She urged Ann to hurry just as David stopped the car at their front door.

"Are you coming too?" Josie asked on seeing him draw up.

"No thanks, I'll pass this time," he replied. "I need to do some essential domestic chores at home." He turned the ignition to drive off. "Next time, maybe, and thanks."

***

Josie hugged and kissed Ann as she welcomed her home, then urged her to hurry; they barely had 45 minutes to get to the party. She rattled off some names of important guests who were going to be present and who were going to make a significant impact on her business. Josie looked ravishing in her black dress; a sight that never failed to tantalise.

Ann dashed out of the shower and swept Josie onto the bed. "Forget the party, we can have one of our own right here."

"Behave yourself and get dressed," Josie said as she jumped off the bed and continued to apply her make-up.

Ann reluctantly complied with Josie's commands. They arrived at the party with minutes to spare. The VIPs from Milan and New York arrived an hour late. Josie was furious but could not complain because she needed their support for sales of her new line of fashion. When all formalities were settled, a team of waiters served liberal amounts of food and wine. Josie proudly showed Ann off to her new clients. An Italian VIP named Matteo took a shine to Ann and stayed with her for most of the evening. He seemed quite dazzled by Ann, much to Josie's annoyance. Tamara Smith seized the opportunity to inflame Josie's temper by commenting that she observed the inspector seemed entranced by Matteo's attentions.

Ann, oblivious to the debate that raged about her conversation with Matteo, discovered that he was an archaeologist who accompanied his brother, Marco, the fashion designer, to the party. Ann had a huge interest in archaeology, both on a personal level and for her work. They soon became engrossed in the machinations of excavation.

Tamara navigated her way around the room to where Ann stood and asked, "Hello Inspector, have you caught any bad guys yet?"

Ann smiled and replied, "Hi Tamara, just as well I can tell the good guys from the bad ones. You might want to tell the bad guys I always get my man."

Ann's remark wiped the smirk off Tamara's face; she turned on her heel and made a hasty retreat.

Josie, who could no longer tolerate having Ann stuck in one place for so long, walked over and took Ann's arm, apologising to Matteo for having to steal Ann from his company, but that other guests wanted to meet her.

When Matteo protested that it was a pity she had to go as they were enjoying their discussion on archaeology, Josie said, "Well, even more reason that I need to rescue Ann, she knows work subjects are banned at my parties."

Matteo held onto Ann's hand and made her promise that she

would keep in touch.

When they were out of earshot, Ann said to Josie, "I hope your behaviour is not because of your conversation with that poison dwarf, Tamara. I saw you speaking to her earlier. She passed a comment to me to get me riled, but I did not rise to the bait."

"No," Josie said with some irritation, "I was just annoyed at your prolonged chat to Matteo who, in case you failed to notice, was not only interested in archaeology he was practically undressing you with his eyes."

"Oh, I think the lady is very jealous," Ann remarked with a smile.

Josie ignored the comment. "I have a host of people who want to meet you, so come along," she said, grabbing Ann's hand and rushing towards a group of people in the centre of the room.

The party continued into the early hours of the morning after which Josie drove them home.

Adam was still awake when they got home. "Dirty stop outs, what time do you call this?" he enquired cheekily. Then he noticed that Josie had her dress on inside out. "Wow, it must have been some party!"

"Don't be so nosey," Josie said, beating him about the head with her scarf.

"What are you doing here anyway?" Ann asked. "Don't you have a home of your own?"

"Don't you love your brother anymore?"

"Yes, I do, but when he visits too often it dilutes the love to some degree."

"Ouch! That was painful." Adam pulled a face. "I thought you loved your brother totally."

"Oh, stop trying to put me on the spot and go get us some coffee."

"I can do better than that," declared Adam, "I can add toasted croissants to the order."

"Sounds wonderful," Josie said, coming out of the shower with a towel around her hair. She sat down at the table and looked at Ann. "Thank God it's the weekend, and will you be free next weekend?"

Ann appeared demurred. "I need to talk to you about the next couple of weeks."

"Sounds ominous," Josie said.

Ann said, "David and I have to go to Moscow on an important assignment in the next three weeks."

Josie stared at her.

"I'll know more nearer the time, but if money for our travel is made available it may be as soon as the end of next week. Why do you need to know if I am free?"

"I thought it would be nice to go to the Lake District and check out the venue for the wedding, that's why."

Adam had stopped what he was doing and focused all his attention on the conversation.

"Dare I ask why you, and not Interpol, need to go to Moscow?" he asked.

"No, you may not. I need to go to Moscow because I am heading up the investigation," Ann replied with a curt nod.

"Don't tell me we may need to postpone the wedding date," exclaimed Josie disconcertedly.

"Yes, there seems to be a possibility that I may not make it on the day," said Ann, trying to inject apology into her voice.

Josie groaned.

"Never mind, Josie, you and I can amuse ourselves instead while the big Chief is away," said Adam in support.

"Don't push your luck, I might ban you from this house indefinitely," warned Ann.

"You would send a search party to find me the moment I disappear because you really love having me around," Adam replied.

Ann smiled because she knew he was right.

"Let's make the most of this weekend, shall we?" suggested Josie.

"Yes, let's get out of London and do some exploring in the countryside," said Adam.

The group were just about to leave when a text message arrived on Ann's phone. It was from DI Roberts. It read: 'Guv, can we meet urgently? Have important surveillance information.'

The look of resignation on Ann's face spoke volumes.

"Don't even attempt to justify what you are about to say," said Josie angrily.

Knowing nothing was likely to placate Josie, she kissed her on the forehead, apologised and walked to her car from where she phoned David to join her at the agreed meeting place in the pub with Roberts.

DI Roberts and his constable were there to meet her when she arrived. They sat down in a quiet corner of the pub. David took everyone's order and went to get the drinks. "Guv," he began, "we have bugged DC Holmes' house and recorded this information." He indicated his tape.

He played back the recording. It was a conversation between Holmes and Tamara. Tamara was heard to say 'That bitch is going to have a heart attack when she reads the Monday papers'. 'Why; has Amy found out that Josie is cheating on her partner?' asked Holmes. 'No, it is nearer to the bone than that', replied Tamara. 'What could possibly be worse than a scandal linked to Ann's partner?' enquired Holmes. 'Classified information that is going to freak her out', replied Tamara. 'How the hell did you access the information?' asked Holmes. 'A very obliging little bird tweeted the information to Amy', said Tamara. 'Shit, that is bad news for me as the CLPD already suspect me of giving you information', said Holmes. 'Aha, but they can't prove anything. Great for Amy if she can dazzle her boss with exclusive information and sell papers', she said. 'Fuck, I don't care about Amy. I could lose my job and never be able to work in the force again!' shouted Holmes. 'Come on, baby, you need me to pay your gambling debts and Amy helps sometimes. You keep your side of the bargain by keeping quiet and Amy bathes in the glory of an exclusive', continued Tamara. Holmes became outraged and the conversation descended into a shouting match. A door was banged loudly and then silence prevailed.

At the end of the recording, Roberts looked up at Ann whose knuckles had turned white as she gripped the edge of the table.

"I don't care if you must bug the whole CID unit. I want the bastard who is leaking information to the media found," she said.

"What are you going to tell Edwards?" asked David.

"I don't know," Ann said, her voice remaining sharp, "but I want you all to keep this recording quiet. I want to catch whoever it is red-handed, and Edwards will mess up and tell everyone. I need you to set up an undercover surveillance so that everyone's movements are reported to me. I want to know everything about everyone, even when they shit."

Roberts reassured her he could devise a system that would encompass keeping tabs on the movements and associations of her team. David pledged his support. They discussed their plans and strategy and eventually came up with a workable plan.

Sleep eluded her that night; she kept thinking about an encounter with Edwards if the morning papers contained the damaging article by Amy Baker. She sent David a reminder to get the newspaper on his way to collect her. It was a miserable night and Josie sulked because Ann had worked all weekend.

Ann was dressed and ready when David arrived at her house. As she got into the car, she saw the newspaper on the front seat. Blazoned across the front page was the headline: 'Police find evidence of human sacrifice and satanic ritual at the Casey house in the forest.'

The article contained information that Ann feared would undoubtedly stifle the progress of her investigation. She bit her lip as she read on, the veins visible on her forehead.

David carried on driving, aware of her anger and the need to remain silent during such times. She got out of the car when they arrived at the police station, failing to return the greeting of the constable at the entrance when they walked past.

Edwards stood waiting at her office door as she walked down the corridor.

As she approached, he growled between his teeth, "Get along to my office!"

"I will do, when my sergeant has fetched me a coffee. Something tells me I am going to need a considerable amount of caffeine for what you have in store for me."

Edwards looked taken aback at her unexpectedly bold reply.

David ran to get the coffee with a look that said he was pleased she no longer allowed herself to be bullied.

"I am not far away if you need anything. Just shout," he whispered.

Ann thanked him and went into Edwards' office.

"Explain this," Edwards ordered, flapping the newspaper article at her.

"I can't explain. No member of my team nor I would jeopardise the investigation by leaking information to the press. You will agree with me that my officers strive for excellence, so I do not see the logic in them cancelling their chances of promotion by currying favour with someone like Amy Baker."

"Have you considered the mole may not be amongst the CID but in the allied units connected to the CLPD?" she asked, raising a brow. "It seems to be someone who works very closely with our team."

Edwards shuffled uncomfortably in his seat as he realised Ann's suggestion made sense.

"What happened to that Holmes fellow whom you suspected earlier?"

"He is no longer seeing Tamara Smith," she replied. "She's sleeping with Amy again."

Edwards raised his eyebrows as if in astonishment that Ann knew so much.

"How do you propose to find the culprit?"

"I spoke to Roberts at our last briefing, and he's come up with a plan to find the mole."

Edwards looked stunned that Ann was one step ahead.

"How did you know that the media would print this article?" he probed.

"I didn't, I just followed my instincts that as Amy had already tried to undermine our investigation she would not stop at a warning but pursue her action for the duration of the investigation."

Ann had managed to turn around a potentially fiery meeting to an amicable understanding. Edwards even offered her a drop of brandy in her coffee.

"What do you suggest we do for damage control?" he asked.

"I think you should call a press conference and redress the balance."

"OK, I'll get that arranged. Will you be around this week?"

"Yes, David and I are planning to have another talk to Sam Cain this week. I think he knows a lot more about the Caseys than he's prepared to reveal."

"Have you heard any more about the funding for Moscow?" Edwards enquired.

"Michael said he'd let either of us know when it comes through. That reminds me, I have a meeting with our auditor" – she glanced up at the clock on the wall – "better dash."

"Call me as soon as you hear from Michael," Edwards reminded her.

She left with a triumphant smile. Gone were the days when she trembled at the mention of Edwards' name. He had become astonishingly approachable and Ann suspected that Michael Heath had played a part in Edwards' change in attitude.

David was busy working on his laptop when Ann walked in.

"Wow, that smile says the boss has told you we have funds to go to Moscow," said David, expressing amazement at her good mood, considering she had been with Edwards for two hours.

"My elation is because I have managed to transform the ogre to a gentle giant," Ann told him, looking triumphant. "I had him eating out of my hand in minutes."

"Good for you; it's about time you were shown some respect from the top brass."

"Thanks. Have you managed to contact Sam Cain for a briefing, yet?"

"No, I waited for you in case you were not available at the same time."

Ann swallowed some coffee and put her mug down.

"I'll ring; give me the number."

She reached for her phone and got through to Sam on the first attempt.

Sam's greeting was brusque.

"Who is it?"

"Mr Cain," began Ann light-heartedly, "why in such a bad mood today?"

Sam bristled with irritation. "Look, I've had a bloody rotten day, and I don't need you, Inspector, to add to my stress."

"I'm sorry to bother you," Ann said, refusing to be intimidated, "but I wondered if you could spare the time to have a chat?"

"I know about your chats, Inspector," Sam said in derisory tone, "they end up getting you arrested."

Two seconds of silence ticked.

"I'll see you without your Sergeant Hughes." Sam's voice left little doubt of his assumed control. "I still have the bruises from the handcuffs he shoved on me when I was arrested."

"Shall we say tomorrow morning, around eleven o'clock?" Ann asked, ignoring his comment.

"Fine; I only have an hour," Sam replied, making it clear he was in control. "The police have wasted too much of my time already."

She turned to David after the call and said, "Sounds like you are not in Sam's good books."

"I don't mind that, I have plenty to do tomorrow." He frowned. "Just mind yourself around that lot. Sam Cain is not as innocent as he professes to be."

Ann blinked and pursed her lips into a slight smile.

"And by the way, Guv," David said, "Peter Drew said we could pop in to see him before lunch."

"OK, let's go now before I get bogged down with work."

Peter Drew was studying some files when they walked into his office.

"I gather we've been keeping you busy with all the forensics information at Nottingham," he said.

"Yes, and thanks, we are grateful to you for all your hard work." Ann paused, studied him and said, "I am here today on another matter."

"Sounds serious. I'll get you some coffee and then we can talk."

They sat around his desk sipping coffee while Ann explained that someone was leaking classified information about the case to the media. Peter listened intently, nodding in agreement at Ann's concern that the leak could jeopardise progress.

"How loyal are the guys in your team, Peter?" she asked him.

"Ten members of my team have been with me for 15 years. The newer members are very dedicated. I believe they are team players and would not jeopardise the integrity of the team for personal gain."

"Do you know if anyone in your squad has a grudge against the CLPD?"

"Not to my knowledge, but if there is I will do a secret surveillance to find the bastard."

"We would be very grateful for that because the leaks are a blight on all our reputations. I don't want you to make the team aware that they are being watched," she instructed. "I don't care whose human rights might be compromised. I just want the culprit caught and prosecuted. I will get the surveillance boys to come and see you about putting taps on your land lines."

Peter nodded.

"I'll need a list of the mobile phone numbers of all your staff please, too," Ann added.

Peter frowned at the prospect of being complicit in spying on his colleagues and employees but reluctantly agreed. She thanked him and promised to keep him posted of any new developments.

"I don't blame him for being reluctant," she said to David afterwards. "Spying on your team is not easy when you've worked closely with people for years."

David nodded in agreement.

"Especially with all the current media hype about phone-tapping."

Ann's phone rang persistently while she talked to David and she felt obliged to answer it, sounding irritated.

"Ann Dixon; who is it?"

"It's Eve Marshall," the voice on the other end of the phone replied. "Have you seen the papers this morning, Inspector?"

"Yes, I have. What about them?"

"There are facts in the article you have withheld from me, and I want to know the reason."

Ann rolled her eyes in exasperation as Eve spoke. David's expression revealed he guessed it was going to be a long call.

Eve rambled on almost incoherently about being deceived and misled. Ann tried in vain to explain to her that the reason for not giving certain facts about her daughter's death was to avoid informing her killer of the police strategy in finding him or her.

She gritted her teeth when she finally ended the call.

"This is exactly what I feared about the impact of the leaks on our investigation." She hunched her shoulders. "Sod it, let's get lunch." She tapped the side of her head. "I've had it up to here with work just now."

They walked to her car. David suggested they head for Pizza One Stop. Ann agreed and swung the car in the direction of Covent Garden where they could reserve a quiet spot in the restaurant. She remembered that Josie had the day off and called her, asking if she wanted to join them. Josie explained that she and Adam were decorating the spare room, were covered in paint and in no fit state to go out. Ann hid her disappointment.

"Who was that on the phone?" asked Adam from the ladder where he was painting the ceiling.

"Ann. She wanted us to join her and David for lunch," Josie explained. "I told her we were unable to as we're painting."

"Any cheeky comments?" asked Adam.

"No, just sounded disappointed and said she would see us tonight."

Adam was concentrating hard on painting around the light fitting.

"I hope she is going to like this aquamarine colour," he said.

"She will." Josie looked up. "It'll be suitable for either a boy's or a girl's room."

"And done in good time for the paint smell to fade by the time the baby arrives."

"I never dreamed I would get pregnant after all Ann's procrastination and then it was you who came with me to the clinic." Josie smiled at her recollection of Ann's reluctance.

***

Ann and David had a busy afternoon setting up meetings with various teams to implement their plan to find the mole within the force.

"What time are we meeting with Jeremy Doyle?" Ann asked.

"Six thirty at the Fox and Hounds in Chelsea." David checked his watch. "It's already 5.45pm and depends on the traffic."

Ann looked momentarily flustered. "Damn, that means I'll need to work at home after the meeting; Edwards wants this report for the briefing with the press at 2pm tomorrow." She turned to go. "Come on, we had better not keep Jeremy waiting."

David sped through the busy roads, arriving 10 minutes late. Ann apologised profusely.

Jeremy grinned as he shook her hand and said, "I would begin to wonder if there was a problem when you guys arrive on time."

Ann laughed.

Jeremy asked, "You're drinking gin tonight, Ann?"

"No. I have a mountain of paperwork I need to do tonight. I'd better keep my head clear."

He smiled over his shoulder as he ordered the drinks, then brought them to the table.

Ann asked, "Do you have any encouraging news for us, Jeremy?"

"Well, our boys in Brazil have established that James has arrived there. We are unable to locate him in Brazil, though. The immigration boys appear to have lost him after his arrival. They suggested that he might have travelled by road to Colombo or Mexico. They were oddly tight-lipped and quite unhelpful – not even tempted by a modest bribe. My boys think they are withholding information and are probably being paid a lot more than we can afford." He drank from his beer.

Ann then proceeded to let him know what they had found out. "We were able to establish that James is a VIP and may be protected by someone in a high position. David and I revisited Susan, James' sister, and she told us that they have an uncle in Curitiba, one of the German settlements in the South Region."

"And?" Jeremy said.

"She said they'd been out of contact with him for a while but James may have gone to live with him. There's no address or contact number."

Jeremy took another drink from his beer and swallowed before replacing the glass on the table. "We have an MI6 operative, Nigel Phillips, who works with DEA agents in Brazil." He frowned and looked serious. "He contacted me and warned me that Muller has ordered a hit on you, Ann."

Ann gazed at him.

"I'm meeting with Nigel to check his credentials," Jeremy continued. "He also has a contact who works with Mossad. The Israelis are interested in Muller because of his links to Hezbollah."

Ann waved a hand. "You know that this is a very high profile and sensitive murder investigation – we cannot allow some unknown Indiana Jones to push his way in without the proper checks."

"OK, and we will need help. If this chap is as good as you think he is, we can use him."

Ann excused herself from the company and headed for the cloakroom.

While she was out of earshot, David said to Jeremy, "Look, I need to meet alone with you. There's information I cannot reveal to Ann. You must trust me on this."

As Ann approached the table, they stopped talking.

"I just need to inform both of you that I will insist on being kept informed of every part of the plan," Ann said as if sensing something had passed between them whilst she had been away. "And if there is no more to discuss, I would like to go home because I have plenty to do."

David pushed his chair back and led the way out of the pub with Ann and Jeremy following close behind.

They parted company outside the door and went their respective ways. Ann was somewhat prickly when she arrived home, a clear indication that she had been left to her own company.

Adam received a text message from David requesting an urgent meeting. He replied that he would see David the following evening.

Ann worked into the early hours of the morning and fell asleep on the sofa. Josie came looking for her and snuggled beside her for the remainder of the short night. David had to hoot continuously when he arrived at Ann's home the next morning as she had not heard the alarm. He always marvelled at Ann's ability to get showered and dressed in 15 minutes. She breezed into the car in jovial mood and did not harp on about the debate of the previous evening.

"Check the briefing room is set for the press meeting this afternoon while I am away seeing Sam Cain, please," she reminded David.

David felt glad to be alone for the morning; he could plan his strategy for Jeremy and ensure there were no loopholes.

Ann scurried about between her office and Edwards' until 10am when she announced she was off to see Sam.

When she arrived at his home, Sam Cain greeted her cheerily.

"Good morning, Inspector Dixon, I see nothing has changed much. As usual, you are reliably late."

"I apologise. There was an accident on the motorway that I did not anticipate."

"So, three murders and nobody arrested as yet," he commented as she followed him inside.

"It's a complex case. We seldom have an instant result in these circumstances."

"Aha," he mocked, "I see even the great Inspector is stumped."

"Cut the crap, Mr Cain. I want to know what you are not telling us. You were close enough to the Caseys and their sister to have gained inside knowledge that would not have been privy to anyone else." She gave him a hardened stare and folded her arms in front of her. "I am particularly interested in the satanic rituals performed by the brothers – and don't pretend you don't know about this. Jake informed me that you know because you spent a great deal of time with the brothers, and apparently their sister, Yvonne, confided in you."

"You must choose your words carefully, Inspector, when you make such statements. I know that satanic rituals were performed but I was not present at any of them." He returned her glare. "My information is second-hand so don't think for one moment that you are going to coerce me to stand up in court and give evidence about rituals I never witnessed."

"That is understood, Mr Cain."

Sam blinked.

"Whatever I say to you today is off the record," he said, "and I trust that you have no hidden recording equipment to entrap me."

"I give you my word on that but, by the same token, I appeal to you to help us catch the Caseys' killer." Ann unfolded her arms. "We have some leads that indicate it may be two killers working together. We know that the satanic rituals are an important part of the killing. Do you know any of the people who participated in the rituals? Did Yvonne ever mention names?"

"Yvonne said there was a doctor who delivered foetuses, but she did not know what happened to them. She did not know the doctor's identity as she said he wore a mask. She was told a doctor would do the abortion to reassure the girls they would be cared for by someone who was medically competent. Tom and George repeatedly raped Yvonne during these rituals."

"I see; go on."

"She said she was drugged for most of the time, so it was pretty much a blur of what really happened. They aborted any pregnancies because of the rapes."

"Why did Yvonne allow her brothers to rape her and not tell anyone who could have stopped it?"

Sam looked at her. "Her father sexually abused her. Her brothers witnessed the father doing this and blackmailed her into allowing them to do the same to her or they would tell her mother." He shrugged. "Yvonne blamed herself for allowing the abuse and was unable to get them to stop until Luke Cowan came into her life." He paused fractionally. "Mr Cowan knows much more than he is willing to tell you. He showed a great interest in the rituals and that is how he met the Caseys. He was only ostracised when he married Yvonne and took her away. The brothers wanted Luke and Yvonne to remain in the family home, but Luke moved to another side of the county. He didn't know what the brothers were doing to her. Yvonne was terrified that if he found out he would leave her. She confessed that Luke had a violent temper. She also said that he indulged in sadomasochism." He swallowed. "He tried to interest Yvonne in the depraved practise, but she declined. This did not discourage him from forcing her to participate in his sick indulgences. She often had to hide the bruises caused by his sick fantasies."

"I'd be interested to find out more about this," Ann murmured.

"If you are desperate to learn more about the rituals, Mr Cowan is your man. The question remains, Inspector, what are you prepared to forfeit to get your answers? If you are prepared to indulge in sadomasochistic sex games, Mr Cowan, without a shadow of doubt, will accede to any request you have. He is addicted to depravity. I am not suggesting you would do such a thing, of course."

Ann became immersed in thought as she contemplated the possibilities.

Sam shuffled his feet and stood up. "If that is all you need to know, Inspector," he said, "I must go now as I have an important meeting at 1.30."

"Of course. Thank you for your time and the information." She hesitated a split second before saying, "All that you have told me will be kept in the strictest confidence." She would need to dig deep into her conscience to justify what she was about to do. But the sacrifice, she told herself, would be worth the reward.

There were both moral and obligatory responsibilities to address and only Ann could decide if her actions compromised her loyalty to the woman she loved. The deafening buzz from the briefing room confirmed that the media were already assembled and probably ready to hurl their accusations at the CLPD. Ann ensured she was not seen before the meeting so as not to upstage the chief. Edwards met with her briefly and went over the facts to ensure he would not be tripped up. He entered the room and called loudly to get everyone's attention. The noise stopped immediately as they waited for Edwards to begin his statement.

Edwards began by saying that he was very disappointed about the sensitive details contained in *The World News'* article. He stated that the media were supposed to work *with* the police, not against them. He pointed out the potential damage that was done by the publication of the article. He said that the public would lose their trust in the police and the media if certain people in the media worked in secret with rogue members of the force who leaked classified information.

"The information you shared with the public about Eve Marshall," he went on, "was withheld from Eve's mother to save her the devastation of learning a member of her ex-husband's family might have murdered her daughter. Without telling her we would never have uncovered the evidence, we did. And please note our investigation points to possibly two killers. They are extremely clever and have managed to send us on a wild goose chase by planting evidence at the crime scenes. We still have a long way to go but had an important breakthrough over the past month." He paused, rocked back on his left foot, and then said, "No matter what your prejudices are against the police, I urge you to work *with* us to solve this case, not against us as has been the case since this investigation has begun. The CLPD must withhold some information to ensure we do not give the killers the advantage of eluding capture."

Edwards' appeal was followed by a moment of total silence. Then the mob of reporters began their onslaught of questions to him.

"Superintendent, will Jake Casey ever regain consciousness and is he one of your two suspects?" Amy questioned.

"The doctors cannot predict if or when Jake will wake up. Items implicating him in the murder have been found but there are extenuating circumstances, which his defence team will put forward."

"If you know about a second killer, why has he not been caught?" she continued.

"It will be possible to arrest him when we find him. Perhaps your informant who so readily provides you with information," Stephen said with some satisfaction, "would be so kind as to tip you off as to the killer's whereabouts."

Amy's face turned red but still she could not resist having a dig at Ann this time.

"Well, DCI Dixon," Amy gave her a waspish smile, "you seem to have lost the knack of catching the bad guys. Don't suppose there'll be any chance of promotion for you in the new year."

"I don't need the promise of promotion to do my job," Ann said. "It's only a matter of time before my team and I solve this case." She treated Amy to a triumphant expression. "If you check my track record you will see I always get my man." She paused for dramatic effect. "Our bonus will be catching the bastard who is betraying this unit."

With her brows knitted and her lips pinched, Amy sat down. The other reporters asked relevant questions, circumspect in their approach. Ann encouraged them to speak directly to her for all their queries and she gave them her word that she would answer as promptly as she could.

When the questions had fizzled out, Edwards drew the briefing to a close. He had handled it admirably and there was a measure of cooperation instead of the usual striving to score points. The media left the meeting satisfied they had gleaned some tangible facts.

Edwards thanked Ann for her support, and she nearly fell over at his invitation to join him for lunch. She declined, promising to be available later in the week. He added that he would hold her to her promise.

"Edwards has undergone a transformation," David remarked to her afterwards.

"Yes, but listen to the best part," – her eyes shone – "he invited me to lunch!"

"Good God, he must be unwell. Did you accept?"

"No, I postponed it till later. Can't let him think I am that easy."

"Come on, grab some of those yummy doughnuts I saw in the incident room."

Her phone rang as David left the office.

It was Josie. "Am I speaking to the grumpy but very sexy Inspector?"

"How dare you speak to an officer of the CLPD like that." Ann smiled into the phone. "Don't you have work to do?"

"I have lots to do."

"Well, let me guess, the laziest man in England is spending the day with you, painting. I must be in the wrong job because my boss expects me at work every day."

"You should be grateful that a famous fashion designer and a handsome, brilliant journalist are decorating your home without demanding a fee."

Ann could hear Adam chuckling in the background.

Ann asked, "Have you two been drinking?"

"Not at all," Josie replied.

"Wait till I get home," Ann said, just as David returned with the coffee. "It's Josie," she mouthed to him, "she's invited us to join her and Adam for dinner tonight. Are you free?"

"Yes, thank you, I would love to come." By the look on David's face and his willingness, he was immensely pleased to have been given a welcome opportunity to meet with Adam without having to concoct a lie to get away from Ann for the evening.

Ann and David tucked into the doughnuts. "Finish your coffee and close the door," she said to him after scrolling through her laptop to check on any matters needing her attention.

"We have work to do concerning the rat in the force. We need to set a honeytrap for Amy and this is what I have in mind."

She lowered the tone of her voice.

"We have an undercover cop called Julie Cunningham. She has done some splendid work for us in the past. Amy will find her irresistible. I will get Josie to organise a party and invite all partners of her employees. To ensure Amy attends, Josie must make sure that she invites the disgraced Italian designer, Franco, who got caught in bed with his male lover by his wife. His acrimonious divorce made headlines around the world. Amy would give her eye teeth to get close to Franco. When Julie gets lucky with Amy, she will be in the house to plant the surveillance devices. The surveillance will at some stage uncover who is giving Amy her information. We just need to wait patiently."

David looked sceptical. "It sounds workable, but what happens if Amy doesn't like Julie and can't get into the house?"

"It will work," Ann assured him. "You just need to think like a gay woman."

David smiled at her mild rebuke.

"Julie will give a star-studded performance; she'll make the plan work."

"So, where do we find this wonder woman?"

"I'll contact her through Michael Heath."

"Will Michael support your plan?"

"Michael won't say no to me." The conviction in her voice matched her air of confidence. "I'll call him right now."

Michael answered immediately.

When she told him that she had a plan to catch the mole in the force, he invited her over to his office straight away.

"Come on, David, you're driving; let's go," she urged.

Michael opened the door and invited them inside. He offered them a whiskey and poured himself one, too.

"OK, let's hear what you have in mind," he said, leaning forward, as they sat down either side of his desk.

Ann told him of her plan. He listened until she had finished.

"It sounds feasible," he said, a little doubtfully, leaning back in his chair. He went on to express his concerns about the surveillance and that if the devices were found Amy may find out that Julie had planted them in her house.

"Amy is no fool and did not get this far in her career by being unobservant," he continued. "She has a nose like a bloodhound. Ann, I know how much we need to nail the bastard who is leaking information, but we need to be cautious that the means do not defeat the end."

Ann blinked and looked across at him. Her arms rested on his desk.

Michael leaned forward again. "I'm going to discuss your plan with Alec Sawyer who heads the undercover unit and get back to you. We need to proceed with care; it's too delicate to mess up now that we have made such progress."

Ann felt a trickle of deflation seep through her. She had thought her plan was workable and that valuable time would be lost by more procrastination. The group talked into the early evening then Ann glanced at her watch and made her excuse to leave.

"Don't worry, I won't keep you waiting," Michael said. "I'll get back to you later this week."

She smiled, shook hands and left with David.

"Damn, I hope this Sawyer guy is not one of those steeped in the bureaucratic soup of delays and reams of paperwork," she said, as David started up the engine.

"Cheer up, Guv; he didn't say no, it was a conditional yes."

"Let's get home before the chef bans us from her dinner table for being late," Ann responded.

A few minutes later a smiling Adam met them at the door. He hugged and kissed Ann and patted David on the back.

"The chef was just wondering if you would be disgracefully late," he said with a broad grin.

"Yes, I would like to have a few words with your chef who makes nuisance calls to an officer of the law," replied Ann.

"I heard that, Inspector!" Josie's voice came from the kitchen.

Ann swung round, grinning.

"Just be careful not to upset the cook," Josie said, "or you may not get any dinner."

Josie and Ann embraced.

"I'll get the wine," said Adam. "What's everyone drinking?"

Adam memorised their requests and went into the living room where he poured the wine while Ann helped Josie bring the food to the table. They dined on Josie's delicious chicken chasseur with buttered new potatoes and French beans, after which Adam left with David, saying he wanted to spend the night at his own flat. Ann felt pleased as it gave herself and Josie time to be alone.

Adam and David continued their discussion on the proposed trip to Brazil into the early hours of the morning.

Ann and Josie finished washing up the dishes and headed for bed. Ann seized the opportunity to inform Josie about her plan to put Amy under surveillance.

"Josie," she said, pulling off her clothes and throwing them into the laundry basket, "do you remember reading that article about our murder investigation last week?"

"Yes, I did, and I remember how stressed you were when your chief tried to pin the blame for the leak on you."

Ann shrugged on her dressing gown and tied the belt. "Well, I need you to be an honorary sleuth to help me."

Josie's face lit up. "Do you really mean that?"

"Don't get too carried away," Ann said as she moved back and forth between the bedroom and the bathroom. "I need you to organise a fashion event with an after-party and I want you to invite Franco. I also want you to invite Amy. I would be even happier if you could send Tamara away somewhere so she is not present at the party." She paused to check that Josie was taking it all in. "I also want you to send an invite to a girl called Julie Cunningham."

Josie stood in her underwear and gazed at Ann.

"Can I ask why?"

"Absolutely not." Ann came back into the bedroom and closed the door. "You only need to follow instructions. No questions, please."

"OK, when do you want this party organised for?"

"I want it done thoroughly, so don't rush. It's more important that it all goes smoothly. We only have one shot at this. There is a great deal riding on this opportunity, so no mistakes."

"I think I can do that," Josie said, pulling off her underwear, "depending on the price of the reward" – she raised her left brow – "like an imminent wedding date, perhaps?"

"We can arrange that for when I get back from Moscow. I haven't forgotten about it. I do still want to tie the knot with you."

Josie shot her a doubtful look.

"Stop looking so insecure," Ann said, observing Josie's clouded expression. "I don't want anyone else." She took off her dressing gown and sat down on the bed, pulling the covers aside. "Does that put your mind at rest?"

They hugged and snuggled in next to each other. Sleep did not come easily to Ann with thoughts and plans bombarding her brain.

Meanwhile, David phoned Jeremy early the next morning to arrange a meeting. He asked Jeremy not to say anything to Ann just yet as he had some explaining to do. Jeremy arranged to meet later that morning; he was keen to hear what David had to say.

Ann had some meetings that did not include David for the morning, so he was grateful that he could get away without telling lies. He met Jeremy at a coffee shop in Chelsea.

Jeremy sounded enthusiastic. "Drag up a chair and tell me all."

"Nigel will meet with you, but you will only meet with this guy, Ben Hajioff, in Brazil," said David. "He'll talk to you but his associate, Rachel Levine, will give you security clearance for him. She has worked with Hajioff and can vouch for him. You will need Ben as he is fluent in Portuguese and knows our double agent with the drug cartels. He also knows the equatorial forest and some of the forest inhabitants. He lived with them when he did the documentary on native American tribes. He trained as a commando before becoming a journalist. He's a valuable ally." Jeremy took a sip of his coffee, listening intently. "I spoke to our Mossad contact, Rachel Levine; her MI6 contact has informed Rachel that James Muller is protected by the drug cartel in Brazil and that he would move heaven and earth for him to stay alive. In other words, whoever pursues him is in grave danger of being killed."

David picked up his coffee cup and considered Jeremy's reaction over the rim.

"You must convince Ann to stick to the request of these agents and not insist on a personal meeting," David went on. "You must dig your heels in on this. I realise this is *her* investigation, but she must follow their protocol as we need their help."

David added, "The difficulty will be convincing Ann of your importance in the Interpol team. I can emphasise that you are needed because you are closely involved with the investigation and have close ties to our contact. I will need to speak to this Ben and check him out before I sanction his participation in this investigation. Give me a couple of weeks. I will then return with concrete information to give to Ann."

"Send me the contact details for Ben and I'll get on with it," promised Jeremy.

The two men parted company with the understanding that they would stay in contact by phone; they feared emails could be read or traced.

David phoned Adam to tell him he had met with Jeremy and had sown the seed about going to Brazil. Adam said that Rachel would get his new identity as Ben Hajioff set up. He told David he needed two weeks to get everything arranged.

"How much is Jeremy going to tell Ann of all of this?" Adam asked nervously.

David replied, "I have asked him to inform Ann on a need-to-know basis – that it is Interpol's jurisdiction so that Ann won't be able to demand to know every detail. Jeremy agreed, so we are safe for now."

"Meet me at the Dog and Duck in Islington after work on Friday," suggested Adam.

"OK," David agreed. "Must rush now before Ann gets back from her meeting."

Ann got back at lunchtime. She went looking for David and found him in the incident room going over some of the forensics reports. She asked him to come to her office.

"I have some feedback from Michael," she said as they headed for Pizza One Stop in Covent Garden.

She continued after they had ordered, "I met with Michael and Stephen about our funding for the Russian trip."

David leaned forward expectantly. "Did we get it?"

"Yes."

"Fantastic news! When do we go?"

"We first have to contact the Russian equivalent of the CID and get a liaison officer to take care of us when we're there. It might take a few weeks." She held up her glass of wine. "Time to celebrate."

They finished their drinks and Ann asked to be dropped off at Peter Drew's lab. David explained that he was meeting with DI Roberts and went straight to the incident room where Roberts was working on his laptop.

David asked Roberts, "Did you get our report on the interview with Susan Muller?"

"Yes, I did, even though Ann muscled in on what should have been *my* interview."

"I know, I couldn't prevent her doing that. You know, when the guvnor wants to do something herself, she just goes ahead and does it."

"I went to Nottingham to look for Mary O'Reilly," Roberts said. "The family moved years ago. They were a disjointed family according to some of the neighbours who knew them. Mr O'Reilly was a drunk and left Mary's mother when she was very young. Her mother had no control over her. She grew up running wild. They remember her being involved with the Casey boys. She had a younger sister, Ellen, who doesn't live in Nottingham any longer. Mary also had an uncle who might know what became of Mary. I left my contact details with the neighbour who said she would contact me if she were able to find an address for the uncle."

"You didn't do so bad," David said. "Ann will be pleased with the information."

Roberts shrugged. "She'll pick holes in my work, she always does. She's never satisfied with anything. I don't know how you can put up with her probing and questioning."

David patted him on the back and whispered, "You just need to practise some patience. Anyway, let's go over the Nottingham information again to ensure we haven't missed anything."

Terence Holmes entered the room singing *From Russia with Love*. He smiled at David and said, cryptically, "Rumour has it that someone is going on a Russian honeymoon."

"Cut the crap, Holmes; I'm warning you," said David angrily.

Holmes smirked. "Aha, you'll have plenty of opportunity for banging her – a dream come true."

David, who had now reached boiling point, lunged forward, punching Terence on the nose. The two men began wrestling with each other on the floor. Papers and chairs went flying as the fight escalated. Their fellow officers watched and cheered as the two men threw punches and kicked each other. David was the better and stronger fighter, but Holmes was a dirty fighter when he sensed he was losing. He bit David's ear until he drew blood. David retaliated by bashing Holmes' head on the floor and managed to beat him into submission. The commotion was heard down the corridor.

Order was only restored when Edwards' voice boomed over the sound of the cheering bystanders.

"What in God's name is going on here?" This was followed by a barrage of expletives.

The bloodied fighters stared at the floor as they were reprimanded. Holmes had a broken nose and David's torn ear was hanging by a piece of skin. The room looked like a bomb site. The floor, broken chairs and files on the table were all blood-spattered.

"Get out of my sight, the pair of you!" Edwards snarled between clenched teeth. "The damages will be deducted from your salaries." He turned on his heel and walked off.

Both men were taken to the nearest casualty department for medical treatment. Edwards phoned Ann to inform her about the fight. She swallowed hard as Edwards criticised her lack of control over her sergeant and suggested she put him on a lead or have him replaced. She was tempted to defend David, but she knew that nothing excused him for fighting on duty. She was shocked but kept her cool and calmly asked which hospital David had been taken to. Ann apologised for her sergeant's behaviour and thanked Edwards for informing her.

She sped off to the Chelsea and Westminster Hospital, preparing the lecture she was going to give David. She made her way to the casualty department where she showed her badge and explained she was looking for Sergeant Hughes. The staff informed her that he was undergoing repair to his ear in the minor surgery suite. Ann managed to track down Holmes who had just had his broken nose reset. He couldn't look at Ann.

"I demand to know what led to this utterly despicable behaviour?"

"It was just a disagreement, Guv," Holmes replied. "David is too sensitive; he doesn't like being teased. He hit me so I retaliated" – Holmes looked down at his feet – "it got out of hand."

"I don't care who was to blame or what it was about, you're a disgrace to the force. And I get hauled into this shit with you, accused of not being able to control you. Edwards wants you both sacked. There will be an internal enquiry and both of you will be severely reprimanded and disciplined."

Holmes apologised and promised it wouldn't happen again.

"Good," she said, "because after this you won't be working for the force much longer."

Holmes lifted his head to look at her but said nothing.

Ann added, "Now go home and stay there until you hear from the Chief."

She fetched a coffee from the machine on the ward and went to wait for David to return from surgery. Meanwhile, she worked on her laptop while the time ticked away.

After a minute or two, Roberts came to join her. He took off his jacket, folded it across his lap, and sat down.

He asked, "What the hell happened today?"

"I believe you witnessed the incident," Ann said. "Why ask?"

"Yes, I did," Roberts said. "I had the unfortunate pleasure of seeing two grown men knocking the shit out of each other. But I didn't see the start of the fight as I popped out to get a drink. When I re-entered the room, blood and chairs were flying everywhere."

"So, why the hell didn't anyone try to stop them?" Ann asked. "From what I hear, the men were applauding the fight as though it was an official boxing match."

"Yes, and quite frankly, only a madman would have intervened. They were knocking the hell out of one another."

"That much is obvious."

A porter went past pushing a bed on which lay a white-faced elderly man, held together with bottles and tubes.

"The men present said that Holmes entered the room singing *From Russia with Love* and then began taunting Hughes who struck the first blow," Roberts tried to explain.

Ann said, "There's no excuse, they were caught brawling a few months ago and I warned both of them then."

A few feet away, two physios were discussing something, looking at some notes.

"I believe you and Hughes are due to go to Moscow in pursuit of a witness testimony. Will the Chief allow Hughes to go along considering his aggression record?"

"I'll do my level best to convince the Chief he has to go to Moscow," Ann said. "He's a good copper, which is what makes this all the more ridiculous, but I have a horrible feeling he'll be disciplined, which is bound to delay our trip." A nurse walked past pushing a trolley full of medicines and bottles of pills. Ann waited for her to go past. "I'm going to see Edwards after speaking to David when he wakes up."

"OK, I'll catch up with you tomorrow," Roberts said, looking up at the black and white clock on the wall opposite. "Got to dash, I have a meeting in an hour."

He stood up and put his jacket on.

Ann drummed her fingers on the table, deep in thought, whilst waiting to speak with David. After a few minutes, the nurse came to tell her that David had woken up and would see her.

When she approached his bed, he tried to sit up, albeit rather groggily. She glared at him, not bothering to ask how he felt.

"What on earth is going on with you with disputes at work and behaving in such a manner?"

David held his heavily bandaged ear and grimaced with pain. "Oh God; my ear, my head – it feels like I have been hit by a bus."

"If it was up to me," said Ann, "I would ensure you were punished. I don't know what Edwards is going to say. He may even stop you going to Moscow. You will be disciplined, that's for sure, and it will impact on our investigation time." She let out a breathy sigh. "We've already procrastinated too much. Why were you fighting?" Her brows knitted into a frown as she studied him. "I do *not* want a stupid excuse, David. Were you and Holmes fighting over a woman?"

David clutched his head in his hands, pulling a face.

"It *was* about a woman but not in the way you think. He implied something in a very lewd way, and it sparked the fight."

"I want to know exactly what he said," Ann continued. "If you don't want to tell me, Edwards will demand that you mention all the details in your statement." She shrugged. "The choice is yours."

There were a few moments of silence in which David appeared to think before he replied.

"Holmes insinuated," he began, speaking slowly, "that you and I were going to Moscow to have an affair. I punched him because I found his remarks offensive and disrespectful to you." He cast his eyes down, unable to look Ann in the eye.

"Why could you not walk away and leave *me* to deal with him?"

David brought his chin up.

"Maybe because we guys settle our arguments differently to women," he admitted, pulling at the edge of the bedcover, "and I couldn't stand by and allow a rogue like Holmes to get away with spreading malicious and untrue gossip."

Ann said nothing.

"Sometimes when dirt is thrown around often enough," David said, speaking with conviction, "it begins to stick" – he levelled his eyes on Ann's – "and that is unfair to the person who is being talked about."

David began drifting off to sleep again as the effects of the analgesia took effect. Ann realised that it would be pointless pursuing the questions. Just then, Edwards popped his head around the door.

"I thought you might be here," he said, and pulled up a chair. "What on earth happened?"

"I believe it was as a result of Holmes' insinuation that David and I were off to Moscow to conduct a clandestine love affair," she explained.

"Good God, that's preposterous."

"My sentiments entirely," Ann said.

"Why can't you control your boys?"

"With respect Sir, I signed up to solve cases for the CLPD, not to teach grown men how to behave."

"Why did Hughes take offence?" Edwards raised a brow and

stifled a laugh. "He's not secretly in love with you, is he?"

Ann smiled, sensing he was making light of it. It was unusual for him to find humour in anything.

"Well, perhaps if I can persuade him to change his sex he might be in with a chance."

"His behaviour was disgraceful," Edwards conceded, "and I believe it's the second fight these two men have had." He clasped his hands in front of him. "And I will not tolerate such lack of control amongst members of my force. They will be disciplined." He unclasped his hands. "I think it may be good to move him to another unit for a while. I will let you know."

Ann nodded.

Edwards added, "What does the doctor say – his ear will recover?"

"The doctor has said he will make a complete recovery. He'll be discharged tomorrow and be back to work next week."

"OK, I'll be off." He headed for the corridor. "See you at my office tomorrow."

Ann was thoughtful as she drove home. She was fearful that David would not now be allowed to accompany her to Moscow. She had not realised how much she had enjoyed working with him until Stephen mentioned separating them. They were a great team and she wanted them to complete the investigation together.

She would have to manipulate the situation to her advantage, to keep David as her assistant, and that meant she would need to play her trump card to make that happen. That was Michael.

Ann called him and told him what had happened. He sympathised and agreed to meet with her the following day.

The expression on Ann's face when she arrived home and walked through the door spoke volumes.

"Goodness, who has died?" asked Josie as Ann sat down.

"Don't you add to my problems," Ann said, rolling her eyes, "I've had a pig of a day."

Adam stopped what he was doing and went to sit next to Ann on the sofa.

"What's the matter, sis? Has misery guts Edwards been on your case again?"

"No," she replied, heaving an exasperated sigh and running a hand through her hair, "it's David. He's in hospital. He had a fight with another officer. A piece of David's ear was bitten off and the other guy sustained injuries, too."

"Bloody hell, I thought coppers were supposed to fight the criminals, not one another. Is he going to be OK?"

"Yes, he'll be discharged soon." She sounded irritated.

"May I ask what the fight was about?"

"No. If David wishes to tell you it is entirely up to him. Besides, you're too nosey when it comes to business about the CLPD."

"That's put *you* in your place," Josie chipped in as she stood in the doorway, hovering between the living room and the kitchen. "Ann gets tetchy when it involves her David."

Ann glanced over her shoulder at Josie. "You can take that smug look off your face," she said, "and keep your opinion to yourself." She twisted her body round in her seat to face Josie, and said pointedly, "And by the way, he is *not* 'my David'."

"Oh blast," Josie said, with exaggerated resignation, "I'll disappear into the kitchen and avoid all the slings and arrows that are flying around here."

"God, you're like a couple of kids, you two," Adam quipped.

Ann's look of vehemence clouded her eyes. She stood up and turned to Adam who got to his feet and stood looking at her.

"Adam," she said sharply, "you took Josie to the fertility clinic… and without consulting me first."

"Well, it was under exceptional circumstances," Adam said by way of explanation, keeping his voice light, "and you must agree, the result was pretty amazing?" he added, with his voice lifted at the end.

"Quite frankly, I feel like doing something equally bloody amazing to *your head*."

Adam visibly stiffened.

"You have the audacity to presume you can waltz into people's lives and make decisions without their knowledge and pat yourself on the back for the consequence of your actions."

"A thousand apologies for acting without your permission." Adam looked incredibly humble. "I did it to help both of you."

"I suppose you know that Josie is pregnant?"

"She told me last night." Adam ran a hand through his hair and tried a smile. "I'm delighted for you both. Congratulations."

"Come on," Ann said in conciliatory tone, "I'm going to take you to dinner – you can drive."

During the dinner at a small restaurant on the High Street, Josie announced that she was going to spend 10 days in New York. Adam said he had a meeting in Paris and would be away for two weeks. They both showed surprise that Ann did not complain about being on her own. But her thoughts were too focused on a mission to discover the truth.

The very next day Ann made an appointment to meet with Luke Cowan. He reluctantly agreed to meet her at his home the next evening.

"I appreciate you making time to meet with me, Dr Cowan," Ann said as he showed her into his living room.

"The pleasure is absolutely mine," replied Luke as he invited her to make herself at home. He offered her a drink, which she accepted.

"I'll come straight to the point, Dr Cowan," Ann said, replacing her cup of tea on the table in front of her. "We have reason to believe that you had been involved in the satanic rituals with the Casey brothers."

"Well, well," began Luke, looking at her thoughtfully, "you certainly have been busy, Inspector." He took a deliberate sip of his tea, placing the cup carefully back in its saucer. "I hope you can back up your suppositions with concrete evidence." He ran his tongue over his lower lip. "Do you really believe I could be bothered to go chanting mumbo jumbo with a group of mindless individuals?" He gave her a deferential smile with a small nod of his head. "I think not."

"I can assure you, Mr Cowan, we do have a reliable witness who saw you with the Caseys during their mumbo jumbo practises, as you call them."

Luke straightened and got up from his seat.

"You can't prove anything," he said, looking down on her. "My lawyer will overturn whatever accusations this witness levels at me."

"I wouldn't be too sure of that." Ann smiled pleasantly and

stood up to face him. "I always get my man."

He blinked.

"Really?"

"I need your help, Mr Cowan." She dug her hands into the pockets of her jacket. "I am not here to accuse you or to fight you. You are not a suspect. Whatever you reveal to me would be confidential."

Luke shifted slightly.

"I want you to take me to the place where they meet for satanic rituals." She took her hands from her pockets and walked to the window. "Don't pretend ignorance" – she turned from the window to face him – "because I have it from a reliable source that you have witnessed these rituals."

"My word," he said, allowing his eyes to travel down the length of her body, "you are very assured about your information, Inspector."

He rubbed the side of his chin, watching her.

"My information comes at a price," he said. "I hope you are willing to pay."

He walked over to where she stood and ran his fingers along her cheek.

She did not resist. Instead, she waited to see what he would do next.

"So, the great Inspector wants my help," he said, and took his hand from her cheek. "Well, for that, I'm afraid you must agree to a forfeit of *my* choosing." He smiled derisively, shifting position and turning away from her slightly. "You see, my help comes with certain conditions, too."

She looked at him.

Luke said, turning his head to her in a beckoning motion, "Let me show you my little secret parlour," he smiled, "it will pique your curiosity."

She followed him to a cellar that was lit by candlelight. It was decorated in dark red and black. There were a collection of whips and handcuffs on a table. A bed covered in red satin sheets stood in the centre of the room.

He turned towards Ann. "See, Inspector," he said, enjoying

himself, "this is my private domain. Not a shred of satanic worship in sight, but I indulge in something much more exhilarating."

In an instant, he reached over and held her face in his hands. He kissed her passionately. She responded at first, then bit his lip and drew blood. This inflamed his passion, and he began to rip off her clothes. She embraced him, raking her nails down his back, drawing more blood. He arched his back with the pain, but her actions only served to arouse him further, which distracted him for a few moments. Ann seized the opportunity to handcuff him, then pushed him onto the bed and tore off his shirt. She reached for a large candle that contained a significant amount of melted hot wax and proceeded to pour it over his chest. The hot wax ran to his groin. His erection stood out, quivering, electrified by his suffering.

He screamed. She pulled him off the bed and chained him to a chair. Then she grabbed one of the whips and began beating him. The bloody welts on his skin sent him into a sexual frenzy. This aroused him further and he begged her to continue to hurt him.

Ann then untied him, and he placed a chain around her neck. He beat her with the whip until she bled. He bit her on her buttock till he drew more blood. He savoured the blood that oozed from her wounds then pushed her onto the bed with her back towards him. He forced her into a kneeling position. He gazed at her exposed buttocks and glistening vagina that inflamed his passion still further. He kept a hold on the chain to control her movement, just as one would control a dog. Then he thrust his engorged penis into her, violently. She screamed... in ecstasy.

They continued their violent engagement with abject, bestial carnality for what seemed hours until they were spent. Finally, they collapsed on the bed, totally exhausted. They slept until the next morning.

"So," Luke said, handing her a mug of coffee, "the Great Inspector has an Achilles heel!"

"Fuck off, Cowan," Ann said. "We had an arrangement. It is business, that's all."

"I'll tell you something else, Inspector, you're a fucking good lay." He took a step back, eyeing her in amusement. "And I'll tell you another little secret – I had to go and have a wank after I first met you." He winked. "You have a splendid body. Shame… it's wasted in your job." He appeared to think for a few seconds. "I wonder what your ladylove would say if she knew you had been screwed by me."

Ann shot him a cryptic look. "Leave Josie out of this. You agreed, in return for my" – she paused fractionally – "payment, to take me to the forest and witness the ritual, so you had better keep to your word."

"Listen to her – so desperate to get the answers she needs, she'll risk anything. What a cop!"

"If you double-cross me, Cowan, you bastard, I really will not stop at anything to teach you a lesson."

"If you didn't make me so fucking randy," he responded, "I would tell you to piss off."

He studied her face for a moment.

"OK," he said, "I'll help you. I will let you know when they have their next ritual."

Ann put her coat on over her torn clothes and ran out of the house to her car.

There were numerous messages on her phone when she switched it on. One was from an irate Edwards who demanded she come to his office. She raced home to shower and change. She was shocked and disgusted at the bruises on her back, neck and thighs, hoping the marks would fade by the time Josie returned.

The following morning, she wore a scarf to her meeting with Michael.

"I'll get my secretary to bring in some hot tea," Michael said, "or would you prefer something a little stronger?"

"No thanks, too early for me; I'll settle for tea."

"Why the scarf?" asked Michael. "Are you going down with a cold?"

"No, I have an unsightly rash; just wanted to cover it up."

"So, your boys have engaged in a bit of fisticuffs," he said, waving her reply aside.

"Yes, and now Edwards wants to move David to another unit, and he didn't even start the fight – and I want him to accompany me to Moscow because he knows the logistics of this case." She looked pleadingly at Michael. "I want you to block Edwards and stop David being moved. Please, Sir, can you help with this?"

Michael smiled. "I will do my best," he said, "but how do I convince Edwards this will not happen again, in view of it *not* being the first encounter these boys have had?"

"It's DC Holmes who needs to be moved," Ann said, "or he will continue to agitate Sergeant Hughes. You need to convince Edwards that it's Holmes who is the aggressor."

"Look, if I can reassure Edwards, then you must be ready to travel to Moscow in 10 days. I have spoken to the Russian CID leader, a seemingly nice fellow called Sergei Kaminsky. I'm going to give you his number so you can update him on the case. I just prepared the way for you in a diplomatic sense. He gave me his assurance that you would be supported every step of the way."

"Thank you, Sir, I am most grateful. I will phone Sergei today."

"By the way," Michael stopped her, "how is Jake Casey getting along? Has he shown any signs of recovery yet?"

"Not much. The doctor says he is stable but still unconscious."

"Do you still believe that Jake was an accomplice rather than the prime murderer?"

"Yes," Ann replied, "because of the many variables in the case. Nothing is clear cut. Either we have a very clever murderer who is *not* Jake Casey, or Jake's cousin, James, committed the murders with his help. We will have to see if we can track down this Saskia in Moscow."

"Good luck, I will certainly support you in all of this," Michael said.

"Thank you, Sir," Ann said, shaking his hand.

Ann spoke to Sergei after having sent him a comprehensive email of both cases and explained the reason for their visit to Moscow. She then had a visual teleconference with Sergei and his detective sergeant, Dimitri Zhukov. The two men were very excited about Ann's visit. They said the case was fascinating and challenging. Sergei reassured Ann that he would arrange their accommodation in Moscow and would have them collected at the airport. She thanked him and promised to phone him nearer the time of their visit. Her next call was to check on David.

"How are you?"

"Not too bad, Guv." His voice came back a little groggy still. "The ear still feels very painful."

"Serves you bloody right."

"Oh no, not more reprimand. You can fight with me when I am better." He was unable to hide his irritation. "Right now, I just want a bit of peace and quiet."

"Alright, you have a week's sick leave. Come into the office at the end of the week. I want to prepare for Moscow now. We travel in 10 days."

Later, Josie informed Ann that she was regrettably delayed for another week. Ann felt relief, seeing the extra time as beneficial for her bruising to fade. She was racked with guilt about her encounter with Luke Cowan and phoned Clive to arrange a meeting.

"What's up?" Clive asked on seeing her as they sat in a small café, drinking hot tea. "You sounded deathly depressed on the phone."

"Oh God, Clive, I have acted so foolishly and recklessly." Ann put her head in her hands. "Please help me."

Clive looked at her.

"What's happened?"

Ann took her hands away from her face, looked over her shoulder and then at Clive before saying in a lowered tone, "I allowed a person of interest in our murder case to have sex with me, in exchange for vital information."

Clive listened intently as she blurted out her foolhardy encounter. He raised his eyebrows as she told him she was going to the forest to meet with her informer to take her to the satanic place of ritual.

"I don't condemn you," Clive said, taking a sip of his tea. "I understand your motivation for doing what you did but I am concerned that you are at some risk accompanying this guy into the forest. If he is the crazy bastard you say he is, what stops him from attacking you and bumping you off?"

"That's why I have you on my side," Ann said, brightening a little and drinking from her cup. "We are going to Treswell Wood, Nottingham. I will tell you when and you are going to follow us and be my bodyguard." Clive put down his cup. "Phew, same old Ann." He smiled. "Still sailing close to the wind. OK, I'll be there for you."

Clive picked up his cup of tea and held it in front of him whilst looking at her.

"Just let me know the details."

***

Luke Cowan contacted her three days after they had met, informing her that the meeting of the Satanists was scheduled for the time of the full moon in two days. Ann insisted on travelling in her own car, with Luke leading the way. The calm weather ensured they had a smooth journey to Sherwood Forest. Luke stopped a few hundred metres from the edge of the forest and got out of his car. Ann alighted from her car and walked over to him.

"OK, Ann, this is no time for heroics as the people who indulge in these practises are serious and dangerous," Luke told her. "The perimeter of the forest where they do the rituals is booby-trapped. They also have lookouts who are armed and dangerous. It is vital for our safety you stay close to me and be very quiet. I will make a sound by which the lookouts will know I am not the enemy, but they must not see you."

She nodded in agreement and followed him as he walked ahead. The full moon broke through the dark that engulfed the forest. They stuck to the thick undergrowth, moving slowly, until they reached a large tree. Luke whispered to Ann that he would help her to climb up the tree, reminding her to be very quiet. He stooped so that Ann could put her feet on his shoulders to climb it. She heaved herself up onto the arm of the first sturdy branch. Luke stuck a knife into the main trunk of the tree to get a foothold before heaving himself up, with Ann helping him to ascend. They sat in the small space on the horizontal branch, giving them an excellent view of the forest clearing. The eerie silence was only punctuated by the hooting from nesting owls. It seemed like an eternity before a grating noise revealed the opening of a hatch that had been concealed by the undergrowth and seemed to lead to an underground tunnel. Hooded figures soon emerged.

The figures, dressed in black, formed a circle around a central altar. One, who was dressed in white, then emerged, and the rest of the group bowed to him, calling him Master. The group began to chant. Moments later, a woman dressed in white was carried out of the tunnel and placed on the altar. She seemed asleep or drugged as she did not protest or cry out. A live goat was also brought into the centre of the proceedings and tied to the side of the altar. The chanting continued for what must have seemed like an hour. The figure in white then walked over to the goat and cut its throat. Blood gushed out. A black-cloaked figure collected the blood in a large chalice. The figure in the white cloak drank from the chalice. It was passed around to each person wearing a black cloak. The remainder of blood in the chalice was poured over the girl lying on the altar. The figure in white then ripped off the girl's clothes and removed his own. He mounted the altar and began to have sex with the girl. The girl woke up from her drugged state and began to scream. Her attacker became more violent in his rape of her and proceeded to sodomise her. The other figures cheered as the attack continued. When the white-cloaked figure had satisfied himself he cut the woman's wrist and proceeded to drink her blood. The girl passed out during her ordeal. The figure in white thrust his hands into the air glorifying Satan. His followers did the same. They carried the girl back into the tunnel and disappeared into the darkness. Just as the last figure descended the steps into the tunnel, the moonlight revealed his face. Ann gasped silently as she recognised the face as that of the DS of the Nottingham division, the man who had led the search in the forest with her team some months ago. They waited until the last of the lookouts had gone before descending the tree. Luke led her safely out of the forest. Stretching her legs from their cramped positions and shocked at what she had witnessed, Ann whispered, "Do you think they killed the girl?"

"That is for *you* to determine, Inspector."

Ann stared at him.

"I did my job and took you to the venue," he said. "Whatever happens next is nothing to do with me." He twisted his mouth into a condescending smile. "We still have the little interlude we had and which may be considered as payment." He stood back from her, wiped his hands down the front of his trousers and said, "You can't deny you have been to my place as your dabs are all over my handcuffs and my candles. Your visit is on my CCTV." He gave her one final smile. "Good luck and goodbye." Then swiftly, he got into his car and drove away.

Ann sat quietly contemplating her dilemma. She could confide in no-one about the events of the past week. No-one would understand her actions, least of all Josie, yet she knew that her trip to the rituals was not a wasted one as it confirmed her suspicions about it being linked to the murders. She just needed time to link these events. She got home in the early hours of the morning and was glad that she was alone and did not need to give an account of herself to anyone. Her bruises had still not faded. She prolonged her shower to cleanse the contamination of her association with Luke Cowan.

***

"Hey, how did you manage to get away without being asked 100 questions?" asked David when Adam appeared at his front door.

"I just told them a white lie about meeting someone at the pub. So, how are you doing, my friend?" asked Adam.

"Painfully well," David replied as he closed the door. He turned back and went towards the kitchen and explained to Adam what had happened.

Adam leant against the worktop and looked at him. "Still defending my sister's honour then."

"That bastard was totally out of line. I had to teach him some manners. Your sister didn't see it that way. She just thinks I'm a thug with no discipline."

"Rubbish – don't let her hardened exterior fool you; she admires your chivalry."

"Anyway," David said with a slight shrug, reaching forward to flick the kettle on, "I managed to meet with Jeremy. I filled him in on Rachel and the MI6 operative. I gave your name as Ben Hajioff. I also gave him contact numbers for them and told him that you would only be contactable in Brazil. I warned him not to tell Ann that the information came via me."

"Sounds good," Adam said as they stood in the kitchen while David poured hot water into two mugs and stirred the coffee. "When do you think you and Ann will return from Moscow?"

"To tell the truth, I may not be allowed to go to Moscow as the Chief wants to transfer me to another unit because of the fight."

"I wouldn't worry, that will never happen," Adam said. "My sister will fight tooth and nail to ensure you go. The plan for Brazil is that you and Ann will be met by Rachel and Nigel."

David drank his coffee and considered him.

Adam said, "I will request that you join me when we go into the forest to meet my DEA connection. We will finalise everything nearer the time. But you must convince Jeremy to only deal with my DEA guys because there are a few crooked ones amongst those in the mainstream." He drained his coffee. "I'd better be getting home now. Speak to you in due course."

David arrived late for work the next morning, much to Ann's annoyance.

"You are appearing before the chief constable for review of your position as a result of your fight with Holmes," she said, and added in a regretful tone, "I hope you will not be moved to another unit or, worse, demoted."

"I hope so, too, Guv. Like you, I want to see this investigation to the end."

"Well, it's a pity you didn't think of that before you behaved like an idiot and put your career at risk."

She gave him an irritated look.

"Now get out of my office, your appointment is in 15 minutes."

David obeyed and left.

The disciplinary hearing was brutal and intense. Worse still, David was none the wiser at the end of the hearing as to what had been decided. The chief constable informed him he would be notified about his fate when a decision had been reached. He expected the worst; the enquiry was gruelling and damning.

Afterwards, he headed for Ann's office needing her support.

"Well, are you in or out?" she asked as he stuck his head around the door of her office.

He slumped in the chair looking as dejected as someone who

had been given a prison sentence.

"I have no idea what they have decided; said they would inform me when they have made a decision."

"Oh, for heaven's sake, cheer up!" She slapped him on the back. "You have a good record and that will tip the balance in your favour."

David pressed his lips together.

"Anyway, you've done me a favour by delaying the Moscow trip because Josie and I want to tie the knot," she said. "If you have no plans on the 12th, that's a week away, I want you to be one of our witnesses."

"I would love to be, Guv; just text me the time and venue and I'll be there."

"And remember, not a word to anyone."

David smiled and nodded.

Ann had been so busy arranging their Moscow trip that time flew and, before she knew it, the eve of her wedding had arrived. Adam and Josie ran around frantically making final arrangements for the wedding as Ann had so little free time. The modest gathering at the venue in the Cotswolds celebrated the marriage of Ann and Josie. David and Adam were the witnesses. Ann hoped that the registrar at the wedding would not remember her name as she had appeared on TV news channels in connection with the murders. The short ceremony was followed by a lavish champagne lunch. Josie looked stylish in a cream silk dress. Ann wore a silver-grey silk suit. They had to put the honeymoon on hold as Ann anticipated her trip to Moscow would follow soon after the wedding. She booked them into another hotel as she had every intention of thwarting Adam's plans to booby-trap their bedroom and enjoyed the look of surprise and disappointment on his face when she ordered a cab to whisk her and Josie to a secret location. He could not resist telling them not to go wild on the wedding night as Josie should remember she was carrying his nephew. He and David sauntered off to the nearest pub with the intention of getting disgracefully drunk.

The three days passed quickly. David was summoned to the chief superintendent's office at 8am on Monday morning.

"I don't know why they are so lenient with you; if I had the chance, I would have had you removed or sacked," said Edwards, glaring at David. "You can remain here and continue the murder investigation with DCI Dixon. DC Holmes has been transferred to Bexleyheath Division."

David nearly collapsed with relief.

"Thank you, Sir, I am very appreciative." He wore a humble expression.

"One more step out of line and you are gone; now get out of my office!"

Suffused with elation and relief, David raced off to Ann's office to share his good news with her.

"Guv, I'm off the hook, they are letting me stay," he beamed.

"That's great news, David. Grab a chair. I am just about to do a video conference with the Russian detectives. Edwards and Heath will be there, too. I want you in on this, so don't wander off."

"OK, do you think we have time for a quick coffee before we start?"

Ann looked frustrated. "Hurry up because Edwards will blow a fuse if we are delayed, and you know how much he loathes you at this moment in time."

David dashed off to get the coffee while Ann made last-minute preparations for the meeting.

Suddenly there was a loud knock on the door. The door opened and Edwards walked in followed by Michael Heath. David appeared soon after.

"Don't even think of bringing that coffee to this office," Edwards said. "What the hell do you think the Russians will say if they spotted you sipping coffee during the video conference? We British are already labelled as lazy and seeing you enjoying a coffee might give them the wrong impression of us, so you can chuck it away."

David scowled as he poured his precious coffee down the sink. Ann wasted no time in getting the conference underway. They got a good satellite link. The Russians appeared on the screen and their CID chief, Sergei, greeted them in his broken English. He introduced them to his colleague, Dimitri. Ann thanked Sergei for agreeing to help the British with their enquiries. Sergei had been sent all the information on the details of Saskia and reassured Ann that they had located the whereabouts of Saskia's parents. The teams made final arrangements for Ann and David to stay in Moscow. Sergei confirmed to Ann that he would meet them at the airport. Dimitri came to the rescue whenever Sergei struggled with his English, to explain.

The video conference lasted two hours. Towards the end, Edwards had shuffled in his seat to send impatient signals to Ann to finish.

"Well, they seemed pretty efficient," said Michael.

"I want to know what happens when we have spent all this money, time and effort and it comes to nothing," Edwards said.

"It won't be a fruitless search," Ann said in response. "Saskia's brother was close to her, and he will lead us to her when we tell him how important it is."

"And what if this whole bloody expensive trip *is* a total waste of time?" Edwards persisted.

"It won't be a waste." Ann was adamant. "We have done our homework. Give us some credit, Sir."

"Anyway," put in David, "the Russian guys sound very committed to helping us."

"Yes, they are very enthusiastic, which is very much in our favour," Ann said. "We leave tomorrow. If there are no further questions, I would like to get on and prepare the paperwork for my trip, please."

She turned to David.

"Get us some coffee, David, my withdrawal symptoms are bad."

David went to the machine and came into Ann's office bearing the Black Gold to which she had virtually become addicted.

CHAPTER 7

Ann and David settled comfortably in their seats as they prepared for their flight to Sheremetyevo International Airport. Just as they emerged into the arrivals lounge, Ann spotted two men holding up a board with her name on it.

"Look," she cried, "there's Sergei and Dimitri!"

The airport was crammed with throngs of bustling travellers. Ann and David threaded their way to their hosts who smiled broadly as they approached.

"Ah, at last we meet in person," Dimitri said and shook Ann's hand as he drew her towards him, kissing her on both cheeks.

Dimitri's English was much better than Sergei's, who spoke with a heavy accent. Dimitri offered them coffee, but Ann declined, requesting to be taken to their hotel to freshen up before joining them at the police's head office. The extreme cold of the Russian winter took their breath away as they emerged from the warmth of the airport building.

"Whatever you do, never take your gloves off outside," Dimitri warned, "even when holding your phone or your fingers will stick to them, like you're permanently attached."

On the road, maniacal yellow taxi-cab drivers tore through the traffic, cursing and swearing and making obscene gestures at other drivers who dared to challenge them.

Ann and David arranged with their hosts to collect them in an hour's time. The hotel rooms were clean, albeit basic, with 3-star rating. They got ready promptly and were soon back in the car heading for the police station where Dimitri ushered them to a large, dimly lit room. They were introduced to the rest of the Russian criminal investigation team by Sergei who declared that he had the best team in Russia. Dimitri smiled, saying that Sergei always thought he had the best of everything. Coffee was brought into the room and the team members took their seats. Sergei was the equivalent of a DCI and Dimitri of a DI.

David helped Ann to display pictures of the murder and a photo of Saskia. The team listened intently. Sergei paused for a few minutes. A few of his officers asked questions that he interpreted for Ann. Ann emphasised that she thought the killings were linked to rituals of the occult that was the key to the murders and that Saskia probably held the clue to who may have been behind these murders.

Sergei informed Ann that they had tracked Saskia's parents to a house near the forest. The meeting carried on for some time as the police got to grips with the essentials of the investigation. They pored over gruesome photographs of the victims while making detailed notes of the investigation.

Ann was in mid-conversation with David when she overheard an officer making lewd remarks about her. She walked over to the officer and, in fluent Russian, rebuked him for his disrespectful comments. A deafening silence prevailed, and all eyes were fixed on her. Dimitri stepped forward and asked what had happened. Ann whispered in his ear. An angry exchange of words followed, and the officer was forced to say sorry to Ann. Dimitri apologised profusely for his colleague's unforgivable remarks and promised it would not happen again. Dimitri suggested they join him and Sergei for dinner. Ann accepted but requested they take her to the hotel first.

"Let's grab a drink before dinner," Ann suggested to David as they walked into the hotel reception.

"You're a dark horse, Guv, fluent in Russian – I never knew."

"It isn't as fluent as I would like. I learned it when a Russian student boarded with us and then learned it properly when I was training for MI6. I haven't spoken it for years, though."

"And that idiot's comments?" asked David.

"If you had heard what he said you would have punched him on the nose."

"Do you think Saskia's parents will help us to find her, Guv?"

"Don't know; they might refuse to cooperate if they think her life is in danger."

Dimitri and Sergei walked in through the swing doors of the hotel. Dimitri looked rather dashing in his dark blue suit, his tall, imposing frame filling every fold of his shirt as it defined his muscular torso. Sergei was less well dressed, having only changed his jacket. Outside, they were ushered into the car and were driven off. Dimitri continued to apologise for his colleague's inappropriate remarks. Ann reassured him she was made of sterner stuff and would not allow it to get her down.

They drove along the Boulevard, the road around the Kremlin that had stretches of park between the lanes, benches and statues of famous writers and revolutionaries. The roads were gridlocked with traffic. It required the skill of a racing driver to negotiate a path out. Sergei pointed out the places of interest and gave a brief history as they continued their stop-start journey. Dimitri spotted a parking slot at the embankment along the river and raced towards it with the tenacity of a stock car driver. The crooked outline of the rollercoasters of Gorky Park loomed across the dark water of the river as they emerged from the car. He suggested they walk the remainder of the way to the restaurant.

The Boulevard was populated with loud teenagers, boozers and prostitutes. A noisy din emanated from the floating restaurant as they approached. A band played Latin American music rather badly. They were intercepted by a waitress who motioned them to a table. Ann and David peered over the menus carefully, not wanting to choose something unpalatable. They settled for a lamb dish. Dimitri and Sergei chose the sturgeon shashlik. Their chosen side orders comprised Azeri pancakes with cheese aubergine rolls, filled with walnut stuffing and served with pomegranate sauce. All the food was washed down with copious amounts of vodka.

Their table was situated at a window, which afforded Ann the opportunity to see the imposing statue of Peter the Great beyond the bridge. Dimitri proposed a toast to the teams from the two countries, clinking their stumpy vodka glasses against David and Ann's.

"Na zdorovie!" said Sergei, which was promptly chorused by the other three.

They discussed the highs and lows of their careers and poked fun at their bullying superiors. The evening passed pleasantly and afforded them all the opportunity to get to know one another a little better.

After a while, Ann announced that she was exhausted and in need of a good night's sleep. The following morning, she woke up with a pounding headache as her body tried to flush out the excess of vodka.

"Never again!" she moaned to David as they met up in the hotel lounge.

David was also the worse for wear and likewise their hosts when they drove up to collect them. They were taken to Sergei's incident room where Ann and David met the rest of the CID team. There followed a detailed briefing on the case and the pair reminded the team that their sole mission in Moscow was to locate and interview Saskia who had vital information linked to the murders. Ann suggested to Sergei he divide his team into units, which would work more effectively in getting results. The meeting continued into the late afternoon. When they had finished, Sergei suggested they dine at a different restaurant to which Ann declined, still tired from the previous night. David, however, agreed and opted to eat at their hotel and meet with Dimitri and Sergei in the morning.

Sergei arrived to collect them the following morning in a well-heated car, and it was a long drive to Saskia's parents' home. Happy banter accompanied them on the journey. Dimitri familiarised them with the odd customs of Russian people. Sergei teased Dimitri for thinking he was more English than Russian.

"My English is perfect compared with Sergei's," joked Dimitri.

The group arrived at midday. Sergei knocked on the door and was greeted by a grey-haired man who called himself Boris. He invited them in and introduced them to his wife, Tatiana. She appeared frightened and nervous at the sight of so many police officers, but it helped to allay her fears when Ann spoke to her in Russian.

Next, they were invited to sit down whereupon tea and coffee was served. Sergei explained to the parents that the two police from the UK were in Moscow to speak to Saskia as she knew the people who were being investigated. Tatiana became very distressed at the mention of Saskia's name. Boris explained that Saskia had disobeyed her parents and, instead of going to university, she went to London since no word had been heard of her. Boris also clarified that he was working for the Russian space programme and was paid very well, so he could afford to educate his children and provide for them. He said they had a son, Yuri, who worked as a scientist and that Yuri still had contact with his sister. They gave Yuri's phone number to Sergei and the meeting continued into the early afternoon when Tatiana – now feeling much happier – served a lunch of herring, gherkins and homemade bread, washed down with a plentiful supply of beer.

Satisfied that they had gained a contact number, Ann and David thanked Boris and Tatiana for their hospitality and left. On the journey they discussed how they would approach Yuri to gain his trust and his fullest cooperation. Ann declined yet another dinner invite with Sergei, opting instead for her and David to eat alone to allow them time to review the details. Ann also wanted to update Edwards and Michael Heath on their progress.

Dimitri managed to contact Yuri who reluctantly agreed to meet with the police. The meeting was arranged for that evening when Yuri had finished work. He lived alone in a salubrious part of Moscow and the interior of his apartment was tastefully decorated. He was fluent in English but very pedantic in his approach. He asked many questions before answering theirs. He paused for a while before informing them that he had not spoken to Saskia for five years and that she was last working at a brothel for a man named Oleg Berezowski. Oleg was also a trafficker of young girls to wealthy businessmen, with a respectable club in Moscow where he lured the girls to dance, after which they disappeared. The police were on his payroll and so he never got caught.

Sergei shuffled uncomfortably in his seat when he heard that the police were involved in such nefarious practises. Yuri went on to say that he knew Saskia had two good friends whom she could trust at the club, a girl called Masha and a man called Vladimir. He said he did not have their contact numbers, but if the police went to the club as clients, they may find these people there. Sergei explained that Yuri would need to accompany them there as he could identify them. Yuri was hesitant to agree until some coercion from Ann.

David and Ann thanked Yuri and agreed to meet with him at the club at the weekend. It was decided that David would go there with Dimitri and Yuri.

The threesome arrived at the club at around 9pm. It was crowded with some very sleazy characters that appeared to be drinking lavish amounts of vodka and champagne. The girls working at the club were scantily dressed, tantalising the men with their curvaceous bodies and enticing them to spend lavishly.

After a little while the men were herded into a dimly lit corner; two women immediately began flirting with them. A large bottle of champagne was placed in an ice bucket on the table. One of the girls sat on David's lap and began kissing him. He played along, much to Dimitri's amusement at his discomfort at the unwanted attention.

Yuri asked the girl if she knew Saskia. She replied that Saskia had left and no longer worked there. He then asked if Vladimir still worked for the club. The girl became very nervous and told him she was not allowed to give information about the staff. Yuri lied to her, telling her that Vladimir owed him a favour and he handed her a wad of notes. She hesitated and looked around uneasily, telling them that they could wait at the back door when Vladimir went off duty at midnight. She then got up quickly and went to another table.

The group stayed until just before midnight, then left and headed for the back door. They waited patiently until, just as they were about to give up, a tall, thin man emerged from the building. He got into his car and drove off. The men followed at a discreet distance and followed him to what they assumed to be his home.

David advised them not to speak to Vladimir immediately, but to meet with Ann the next morning and first discuss a strategy.

Ann waited for David to get back as she was eager to hear how they had got along. She was pleased that David had exercised caution about approaching Vladimir.

The team met the next morning at the incident room. It was decided that, as Yuri knew of Vladimir, he should approach him about Saskia's whereabouts. When they asked Yuri, he was hesitant as he said it would place him in danger. Ann's unique persistence skills were rewarded and he finally agreed.

The team parked their car some distance from Vladimir's home. When he emerged to get into his car, Yuri stopped him and asked if he could spare five minutes to talk.

"Do you think I am Saskia's keeper?" Vladimir retorted angrily.

"Saskia has gone away. She no longer works for Oleg."

Yuri could tell he was lying. Then Vladimir pushed past Yuri, got into his car and sped off.

The team met with Ann at lunchtime. Dimitri suggested that they deal with Vladimir Russian-style. He proposed that they kidnap Vladimir's wife and children and force him to tell them where Saskia was being held. Ann opposed the idea.

"Ann, with respect," Dimitri began, "sometimes it calls for drastic measures if you want a result."

She pursed her lips.

"We will ensure the wife and children do not get hurt," Dimitri ensured.

She looked to David for support.

"It's your call, Guv," he said. "Sounds plausible to me if we need the information and they guarantee the family's safety."

"And when it goes wrong, it's *my* neck on the line," said Ann.

Dimitri said, "It is, how you say, killing two birds with one stone."

After some reservation, Ann finally agreed. They decided not to share the kidnapping plan with the rest of the CID team in case there was a mole in the police.

Dimitri and Sergei chose a disused building normally kept as a safe house. The kidnapping was scheduled for the next evening. They had already removed Vladimir's wife and three children from the house when he got home that evening.

The police took him at gunpoint. He swore and cursed all the way to the safe house. They took him into a separate room, next to the one where his wife was held. The team had a recording of his family's distress. He did not know they were the police, which intensified his fear. They told him that Oleg had taken Saskia from her family who had hired them to find her, even if it meant killing him and his whole family. They began beating him to prove that they meant business.

Vladimir denied all knowledge of Saskia, but when the screams of his children became intolerable, he agreed to give them information. He told them that Saskia was Oleg's mistress and lived with Oleg. He said that Oleg operated his human trafficking from a disused factory that he had renovated to suit his needs. He also said that Oleg had a helicopter that was kept on the roof of his building. He showed them on a map where the factory was located. He also knew how many armed guards were in the building and drew a map of the layout of the building. He told them that the only way into the building would be if they posed as clients interested in buying the girls who were on offer. He also said that the girls were sold for up to a million pounds each.

The interrogation went on for hours. Dimitri looked triumphant as they emerged from the building.

"Sadistic bastard," David said. "I hope you are not proud of the despicable method you used to extricate the information."

"You English are too soft," Dimitri said. "You should have been in the Russian Army. It would toughen you up."

David returned to the hotel where an anxious Ann waited.

"Got our information," he said, "but it was pretty tough for Vladimir."

Ann looked anxious. "Oh God, did they harm the children?"

"No, they just frightened them until their screams got him talking."

"I wish this was over; can't stand the tension." She looked at him, distress flickering in her eyes. "Come on, let's get some coffee sent to the room. I want to phone Josie and Adam."

When she got through to home, the voice on the other end of the line said, "Oh, someone must be missing me. What's with the early call?"

"I miss you so much," Ann said. "I wish I was home already."

"We miss you, too, even the baby," Josie said. "He just kicked when I mentioned your name."

Adam interrupted the call. "Hi sis, are they treating you well over there? When are you going to be back? We miss you."

"We're going to be awhile yet. You just take good care of my family."

"How is David?"

"He's working really hard."

"Tell him to take care of you."

"Will do. Speak soon. Love you lots." Ann clicked off the phone feeling a slight emptiness.

Ann and David met with the CID team the next morning. They did not reveal how they got their information but told the team that they knew where Saskia was being held. Ann spoke first. She informed them that David would pose as a client to buy the girls. Dimitri would act as his bodyguard. The team agreed. Sergei proposed that they access the building via an access hatch outside the protective fence surrounding the building. This hatch was situated in a disused area frequented by tramps. It had a lock and chain and was usually left unguarded; Oleg probably believed it posed no risk – only tramps regularly hung out at the area.

Sergei said, "David has 10 seconds to get from the outer door to the inner door before it shuts. We have no code to open the inner door."

"Who supplies funds for the girls?" Ann asked.

Dimitri held up his hand. "In Russia everyone needs a oligarch to take care of them. It is like a fixer who protects and provides when necessary. Our oligarch will give us the money. He has an old score to settle with Oleg. Money no problem."

"Thank God for that," Ann exclaimed. "Can you imagine what Edwards would have said if we asked for that kind of money?"

"His words would have been unrepeatable, to say the least," David said.

"I'll get David fitted with a designer suit," Dimitri said.

"Has anyone asked Vladimir to tell Oleg he will be away for a few days?" Ann asked.

"Yes, we got him to tell Oleg he was away as his mother is ill," Dimitri said. "Oleg accepted without question."

Ann nodded, pleased.

"OK, we'll schedule the assault for when the next sale of girls take place," Dimitri proposed. "Our computer geek has hacked into his secure site and has booked David a bidding slot as Alfred Gray."

The following hours were spent studying the arrangements in trying to anticipate potential problems.

"This is the final blueprint for our plan," Ann began. "David and Dimitri will enter the building with all the legal papers as potential clients. According to Vladimir, David will be shown to the viewing room where he will remain for an hour, choosing a girl. When he has made his choice, he will be shown to another part of the building where he will be given his phone and access to his laptop to transfer the payment for the girl into an offshore account. When he has done this, he will send a text message to myself and Sergei giving them their cue to attack. Dimitri will have joined David by this time, so he needs to send a coded message on his radio in case the phones are not working. David then announces that he needs to use the toilet, which is in the corridor opposite the door and security access to Oleg's apartment. Vladimir has given us the access code for the first door. The inner door will open but closes in 10 seconds when you have passed through the outer door.

"David will have to run like hell to get inside the apartment – we don't have the code for the inner door. Then, David will need to wait until the guard at the door does his half-hourly checks of the lower end of the corridor to get through the outer door. Sergei, you and your men will enter the tunnel via the disused car park. It is a 10ft drop so you will need ropes and fluorescent sticks to light up the tunnel. Prepare yourselves for fierce resistance."

Everyone nodded their approval of the plan. Ann added, "Please do say if there is anything you are concerned about."

Next, Sergei addressed his officers. "All your phones will be confiscated for the next three days except Ann's, Dimitri's and mine. Our officers will stay at a safe house and won't be allowed out in case we have a traitor amongst them."

David, Ann and Dimitri watched him speak, assimilating the information.

"On the day, at 7pm," Dimitri said, "Ann will travel with her team, all posing as the food delivery guys. She will hijack the real delivery men and tie them up in the back of the van. She will wait for David's signal and alert Sergei that she has started the assault on the entrance to the building. This should coincide with the time that David reaches Oleg's private suite."

He made a small movement with his hand.

"I will have to go in disguise as some of the guards are ex-soldiers and may recognise me," he explained. "Sergei has arranged for a make-up artist to disguise my face."

"OK, lads," Ann said, turning to head for the exit, "that about sums up everything. Time to head for home."

David followed her and hailed a taxi as they got to the street. "Rather exciting, wouldn't you say?"

"Yes, and bloody dangerous, too. Some of us could be killed."

Later, David was taken to the tailor for his suit and Dimitri visited the make-up artist. The rest of the team checked their firearms to make sure they were in good working order. Ann rechecked the schedule and ensured that everyone was familiar with the plan and timing.

David's suit was delivered on the morning of their departure. It was decided that Ann would go with the team in the food van and Sergei would accompany the team to the access hatch at the tunnel. David sauntered up to Ann wearing his chic grey designer suit with a royal blue shirt and gold tie. Ann gazed at him for a while, surprised that she had never noticed how handsome he looked; his muscular torso accentuated the lines of his immaculate suit and his groomed dark hair added the finishing touches. She sauntered up to him and adjusted his tie.

"Looking very handsome, Sergeant Hughes," she said. "You had better not get used to this life. Remember, it is only pretend." She smiled at his discomfort. Dimitri joined them, appearing mean and rugged. The make-up artist had done a great job.

"It's so bloody good; I am sure your mother would not recognise you," David observed.

"You look damned good, too," replied Dimitri, who glanced at his watch and said, "OK, we need to get going; we have to be there at six o'clock."

Ann waved to them and wished them good luck as they drove off in the smart black Bentley.

She phoned Josie and Adam to reassure them she was OK before starting her preparations for the assault. She then phoned Sergei to check that his men were ready. Satisfied that the plan was ready to be mobilised, she took a taxi to her rendezvous with her unit. Checking the map with the driver, they set off on their journey. They waited in a siding for the food van, which was scheduled for around 6.30 in the morning. It would take them 30 minutes to get to the factory. Their assault would be synchronised so that they would reach the gate of the compound simultaneously with Sergei's task force entering the tunnel via the disused car park. Ann organised the roadblock minutes before they spotted the vehicle entering the road they were patrolling. The van stopped at the roadblock. Ann, dressed in army uniform, instructed the driver to get out of the van, explaining in fluent Russian that they were authorised to check all vans for a fugitive on the run. The driver and his companion got out of the van. They were despatched swiftly by one of the police officers while the other police officers subsequently entered the van and crouched out of sight on the seats. Ann and the Russian sergeant sat in the front seat. The sergeant took the steering wheel. They synchronised their watches and sent a message to Sergei informing them they were on their way to the compound. He acknowledged their message. Meanwhile, David had already arrived at the compound, alighting from the Bentley. Dimitri followed him into the building. He was apprehended at the entrance and was asked for his papers.

A man dressed in a smart silk suit read through the papers and waved David into a hallway. A guard blocked Dimitri's entry and asked why he was with David. Dimitri explained he was David's bodyguard. The man in the suit motioned for Dimitri to follow David after checking Dimitri's credentials. They took David's laptop for safekeeping and told him he was only allowed the use of his laptop to transfer the money if he chose to purchase a girl.

David nodded his agreement and followed the man who led him to a kiosk. Dimitri was told to stay outside. The cubicle comprised of a window that looked out onto a centre stage. David sat silently, going over his role's strategy in his head. A bell sounded and 10 beautiful young women stepped onto a carousel in the centre of the stage. The carousel had vertical poles along the whole of its circumference. The girls wore no clothing except diaphanous gowns. A second bell rang and the girls each grabbed hold of a pole to begin a ritual of dancing. Their acrobatic actions were designed to show off their bodies' most intimate details to whet the appetites of their potential buyers.

David watched the girls for a whole hour before pressing his buzzer indicating that he had made his choice. A man appeared at the door of his cubicle and escorted him to another room. A smiling official met him who assured him he had made a good choice. He was handed back his laptop and began the process of transferring the £300,000 into Oleg's account. When he had finished, he asked to be shown the way to the toilet. He was pointed in the right direction and walked slowly, observing the guard who sat watching the entrance to Oleg's private quarters.

David entered the toilet and held the door ajar to watch the guard while he carried out his routine checks along the corridor. David rushed to the door, punched in the code and observed the inner door opening. He raced to get through it in the 10-second time span.

The suite seemed empty but, as he approached the living room, he saw a young woman sitting in a chair. She let out a gasp when she saw him and was about to scream when he moved forward and covered her mouth with his hand. She tried to struggle free. He spoke to her in a low voice telling her he was sent by Yuri. The mention of his name seemed to calm her, and she went silent.

With his back to the door, David didn't see the large hulk who crashed into him. The next thing he knew he was being catapulted across the room with mighty force. He picked himself off the floor and came face to face with a monster of a man. The bodyguard had found him. The giant figure lumbered towards him and lifted him into the air like a rag doll. He was literally thrown across the room where he smashed into a large mirror that shattered on impact. He quickly picked himself up and, using his body like a missile, lunged at the man. Instead of pushing his attacker from his feet, the man appeared to bounce off like a rubber ball. David grabbed any heavy missile he could find and threw it at the guard. His kicks and punches made no impact and the relentless assault on him continued. David then jumped on his assailant's back and sank his teeth into the big man's ear.

His attacker groaned in pain but continued punching David, getting the upper hand. He then held David in a headlock and began tightening his chokehold. David knew he had very little time before he would pass out. In one last desperate effort, he grabbed hold of a shard of the broken mirror on the floor and plunged it into his attacker's neck. A fountain of blood spurted from the hole the glass had made and, after a few seconds, the guard slumped to the floor – dead.

A man rushed into the room and called the girl by her name, Saskia. She had been cowering in a corner during the fight. He spotted David still lying on the floor. He took a shot at David with his gun, grabbed the girl by her hand and rushed out towards the escape tunnel. David was bleeding profusely from a wound in his chest. Just as he was despairing at the lack of backup, Dimitri entered the room.

"Where the hell have you been?" David demanded breathlessly.

Dimitri walked over to the dead guard and let out a whistle.

"Bloody hell; looks like you didn't need my help." He wore a look of amusement. "You killed the giant on your own in the Bible," he joked.

"You bastard!" David croaked, coughing up blood. "I am dying here, and you have time to joke?"

Dimitri merely looked down at him.

"Come on," David spluttered, "I think Oleg has taken Saskia and they're headed for the helicopter. We must stop them."

Dimitri helped David to his feet, and they hobbled along the corridor towards the helipad. They heard gunfire behind them. The wind generated by the helicopter engines nearly knocked them off their feet, and they ran towards it as it tried to take off, grabbing hold of the feet, clinging on as the machine hovered over the helipad.

The occupants in the helicopter began shooting at them. Dimitri began firing at the blades of the helicopter. Just when it seemed they were losing the battle, Sergei, Ann and the other officers appeared and managed to abort take-off. The pilot and Oleg were handcuffed and led away.

"Why on earth did you take so long?" David gasped.

"We had heavy opposition in the tunnel," Sergei replied. "We also had one hell of a fight with the guards at the front of the building. Not exactly a walk in the park."

"Come on," Ann urged, "we'd better get David to the hospital. How many dead amongst our chaps?"

"Five, I think," Sergei replied.

"Pity, there should have been none."

"Too bad, that's how it is," Dimitri said. "Our timing was perfect. We ambushed the van, got through the gate and surprised them. The captured guards were placed in handcuffs and put into police vans."

Ann accompanied Saskia to a safe house. David was sent to hospital. He had been shot in the right lung. Ann's fluent Russian helped to win over Saskia's confidence. A policewoman was then left to stay with her; Ann wanted to ensure that she had got over the shock of events that day before questioning her.

Ann declined Sergei's offer of vodka, wanting only a shower and a comfortable bed. She phoned Michael Heath to inform him that she had managed to find Saskia.

"Bloody good job," he said. "I hope Hughes did his bit."

"He was a hero, Sir. He got pretty badly injured; he's in hospital. We lost five officers."

"That's grim," replied Michael. "When will you be back?"

"Another couple of days, probably just as soon as David is well enough to travel. I will need you to arrange our papers to enter the UK, Sir."

"That will not be a problem," Michael said. "I will get them couriered to our embassy in Moscow where you can collect them."

"Thanks. I'll keep you posted."

The following morning, Ann and Dimitri went to check on David.

"Feels like I've been in a cement mixer," David groaned as they approached his bed. "A few broken ribs, lots of tissue damage and a lot of pain."

"Don't worry," assured Dimitri, smiling, "you won't die, and you killed Goliath."

"You were supposed to be my bodyguard," David said cryptically. "You arrived *after* the fight."

"Any idea when you'll be out?" Ann asked, not giving Dimitri any chance of explanation.

"They said I'd be here for a week," David replied.

"OK, I'll use the time to interview Saskia and visit you each day to keep you posted," Ann said. "I've reported to Michael who sends his best wishes."

"We can start the interview with Saskia this afternoon," said Dimitri.

"Does Sergei want to be present?" she asked him.

"No, he's recovering from a hangover and won't be at work till tomorrow."

Ann nodded in understanding.

"Come on, Ann," Dimitri began, "let me take you to lunch. Then we can meet with Saskia."

They mulled over the details of the forthcoming interview during a lunch of char-grilled beef burgers with rocket salad and French fries. They informed Yuri that they had found and rescued his sister. He was elated and wanted to see her urgently. Ann informed him they may ask for his presence; Saskia might be more willing to talk if her brother was in the room.

In the interview room, Saskia looked frail and anxious as they came through the door. Ann spoke to her in Russian, informing that she would only proceed with the interview if Saskia felt well enough to do so.

Saskia objected to Dimitri being present when Ann explained that it was imperative Dimitri remained in the room. Ann made her aware that the information they required was nothing to do with her time spent with Oleg, they needed to know about her time in England.

Saskia became distressed and refused to answer Ann's questions. As Ann had anticipated, she told Ann she would only speak if her brother was present.

Ann motioned Dimitri to follow her as she exited the room.

"We will have to get Yuri to be present when we talk to her. Can you phone him and ask if he is free to join us tomorrow?"

Dimitri nodded and took his leave.

Later, Sergei contacted Ann and asked her to join him for a working dinner. She was disinclined to agree, not wishing to be part of his lengthy drinking episodes. He chose a relatively quiet place and Ann was glad that Dimitri had been invited, too. She informed Sergei that they would only interview Saskia when her brother could be present. He appeared irritated at the delay and asked when her brother would be available.

Dimitri interrupted and confirmed, "Yuri has agreed to be present tomorrow afternoon."

Ann asked if they had released Vladimir and reunited him with his family. Sergei confirmed that this had been done and the family had moved to a safe house outside of Moscow. They would give Vladimir a new identity and move him to a place in Switzerland. He had agreed to testify against Oleg who would be charged with human trafficking, drug dealing and murder. Ann stated that if Saskia agreed to testify against the Casey brothers she would be flown to England and resettled somewhere of her choosing within Europe.

Soon after dinner, Ann explained that she needed to see David. Dimitri accompanied her to the hospital. They found him sitting outside of the bed.

"You seem to be recovering well, Sergeant Hughes," said Ann.

"Everything still hurts like hell," David said, shifting his position whilst bunching up his features in obvious discomfort.

Ann removed her shoulder bag and placed it on the bed.

"How did you get on with the interview?" David asked as he resettled in his chair.

"She's too traumatised to talk," Ann replied, drawing up another chair to sit opposite him. "She wants her brother to be present; he's agreed to be there tomorrow."

"Be interesting to hear her side of the story."

"Yes, I'm quite sure her version will be rather interesting." She looked at him. "You must be bored in here."

"Not too bad. Josie and Adam call regularly. Josie's excited about the baby, and Adam, too."

Ann laughed at that. "They're like a couple of teenagers at times." She looked thoughtful for a few seconds, glancing down at the bedcover. "Sometimes I wonder if they *should* spend so much time together."

David said nothing.

Ann picked up her bag and got to her feet. "I'd better let you get some rest now. I'll be back tomorrow to brief you on the interview."

Ann updated Edwards on their progress when she got back to the station.

Edwards informed her that preparations had been made for Saskia to be brought to London and that Ann could collect the papers from the embassy in Moscow.

She phoned Josie. "A little bird told me you have been phoning Moscow every day but, strangely, *I* didn't get a single call," she said.

"Oh, you're jealous I've been calling David to see how he is."

"You and Adam should let David recover, not bombard him with calls."

"So, who's rattled *you*? You shouldn't be causing anxiety to a woman in the late stages of her pregnancy, Inspector."

"Just you wait until I get home," Ann said with a hint of a chuckle. "I'll deal with you then."

"When *are* you coming home?"

"I think middle of next week if David is fit to travel."

Ann lay awake for a long time after the call thinking of her new role as a parent, with some trepidation. In the morning, she was in the middle of eating brunch when Dimitri came to collect her.

"Sorry I'm so late," she said, "I didn't get to sleep until the early hours of the morning and then I woke up late."

"Don't worry, I'll have some coffee while you finish your meal," Dimitri assured her.

Ann smiled her thanks and carried on eating.

"Yuri will be with us at 2pm," Dimitri added. "We set up the tape in Saskia's room."

"It will be better if I go in with Yuri," Ann said. "You'll be able to listen to our interview in the next room."

Dimitri agreed and, after she had finished eating they went to meet Yuri, took him to Saskia and left them alone for a while. When he indicated that it was alright for Ann to join them, she did so. Saskia had been crying and Yuri was also tearful.

Timing her questioning carefully, Ann began by telling Saskia that George and Tom Casey had been murdered. She explained that she needed to know if there were other men who joined their parties at the house and whether Saskia knew any of them.

Saskia hesitated for a long time before answering. She told Ann

MURDER MOST EXTREME

that she met George Casey at a local pub. He invited her to his home where she was introduced to his brothers Tom, Jake and Nathan. During her association with the brothers, she was thrown out of her accommodation as she was not able to pay. George offered her a room at his family home. In return, she kept the house clean and did the shopping to earn her keep. This worked fine for a short while, but then one night Tom seduced her. The brothers, she explained, had parties at their home to which they invited lots of foreign girls. The parties would go on till the early hours of the morning and they had sexual orgies with the girls, including herself.

She took a breath and steadied herself for a few seconds, trying to maintain her composure before continuing. She explained how she had become pregnant and was very worried; she had no job to support a baby. She was then approached by their cousin, James Muller, who said that if she was prepared to abort her baby to help medical science, she would be paid. Saskia described how she readily agreed – she thought it would help her out of a dilemma and believed she was doing something good for medicine. The baby was subsequently aborted at 24 weeks and taken away. After that, they continued to have sex with her, and she fell pregnant again six months later. The same offer was made to her, and the baby taken away.

Her cousin, Olga, who had come to England also found herself in financial difficulties. She sought help from Saskia who asked the brothers if Olga could stay at their home. They agreed, but soon they were having sex with Olga and got her pregnant, too, aborting and taking her baby away, also. This happened four more times.

Saskia explained how, one day, she heard Olga having a heated argument with James about the abortions during which Olga told him she was not going to have another abortion and threatened to tell the police. James, she said, grabbed Olga by her hair and warned her that if she went near the police, he would kill her.

Saskia appeared to stiffen whilst reliving the experience. The same night, Saskia said she found a tunnel leading from the house to the forest. She realised she was following the brothers who were wearing black hooded cloaks. They gathered around a tree trunk in the forest and placed Olga's body on the tree trunk. Olga seemed

233

drugged as she lay very still. Another hooded figure in red appeared and all the others called him 'Master' and chanted as he approached. The master got on top of Olga and began having sex with her. When he had finished, he plunged a dagger into her chest and cut her throat. He collected her blood in a cup, drank it and passed the cup around to the other figures. They cheered and gave thanks to Satan. Tears began rolling down Saskia's cheeks as she recalled this event. She was shaking and asked to be allowed to stop. They gave her a break for an hour before asking to resume the interview.

"Did you see what he did with Olga's body?" Ann asked as gently as she could.

"No. I had to hide before they spotted me," Saskia replied. "I waited until they'd all gone out the next day, then I took some money belonging to George Casey and bought a ticket back to Moscow."

Saskia then proceeded to tell Ann that there were some Irish girls who were also made pregnant and had had their babies taken away. Ann asked if all the brothers were present at this meeting in the forest. She said that Nathan never got involved in any of the sexual acts or the meeting that night. She saw Tom, George, Jake and James dress in the black cloaks but did not know the identity of the master.

Ann enquired if there were any other names that Saskia remembered and she replied that the brothers did not allow any other men to join their circle of debauchery.

At that point, Yuri asked for the questioning to stop as he thought his sister was becoming distraught. Ann agreed, apologising for putting Saskia through such a rigorous interview, assuring him of her safety. He thanked her for all she had done to rescue his sister and left.

Dimitri shook his head at what he had heard when Ann joined him in the next room.

"Shit," he said, "I thought the Russians were sadistic bastards, but the English don't seem far behind."

"If she agrees to testify, I'm going to nail that bastard James Muller's arse," Ann said. "Problem is, we need to find him first. Come on, let's go tell David."

Once they'd caught up with David he asked, "Well, did she spill the beans?"

"Every gory detail," replied Ann. "James Muller – top of the hit parade."

"Have you told Edwards yet?" David asked.

"No, I'm going to phone him when I get back to the hotel. And you hurry up and get better, we have a great deal of work to do."

When she phoned Edwards, on the one hand he sounded relieved that her witness had given her the information she needed but he did not compliment her on her achievement. Michael Heath, on the other hand, was chuffed about Ann's success and showered her with compliments. Dimitri stayed with David after Ann had left.

"Your boss is quite some woman," he said. "Tough as the best of my Russian guys. She's good-looking and has a great body, too. How do you keep your mind on your work?"

"She is great to work with," David replied cautiously, "and her conduct demands respect and the cooperation of her team." He let out the lightest of chuckles. "A guy doesn't dare think of anything else."

"Come on, you're a man first and foremost. You can't say you haven't noticed her legs and her gorgeous figure?"

"Look," David said with an emphatic gesture of his hands, "stop right there. Ann is married to a lovely lady, and they are expecting a baby. And I'm warning you, don't breathe a word I told you about this."

Dimitri arched his brows, ignoring David's threat. "What a shame. Doesn't she like guys at all?"

"No, and don't go stirring up trouble by assuming anything." He studied Dimitri with a frown. "Enough about Ann; let's talk about something that will be of greater interest to you."

Dimitri regarded him.

"Ann wants you to travel with us because I am not fully recovered and Saskia will need protection. I want you to meet Ann's brother, Adam. He's a journalist with a great deal of experience in capturing fugitives. He has international links with important people. When Ann and I go in search of James Muller in Brazil, Adam will be joining us, but Ann doesn't know about this." He paused to make sure Dimitri was listening. "I will ask Adam if you can be included in our team as we will need your army skills. You must remember not to speak about any of this in Ann's presence. I'll find the time when you're in London to get Adam to speak to you in private."

Dimitri nodded.

David added, "Speak to Sergei and warn him that Ann wants you to accompany us to London."

Dimitri waved away David's words with his hand. "Sergei won't stop me going, I have some leave owed to me and he won't need to find the money for my ticket; I was saving to go to Italy for my leave, but I'll go to London instead."

"OK," David nodded, "but remember – not a word to Ann until I have spoken to her."

***

Ann made the final arrangements for their return to London and was assured by the doctor that David would be fit to travel. David persuaded Ann to have Dimitri accompany them to London, too. She agreed, albeit reluctantly, telling David she was sure that he had conspired with Dimitri to accompany them. She arranged with Michael to organise a safe house for Saskia and accommodation for Dimitri, thanked Sergei for his help and support, and departed.

They arrived to a rainswept London. Michael and Edwards met them at the airport; they took Saskia to the safe house and the female Russian policewoman stayed with her. Ann, David and Dimitri were driven to Ann's home. Josie beamed at the door when she saw Ann. She hugged and kissed her while David and Dimitri exchanged glances, David's more as an 'I told you so'. Adam appeared a few minutes later, Ann made the introductions and invited Dimitri to make himself at home.

"Wow, sis," Adam greeted her, "I see you've managed to steal the best officer in the Russian police."

Dimitri and David laughed.

"You must be starved," Josie interrupted them. "Come and sit down; I've cooked dinner."

She ushered them to the table then grabbed Ann by the hand and led her to the kitchen where she embraced her. "I have missed you so much."

Ann did not pull away as quickly as she usually did but pressed Josie close and reciprocated the feeling. This propelled Josie to take hold of Ann's hand and place it on her stomach.

"Feel the baby kicking."

Ann indeed felt the baby move and smiled.

"Only a month to go," Josie said.

Ann kissed her again.

"Hey, does anyone care about the starving lot out here?" Adam shouted.

Ann gritted her teeth.

"Perhaps if the fellow with the big mouth volunteered to help, he might not starve!" Ann shouted back.

Adam rushed to the kitchen to help them carry the food to the table. David served the wine and the evening passed convivially enough.

After the meal, Dimitri was taken to a bed and breakfast near Ann's home. Adam offered to take David home, which he accepted. During the journey, David updated Adam on his conversation with Dimitri and they agreed to set up a meeting with him. As David was still recovering, he was not expected to attend at work for another week.

Josie noticed the bruises on Ann's body as she came out of the shower.

"Oh God, look what they've done to your body!" she exclaimed.

Ann swiftly reached for a towel to hide the marks.

"It's nothing, just a few bruises," she said a little too brusquely, relieved that the trip to Moscow had given her a convenient alibi. They talked about the imminent birth until the early hours of the morning.

When Ann arose to go to work she felt the absence of David and his prompt arrival in the morning. Her office had a cold emptiness about it with her in-tray stacked high with mail. She leaned back in her chair and savoured the cup of coffee that had been brought to her by one of the junior staff.

The ringing of her phone jolted her. It was Michael.

"Can we meet with Stephen this afternoon? He's rather keen to hear the tape."

"Where are we meeting?"

"My office is more private. Say around 2.30?"

She agreed and Michael arranged for lunch to be brought to his office for their meeting. Ann played the interview recording with Saskia. The two men listened in silence at the revelations on the tape. Michael praised Ann for her diligent work and success in rescuing Saskia. She paid tribute to the Russian police and expressed regret at the loss of life for which Edwards was quick to condemn her, despite her explaining how the rescue had occurred in exceptional circumstances.

"What happens next?" Edwards asked impatiently.

"Well, we need to have another search of the Casey property in Nottingham," Ann replied. "We must find the link to the forest and get SOCO to examine the garden and the basement again. If they were killing babies, there must be human remains on the property."

Edwards stared at her as if expecting more.

"I'll get my team to hear the tape and we will plan our next move from there," she said. "Can both you and Michael be available at the incident room tomorrow morning at eight o'clock, please?" They agreed and she left.

Meanwhile, Adam, David and Dimitri met at David's flat. David supplied the beers while they chatted. Adam filled Dimitri in on their plan and asked him to add his thoughts.

"How much does Ann know about your involvement, Adam?" Dimitri asked.

"Nothing; she'll do her nut if she finds out and demand that I'm pulled off the job."

Dimitri rubbed his chin thoughtfully.

"Look, I'll arrange a meeting with our MI6 man," Adam continued, "and work out a plan to include you. Your military background will be a bonus to our mission."

Dimitri nodded.

Adam asked, "Do you think Sergei would agree to your involvement in this, and if so, who would pay for your airfare and other arrangements?"

"You forget I have an oligarch who will fund me and I will use my leave to stop questions being asked by powers above Sergei."

"We need to have your total commitment because it's going to be a major project, especially as Mossad is involved," Adam said. "They will insist on a strong commitment with attention to detail because they want their man, so no mistakes," Adam warned him, looking at him closely. "I also want to organise a meeting with us, MI6 and Rachel, our Mossad link, while you are here."

Dimitri agreed.

Adam turned to address David.

"David, you will need to dream up a plausible excuse to get away from Ann for a few days. Be bloody convincing so that Ann's antennae don't rumble you."

Dimitri smiled. "Your sister is an incredible woman," he said, and added a little ruefully, "I wish she didn't have someone in her life. Perhaps I could have changed her mind."

Adam grinned. "Wild horses would not be able to drive her away from her commitment to her relationship with Josie," he said, "especially with a baby on the way."

Dimitri managed the semblance of a smile and looked regretful.

Adam said, "Well, we had better leave now to get home and avoid a thousand questions before Ann gets there first. And Josie is preparing dinner."

"Give me some time to shower and change, then I'll join you," David said.

"Get a move on with it – we'll wait in the car."

When they arrived at Ann's home, Josie asked, "So what have you boys been up to all day?"

"Just driving around," Adam replied with a laconic smile. "We showed Dimitri some of the sights and then stopped off for a pub lunch."

"OK, well, make yourselves useful," Josie said. "Set the table. Ann will be here in half an hour."

David was about to take a seat in the living room when Josie added, "David, you can serve the drinks while we are waiting."

Ann arrived carrying a stack of files. Adam took them from her then kissed her on the cheek. "Good day at the office, sis?"

"Frantically busy and I missed having David around." She

turned towards him. "I want you to come to the team meeting tomorrow, David," she said.

"There will be no talk about work until after dinner," Josie ordered to which Ann relented.

"So, how did *you* spend today?" she asked Dimitri.

"I had a very interesting day," he responded. "The boys showed me around."

"Good," Ann said, immediately relaunching into a work topic, "you are welcome to join us at the CID meeting tomorrow. We will discuss our time in Moscow and reveal the contents of the tapes."

"I will look forward to meeting your team," Dimitri replied.

Josie frowned at her.

"Sorry, I just wanted to catch Dimitri before he was whisked off by Adam," Ann said, noticing the black look on Josie's face.

***

"Good morning team," Ann greeted those gathered. "I would like to introduce you to Detective Sergeant Dimitri Zhukov. He played a significant role in the rescue of our witness, Saskia, in Moscow."

Dimitri stood up in acknowledgement of Ann's introduction.

"I am going to play the relevant parts of the recording of my interview with Saskia," Ann went on. "This young woman is very nervous and afraid. She will remain at the safe house with a Russian female member of their CID team. The man who was her lover and kept her a virtual prisoner was arrested. Sadly, five of the squad members died in the rescue of Saskia. I have passed our condolences and gratitude to their families." She paused for a few seconds, looking at them, and then said, "The whole recording is too long to play in full, but you will gather enough information from the parts I am playing."

The team listened in silence and only voiced their opinions when the parts about sacrificing the foetuses were revealed. Ann called them to order, appealing for patience. When the tape had finished, some members of the team flung a barrage of questions at Ann.

"What's the next step, Guv?" asked DI Tobin.

"Well, we need to visit the Casey family home. I am sure there are remains of the babies under the floor or in the grounds. They must have buried them somewhere. I will speak to the CID squad at Sherwood Forest," Ann told him. "I will also meet with the forensics archaeologist. The murderer of the babies is James Muller according to Saskia. He may also have murdered her cousin, Olga. Whatever the search uncovers in Nottingham, it will point us in the next direction. And a trip to Brazil is on the cards, as we have no guarantee that Muller will return to the UK."

Tobin nodded.

"By the way," Ann began, looking at Tobin, "has Jake Casey woken up yet?"

"No; he's stable, but still unconscious."

Ann walked back to her office with Dimitri and David. On the way she collected coffee from the machine for all of them and invited Dimitri to join them in the office.

"Your team are very enthusiastic," commented Dimitri.

"They are eager to solve the case," Ann said, looking at him. "We've been severely criticised by the press on our delay. I'm glad we found Saskia; I'm sure we'll find clues in Nottingham, too, and I'm sorry you won't be here when the search takes place."

"But I will be here for two weeks," Dimitri replied, smiling pleasantly. "Perhaps I'll go with them."

"What about you, David?" Ann asked. "Will you be well enough to go to Nottingham?"

"I have another week of sick leave, Guv."

"Damn, I could have done with you."

"Dimitri would be a good replacement."

"Don't shirk your responsibilities, Hughes," Ann said, smiling at his discomfort. "All that play-acting in an Armani suit could go to your head."

She quickly adopted a more serious tone.

"Get me the forensics archaeologist on the phone. Let's arrange a meeting. Also, I need to speak to the Nottingham squad."

She managed to arrange a meeting with the archaeologist in two days' time. The Sherwood Forest DCI said he would organise a SOCO team to meet with Ann at the house in three days.

"Pain or no pain, I want you at my meeting with the

archaeologist," Ann said to David. "And don't look so miserable, I will bribe you with dinner tonight."

David left with Dimitri while Ann had a chat with Edwards.

***

The archaeologist, Phillip Chambers, stretched back in his chair after listening to the tape.

"You've got a bloody complicated case," he said. "How sure are you that we will find human remains on the property? What if they were dumped in the forest?"

"I am damned sure we will find remains around the property," Ann said, "because those pig-headed murderers thought they were unstoppable and that nobody would dare to descend on their property while they were living there."

Phillip acknowledged her reply. "Sounds feasible," he said. "When do we start?"

"Tomorrow. I am meeting with the Nottingham CID who did the first search. We'll need to check out the forest where they had their satanic meetings, too."

Ann looked at him steadily.

Phillip said, "I will call you when we arrive, and you can inform Nottingham of our involvement."

Ann nodded. "Yes, we will keep in touch and make the final plans when we meet in Nottingham."

***

"She's like a child going to the fun fair when she goes on these missions," said Josie as she noted Ann's hyperactive frame of mind.

"Hmm," Adam snorted, "she never takes her beloved brother anywhere on her adventures."

"Has anyone reminded you that you are *not* a member of the CLPD?" Ann replied. "And as an imminent uncle, you also have paternal responsibilities."

"Quite right, too. Come on," Josie said, "I'll start putting the dinner on the table."

After dinner, Adam suggested the men accompany him to the pub as Josie and Ann had declined the invite. Ann helped Josie with the washing-up when they then retired to bed whereupon Ann rubbed Josie's large abdomen.

"Not long to go now," she said, with genuine tenderness.

"Are you going to be with me at the birth?"

"I will do my utmost to be there, my darling," Ann replied.

Josie seemed to accept this and did not respond.

"Hey, we talked about you setting up Amy to find the rat who is their informant," Ann said, seeing Josie's slightly clouded expression. "Do you think you will be up for arranging that soon, because we don't want classified information getting out, especially with our new quest in the investigation?"

"I'm sorry, I haven't been able to arrange it yet. So many things have happened that have prevented me from setting up the perfect scenario." Josie appeared a little forlorn. "But I will get onto it soon when you leave for Nottingham." She lifted her head and said more brightly, "You can pay me in kind, in advance."

"Devious little madam," Ann said. She smothered Josie in kisses. "You always know which buttons to press."

Ann and Dimitri set out early the next morning. Ann outlined the plan to search the Casey property. She updated Dimitri about what the police had discovered during the last search. He added his views and made a few suggestions about finding the tunnel based on his experience when he served during the Serbian conflict.

"When do you suppose you will travel to Brazil?" Dimitri asked.

"A great deal will depend on our findings at the Casey home," Ann replied, "as well as finance and the assembly of our task force."

Dimitri glanced briefly across at her.

"Anyway, you need not concern yourself with our mission in Brazil. Your team have helped enormously by assisting us to find Saskia."

"I disagree." He braked slightly and glanced in his driving mirror as the car in front slowed to indicate. "This case is as much ours, too, because if Muller *has* murdered Olga, who is Russian, you cannot exclude us from further involvement in the case."

Ann blinked. She wore an irritated expression.

"Hmm, forgive me for thinking that David Hughes has opened his big mouth to persuade you to speak to me about Brazil."

Dimitri's hands tightened slightly on the steering wheel. "Yes, David and I talked, but I decided that we should be part of the Brazil trip as a Russian national has been murdered and we have as much right to have a say in the matter. Let's face it; Muller's capture will not be a walk in the park. You will need personnel skilled in armed combat. I have a military background and have seen active service for many years." He frowned. "If you are taking on the drug cartel, you will need the expertise of guys who can do the job and survive. Your two DEA guys and the Mossad team will need some extra help. I have some leave and my oligarch will finance my trip."

"Bloody hell, you *have* been well informed. I am not refusing help, but it's not up to me." Ann looked ahead. "My Super, the MI6 and Interpol chaps will need to consider your involvement." Ann turned to look outside of the passenger window. "Anyway, your wife will be appalled if we drag you into this dangerous mission. What will we tell her if you are killed?"

"I am divorced." Dimitri glanced in his rear-view mirror. "I have two teenage children who live with their mother. I have a very good relationship with my ex-wife. She knows my work has many dangers."

"I am not promising anything," Ann said. "You will need to wait until I have spoken to my superiors." She faced him. "We are approaching Nottingham. We will rendezvous at the Casey home. Watch out for the turnoff towards the forest."

When they reached the Casey property the Nottingham DCI, SOCO and the forensics archaeologist met them. Ann introduced Dimitri to the assembled group and gave a brief account of his involvement in the case. The group was split up into teams, with Ann suggesting that they should start their search in the cellar where she believed they might locate the entry to the secret tunnel. The archaeologists began their search using ground-penetrating radar in the rose garden and the grounds of the house.

Ann surveyed the walls of the cellar, looking for a possible concealed entry to the tunnel. She leaned against the side of the bookshelf and accidentally pushed a lever that resulted in a grinding noise as the bookshelf moved aside and gave way to the mouth of a gaping dark tunnel. There were excited shouts as the officers rushed towards the sound. Calls for lights followed as the officers gingerly proceeded into the tunnel. They walked into spider webs thick with dust and dirt as they made their way cautiously down the tunnel. Solid steel frames securely supported the roof and tunnel sides. The tunnel continued for half a mile before they reached the end.

"Look for a lever," Ann instructed, looking up towards the roof of the tunnel. "It must be the exit hatch just above your heads."

They shone their torches, searching anxiously for a lever.

"Here; this must be it!" exclaimed one officer, pulling on a long steel handle.

A grating sound and a moving shaft revealed the exit to the tunnel. They clambered out into the forest and found themselves at the cut-off tree trunk used by the Satanists in their rituals.

"Right, get SOCO to take samples of everything on the altar. Get us some better lighting. We need to examine the inside of the tunnel properly," Ann ordered.

The SOCO teams split themselves into groups so that there were officers collecting and photographing samples in the cellar, in the tunnel and in the forest. Ann returned to the archaeologist, anxious to know if they had located any human remains.

"The tunnel led to the forest. Any luck on your find, Phillip?" she enquired.

"I am afraid not, Ann," he replied. "We've checked the ground at the front and side of the house."

"Oh, I've just had a thought," Ann said. "These Casey brothers did not respect life but, according to their neighbour, they were very meticulous about their rose garden. Why would a bunch of murderers care about gardening so much?"

"You have a point there. I'll start with the rose garden in the morning. I'll have to wrap up now as the light is fading. Care to join me for dinner?"

"Thanks, but I already promised to have a drink with the Nottingham squad," Ann replied politely.

Ann collected Dimitri and went off to the pub. She left for her hotel as soon as she knew Dimitri was comfortable amongst the other officers. Early the next morning she collected a rather hungover Dimitri and drove to the Casey home. Phillip already had the equipment lined up to search the rose garden. Ann's hunch was duly rewarded as the radar revealed a vast collection of human bones beneath the soil.

The large area was divided into rectangular grids. The forensics archaeology team set about excavating the ground. They worked with trowels and brushes, carefully sweeping away the sand around the bones and using sieves to sift the soil. Ann greeted the find with a mixture of triumph and sadness – there were so many skeletons of babies. Three hours later, they uncovered the skeleton of an adult.

"How long do you think they have been buried?" she questioned.

"I would hazard a guess at 10 years," Phillip told her.

He examined the pelvis of a skeleton and declared it was that of a female.

"Do you know whom the skeleton might have belonged to?" he probed.

"I don't know but it might be Olga, the Russian girl, or an Irish girl who went missing after she met the Casey brothers. God knows whom they ensnared in their den of iniquity."

She surveyed the scene.

"How long do you think you will take to unearth the entire area?"

"Probably two to three weeks," Phillip informed her.

"OK, I'll hang on for a few days until SOCO has completed their work, then return to London," she responded. "We'll await your findings with great anticipation."

The team gathered at the pub at the end of the fifth day of the search. They were in buoyant mood and toasted their success with copious amounts of alcohol. Ann was shocked at Dimitri's consumption of alcohol. She intervened when she thought he had drunk too much and frogmarched him to the car to the cheers of the other officers. Dimitri was barely able to stand when they got to their hotel. He put his arm around Ann's shoulders to steady himself. When they got to his room, Ann opened the door, but Dimitri paused and leaned with all his weight against her. He embraced and kissed her, muttering endearments in Russian. His powerful arms held Ann for a few moments before she was able to break free and push him away. She led him to the bed and hastily left the room.

She stood outside his room momentarily catching her breath and chiding herself for allowing him to kiss her. When she got to her room, she phoned Josie.

"How are you, my darling? I miss you and the baby."

"Uncle Adam and I are just sitting here talking about you. When will you be home?"

"On Sunday."

"Was your trip successful?" Adam yelled down the phone from his position further away.

"It was fine," replied Ann stiffly, with obvious annoyance.

It was a very subdued, embarrassed Dimitri who joined Ann for breakfast the next morning.

"I am so sorry about my behaviour last night," he groaned, hanging his head low. "Please forgive me, Ann."

"So, the alcohol did not affect your memory." It was a statement, not a question.

He looked up at her.

"I will never cross that line again."

"You know, I thought you were different," Ann said, disregarding his pledge. "All the men I have met disapprove of my relationship and are under this misguided belief that if I slept with them, I would change my preference in an instant. I want you to remember that our relationship will only be a professional one. You are not my friend. Please remember that."

They finished the breakfast in silence and journeyed to the excavation site. Phillip had found a third adult female skeleton. The neat back garden looked like a bomb site with heaps of soil, sieves, bags and men milling about with equipment and cameras. Ann collected copies of the photographs taken at the house and set off with Dimitri back to London. Ann's first stop was at Edwards' office. He was very pleased with their progress and even managed to compliment Ann on her find. He arranged a meeting with Michael

Heath later that day. She asked David to be present at the meeting.

Michael invited them to join him for lunch at his private members' club. He gushed with pride as Ann revealed their findings.

"We'll have a meeting with the team as soon as we have all the information from SOCO," she advised. "The forensics team will take at least three weeks to process their findings. We will release the information as it unfolds."

"What is your next move?" asked Michael.

"Well, based on the information we have, Saskia's testimony and what we find at Nottingham, we have a strong case to go after James Muller."

"I don't know where the hell you think the funds are coming from," protested Edwards.

"Oh God, be reasonable, Stephen," intervened Michael. "We are on the brink of achieving the most amazing result and all you can worry about is the cost."

"There is another issue I wish to discuss with you," Ann said. "Going after Muller will not be easy. We have assembled a good team, but I had a request from Dimitri who wants to join us because he says if Saskia's cousin, Olga, *has* been murdered, then the Russians have a legitimate role in joining us."

Edwards exploded with rage.

"Why on earth does *he* want to tag along and who is going to pay for *him*?"

"He has leave and will be funded by an oligar–"

"Hold on; before we all get hot under the collar," Michael interrupted, "let's check with MI6 and Interpol if they will allow Dimitri to join us."

Ann turned to look at Michael.

"Ann," he said, "you brief Tobin and the rest of the team sometime tomorrow. Take the rest of the day off. You have earned it."

"Thanks, Sir. I'll keep you posted."

At that, Ann and David left together, with Michael also leaving for home, giving Edwards no chance to interfere further.

"This is all your fault, David," Ann said to him on the way. "You couldn't keep your trap shut. You just had to share classified information with Dimitri who did not hesitate in telling me about the great Brazilian adventure."

"He was persistent in his questioning."

"Yes, and while he tightened the thumb screws, you simply could not stop yourself spilling the beans."

"Sorry, Guv, I just thought he might be useful, owing to his experience."

"You could have had the courtesy to ask me before speaking to him."

David looked contrite. "I *am* sorry, Guv; it won't happen again."

Ann merely glanced at him, seeming to accept his apology.

David said, "I have good news for you, though. Josie got Julie to hook up with Amy. She swallowed the story hook, line and sinker and Julie was able to plant the bugs in Amy's home. We have gathered interesting information but not been able to nail the informer."

"Great, I'm sure we will find the mole," Ann said. "You'd better collect Dimitri on the way home."

When the group arrived back at her home, Josie was delighted to see them so early, and especially Ann.

"Where is Adam?" she asked.

"He'll be home at six," Josie replied. "He went to meet a friend."

"You and David keep Dimitri company," Ann instructed. "I have some paperwork to do."

Just after six, Adam entered the house.

"Hey, this is nice," he said. "Did you enjoy the hospitality of the northerners, Dimitri?"

"I did. They are very much friendlier than the people in London."

Ann joined them, hugging Adam as she entered the living room.

"Dinner smells great," said Adam, sniffing the air.

"Yes, you can do the salad and get someone to help you serve the dinner," Josie suggested, sinking into an armchair.

"We might have to carve out room for your tummy at the table," Adam observed, patting Josie's growing abdomen.

"Come on," said Ann, "stop messing about. I'll help you with serving the dinner."

After dinner, Adam took Dimitri and David home while Ann stayed behind with Josie and cleared up, catching up on their news.

Meanwhile, the boys stopped off at the pub on the way home.

"Wow, your sister is frightening when she's angry," Dimitri said.

"And what caused her anger?" Adam asked.

"I was drunk, and I kissed her," Dimitri confessed.

"What? Are you insane?" Adam's eyebrows shot up. "You're lucky you escaped with your balls intact."

"She waited until I was sober to inflict her venom."

"Look here, my friend," put in David, "don't you ever do that again." His voice became stern. "Ann does not deserve such disrespect. I told you she is committed to her relationship. Forcing yourself on her will alienate you. You don't want Ann to be your enemy, I promise you."

"Sorry guys, it won't happen again." He looked away, appearing shamefaced, and then back at David. "I talked to Ann about the Brazil trip."

"Yes, you bloody idiot *again*," David said. "She wiped the floor with me about that."

"I don't believe in beating about the bush as your English say. I approached her head on as I want to be included in your team for Brazil. She said she would check with her superiors and get back to me."

"We can expect a meeting with all involved quite soon," Adam said.

"Yes, I think she will want to meet while I am here," Dimitri replied.

Adam said, "I had better warn Rachel at Mossad. She'll want to be present at the meeting."

The men chatted late into the night, making tentative plans for their roles in the Brazil trip.

In the morning, the shrill ringing of the phone jolted Ann from her sleep.

"Have you seen the papers?" It was David.

"No, why the hell would I be reading the papers at this time *and* on my day off?"

"Get hold of a copy of *The World News*; you'll see what I mean. See you later."

Curiosity piqued, Ann hurriedly dressed and dashed to the local newsagent to buy a newspaper. Emblazoned on the front page was the heading: 'Russian woman provides police with vital information regarding family serial killing'.

As she raced home, she couldn't stop the flurry of expletives circling around her tongue.

"Fucking Amy. I could kill her!" she shouted out when she got home.

"What on earth is going on?" Josie asked, looking bleary-eyed as she walked down the stairs.

"Read this!" ordered Ann, slamming the paper on the table.

"Oh, I see." Josie peered at the print. "I guess Edwards will have your head for this."

"You can bet on it and it's that rat who is to blame. When we catch him or her, I will personally deal with them."

The doorbell rang. Ann went to the door.

It was David.

"I don't care what methods you employ," Ann said, "I want the bastard who is leaking this information caught. And this places Saskia in grave danger."

"Julie has put the bugs in place, Guv. It will just be a matter of time before we catch the mole."

Ann's phone rang. It was Edwards blaming her for the newspaper headlines. She explained that her team were in the process of catching the informer. He ignored Ann's explanation, berating her for her incompetence. She slammed down the phone, vowing to punish Edwards for all the abuse she had endured. Josie and David calmed her down and pledged their support.

Ann then received the results from SOCO following the search at Nottingham. She called a team meeting requesting that Edwards and Michael also be present.

"We have the results from Nottingham," she said to the assembled group. "Numerous samples of human and animal blood, hair and skin were found in the cellar, tunnel and the altar. There was writing in Russian on the wall inside the tunnel that read: 'They have killed my babies, and I am afraid they are going to kill me. Someone, please help me. Olga.'" She dug her hands into her pockets. "Olga is Saskia's cousin and someone Saskia believes had been murdered by James Muller. The forensics team are still busy finding out the identities of the three adult female skeletons found in the rose garden. There were 35 foetal skeletons found with items of clothing, knives and pairs of gloves. The foetal skeletons had knife marks on the frontal surfaces of the cervical vertebra suggesting their throats were cut, possibly during the rituals." Ann paused, removed her hands from her pockets and took a deep breath.

"Two of the female victims had knife marks on their ribs and sternums suggesting the knives were plunged into their chests. They will have died instantly due to a puncture of their aortas. The third woman was strangled, and a ligature was found around her neck."

Silence was followed by sighs of indignation and whispers of disbelief that such barbarism still existed.

"Please keep your opinions to yourself," Edwards said loudly. "You are here to solve the crime, not to express your personal feelings."

The team asked numerous questions and Ann tried to answer them as best she could.

"Have you been able to track down Mary O'Reilly?" Ann asked Tobin.

"No, Guv, but we've spoken to neighbours who knew her cousin – both girls had not been seen for the past 10 years. Family have said that the girls were very wayward and left Ireland to live in London. They stayed with an aunt in Nottingham for a while but when they got involved with the Casey brothers, they had an argument with the aunt who threw them out. We have put numerous appeals in the papers with their photographs, but nobody has come forward yet."

"Have you checked the death register?"

"Yes – no luck. Not even in Ireland," Tobin responded.

"OK, we will let you know what happens next. We have a mole in our midst. Further information will not be released. You will all be informed on a need-to-know basis."

The team dispersed and Ann, David, Edwards and Michael proceeded to her office.

"Well, that went well," said Michael. "When do you think you will hear from the archaeologist?"

"Phillip said that the strontium tests on the bones of the women would ascertain where they lived," Ann replied. "The reconstruction of their faces will take another two weeks. I will call you as soon as I hear from him."

"When are you going to find the mole in your team?" Edwards probed, a frown furrowing his forehead.

"Just as soon as the little bug we placed in Amy's house delivers the golden goose, Sir," Ann replied.

"I will arrange a meeting with MI6, Interpol and Mossad," Edwards said. "I believe your Russian chap wants to join us."

"Do you think he's up to the job?" Michael enquired.

Ann replied, "Yes, he's very skilled. I think he'll be an asset to our team. He also believes he has a right to be with us because two Russians are involved in the case."

"Alright, let's arrange a meeting for early next week."

"OK, will keep in touch, Sir."

***

"That bastard, Edwards, is like a growling dog with a bone," Ann complained.

"You shouldn't let him get to you, Guv," David said. "He's jealous of your success. His record as DCI was unimpressive. He wished you would fail but all your hunches have paid off. He's especially miffed because you are a woman. Don't allow him to get to you. You are so close to getting a result."

"I suppose you're right, but what the hell," she said, attempting to shrug off her annoyance. "Come and join us for dinner."

As Ann walked through the door, Josie said, "Thank goodness, you seem more cheerful."

Ann slipped her bag off her shoulder and went to hang up her jacket. "Yes, we had a good team meeting," she said, turning back towards Josie. "I've invited David to dinner. Do you mind?"

"Of course not, silly. David is part of the family now. He's always welcome." Josie followed Ann into the kitchen. "I wanted to ask if he could be godfather."

Leaving Ann to ponder this, Josie approached the cupboards and busied herself taking out plates and bowls. "Adam wondered if it would be nice to ask David as he was a witness at our wedding," she said.

"Amazing how decisions are made over my head," Ann said, shaking her head, "and I'm always the last to know."

She turned to David. "Do you see how I am passed over, David?"

Just then Adam walked in with Dimitri. Josie went to the fridge, took out a carton of double cream and a block of butter and placed them on the kitchen worktop. She did not speak.

"Did I hear reference to me?" Adam asked.

"Yes, and do you think I enjoy having you make suggestions without consulting me?" Ann remarked.

"I would never assume anything without consulting you, sis," Adam said.

"Don't play the innocent. Josie says you suggested we ask David to be the baby's godfather."

With a light movement of his hand, Adam waved away the notion. "Oh, that," he said. "Of course I would have asked you first. It was just me thinking aloud."

"Well," Ann threw him a defiant stare and said, "this is *our* baby, so keep your thoughts to yourself. Josie and I will make our own choice."

"Come on, stop bickering," Josie urged, turning back from the hob where she had been stirring the contents of a large pot. "Dinner is ready." She peered into the pot with an approving sniff.

***

Michael convened the meeting for the Brazilian mission with all parties concerned. Two members of Interpol and Mossad also attended. Rachel was not at all like Ann imagined her to be. She was a rather short, stocky woman with a flat nose and protruding chin; it was only when plans for the trip unfolded that Rachel's talents emerged. She was very well informed about James Muller's history and his criminal background. She stressed that it was a dangerous mission and everyone on the trip would be expendable. She expressed her concern that Ann had very little army experience. Ann informed her that she had trained with the special forces when she opted for the army before joining the CLPD. Dimitri hastily added Ann's impressive role in rescuing Saskia.

They spent many hours working out a strategy for kidnapping Muller.

"We must take him alive at all costs," Rachel said. "There will be nine members in the group. The ninth man, Ben Hajioff, will only join us in Brazil. He has local knowledge and speaks the language. He is also ex-army."

They prepared for every emergency and agreed to leave in a week. Rachel informed them that her spy had confirmed Muller was still hiding in the jungle near the Colombian border.

"We need to get him before he decides to move elsewhere," Michael suggested.

When the meeting ended, Michael invited them to dinner. The group were more relaxed and became better acquainted. The wine flowed freely, and they went home quite inebriated. Ann hid her fear that she might be killed on the Brazilian mission by drinking more than usual. Rachel met with Adam and updated him on the mission.

David called at Ann's house three days after the meeting to give her the good news. He rushed in through the door, chattering excitedly.

"Calm down, Hughes," Ann said, "I can't understand a word you're saying."

"We got him, Guv. We've nailed the mole."

"Really, are you sure?"

"Yes, Guv, you'll never believe who the culprit is."

"Come on then, don't keep me in suspense. Spit it out."

"It is Sergeant Neil Havers. He's the detective constable working with DI Mason. We've got him, Guv, the evidence is irrefutable. I've sent a report to Edwards and Heath."

"I would love to see Edwards' face when he finds out," Ann admitted.

"Well, this will help take the heat off you, Guv."

Ann smiled at that.

"Come on, David, join us for dinner. Josie has cooked a great meal."

"Hey," Adam burst in, after rushing down the stairs, "I couldn't help overhearing what sounds like terrific news."

"You should keep your nose out of police business," replied Ann, hitting Adam playfully on the head.

"Couldn't help overhearing since you both spoke at the top of your voices."

"Hurry up and sit down," Josie said, "or the dinner will be stone-cold when you get to eat it."

***

The meeting of the members of Ann's task force took place at a private room at Michael Heath's gentlemen's club. Michael, Edwards, Ann, David and Dimitri met with Roger from MI6 and Joe and Reece from Interpol.

"You've been briefed by Ann and about this very complex case," Michael said to the assembled team. "I am now going to set out our preliminary plan for when we get to Brazil. We all travel to São Paulo. We will be met by the Mossad operatives, Rachel and Abie. We meet up with the DEA chaps, Eric and Douglas in Manaus. Our internal flight will leave for Manaus on the evening of our arrival in Brazil. We have told the Federal Government of Brazil very little because they will offer no help and we cannot risk a leak if there are any drug cartel contacts in their government. We know that our suspect lives in a compound near the Brazil–Venezuela border. He is protected by the drug cartels living in the compound. We also know that Muller travels with an armed escort to rendezvous points with a terrorist cell 10 kilometres from the compound every three days." He cleared his throat. "We cannot attempt to take him on his route out of the compound because, beside his armed escort, there are armed men all along the route. We will be outnumbered. We must draw up a plan to take him *in*side the compound. We are sure that we can pull this off because our team is skilled in SAS combat."

He looked at them steadily.

"You will all endeavour to protect Ann if needs be. She is

competent but perhaps not at SAS level. It will be a highly dangerous mission. There is the possibility some of you may not return. Now, I would welcome any thoughts and suggestions you have?" he asked, raising his voice at the end.

"How are we going to get out once we have captured Muller?" David asked.

"The DEA guys will arrange a Land Rover to get you to an airstrip where a plane will pick you up. Mossad are responsible for supplying the plane that will ferry you to your destinations and to safety."

"What arrangements have you put in place if we have hostile fire from the cartels and the plane is unable to land?" Ann asked.

"The backup plan is to escape by river. The DEA have local connections in Icana on the Icana River where a boat will be kept in reserve. Please remember: the cartels will *not* spare your life if they find you. You must kill them on contact. One of our Mossad agents, Ben, has a comprehensive knowledge of the forest. He will be your guide. He speaks the local tribes' dialect and will have one tribal member with him. You leave in a week. It will give you enough time to coordinate everything and iron out any potential problems."

After the meeting, Ann staggered into her house after having consumed a good deal of alcohol during the six-hour meeting and which she had deliberately done to disconnect herself from the thought of her possible death on the mission.

"Good gracious, I have never seen you so out of your head on drink," Josie said, helping her onto the settee.

Ann mumbled a few incoherent words before passing out. David apologised for Ann's condition explaining that the meeting had continued for longer than intended and with the drink flowing freely.

"But I have never seen her so drunk as this," Josie exclaimed.

"Don't worry, I think she just freaked out at the prospect of our trip to Brazil," David responded.

"That's odd because Ann never panics about anything," Josie said. "Why is Brazil so different?"

"She probably doesn't like the prospect of leaving you in your condition," David replied.

Even so, Ann's reckless inebriation troubled Josie. She waited for

Adam to get home, which was not until the early hours.

"Hi Josie, have the ghosts chased you out of bed?" he asked on seeing her awake in the middle of the night.

"No, I waited for you. We need to talk."

"Sounds serious. A woman in your condition should not be engaged in serious talk."

"I am concerned about Ann. She arrived home extremely drunk tonight. Why would she do that? The Brazilian meeting must have worried her. Did she drink like that to cope with the stress?"

"Don't be ridiculous. When has Ann ever allowed the responsibilities of work to force her to resort to alcohol?" David looked steadily at Josie. He wanted her to believe him. "It was an important meeting, and she simply joined the lads afterwards to relax and overdid it a bit, I guess."

Josie pursed her lips. "I think she's really worried about something."

"I tell you what," Adam began, "how about I find out discreetly how the meeting went, then you can relax?"

Josie agreed.

As dawn broke, Ann sauntered into the kitchen.

"Hi sis," Adam greeted her. "I've made you a delicious breakfast. Are you going to join me?"

She just swallowed.

"Good meeting last night?"

Ann's tone was curt. "Mind your own business. I am not in the mood for conversation."

"Well, your inebriated state worried Josie last night. She thinks you drank excessively because of something to do with your meeting about Brazil."

"Yes, and no doubt you fuelled her insecurities by agreeing."

"On the contrary – I reassured her and defended your corner."

"Very good of you but I will sort out matters with Josie myself."

David hooted on the car horn from outside.

"Excuse me, I need to go." Briskly, Ann took hold of her coat and slammed the door behind her, making her irritation clear.

She briefly thanked David for being prompt.

"We need to get the team to the incident room for 2pm," she pressed. "The forensics report is ready. I want everyone, including Heath and Edwards, at the meeting."

The incident room was crowded. Everyone was keen to know the archaeologist's findings. Stephen Edwards addressed the meeting.

"Allow me," he began, "to introduce Phillip Chambers, the archaeologist who has done sterling work on the remains found in the garden of the house belonging to the Casey brothers."

He showed photographs of numerous skeletons of infants and three partly intact adult skeletons, which were taken at the excavation site.

Absolute silence prevailed as Chambers began revealing his findings.

"I must hand it to the brothers," he said, tilting his head, "their gruesome secret would never have been discovered because only the outer rim of the garden had real roses. The centre of the garden, where they buried the remains of their victims, consisted of a removable plate with artificial flowers. The garden always looked immaculate because only the centre was disturbed, but the replacement of the artificial flowers ensured their secret was not uncovered." He spread his hands as he spoke and looked at his audience.

"The head of the forensics team revealed that DNA isolated from items in the tunnel, the cellar and the car, which contained the body of George Casey's daughter, belonged to the same person." He nodded towards Ann. "Ann had managed to secretly obtain hair samples from the brush and toothbrush in Susan Muller's bathroom. The DNA at the time indicated that the DNA in the car belonged to Susan's sibling. Since it was known that James Muller used Jake's car, it was concluded that findings at the burial site were linked to James Muller."

Phillip also informed the team that he used strontium to trace the places where the women lived. One woman was traced to Minsk, Russia, and the other two to Donegal in Ireland. Two reconstructed faces stared out from the plinth they were placed on.

He looked down at the faces and indicated further with his hand.

"These are the reconstructed faces of the dead women. Dimitri will arrange for Saskia's aunt and uncle to identify this face and we will check their DNA to establish if it is that of their daughter, Olga."

Looking up at them, he asked, "How much information does your team have on tracing the O'Reilly family?"

Tobin replied, "We will need to obtain the DNA of Mary's parents and get them to identify the face. Hopefully they will help us to confirm whether Ellen O'Brien, Mary's cousin, is the other victim."

"We have sufficient evidence to justify our need to pursue James Muller," Michael said. "We have a task force that will be headed by DCI Dixon. We want to bring Muller to the UK to be charged and stand trial. The Israelis want him, too, but we have priority. The Israelis will argue that they need to question and prosecute him as his terrorist ties are greater. We will leave that to MI6 to settle. I state again, we have assembled a very capable task force."

He cleared his throat.

"The men and women have served in the special forces in their respective countries and undoubtedly will execute their task to the best of their ability. The mission is fraught with danger as they will need to capture their quarry in drug cartel territory. You will appreciate that, in the interests of the safety of the task force, we cannot reveal more information." Michael skimmed around the faces. "I also want to inform you that we have found the mole amongst us who has been leaking classified information to the tabloids. He has been dealt with accordingly."

"If there are no questions, you are free to go," Edwards said, thanking them and closing the meeting.

The team dispersed, leaving the senior members to continue their discussions. Michael informed Ann that he would let her know when the rest of the task force had decided on a date of departure.

Ann returned to her office with David and Dimitri, informing Dimitri that he could contact Sergei from her office while she sent David in search of much needed coffee.

Sergei popped up on her Skype screen.

"You have stolen my sergeant, Ann. When are you sending him back?"

Ann laughed briefly. "I think he has got used to the lazy British life, lying about all d—"

Dimitri cut in on the conversation.

"These English women tell so many lies, Sergei," he said. "You should not believe them."

He then continued the conversation in Russian, updating Sergei on all the latest findings of the investigation. On hearing of Dimitri's trip to Brazil, Sergei expressed his opinion with expletives.

Ann reminded him that he ought to mind his language. He apologised and continued the conversation. Dimitri informed Sergei that he would be returning to Moscow in a few days and would return to London to join Ann for the Brazilian trip.

David entered bearing coffee and doughnuts just as Dimitri completed his call.

"David, you and Dimitri can take a photo of the bust of Olga and get Saskia to formally identify it," Ann instructed. "Also, get Sergei to take samples from Olga's parents, if she is the girl in the photo, and get him to send it to forensics. I have a few things to tie up and I'll see you later this evening."

She tucked into her doughnut. Her mobile rang. It was Josie. "How is the hangover?"

"There was no time to have a hangover," replied Ann. "We had an important forensics meeting. Just finished and in the middle of having my first bite of food since last night."

"Have no fear of starving," Josie said, "Adam has invited David and Dimitri to join us tonight; he's treating us to a meal."

"Really?"

"He said something about making amends for your encounter this morning."

"Oh God, I wish Adam would just back off and leave us in peace for a while. I wanted to have some quiet time with *you* tonight. Do we have to go with them?"

"Come on, cheer up. He means well. Do it for me, please."

"If I have to," said Ann, with a heavy sigh. "I have no idea why I let you and Adam bully me into doing things I don't want to do. See you later. Love you."

She completed her report on the findings at the meeting, went to Michael's office and knocked loudly on his door.

"Sterling work on your case," Michael said. "Edwards is most impressed but refuses to tell you to your face."

"All that matters," said Ann, "is that we achieve a good result."

"Are you ready for Brazil?" Michael asked her.

"Ready as I'll ever be. I am also fearful."

Michael raised an enquiring brow.

"My partner is expecting our first baby and the prospect of me possibly not returning leaves me with sleepless nights."

"Yes, it is worrying, I understand, but you have a bloody good team. The boys will protect you with their lives."

Ann looked at him, hoping he was correct.

Michael asked, "Can I tempt you to dinner?"

Ann gave him a small smile of appreciation. "That would be nice, but my brother is taking my partner, me, Dimitri and David to dinner. How about I reserve an evening for us next week?"

***

Adam chose an expensive restaurant in Mayfair for their dinner.

"This is so lovely, thanks Adam," said Josie.

"You do realise," Ann said, "Adam will be penniless after this meal."

"On the contrary – I had a win on the horses so I shall not be skint. Would you ladies like to join us for after-dinner drinks?"

"No thanks, Josie and I want to spend some time together, so we shall love and leave you," Ann replied.

"Can you imagine how Adam will fuss over the baby when it is here?" asked Josie as they clambered into the car.

"I dread to think what he will be like. I doubt whether you'll be allowed to hire a babysitter. He'll want to spend every minute with the baby."

"Such a shame he hasn't met anyone," Josie sighed, "he would make a lovely dad."

"He never really got over Rachel. I think he's in denial about his feelings for her, so he hangs around us to escape the truth." Ann snuggled up next to Josie. "Anyway, I thought we wanted to get away from the men tonight to spend time alone together, so no more about

Adam's love life."

They talked about the future of their unborn baby until sleep overcame them.

CHAPTER 8

Dimitri left for Moscow the next morning; he looked the worse for wear after a heavy drinking session. Ann and David were summoned to Edwards' office where Michael was also present.

"You leave for Brazil in three days," he told them. "Your code name for the mission is 'Jaguar'. You will identify your assault team by that code. You will fly to Rio de Janeiro where you will rendezvous with Dimitri and MI6. Mossad and the DEA chaps will be at Manaus to meet you. The MI6 fellows will be solely in charge of intelligence and surveillance. Mossad has three agents to ensure the assault crew is full quota." He rubbed his right temple. "Prepare yourselves to travel by boat to the forest. You will be taken by helicopter with your captive to San Carlos in Venezuela. The rest of the journey will unfold when you get to San Carlos." He coughed and raised his chin.

"You both can take leave from today; I'm sure you have a great deal to prepare."

"Good luck," said Michael. "I have no doubt that you will succeed. You have proved yourselves in the past and I am confident you will get your man and bring him to justice."

"We will do our very best, Sir," Ann responded.

When Ann and David walked in through the front door early, Josie asked, "Have you been sent home for good behaviour?"

"You will be happy to know we are on leave as of now," Ann replied.

"Oh," Josie said, looking surprised. "Does this mean you will be leaving soon?"

"Yes, in three days," Ann replied.

***

When the day of departure arrived, Josie did not hide her uneasiness. She was tearful as she kissed Ann goodbye. Ann promised she would be home soon and reassured her that she had left Adam to take care of her.

Even though she appeared in control, Ann suppressed her fears and doubts about the trip. During the flight she slept most of the time. David read then fell asleep for the remaining journey. The plane touched down at Rio de Janeiro in the early hours of the morning. They cleared passport control and walked to the agreed meeting point. Two men approached Ann and David and called out the code word, Jaguar.

"You must be Ann. We are Eric and Roger," said one of the men.

"This is my Sergeant, David," Ann said, shaking their hands.

Dimitri approached them wearing a broad smile.

"We only have an hour to our connecting flight," Eric said. "Let's head for the domestic departure lounge."

During the flight to Manaus, the group became better acquainted. They landed at Eduardo Gomes International Airport, Manaus, in the late afternoon. The group made their way to the designated meeting place where they were next met by a motley group of people identifying themselves by revealing the operation code. They introduced themselves as members of the Interpol team and two members of Mossad. The team was missing Ben from the Mossad team. They were told he would be joining them the next day. Ann was grateful for the added female presence of Rachel.

"Let's head for the hotel," Ann suggested, anxious that their presence did not arouse suspicion.

They stepped out of the airport building and were enveloped in the suffocating, cloying tropical heat.

Manaus was a pocket of urbanity nestling in the middle of a large jungle. The profusion of exotic sights and sounds as they drove along the busy streets was seductive. Two taxis ferried them to 10 de Julio situated near the Teatro Amazonas – which was built during the rubber trade and was now an opera house – a rambling building with large sterile rooms and basic communal shower units.

A long session cocktails and beer consumption preceded a large dinner. The team discussed the preliminary assault plan, adding backup plans for every eventuality. They were in constant contact with Eric and Douglas, the DEA team. The group were informed that Ben would join them in the forest; he had to brief two members of the Yanomami tribe to be their guides in the forest. Eric and Douglas had stashed the weapons for assault at a place near the forest where they were to rendezvous.

The next day they were flown by helicopter to Boa Vista along the Rio Branco River. They were taken to a disused warehouse where they met with Eric and Douglas and were supplied with their weapons: sniper rifles, MAC-10 submachine guns, army revolvers, grenades, a rocket launcher and a collection of knives. The team checked and tested the weapons to ensure they were in perfect working order.

As it would take 12 hours to get to the part of the forest where James Muller was in hiding, they decided to leave at midday.

"Night falls quickly in the tropics," Eric told them.

A simple meal of beans and bread was served for dinner with beer, while the team made final arrangements for the assault.

A boat was moored on the river equipped with food and supplies for their journey. An ex-drug cartel member, Luis, who was trusted by Eric and Douglas, was assigned to take them to their destination. The boat was rather dilapidated and looked as though it might sink at any moment. The upper deck comprised of a table and basic cooking facilities. The middle deck had an array of hammocks while the lower deck had a primitive toilet. Luis advised them to stay in the middle deck as too many people on the upper deck might alert some drug cartel members who may be patrolling the forest. They began their journey in the darkness of the Amazon. Some of the team members spoke quietly to one another to calm their nerves. Other members of the team snatched a few valuable hours of sleep. Two stayed awake to keep watch. Ann, however, was unable to sleep. She kept thinking about Josie and hoped she would be back alive and in time for the birth of their baby. Rachel sensed her apprehension and reassured her that they would succeed. They reached their destination at around 8pm that night. The team communicated with Ben and his natives by mimicking animal sounds known to Eric and Douglas.

When they alighted from the boat there were three men waiting on the bank, two Yanomami Indians and a man wearing a black ski mask. The code was exchanged. After walking a little distance away from the group, Rachel returned and informed them that they should spend the night on the boat and would be collected at 4am the next morning. They had a brief meeting before retiring to bed.

Eric told them that they were given inside information by an ex-drug cartel member who had been a guard in the compound where Muller lived. He told them there were 50 guards on each shift. The compound was surrounded by barbed wire. The building had a flat roof where 10 of the guards kept watch day and night. The back of the building had a 2-metre-high wall. The inside of the wall housed live alligators, which led all the way to the back of the house. The ventilation shaft access was on the roof. It was decided that the guards would be engaged with knives and darts to disable them. Firing would alert the whole compound and give the guards time to call for further help from guards stationed at a recess a mile away. The cacophony of animal sounds deprived them of sleep and the heat added to their discomfort; they were relieved when dawn broke. Breakfast consisted of cold beans, bread and hot coffee. The Yanomami Indians appeared at the meeting point. They informed the group, in their broken Portuguese, that Ben had gone on a reconnaissance of the forest and would join them later.

Furthermore, the group were warned about the dangers of the forest and instructed to watch out for snakes and other dangerous wildlife. The heat had begun to rise as they walked through the damp undergrowth. Dappled sunlight stole through the canopy. They stopped only for toilet breaks and brief periods of rest. Ann went off a little distance from the group to relieve herself. Just as she began to squat, she noticed a snake sliding towards her. She froze on the spot, terrified, whilst willing herself to remain calm. Eye to eye for a few brief seconds, they stared at each other. Then, with a quick movement, the snake lunged towards her just as a strong pair of arms grabbed her. She was thrust to safety and the man holding her back then spun around with a machete, cutting off the snake's head in one swoop.

Ann could hardly believe her eyes when she realised that the man called Ben Hajioff whom she had only previously met in the dark was none other than Adam.

"What the hell are you doing here, Adam Dixon?" asked Ann in bewilderment.

A blackened face stared back at her, grinning.

"Shouldn't 'Thanks for saving my life' be your first words, sis?"

She did not reply but hugged him with relief.

"Who is with Josie?" Ann asked, her eyes darting anxiously to his face.

"Josie is in the safe hands of a private midwife who is living in the house," Adam reassured her. "She wanted me to come on the trip to keep an eye on you."

"Oh, I see, well in that case she's got some explaining to do when I get home."

Ann looked indignant.

When they approached the rest of the group she said, "You bastards, you knew all along. Now I know why all the secrecy surrounding this mysterious Ben who never took off his ski mask or spoke." She placed a resentful hand on her hip and turned toward David. "I suppose *you* knew all about Adam's involvement from the start. You know, I had this gut feeling that your meeting in London was a subterfuge for scheming." She continued to point her finger at him. "I will recommend that you return to the beat."

"Sorry to disappoint you, Guv, but it was the big Chief who sanctioned it."

"He is right, sis," Adam said. "We planned this to ensure your protection." He looked at her. "I've been on dangerous missions in the past. I did a great deal of work with the Mossad agents, especially Rachel. I am an honorary Mossad agent. Capturing Muller is no walk in the park." He rubbed his thigh. "He will not stop at anything to avoid being kidnapped. Besides," he went to her and hugged her, "who would have rescued you from that snake?"

For a moment Ann looked bemused, taking in all that her brother had just said.

Adam's expression turned to one of pride. "Meet my Indian guides, Gongalo and Gustado."

Douglas said, "OK, now we need to assign tasks to all of you. I suggest that David, Dimitri, Eric, Ann and Gongalo take the rear of the building. Gongalo is an accomplished knife thrower and Gustado is handy with the darts. I want Alex, Rachel, Joe and Reece to man the rifles and the ammunition. You can prepare your camouflage suits and get into position on my signal. Not a single shot is to be fired." He studied them with a serious expression. "We need to take out the guards with sniper fire. The big guns must only be used if they manage to summon reinforcements, but we cannot let that happen as it will jeopardise our kidnap plan. Clive, Abie and Roger have organised our escape from the building by helicopter." He became brusque. "Does anyone have any questions?"

First, everyone nodded, agreeing to their roles in the mission. The sniper squad asked about their rescue. Adam reassured them that he and Gustavo would monitor and help them to the second helicopter.

It took 10 hours of walking to reach the edge of the forest near the compound. The compound was visible from their vantage point. Their binoculars allowed them a good view of the building and the guards. A truck arrived at the gates and stopped in the grounds. Two men with their hands tied behind their backs were roughly pulled out, pushed to the ground and kicked violently. Another truck was parked in the grounds. The men were tied to the back of each of the vehicles with a rope. The drivers climbed in the vehicles and drove off with the men still attached to the vehicles.

Within minutes the stones in the ground had torn and battered their bodies. The vehicles continued driving, even though it appeared that their victims had died in the merciless torture. Their bloodied and beat-up bodies were finally cut loose, picked up by a farming tractor and dumped on what looked like a cultivated patch of land in the compound. Two men promptly chopped up the bodies with an axe then climbed into a tractor and ploughed the two bodies into the ground as though they were compost.

"I am glad you witnessed that," Douglas said. "You see there is no room for error. These guys cannot even spell the word 'mercy'. The buzz words are 'kill on sight'. Do your job to the very best of your ability."

The team waited until around midnight when the lights in the building were extinguished. It was thought that the guards became more complacent once the lights were out. Dimitri aimed his knife at the guard smoking a cigarette behind the back wall. The knife struck its target and the guard fell like a stone. A dart fired by Gongalo brought down the second guard at the side of the wire. The remaining eight guards fell like flies as the darts and knives hit their targets.

Ann ran towards the compound and clambered up the wall. She signalled to the sniper team using her torch. A few seconds later guards on the roof fell over as the bullets hit home. Rachel followed next and helped Ann secure the cable. The rest of the team at the rear followed Ann onto the wall. David fired the grappling iron into the wall of the building. The iron had wires leading from it. Wheels were threaded onto the wire and one by one the team slid across towards the building.

Dimitri reminded them to draw up their legs as they slid across to avoid being brought down by the alligators that were languishing in the yard. Ann located the access point of the ventilation hatch. She opened the lid and cautiously crept inside, shuffling along on her belly. The rest of the team followed, pulled on by the sound of a television coming from one of the rooms. They had been told that Muller's room was the one at the rear. They moved more cautiously as they realised they were in the ceiling of his room. The group spotted him through the grate of the ventilation exit hatch sitting in an armchair watching television. The access point was behind the chair.

Ann opened the hatch carefully and slid out onto the floor. Muller swung around as he heard the thud. Ann used the Taser and he fell after a few seconds. The rest of the team piled into the room. They checked the remainder of the room for the presence of guards then peered out into the corridor where they observed two guards playing cards with their backs toward Muller's bedroom door.

Eric killed them with his pistol, which had a silencer. The men slumped forward. The team penetrated the rest of the building, shooting the guards they encountered. Douglas and his team had killed the guards at the front and at the gate of the compound and finished off all resistance they encountered on their way into the grounds of the building. Confident that they had secured the building, they went inside in search of their teammates.

Dimitri and David had succeeded in getting Muller onto the rooftop. Ann remained in the building to meet with Douglas and the team. The helicopter hovered over the roof while they managed to strap Muller into the harness. David hung onto the harness and was winched up with Muller. A second helicopter arrived to pick up the rest of the team.

During their exit, an enemy helicopter arrived and began shooting at them. Douglas and Adam positioned their air-to-surface missile and blasted the helicopter out of the skies. The commotion had alerted the reserve guards further down the forest. They raced to the compound in their jeeps. They began firing at the team on the roof. The airlift seemed to take ages, especially with the guards at their heels. The engine of the helicopter spluttered as if it was about to fail but sprang into life at the last minute. Adam and Douglas were still on the roof when the last man was winched up into the helicopter. They stood their ground, firing at the guards who clambered up.

The helicopter swooped down to pick up the two men, but their attempts were thwarted by the gunfire from the guards on the ground. Just then, Adam flung a grenade at the group of guards who had been firing at the helicopter. It felled them instantly and the helicopter was able to collect Adam and Douglas safely.

Nobody uttered a word until they had crossed the Venezuela border, when whoops and cheers arose at the relief of a successful mission. Muller had begun to regain consciousness. They landed at San Carlos and were taken to a safe house. Muller was placed in a locked room in handcuffs. Muller demanded to know why he was being taken into custody. Speaking through the grille, Ann informed him that he was wanted for suspected multiple murders. He smirked and replied that he had good lawyers who would get the charges quashed.

"Good luck with that, Mr Muller," Ann said, "we have a very strong case against you." She regarded him with a defiant stare. "Let's see what the jury says."

Once she had returned to the team, she addressed them.

"You have two hours to eat and freshen up, then we fly to Asunción."

While the team relaxed, Ann asked for a connection to Michael Heath.

"Hello Sir, we are in San Carlos with our quarry," she said to him.

"Well done, Dixon," Heath said, "I am proud of you. Any idea when you'll be back?"

"I think in a few days, Sir. I'll give you plenty of notice to organise the reception committee."

The next call was to Josie.

"Oh, my darling, it is so good to hear your voice," Josie said, sounding almost tearful. "I've been out of my mind worrying about you."

"Well, just remind me to strangle you for scheming with Adam," Ann breathed into the phone.

"Oh that." Josie sounded dismissive. "We were only thinking of your welfare."

Ann ignored the remark. "How are you and the baby?" she asked Josie instead.

"We're doing well, but I am finding it more difficult now to move around. My feet are swollen. I can't wait for the bump to be born. Get here quickly, though, please."

"See you in a few days. Love you lots," Ann replied.

The Mossad team organised a plane to get them to Asunción. They spent a night there before continuing their journey to Barbados. Ann had to fight very hard to convince Mossad to allow her to take Muller to London. Rachel cast her vote in Ann's favour. Adam thanked his Indian guides and parted company from them.

The Mossad team left for Israel. Ann, Adam, David, Dimitri and Muller took off for London the next morning. They each took turns to watch Muller in between short periods of sleep.

Michael, Edwards and some of the CID team met Ann at the airport where they bundled Muller into a police car and sped off to the holding cells. Michael patted Ann on the back and congratulated her and her team on their outstanding performance. They went to Michael's office where they had the debriefing of the whole assault mission.

Three hours later, a relieved Ann headed for home, the others having already arrived. Josie flung her arms around her as she entered the house. Adam joined in the hug. David and Dimitri seated themselves on the sofa while Ann and Josie had a catch-up. Adam served the drinks and they recapped on their Brazilian adventures during dinner. Adam filled Josie in on his miraculous rescue of Ann.

"Yes, but don't think your heroism lets you off the hook," warned Ann.

"Come on, Guv, if he hadn't rescued you, you wouldn't be here with us now," David chipped in.

Ann gave him an admonishing look. "You keep out of this, David Hughes," she chided, "you're in enough trouble as it is."

***

Ann scheduled the interview of James Muller for 8am the next morning. David watched from the next room. Ann switched on the recording tape.

"It is 8.33am on the 30th of October 2005. People present in the room are the accused, James Muller, and DI Tobin."

She looked up and addressed the accused.

"James Muller, I must warn you and caution you that I am charging you with the murders of Olga Mironov, Mary O'Reilly and Ellen O'Brien." She glanced down at her notes. "I am also adding the charges of suspected murders of Tom and George Casey on the 14th of July and 2nd of August 2005." She looked up at him before scrutinising her notes. "Your car, found in the lock-up garage of Jake Casey, contained the body of Elaine Casey who had been murdered at the Casey home in Nottingham. We have found your DNA in the car." She studied his face. "I also have two witnesses who will testify that you murdered some of the foetuses aborted by the women who your accomplices held captive at their home."

"Excuse me for being a touch obstructive," James Muller said, "but I have been living in Brazil for the past few months."

"On the contrary, Mr Muller," Ann responded, "your sister told us that you only left the UK in June of this year. We have also checked and found that you travelled out in June on a Brazilian passport using the name Carlos Mendes."

Muller shifted in his seat and his voice grew loud. "I demand to have my lawyer present."

"Yes, of course, after this interview." Ann continued to watch him closely. "We have a witness to the satanic rituals that you and your cousins performed in Nottingham's Sherwood Forest. We also have the remains of three women used in the rituals and murdered by one or two perpetrators during the rituals."

"Stop looking at me." Muller put up his hands as if trying to defend himself against the barrage of words landing on him. "I had nothing to do with any murders. My cousins are to blame for all that happened." He lowered his hands and pointed his finger at Ann. "And by the way, how the hell do you think it was me? I did not give any permission to collect my DNA."

"We visited your sister, Susan, and obtained her DNA," Ann replied, remaining calm. "The DNA in your car revealed that you were siblings. We will be taking DNA samples from you in due course." She stared at Muller who had stopped pointing. "You were living with your sister and she was unable to provide an alibi for your movements around the time of the Casey family murders."

Muller began to panic and demanded again to have his lawyer present. It was another six hours of questioning before Ann terminated the interview and instructed the officers to take Muller back to the holding cells. She then met with Edwards and Heath and discussed the details of the interview. She called a team meeting in the incident room later that afternoon. The team applauded as Ann and David entered the room. It was such a different atmosphere than to what Ann had been used to in the past.

The team were in jovial mood. "Great job, Guv!" they called out in unison.

"You bastards!" she responded. "I nearly lost my life having to prove I had balls."

"The drinks are on you at the pub tonight!" put in Tobin.

"OK, it's a date," agreed Ann.

Ann then proceeded in giving a brief talk on the mission and the capture of James Muller. She informed them that after they had confirmed his DNA, Muller would be implicated in the murders of the three women at the Casey family home.

"Saskia will testify to Olga's murder," she added.

"Jake Casey has regained consciousness," Tobin said. "He is in rehabilitation under guard."

Ann looked surprised. "Gosh, that is extremely good news. I'll see him later. How is his memory?"

"Not great," Tobin replied, "but he remembers being in custody. He's unable to walk unaided, however, we have received the DNA samples from Olga's parents." He looked very pleased. "It is a match. She is their daughter. We also got the samples from Ireland. The other female body is Ellen O'Brien, Mary's cousin."

"Come on, David," Ann said, turning to go, "let's get some food and then go and see Jake."

***

Jake Casey sat in a wheelchair beside his bed.

"Do you remember much of what happened before your accident?" Ann asked him.

He shook his head.

"Not much, except that I was in a holding cell."

"Do you remember me asking you if you could decode a book we found at your brother, Tom's, house?"

"Vaguely, yes."

"Can you help to decode the book?"

"My memory is not fully functioning yet, I'll need time to recover, but, yes, I can help with the decoding."

Ann nodded, pleased with his helpfulness.

"You *do* know that the evidence against you still stands?" she asserted. "We have arrested your cousin, James, and are hoping he can cast some light on the murders."

Jake shrugged.

"Huh, James would sell his own mother to protect himself."

"OK, we'll leave you to rest now. I'll be back to question you again later."

After they had left him, David asked, "Do you think he is pretending not to remember?"

Ann blinked, looking thoughtful.

"I think, in view of his accident we need to give him the benefit of the doubt. If he knows his sentence will be reduced, he may cooperate more willingly."

After David had dropped her off at home, she saw that Josie was home alone. Josie told her that Adam had taken Dimitri for a drink.

"That's good," Ann said. "We need to be alone. Let's snuggle up and eat ice cream in bed."

"Sounds decadent, but lovely," Josie said and looked at her protruding abdomen. "I don't think I'll grow any bigger now."

Ann followed Josie's eyes. "You *have* got rather large, I agree."

"Only one week to go."

Ann said, "I will be away for a few days this week. I'm needed in Nottingham. I'll be meeting with their CID about the skeletal remains."

Josie frowned.

"That's just great then, Adam is also going away to Scotland, leaving me alone."

"I won't be far away." Ann kept her tone light, following Josie to the stairs. "The CLPD will fly me home if there is any urgency."

Josie stopped and turned to look at her over her shoulder.

Ann added, "And I have asked David to stick around if you need him."

Josie shrugged and continued up the stairs to the bedroom. She didn't speak.

"Ask him to sleep here if you are worried," Ann said. "I won't miss the birth, I promise you."

Josie, standing at the top of the stairs, turned slowly to study Ann.

"I sent the health visitor away because she is too bossy," she said, resting her hand on the stair post. "I don't want David here, only you."

Ann said nothing, just tumbled into bed with Josie, both falling asleep almost instantaneously.

The next morning Ann started out on her journey early and reminded David to check on Josie from time to time.

In the late afternoon, Josie received an unexpected call from Jake. He sounded desperate and anxious. He asked her to collect him from the rehabilitation unit. She protested and told him that she could no longer meet with him. He became persuasive and said he needed her to take him to collect a book to help him decode it for Ann. Josie relented and agreed.

When she drove out to the rehabilitation centre, she found Jake in his wheelchair in the car park.

"Quick," he said, "we need to get away."

"Why the urgency? What's up?"

"Just trust me," Jake replied. "I want you to drive me to a safe locker to collect a book that I need, to decode another book for Ann."

Josie did as he requested, folding up his wheelchair and helping him into the car.

After he had collected his book, he said, "Drive me to your home; I want to talk to you."

Jake was so insistent that Josie obeyed. She wheeled him to the living room and went to the kitchen to make coffee. Then she heard voices coming from the living room. She went to investigate, startled when she saw a man dressed in black and wearing a ski mask. He had a gun and was threatening to shoot Jake.

"Where is the code book?" shouted the man.

Jake denied having the book. There was a crack as the man shot him in the knee. Jake screamed in agony, still denying having the book. The man shot him in the other knee. Josie, terrified, grabbed a kitchen knife and lunged at the man in the ski mask. He grabbed her by the hair and tied her hands behind her back.

"You just be patient, my love," he said to her, "I'll deal with you later."

"Kill me, but don't harm her," pleaded Jake.

"Even better," said the man, "you can watch while I enjoy her."

The man then proceeded to pull off Josie's clothes, rape and sodomise her.

She screamed throughout the ordeal.

"You're harming my baby!"

She managed to free her hands and grab her assailant's hands.

She lunged forward to strike him but missed. He knocked her on her head with the butt of the gun and she passed out.

"You bastard," said Jake, "I'll never give you the book now."

His assailant shot him in the head and fled.

***

David stopped at Ann and Josie's house on the way home. He rang the bell but there was no answer. Knowing it was unusual as he was expecting Josie to be around at this time, he went around the side of the house and peered through the window. He saw Josie lying on the floor. He managed to kick down the door and rushed inside. She was still breathing but unconscious. Jake was dead in the wheelchair. Rapidly, he rang for the emergency services.

Then he rang Ann and informed her that Josie was hurt and had been taken to hospital and to get back to London immediately. He also informed Heath and Edwards.

The house resembled a bomb site when the police and emergency services arrived.

David and Ann accompanied Josie at her hospital bedside where she was still unconscious.

David met Ann's eyes. "I am so sorry that I got to Josie so late," he said, "I had a lot to do at work."

"It's not your fault, David," she said. "I don't know all the details yet."

Josie was soon taken straight to the operating theatre.

Ann slowly walked to the waiting room where Michael Heath joined her. The surgeon came out of theatre and told Ann that Josie had no brain activity because of having been starved of oxygen for too long. He said he had delivered the baby, a boy, who was safe and well and was in the nursery. He asked Ann if she would consent to donating Josie's organs and that there was a young woman who needed a heart urgently. Ann nodded in agreement, sobbing as she realised the hopelessness of the situation.

Michael said, looking at her, "I am so sorry. We think Jake phoned Josie to fetch him, doing a runner when the officer guarding him went off duty; there was a delay before the arrival of the relief officer. The perpetrator must have followed them from the rehabilitation centre," Michael explained. "Yes, but I need to ask Adam how Jake knew Josie. She will have confided in him," said Ann.

"Perhaps your brother may know why Josie befriended Jake. Sometimes partners find it easier to confide in the in-laws instead of their nearest and dearest," Michael continued.

Ann was inconsolable when the surgeon informed her that Josie had passed way. She returned to the unit to spend some time with Josie's body. Adam arrived much later that evening and wept uncontrollably.

"We have arranged for you to stay at a hotel until SOCO has finished their work," he said. "We will leave a police officer on a 24-hour guard at your house. David can accompany you to collect whatever you need once SOCO gives us the nod," Edwards informed Ann.

Ann joined Adam at the nursery. "Oh, he is so beautiful," Adam said. "Have you thought of a name?" He paused and looked at his feet. "Josie wanted to call him Adam."

"I want to change that to Joseph Adam," Ann said.

"Sounds great. Josie would have loved that."

"Pity she is not here to know."

"I'll help you to raise him; I promise you, sis."

Adam accompanied Ann to her hotel and offered to stay the night. Feeling suddenly and terrifyingly lonely, she accepted his offer.

When she had composed herself, she concentrated her thoughts on finding Josie's attacker. Despite being reluctant to take time off work, she accepted compassionate leave and another DCI was brought in to manage the case. David and Adam spent a great deal of time with her.

Once again, she mulled over the idea of returning to the house to see the crime scene for herself, and one evening she steeled herself to go.

The officer guarding the house was nowhere to be seen. She let herself into the house and made for the living room. The house was in total darkness. She heard a door close, and she dived behind the sofa. She fell next to an object. She began to explore the object with her hands in the pitch blackness. As her hands travelled over the object, she was able to make out that it was a body. She ran her hands over the chest, encountering metal bars on the shoulders; she realised that the body was probably that of the police constable who was left to guard the house. Her hand moved over the victim's chest where she found a sticky wet spot. Her fingers followed the wet spot up to the victim's throat where the sticky trail led to a gaping wound in the neck. A second noise in the darkness made Ann hold her breath and crouch down low. Silence followed. She saw the beam of torchlight flitting across the room.

A sudden message bleep on her phone pierced the silence. Unable to see in the dark, her fingers fumbled around for her phone to switch it off. At that moment, a dark figure suddenly lunged towards her. She rolled out of the way just in time and somersaulted back onto her feet. Her eyes adjusted to the dark and slivers of moonlight helped to outline the shape of her attacker.

Ann kicked her assailant off balance and then flung a chair at him, after which they exchanged vicious blows. Her assailant was strong, but Ann stood her ground, raining a series of attacks on him, denying him any advantage. In an unguarded moment, Ann was kicked forwards and landed on her stomach, hitting her head. She was momentarily dazed, giving her assailant time to hold her neck in the crook of his arm.

"If you don't keep still," he hissed, "I'll break your neck."

He managed to tie her hands behind her back.

"Do as I say," he commanded, "and you won't get hurt."

He dragged her backwards across the floor. The ski mask he was wearing hid his face, but she recognised the voice.

"What the hell are you doing in my house?" she demanded between gritted teeth without revealing that she knew his identity.

"I came back to collect an item belonging to me," he replied. "I wouldn't want your lads at SOCO tying me to the crimes."

"You murdered my partner, and I will not let you get away with that."

"Oh," he mocked, "but it wasn't personal. Your partner just got in the way," he laughed. "Mind you, she was a fantastic screw." He stood back and chuckled again. "Let's face it, two women fumbling about can hardly be called fucking. If you had a bulging cock like mine, you'd know what I mean. I bugged the Casey brothers' phones and their houses; I knew exactly where they were and what they were doing."

Her assailant hog-tied her and suspended Ann by her arms.

"You just hang there," he instructed in a menacing tone, "and let me find what I came for – then we'll have some fun."

"Why did you kill Jake?"

"Only Jake had the ability to decode the book that would have implicated me for the murders linked to the rituals, and he refused to give it to me," the man said.

Ann went silent.

"You must speak to James Muller," he said, "he should shoulder the blame for killing the girls."

"Did you murder the Caseys?" Ann asked.

"Got it in one," he replied with a cynical leer. "I did and, if I had the chance, I'd do it all over again. They deserved what they got."

Ann narrowed her eyes. "Why?"

"Simple," he replied, "they abused my loved one when she was pregnant with my baby. They aborted the baby and sacrificed it in their satanic rituals. She died because of septicaemia after that abortion. I was away at the time but I returned in time to hear it from her before she died." He smiled and said in mock seriousness, "I decided then that no sentence would do justice to the punishment I had planned for them." He rocked his head back and thrust out his chin. "And believe you me, I delighted in every aspect of the torture I treated them to."

"Did you kidnap and kill Elaine Casey?"

"Yes, and that was my pièce de résistance," he smirked. "First, I got her father to screw her. You should have seen his face. He was terrified I would kill her right there at his house, so he didn't have a choice but to fuck his own daughter." He lowered his voice. "Before he died, I whispered to him that I was going to rape and kill his little girl. And boy, did I enjoy her!" He scrunched up his face at the memory. "I tortured her for hours and then screwed her in every way

I could. Such sweet revenge."

"You're a rat," Ann said, "but you won't get away with it."

"Oh indeed," he sneered, "I *will* get away with it," and then he paused for dramatic effect, "because you won't live to tell them what I have told you; that's why." He took a step nearer to her and held his face within an inch or two of hers. "And how could I pass up a chance to screw you first?" He stepped back from her. "But before I enjoy that little delight, I must find the clasp of my watch. When I wrestled with your partner, she tore my watch off and the clasp was lost somewhere in this room. It quite possibly will have some of my DNA."

He began searching for the missing item and did not notice the two men entering the room.

Luke was strong but their combined strength pinned him down and knocked him out. David and Adam looked down, first on him, and then turned their attention to Ann.

She was bruised, battered and covered in blood. They untied her and covered her with a throw from the sofa.

She looked down at her assailant. "You deserve to die," she said to his inert form, "you rotten piece of shit!"

They pulled off the man's ski mask.

"Luke Cowan," gasped David. "I don't believe it!"

"How did you know where to find me?" Ann asked them.

"We put a bug in your car and were able to trace you," David replied. "I suspected you would return to the house to look at the crime scene."

"How much did you hear of Luke's confession?"

"We heard most of what he said." He indicated to Adam. "Adam suggested we wait to see his next move before we stepped in to help."

David offered Ann his handkerchief to wipe the blood that ran down her forehead.

Ann said, whilst wiping the remaining traces of blood from her face, "I recognised Luke's voice but didn't make him aware. I wasn't sure what he would do." She put the handkerchief aside and suddenly looked alert. "We must find that watch clasp."

During their search, throwing extra light on the floor and table surfaces, Ann accidentally knocked over a flowerpot on one of the tables. She bent to retrieve it and replace the soil in the pot when she found the metal clasp.

"Got it!" she yelled while holding up the prize. "This looks like the clasp of a watch."

It appeared to have dried blood and skin on it, and she carefully placed it in a clean freezer bag and labelled it.

Once again, the house was soon buzzing with police and paramedics. Luke Cowan had recovered and was taken away by the police. Edwards and Heath arrived also.

"Good God, Ann," said Michael, "you were very nearly killed."

"I'm sorry, Sir, I just had this gut feeling that the murderer would return to the crime scene."

Adam joined them. "Who will take care of Ann?" Michael asked.

"I'll take my sister to the hotel," said Adam.

He broke the silence in the car.

"Josie loved you with all her heart," Adam said. "Her meeting with Jake was simply to buy his silence. But she felt guilty as hell about it and about the accident *and* how she was manipulated to communicate with him." He looked at her in earnest. "She never slept with him or encouraged anything beyond dinner and a drink; that I *do* know." He rubbed the side of his temple. "I think she collected Jake from the hospital at his request and that it had something to do with the code book that he promised you he would decode. Perhaps he felt vulnerable in hospital and needed to be at a safe location to do that." He paused and swallowed. "I believe he was watched and followed. After all, if the murderer got to Jake in jail, what stops him from watching Jake at the hospital? Josie was the only neutral person he could trust. There was no way you would allow him out of hospital unguarded."

Ann studied his face. "I should have been at home and not gone to Nottingham when I did." Her voice came out little more than a lame squeak. "She asked me to stay and I didn't listen."

She buried her face in her hands.

"Oh God, Adam, I am to blame for causing her death."

Adam embraced her, trying to comfort her.

"Adam," Ann said, "there is something I must tell you. I overstepped the bounds of my authority by entering an illicit deal with Luke Cowan," she admitted, bowing her head. "I had sex with him, sadomasochistic sex."

"I know," Adam said. "Cowan was mouthing off about it when they put him in the police car," he added.

Ann looked up at him, astonished.

Adam said, "I overhead your conversation with Luke before David joined me. Thank God David didn't hear it. Why in God's name did you do such a thing?"

"It was the only way I could find out more about the satanic rituals. I knew there must be a tunnel to get from the house to the spot where they performed the rituals. He agreed to take me there if I had sex with him. I learned from Sam Cain that he would do anything for sadomasochistic sex. The only problem is, if he reveals this to Edwards, they will find my DNA at his home and my visit is on his CCTV."

Adam's eyes darkened. "You are *not* going to be implicated in any of this," he said, anger rising in his voice. "That bastard deserves what he gets and he's not going to drag you down with him."

"No, Adam," Ann protested, waving her arm, "I am guilty and must own up to what happened."

"This is the one time I am not going to listen to you, sis," Adam said with vehemence. "If it becomes public knowledge, your career is over. And that piece of shit is not worth the sacrifice."

Ann studied him, mulling over everything that had happened.

"I feel so ashamed," she said, clenching the air in front of her. "I betrayed and cheated on Josie; my punishment was her death."

"Stop thinking like that!" Adam gripped her shoulders and shook her. "You did what your instincts dictated, OK? No-one knew that he would murder Josie in the process. Look, life happens, shit happens and sometimes we have no control."

When Michael Heath asked Ann to call at his office she felt herself trembling at what he was going to reveal.

"I think you know why you have been called to see me," he said as she entered his office and waved for her to sit down.

"Yes, Sir, I can explain."

"No need," Michael said, "your brother called to see me last night."

Ann bit her lip and frowned.

"With respect, Sir," she said, "I don't need my brother to fight my battles." She became indignant. "I am quite capable of shouldering the responsibility of what happened myself."

"Ann, I fully understand why you acted as you did," Michael said. "It was in extraordinary circumstances and your actions achieved a phenomenal result."

Ann nodded.

"However," Michael continued, "Edwards and the chief constable will not see it like that. They will condemn you and demote you."

Her limbs felt rigid. It was what she had expected.

"Your brother had my permission to remove all evidence of your presence at Cowan's house," Michael went on, "including the CCTV evidence."

Ann said nothing.

"If Cowan makes an allegation, no evidence linking you to having been at his home will be found." He tapped his pen on his desk as he spoke. "You must give me your word that you will accept my ruling and that you will not blame your brother for his intervention."

She stared at him, the comprehension of his words slowly absorbing.

Michael said, "He would give his life to protect you and I agree with him – you are worth the sacrifice. How did Cowan manage to get all those alibis from the women for the murders he had committed?"

"How did Cowan manage to have alibis for the time of the murders when he said he was with various women?" Michael asked.

"I questioned a few of those women who gave him alibis and I believe he paid them and bribed them with all kinds of gifts and terrified them with threats of revenge if they went against him," Ann replied, still unsure of what she should say.

Michael came around to her side of the desk and placed a hand on her shoulder.

"You have been put forward for promotion for Superintendent," he said.

Ann swallowed and moved away from him.

"In view of the circumstances, Sir, I will decline the promotion," she said evenly, and looked at him. "And I would ask that you don't pressure me to accept."

***

Adam was waiting for her outside Heath's office.

Ann greeted him with a hug but did not speak.

David spotted them as they got into the car and walked over.

"Fancy some lunch?"

"That would be nice," replied Adam.

David chose a quiet little bistro near Kensington.

"I believe congratulations are in order, Detective Inspector Hughes," Ann said, kissing David on the cheek. "That calls for champagne."

"Allow me to treat *you*," declared Adam, shaking David's hand vigorously. They sat at a table and ordered food.

David turned to Ann.

"Surely they are going to give you the Super's post, Guv?" he asked while swallowing down a forkful of his fillet steak and chips.

"They did and I turned it down because I want to keep my hand in the active side of the investigations," Ann replied, cutting into the gammon on her plate.

David chewed on his food for a while.

"Shame not to have you as our boss," he said, "but great to still be working with you in the field."

"You'll be replacing DI Tobin," said Ann, and took a gulp of champagne.

During the meal they discussed Cowan and Muller's impending trial. David informed them that both men would get three life sentences with no chance of parole. Besides the overwhelming DNA evidence, Saskia's evidence would seal their fate. The bite marks on Josie's buttocks were a match to Cowan and his DNA was found on the clasp of his watch.

The chapel for Josie's funeral at the little crematorium the following Friday was packed with police officers. Every member of her team had made the effort to attend. Josie's sister, June, and brother, Martin, were present but kept their distance. Ann held the baby, with a nanny on hand for help. The solemnity of the funeral and the support of her colleagues touched Ann greatly. She did not hold back her feelings but allowed herself to express the grief she felt so very deeply. Holding onto the baby was her only tangible reminder of the woman she had loved so dearly. Her team shared that grief and lent their support throughout the ceremony. Edwards delivered a heartrending speech that moved Ann to tears. She could hardly believe that the man who had initially hated her could demonstrate such an understanding of her loss.

When everyone had left, Ann, Adam and David stood at the door of the crematorium sharing a group hug. Adam whispered softly, "Sis, we will always be there for you and Joseph."

Roy Peter Du Toit

In loving memory of my beautiful friend
28/7/56–15/5/14

My grateful thanks to:
Jirka Bartak &Teagan Whealon-Mortimer for their invaluable
technical computer support during the compilation of this book.

Printed in Great Britain
by Amazon

46124079R00169